CW00485986

Polly Courtney, 28, lives in London where she divides her time between writing and sports-related projects. Her first novel, *Golden Handcuffs*, exposed the truth about living and working as a 'high flyer' in the square mile. In stark contrast yet with some surprising parallels, *Poles Apart* is an eye-opening depiction of what it's really like to be a young migrant in London today.

Polly Courtney

Poles Apart

Copyright © 2008 Polly Courtney

The moral right of the author has been asserted.

Apart from any fair dealing for the purposes of research or private study,
or criticism or review, as permitted under the Copyright, Designs and Patents
Act 1988, this publication may only be reproduced, stored or transmitted, in
any form or by any means, with the prior permission in writing of the
publishers, or in the case of reprographic reproduction in accordance with
the terms of licences issued by the Copyright Licensing Agency. Enquiries
concerning reproduction outside those terms should be sent to the publishers.

Matador
9 De Montfort Mews
Leicester LE1 7FW, UK
Tel: (+44) 116 255 9311 / 9312
Email: books@troubador.co.uk
Web: www.troubador.co.uk/matador

ISBN 978-1-84876-005-9

A Cataloguing-in-Publication (CIP) catalogue record for this book
is available from the British Library.

Mixed Sources
Product group from well-managed
forests and other controlled sources
www.fsc.org Cert no. TT-COC-2082
© 1996 Forest Stewardship Council
FSC

Typeset in 11.5pt Bembo by Troubador Publishing Ltd, Leicester, UK
Printed in the UK by The Cromwell Press Ltd, Trowbridge, Wilts, UK

Matador is an imprint of Troubador Publishing Ltd

Thanks to the real Marta, whose story inspired me to write Poles Apart, and to everyone else who helped make it happen.

PROLOGUE

"HAH! DRINK UP – you're using the wrong hand!" squawked Rosie, quick to point out Holly's error. "It's European Drinking Regulations here, you know. In the first half of the hour, you drink with your left! Don't you know anything?" She gleefully filled Holly's glass and sat back in her chair to watch, pouting.

Obligingly, Holly downed her red wine. She was good at drinking games, but this evening, new rules kept creeping in that everybody else seemed to know about except her. *European Drinking Regulations*, for God's sake. They were so cliquey, the South Kensington lot. She had never warmed to them. If Tash hadn't begged her to come over tonight, she would have made up an excuse and come round to see the place another time.

They were playing an intellectual version of twenty-ones, which involved turning your number into a roman numeral, then converting I, V and X into 'ooh', 'yeah' and 'not there' respectively. You could tell they were bloody Oxbridge, thought Holly.

"Ooh, not there!" Tom moaned loudly.

"Not there!" shrieked Plum. Holly watched as the girl flicked her hair in the direction of Jack, Tash's boyfriend. Plum (real name Victoria) had no morals – but then, as far as Holly could tell, neither did Jack. She wondered whether they'd ever actually done anything behind Tash's – "Oh, not there, ooh, yeah!" she said, just in time.

"Hesitation!" chimed Rosie and Plum triumphantly. "You can't say 'oh'! See it away!"

Holly knocked back more wine, white this time. Jeremy, sitting opposite, was looking down his long, unattractive nose at her, swilling what looked like Port in his glass. Some house-warming, thought Holly.

"Not there, not there, oooooh!" cried Tash hysterically, before realising that the joke was on her. She sulkily polished off her wine. Emerging from the bowl-sized glass, she waved her hand. "Ooh – I forgot to tell you! I have some news! *Bad* news," she said dramatically. "As of next week, this lovely, beautiful house that mummy and daddy have given me will not be mine any more!"

The others around the table acted suitably shocked and surprised. This was Tash's style: melodramatic. Holly had got wise to it, having lived with Tash during their second year at university. She had famously reported an intruder to the police when the electrician she'd booked came round to change the light bulbs.

"No! I've been told that I am to share it..." A long pause... "With a Polish girl!"

Again, astonishment all round.

"She's from a small village just outside Warsaw – called Loopoopski or something – and mummy is allowing her to stay for as long as she wants! Oh – and listen to this. They're charging her fifty pounds a week. For a place in South Kensington!"

There were gasps and shaking heads. "Fifty pounds!"

"Who is she?" asked Plum, as though referring to a nasty disease.

"Mummy used to help organise foreign exchange trips, *ages* ago," Tash explained, "and she stayed in touch with one of the teachers. So this is the teacher's daughter."

"Does she have a name, this teacher's daughter?" asked Holly, fed up with the undertones of this conversation: the implication that this girl wasn't good enough for South Kensington.

"Marta," Tash replied. "Oh and don't ask me to pronounce her surname—"

"Polovski?"

"Smithovski?"

"Powchowska?" came the helpful suggestions from round the table.

"Oh – it is something like that. Dabrowska! That's it!"

"We've got a Polish bagel shop just opened near us," Jeremy announced, as though this was interesting.

"They're everywhere, Poles, these days," declared Jack disdainfully. "The government's letting them in to do all the jobs we

Brits don't want to do." He snorted. "Still... she'd better be bloody attractive." He yelped as Tash presumably pinched him under the table. "Sorry." He flashed a cheeky smile at Plum.

"Actually, I have a photo," said Tash, pushing back her chair and stretching out to the antique dresser. "She looks... well..." she screwed up her face, squinting. "Polish."

Holly leaned forward to get a glimpse of the photo, which Jack was eyeing up approvingly. The image was of a tall, leggy girl in tight jeans and a sweatshirt not dissimilar to the type Holly had worn as a teenager. It may even have *been* from the early nineties, she thought, cringing at the lurid colours. The girl had long brown hair cut in no particular style and a pale complexion. Despite the amateurishly taken photo – snapped outside what looked like a concrete bunker – it was impossible not to be drawn by the girl's eyes: icy blue, turning up at the edges in a momentary smile.

"Well, I think it'd be nice to have a housemate," declared Holly. "It's a massive place – you'd rattle around in it on your own."

"I'm sure I'd find things to do," replied Tash, talking more to her boyfriend than anyone else.

"I can't believe your parents are letting an Eastern European immigrant be their first tenant!" squealed Rosie.

Tash shook her head, rolling her eyes. "Frankly, neither can I."

1

"LOOK, IT'S NOT AS IF I'm going into space," joked Marta, trying to lighten the mood. "It's only a short flight away."

Her parents smiled and glanced at one another. The smiles didn't reach their eyes. What Marta had neglected to mention, and what they were all thinking, was that short flights cost money. She wouldn't be popping back for a weekend any time soon.

Her best friend, Anka, was avoiding eye contact. Marta could tell she was about to cry. Marta's brother and sister were just staring at her.

"God, stop being so morbid, all of you!" cried Marta. "We all have phones, don't we? And email? Well, sort of," she added, remembering the last time she'd tried connecting to the internet in Łomianki library.

Marta glanced up at the departures board and the others did the same. Her flight was boarding. "I'd better go through," she said, suddenly feeling worms in her stomach. This was it. She was about to leave her country. This was the last time she'd see mama and tata, Anka, her brother and sister – for at least a year.

They were so close, their family – sometimes too close, in their little townhouse. She couldn't imagine them not being around her. Mama running up the stairs to chase her brother out of bed in the mornings, tata chiding her sister for not taking long enough over her homework, the five of them sitting down to dinner together every night – pierogi or gołąbki – and her brother whinging that he wanted to watch TV... this was life, for Marta. It had been for the last twenty-two years.

Anka stepped forwards and finally dared to look Marta in the eye. There were tears in hers. "Będę za Tobą tęsknić , Marta." I'll miss you.

Then she pulled away and delved in her bag. She'd dressed up for the occasion, Marta noted. Anka always looked stylish, but today she had on long drainpipe jeans and a tight sparkly black top beneath the old brown coat she always wore. The glittery eye shadow had gone to waste, thought Marta, watching it stream down her cheeks.

"Open this when you get there, OK?" Anka instructed, chewing on her bottom lip to stop her jaw wobbling. It was a sizeable parcel, wrapped in what looked like magazines and brown tape. "Sorry about the paper."

Marta hugged her. She could feel Anka's body heaving with every sob. She was determined not to cry, not to falter; she wanted to leave them with an image of strength and resolve. But to Marta's dismay, she felt her eyes welling up.

They had been best friends ever since Marta had rescued Anka from a group of girls in the playground who'd been calling her 'fatty'. Fifteen years later, Anka was now one of the skinniest girls in the town, and perfectly capable of fending for herself – but looking back, that first encounter had been a strangely accurate reflection of their relationship over time.

They were both vivacious girls, and intelligent too – one of them always coming top of the class at school – but Marta had always been the brave one. When it came to trying new things, taking risks, letting go, it was always Marta. When they left school, Marta applied to universities and got a place to study marketing at the prestigious Szkoła Główna Handlowa in Warsaw – one of the best in the country. Anka wasn't sure about leaving Łomianki, so she stayed and got a job at the bakery. She was still working there three years later.

It was fair to say that Marta was braver than most people in Łomianki. With a population of only nine thousand, it was one of those places where people reacted badly to change. When Poland had joined the EU in 2004, national newspapers had been bursting with stories of young men and women starting new lives in new countries – of couples fleeing the drab, grey streets in search of adventures abroad – but not the local papers. In Łomianki, deserters were frowned upon. In Łomianki, doing anything different was seen as a sin. The old folk – of which there were many – looked badly on those whose son or daughter had moved away. It was that, as much as anything else, that had made Marta desperate to leave. She had to get out of this place. There was so much of the world she hadn't seen – so much that she was finally being *allowed* to see – and she wanted to explore.

"You'll miss your flight," mama warned, with a note of what sounded like hope in her voice.

Marta turned to her parents. The churning in her stomach was getting worse. She couldn't believe she was actually leaving them. What if things changed, in her absence? What if tata lost his job at Polkomtel, and mama had to teach more classes at the university? What if they had to move house? The routine would change, and she wouldn't be there to know. All her life, they'd been there, strong and reliable, there to support her. But now, their faces pale with concern and lack of sleep, they looked fragile. They looked *old*, thought Marta. She had never considered the possibility that her parents weren't immortal.

She braced herself and switched on a smile through the tears. "What's this?"

Tata was holding out a parcel – this one smaller than Anka's and more neatly wrapped.

"And this," mama added, producing what looked like a sack of potatoes bound in reams of plastic tape.

"That's not going to fit in my hand luggage!" exclaimed Marta, already guessing the contents. It weighed several kilograms.

"It fits. I tried it this morning. You just have to leave half of it sticking out–" mama demonstrated, stuffing the end of the enormous package into Marta's rucksack. "There!"

Marta pocketed the small package from tata, and went to hug her brother and sister. Even Tomek had a forlorn expression on top of his moody teenager look. Ewa was frowning. Poor girl – she was only twelve. She'd miss her big sister.

"Right, I'm off to London!" Marta announced purposefully. She balanced the precarious load on her back, and hugging Anka's parcel, set off towards the departures lounge.

"Don't forget the magazines!" yelled Anka. "Remember – lots of pictures and not too many words! I want to practise my English style!"

Anka loved fashion. It was a pity she never had any money to buy or create her own. Marta had tried to persuade her to get into dressmaking, or to do a course at university, but Anka hadn't had the confidence. Marta turned, smiling through the tears. "I'll send you some for your birthday!"

2

MARTA FOLLOWED the line of passengers across the damp tarmac and up the steps onto the plane. The wind ripped through her flimsy jacket, driving the sleet at her raw flesh. It was cold, even for Warsaw. She paused as she entered the aircraft and breathed her last breath of Polish air.

"Welcome aboard," chirped the air hostess.

Marta smiled nervously, holding out her boarding pass, which the woman ignored. It was her first time on an aeroplane. In fact, it was the first time anyone in her family had flown. Before 2004, travelling out of Poland had been impossible, and until recently, flights had been so expensive that the only option for getting across Europe had been a twenty-hour coach trip through Germany and Holland. Now there were at least a dozen flights from Warsaw to London every day.

The butterflies were getting worse, and now her hands were shaking too. She couldn't tell what was making her nervous. Was it the safety instructions that informed her that 'in the unlikely event of an emergency, oxygen masks would drop from above'? Was it the fact that the wings of the plane seemed to be made from flaps of metal that didn't look very securely fastened? Was it the fact that mama and tata weren't here? Or was it just a fear of the unknown?

Marta had prepared herself as well as she could for her new life, reading books and magazines about London that mama had borrowed from the university. There was a book called 'A-Z' that had maps of every street in London, including the one she was going to live on, and there were some old copies of a magazine called 'Time Out' that listed all the concerts and shows happening around the city. There was so much going on – not just organised fun that you got in

Warsaw – the opera and theatre – but real, spontaneous entertainment. Rock concerts, comedy nights, festivals – even live music events put on by ordinary Londoners… there was a sense of freedom about the place that Marta longed to experience.

The excitement mingled with her nerves. Marta was determined not to be daunted. She wasn't the first Pole to move to England, and she had a better chance than many who came over – as her parents kept reminding her. The thought of her parents brought on a fresh wave of home-sickness. "Stop your worrying," mama would scold in her no-nonsense way, whenever she voiced her doubts, as tata hit her playfully on the back of the head. God, she'd miss them.

An air stewardess came strutting down the plane, clicking a tiny machine with her thumb – once for every passenger. There was a general rustling as people squirmed in the confines of their seatbelts and crew busied themselves behind a yellow curtain at the front. Marta didn't want to think about the 'unlikely event of an emergency'. She had once read that the chance of survival in a plane crash was zero; they just put in safety procedures to make passengers feel at ease. She didn't feel at ease.

Marta wondered how many of the people on this plane were travelling on a one-way ticket. The price of a flight to London was nearly double that of the return to Warsaw, which suggested that most people were going one way: out of Poland. Word had it that nearly a million Poles had fled to England in the last three years – although the authorities would claim that the figure was less than half of that. If the passengers on this plane were a representative sample, there were a hell of a lot of twenty-something-year old Poles in London.

It made her angry that the government was trying to stop the young people leaving. What did Poland have to offer them? No well-paid jobs, that was for sure. Marta thought back to her home town – the grey buildings, the old faces with their blank, disparaging eyes. She loved its familiarity, but at the same time she loathed it. The place was depressing. Most of the people her age had moved away, either to other parts of Poland or, more commonly, to Europe. The only ones left were the old folk and those with no sense of adventure.

It was a risk; she knew that. A girl from her class had moved to London with her boyfriend after graduating. They couldn't even afford to pay for a room in a hostel, so she'd taken a job as an escort. She'd run off with one of her clients who had turned violent, tried to kill her then stolen her passport so she couldn't go back to Poland. Nobody knew what happened to Beatrycze after that.

Marta was determined that she wouldn't fall into any of the traps. She knew that the streets of London weren't paved with gold, that she'd have to work for her money. She didn't expect it to be easy, and she was grateful for the generosity of Penelope and Henry, mama's friends, who were letting her stay in their house with their daughter. She was prepared for the worst, but she was confident she could make a good go of it.

The plane wheeled around on the runway and quickly started picking up speed. Marta watched the metal panels on the wing, wondering whether they were supposed to flap up and down like that. There was a tremendous roar, and suddenly the whole aircraft seemed to be shaking itself to pieces. Just as the noise became disconcertingly loud, Marta felt herself tipping backwards. She twisted round in time to see the ground tilt and then drop away, very quickly. They were airborne.

She watched the drab buildings shrink beneath her until they looked like a sprawling mass of concrete. The nerves were just flying nerves, she told herself. Once she landed, she'd be fine. The guide books had taught her everything she needed to know about London: how to use the buses, where to live, how to ask for a second helping. She didn't know how long she'd stay. Maybe a year, maybe more – maybe forever – she didn't need to decide yet. Her plan was to make money, send some back to her parents each month, and keep a little aside for herself.

Marta sank into her seat and shoved her cold hands into her pockets. Her fingers curled around something soft and papery. Tata's gift. She turned it around in her pocket, poking at the flimsy wrapping. In the end, her curiosity won over her self restraint and she pulled it out, scratching away at the paper.

She could hardly believe it. Marta put the notes back in their little pouch, then brought them out again and counted a second time, discreetly. Tata had given her *one hundred English pounds*. That was nearly six hundred złoty! How could he possibly afford that? What would he use to feed Tomek and Ewa this month? Marta felt a lump in her throat.

There he was, confidently assuring her that she could make a good living in England, and all the while he was sacrificing a week's wages to help her out. Dear tata. He was still looking after her, even now.

The little seatbelt light above her head went off, and passengers all over the plane sprung into action, standing up, wandering around and colliding in aisles. Marta thought about the parcels stowed away above her head. The air hostess had laughed at Anka's attempts at packaging as she'd stowed the patchwork lump in the overhead locker. Marta smiled, picturing Anka amidst a roomful of fashion magazines, wrangling over which pages she would least mind turning into wrapping paper. She unfastened her seatbelt and reached upwards.

It wasn't even necessary to open mama's present. Marta knew what it was. She peered through the tear she'd made in the paper and caught a glimpse of the Drożdżówka label. Her favourite cake. This wasn't the first food parcel mama had made for her, but it was certainly the largest. Mama had a knack of cramming more food per cubic inch than any food manufacturer had ever achieved.

"Anything to drink for you madam? Anything to drink?" asked the perfectly proportioned air hostess, whose makeup appeared to have been applied with a spatula and a felt-tip pen.

Marta carefully noted other passengers' reactions. Was it free? Someone behind her was noisily rifling through change in his pocket. No, it wasn't. "I'm fine thanks." She smiled sweetly.

Anka's present sat in her lap, a picture of catwalk perfection and brown sticky tape. She was supposed to wait until she arrived, but she didn't see what difference it made opening it now or later. Marta hesitated, and then tore at the glossy paper.

She nearly screamed. It was a Malina Q jacket! A gorgeous, turquoise puffy jacket with a faux fur hood lining – the type she and Anka had been drooling over for months! *All* the rich girls in Warsaw had these. Neither Anka nor Marta had ever been serious about owning one. They cost nearly three hundred złoty! Marta hugged it against her face, discarding the sticky magazine pages on her lap. The English woman in the next seat was looking at her strangely, but Marta didn't care. She had a Malina Q jacket. Dear Anka, she thought, as a tear rolled down her cheek and onto the bright blue fabric, sinking into the fur lining. She was really going to miss her best friend.

3

"I SIT?" said a voice above Marta's head.

She glanced up to find a young man about her own age looking at the seat next to her and pointing at her luggage.

Marta smiled at his improvised sign-language and moved her bags, counting herself lucky for ending up with such an attractive travelling companion. The coach was filling up, and there were some very dubious passengers squeezing down the aisle. This guy, though, he was intriguing. Through the dusky complexion and stubble, there was something about him that caught Marta's eye: a wariness that seemed to match her own.

"Did you just fly in?" she asked, in her own language.

He looked at her, startled, and then his features melted into a smile. "Yes." He removed his grubby baseball cap and ran a hand through his hair. "How did you know I was Polish?"

Marta shrugged. She wasn't going to tell him she'd spotted his insecurity. Having spent the last hour watching passengers rush around Luton airport, Marta reckoned she could spot Poles from Brits without hearing them speak, with near one hundred per cent accuracy. It wasn't just the way they dressed, which, she was beginning to realise, was very different; it was the way they moved, the way they expressed themselves. There was something furtive about this guy, as though he didn't belong.

"I'm Marta," she said, smiling.

"Lukasz." He half-heartedly offered his hand and then turned the gesture into a scratching of his knee. The coach pulled away from its bay, manoeuvring through the sluggish airport traffic.

"You're here for good?" she asked.

"Maybe. Who knows." It was Lukasz's turn to shrug. "I've never been to England before."

"Me neither. It's weird, finally being here."

Lukasz nodded, looking past her and through the coach window. Marta did the same. They were on a main road now, rolling steadily through flat English countryside sliced up by grey motorways. It felt strange to be on this side of the road. In fact, everything felt strange. The tarmac was the wrong colour, the lamp posts were different, there were neat green hedges between all the fields… this was it. This was England, at last.

"Do you speak any English?" asked Lukasz.

"Yes, although not perfectly," Marta replied, the worms returning to her stomach. Her teacher at school had believed in the phrase: 'Understand what they say; you'll pick up the rest.' This meant that Marta could translate almost anything from English to Polish and almost nothing the other way round. She could read signs, take instructions, understand conversations, but she couldn't join in – not confidently, anyway.

"I don't," Lukasz confessed. "But it doesn't matter, apparently. I'm staying with a friend who's been here two years. He says that the language is no problem. He's promised to find me a job."

"You don't know *any* English?" she asked, shocked. Surely he couldn't consider migrating without speaking a word of the language?

He shook his head. "It's fine. Gabrjel says he got work the first week he arrived. He didn't know any English then – still doesn't."

Marta frowned. "What sort of work? Something involving not speaking, presumably?"

"Construction, mainly. Some odd jobs – maintenance, gardening…"

Marta nodded. She wasn't sure she'd fit in too well on a construction site. Nor was she sure that Lukasz and she were working towards the same goals. He had his sights set on menial jobs that earned good money but required no intellect; she wanted to use her brain, her marketing degree. Perhaps Lukasz and his friend hadn't been to university.

"Gabrjel was a qualified doctor," he told her, as though reading her mind. "He had a job lined up at the hospital in Wrocław for three thousand złoty a month. Here, he gets nearly two thousand *pounds* a month – that's twelve thousand złoty! For lugging bricks around."

Marta nodded. The story didn't surprise her; it just depressed her. Back home, she was always hearing about qualified graduates moving to England to do unskilled work for five times the salary. The problem she had was that she didn't *want* to do unskilled work. She had skills. She wanted to use them.

"What are you planning to do?" asked Lukasz.

Marta hesitated. She didn't want to aggravate the guy. "Not sure yet. I'll find something."

Lukasz nodded. "You're lucky, being a girl. You can always get au pair work. The money's OK and they give you a place to live."

"Yeah." Marta nodded. The chances of her becoming an au pair were lower than the chances of her getting work on a construction site. There was no *way* she'd stoop to becoming an English family's slave.

"Or you could work in a Polish bakery – apparently they're springing up all over London."

Marta gritted her teeth and nodded again. She would rather move back to Łomianki than spend her days smearing cream cheese on bagels.

Marta felt more anxious than ever about her prospects of finding good work, despite the fact that her companion was someone who hadn't even bothered to learn English. She brought the conversation to a halt and delved into her bag, extracting the scratched old CD player she'd had since she was twelve. Inside was the disk her mother had cobbled together from snippets of English radio four years ago. She nearly knew it off by heart, but that didn't matter. She needed to hear the language – needed to remind herself that she still understood, still had the skills, still had the ability to make something of her time in England. Marta pulled the earphones over her head and leant against the juddering window.

It must have been forty-five minutes later – half of the CD – when the coach finally pulled up. They were inside a massive, fume-filled bus depot. People towing suitcases and screaming children filled the concrete walkways, colliding like atoms under a microscope. Deafening announcements echoed off every surface. Around her,

11

people rose in their seats, hitting others in the face as they hoisted rucksacks onto their backs.

"Well, good luck," said Lukasz, with none of the confidence he'd had before. His eyes were jumping all over the place. "Maybe keep in touch?"

Marta smiled. Beneath the macho, stubbly exterior was a very anxious young man. "Maybe."

"Here's Gabrjel's number – that's where I'll be staying," he said, ripping off part of his cigarette packet and scrawling on it in biro.

"Thanks," said Marta, doubting that she'd ever call the number. "Good luck, Lukasz."

He smiled. "Enjoy England."

4

THE QUESTION WAS, *which exit?* If you wanted to visit a science museum, or in fact any number of museums, there were signs saying where to go. But Marta wanted to go to Egerton Square. All she had was an address. She was beginning to wish she'd kept hold of that book, 'A-Z'.

"Are you OK?" asked a soft female voice that came straight from an English listening test. A well-dressed young lady – probably not much older than Marta – was peering down at her and exuding an expensive-smelling perfume. "You look *lorst.*"

It occurred to Marta that she probably did appear rather pathetic, standing in the station concourse staring at signs and clutching a giant food parcel. She found herself offering up the scrap of paper with the scribbled address.

"Ah, OK," she uttered, nodding, while Marta studied her flawless exterior: glossy, chestnut hair, a natural tan, leggings sprayed onto exceedingly skinny thighs with a pair of high-heeled boots like the ones Julia Roberts wore in Pretty Woman. Marta glanced down at her beloved Malina Q jacket. It shone back at her, brilliant and turquoise. Maybe Warsaw was nothing like London.

"You need Exit 1," the woman explained, brushing a lock of hair off her face with utmost elegance. "With your back to South Ken, head east along Brompton Road until you reach Egerton Terrace. Your road should be just off there."

Marta expressed her gratitude and watched as the figure sashayed sexily up the steps of the station. Now *that* was how she would look in a few weeks. Marta reached down for her leather suitcase, still clutching the parcel, and headed for Exit 1.

Her disbelief reached new heights as she turned the corner into Egerton Square. The whole area was like nothing she'd ever come across. She knew South Kensington was an up-market part of London, but this – this was incredible. Every house on the road had its own set of pillared steps leading up to a double front door, like the White House or some place of worship. Each one was unique, too: one covered in ivy, the next clad in stone, another... Oh my God, thought Marta. That was number fourteen.

It had flames outside the front door. Two enormous, flickering torches either side of the Grecian columns, lighting up the front of the house in the twilight. *She was going to live in a place with flames outside the door.* Marta nearly laughed out loud. She couldn't wait to tell Anka.

As she approached, the worms suddenly returned to her stomach. Was it an embassy building or something? Would she be expected to behave like English royalty? Or worse still – oh no. Was she being invited to live here on the premise that she would look after the place? Would she be expected to cook and clean for the girl, Penelope and Henry's daughter? She rang the bell.

Within seconds, Marta found herself inside a vast, marble-floored atrium, playing an elaborate game of kissing, shrieking and arm-throwing.

"Hi, hiiiiiii!" wailed the tall blonde who had opened the door. "You must be Marta! I'm Tash!"

"Here! Let me take your jacket," offered a smaller girl with a face like a horse, removing the Malina Q coat gingerly as though it might have been contaminated. "My name's Plum, by the way. A school nickname that stuck." She let out a deafening hoot of laughter and kissed Marta on each cheek with great panache.

"Come in! Come *in!*" urged a young man as he slipped a hand around her waist and guided her away from the door. Marta stole a closer look at the guy. He was gorgeous. Lean but toned, with the most incredible jaw line she'd ever seen.

Marta stood, trying to take it all in. The blonde, she ascertained, was the daughter of Penelope and Henry: her new housemate. It took a lot of restraint not to just stare at Tash. She was striking. Not beautiful, but striking. Her face was pale like a china doll's, and her eyes were heavy with well-applied makeup, set off by a pair of pearl earrings. She wore a soft, blue cashmere V-neck with a matching scarf, even though they were inside. And of course, she had the obligatory knee-high boots.

"Let's go through to the kitchen!" suggested the horsy-faced girl. Marta made a mental note to look up the word 'plum' in her dictionary; she was sure it was a type of fruit.

"I think a drink is in order," suggested the good-looking guy. He caught her eye and smiled, cheekily.

"Sorry – how rude of me! This is Jack," announced Tash as she led the way through the echoing hallway. "My boyfriend."

A little cloud went in front of Marta's sun.

"And that's Jeremy," she added, motioning towards the back of the group.

Marta's hopes rose momentarily, and then plummeted. Jeremy's head was too large for his willowy body, and his nose too large for his face. He nodded in her direction, all the time looking down his huge snout as though finding the whole situation rather distasteful. "Ve'y nice to meet you," he said.

Marta smiled uncertainly. They entered an airy room with high ceilings, vast, polished surfaces and lots of matching sets of kitchen implements in chrome and black.

"So! What will you drink?" asked Jack. "Vodka?"

There were screams and whoops of laughter. Marta opted for a gin and tonic, like everybody else. It came in a frosty iced glass with a perfect slice of lime. On Tash's suggestion, they retired to the 'drawing room': a room with no drawings in it – only one very expensive-looking oil painting of an old man looking constipated. They were allocated seats by Tash around a table on upright, red cushioned chairs.

"So, what's it like, being Polish?" asked Plum, excitably.

"What an absurd question!" Jack exclaimed, before Marta could open her mouth.

"Well, I just meant –"

"How is she supposed to answer that? She's been Polish all her life! It's not as though she suddenly found herself liking dumplings and wearing furry coats and adding 'aski' onto the end of all her words one day, is it?"

15

"Don't be racist!" cried Tash, looking outraged.

"I wasn't," Jack replied in a clipped tone. "It's fair to say that those are characteristics of life in the ex-Soviet block. And besides, Polish is not a race. It's a nationality."

Marta felt like a child, with everyone talking about her as though she wasn't there.

Tash pulled a nasty face at her boyfriend, then switched on a smile. "So Marta, whereabouts in Poland are you from?"

Marta opened her mouth, but nothing came out. They were all staring at her, waiting for an answer, and for some reason, she couldn't remember a single word of English. "Łomianki," she said, finally, knowing she should follow it with something, but not sure what.

"Is that near Warsaw?" asked Tash after an awkward pause, speaking slower and louder now.

"Yes."

She wanted to elaborate, but her mind was blank, and even in Polish she couldn't think of anything to say.

"It's nice," she added, finally. They all smiled and nodded understandingly. This was not going well.

"So, where, are, you, planning, to, work, in, London?"

Marta hesitated. She wanted to explain that she'd graduated from one of the top Polish universities and wanted to join the marketing department of a large UK firm, but for some reason, all her vocabulary was missing.

"I… So…"

"Will you get an au pair job?" asked Tash brightly, unable to hide the sympathy from her voice.

Marta's anger started to burn. Firstly, she resented the assumption that she, as a Polish girl, could only hope to get work as a nanny for English children. And secondly, Tash was implying that Marta should find somewhere else to live – after only five minutes in the house. She was getting the distinct impression her host didn't like her.

"No," replied Marta, determinedly. "I have a degree in marketing from Poland, and I hope for using that. I will get a job in an office."

She was surprised by the eloquence with which she delivered her answer – but not as surprised as the others. There was a short silence while they all took in the facts: Marta *could* speak English, and Marta did have a personality.

"Wow, marketing!" gushed Plum, clearly feeling the need to say something.

"It's a novel idea, actually *using* your degree in your job," mused Jeremy, speaking for the first time. He was swilling his gin and tonic around in ever-increasing circles, watching the vortex deepen.

"I don't know – I may not have done any philosophising or economising since I graduated, but I've experienced plenty of office politics," offered Jack.

"Jack did PPE at Oxford," explained Tash. "That's politics, philosophy and economics," she said, expressing each syllable slowly as though Marta were lip-reading. "He works at Goldman Sachs now. He's an investment banker."

Marta nodded. There was something about these people that made her feel silly. They were the same age as her, but somehow they seemed... superior. It was as though they felt sorry for her – and not just because she was new to this city. Marta found herself thinking of Anka, her trusty, humble best friend. Why couldn't they be more like her?

The conversation remained stilted.

"So, d'you know anyone here? D'you have any contacts to get you into marketing?" asked Jack, raising an eyebrow. He was gorgeous, but he knew it.

"I..." She trailed off. She had planned to do all the usual things that people did when looking for a job: trawl the newspaper advertisements, call up companies, maybe look on the internet. That was how it worked back home, at least. But somehow she felt reluctant to disclose her intentions to her companions in case this wasn't how things were done over here. "I have some friends who have come to England," she told them, smiling confidently.

It was only a white lie; she *did* know some people who had come over to England, it was just that she either hadn't kept in touch with them or they'd returned to Poland. The fact was, Marta had nobody to help her over here. She'd manage, though. She always did. A week was what she'd set herself as job-hunting time, and that was all it would take.

"I'm sure you do," said Jack, looking at her quite intensely. "And if you need any more..." He winked at Marta and smiled.

5

MARTA LEANT AGAINST the cold stone wall, listening to the rhythmic slosh of the Thames beneath her. The speedboat zipped off into the distance, heading towards the huge tower with the pointy roof. Canary Woof. It was an office block, according to Tash. The mirrored sides were giving a warped reflection of the near-perfect sky.

To her left was another incredible sight: the big wheel. It had a proper name, but Marta couldn't remember it. If you watched really carefully, and aligned one of the bubble-like carriages with a fixed spot in the distance, you could just about make out its movement: twenty degrees every minute, she calculated.

Marta was in the shade of Tower Bridge and the stone wall was making her cold, but she didn't care. She was in London, and she'd never felt happier. There was something about this city, a vibe, that made her feel free. The place had history, but it wasn't oppressive history. And people didn't cling to it. They got on with life, started afresh, went about their business. Maybe it was because they'd never had communism, thought Marta. Whatever it was, she was ready to make her mark.

Just one day, she'd allowed herself. One day for exploring, seeing London. She had taken ten pounds from tata's stash, although so far she hadn't spent anything. The tourist exhibits were out of the question, and she was avoiding public transport. It wasn't just because of the money; it was because Marta wanted to see London properly. She wanted to go at her own pace, see the streets from ground level, discover back alleys that not even Londoners knew about.

Marta could only guess how many miles she had walked today. Setting off at eight this morning, she'd cut through Hyde Park and walked amongst grey suited commuters, battled through crowds on Oxford Street, slipped through the ghost town of Holborn, got involved in a Japanese tour around St Paul's Cathedral and wandered through a bleak part of town where every shop sold expensive suits or sandwiches. Eventually, she had crossed the river and followed it along to the cobbled streets of Tower Bridge.

It was nice to have time to think. The last few days had flown by in a mad, stressful blur, with no time to mull over what was happening. Despite her elation at finally being here, Marta found herself missing her home town. She hadn't expected to. There wasn't much there to miss, but strangely her mind kept bringing up images of fur coats, cold wind and brusque shop keepers. Crumbling roads, signs in Polish. Soup. Sleet. Most of all, though, she was thinking about the people.

Tash had done her best to welcome Marta into her home – if you could call it that. It was an incredible place, and Marta knew how lucky she was, being allowed to live in it. But she felt uneasy. It wasn't just because of the risk of breaking a crystal ornament or knocking a chandelier – it was because of Tash. Tash was very different to Marta. She was different to every girl Marta had ever met. She was rich, of course, but that wasn't the only thing. She was… hmm. Marta couldn't think of the word. She seemed to need constant reassurance, not just in terms of how she looked and whether her clothes looked good, but in conversation, too. She had to be the centre of attention – everyone's attention, but especially her boyfriend's. Not that Jack seemed particularly enamoured with her. Perhaps Tash sensed that. Perhaps she knew, too, that her friends weren't real friends – they were just a group of similarly elevated people, one of whom fancied her boyfriend. Poor Tash. She was insecure. That was the word. Insecure.

The water was lapping more gently now, and Marta became aware of a presence behind her. She turned round. A young man in a fluorescent yellow jacket was parking a dirt cart up against the wall. She watched out of the corner of her eye as he set about sweeping the area and emptying his load into the cart.

A pleasure boat chugged along the river, blasting out unintelligible commentary to a group of six windswept passengers. She smiled. The street cleaner crept into her field of vision, hoisting himself onto the wall further down and bending over something in his lap. Sandwiches. It was lunchtime. Marta half-watched as he unwrapped the tin foil and wolfed it down in record time. He screwed the tin foil into a ball and lobbed it into his cart, where it made a satisfying thud against the bottom.

Marta prised herself away from the wall, contemplating getting some food for herself. As she did, something caught her eye. A blur of red and white. She took a proper look in the workman's direction. He was reading a magazine. And sure enough: across the top of the cover page was the distinctive Polish flag. *Polski Express,* read the title.

"Cześć!" she said, impulsively. It was still a novelty meeting fellow Poles, even though there were over a million of them over here.

The guy met her eye, expressing no surprise at hearing his own language. "Cześć," he replied, checking out Marta's legs.

"Er, are you done with that?" Marta asked, at exactly the moment he hopped off the wall and tossed the magazine into his cart.

He chuckled, taking another look at Marta's legs. "Looks like it, doesn't it?" He bent down and fished out the supplement, wiping some mayonnaise from the cover with his sleeve. "Want it?"

Deciding it would be rude to decline, Marta nodded. "Thanks."

"You new around here?" asked the man, addressing her breasts this time. Marta was beginning to wish she hadn't started this conversation.

"I arrived yesterday. I'm not... not based here. I'm staying, er, somewhere else," she stammered. Admitting she lived in South Kensington would be like saying 'I'm very rich'.

"Huh. Aren't we all?" The guy rolled his eyes. "Anyway, I'd better get off. Enjoy," he said, nodding at the soggy magazine in her hands and taking one last look at her legs.

Marta forced her mouth into a smile. "Bye."

There was only one reason Marta had asked for the magazine. It was something she'd seen on the back cover. An advert. Spreading the supplement out on the wall, Marta carefully extracted the staples and pulled off the cover, reading the text as she did so. She folded it into eight, shoved the page in her pocket, and set off in search of food. Today wasn't going to be entirely unproductive after all.

6

"MARTA? MARTA, oh thank goodness you're there. Would you be a sweetie and open the fridge? Only I've just done my nails, and I *need* my skinny latte before I do anything! Could you…?"

Tash rushed across the lounge and dramatically revealed her manicured fingers. She was wrapped in a blue silk dressing gown, her head engulfed in swathes of white, fluffy towelling.

"OK," said Marta, putting to one side the recruitment section of the local newspaper, which was turning out to be less than inspirational. The only offers of employment seemed to be for shop workers and bus drivers, and it was depressing how many ads were so obviously directed at Eastern Europeans.

"Oh, thank you Marta!" gushed Tash, fanning her pearly nails in front of her face. "I can't survive without my skinny latte in the mornings, and I've got *such* a busy day today!"

Marta nodded. She was dubious of the fact that Tash would die if she didn't have her morning coffee, and she also doubted the industriousness of her day.

"We're doing a girlie sesh," Tash explained, shepherding Marta out of her seat and into the kitchen. If she hadn't just done her nails, thought Marta, she probably would have physically lifted her out of the chair. "It was Plum's idea – you remember Plum? We're shopping all morning, then having a boozy lunch at the Rose Tree and then she's booked us for some beauty treatments – probably shouldn't have done my nails really, but you know what it's like when they really need doing… Now if you could just get the milk out–"

Marta dutifully opened the fridge, nodding as Tash prattled on.

The truth was, she *didn't* know what it was like, caring so much about trivial things like nails. She couldn't relate at all to Tash's mindless drivel, or in fact to anything going on in Tash's life. She reached inside the fridge and pulled out the nearly-empty container of milk.

Tash let out a cry of anguish as though she'd just learned some tragic news. "Oh no!"

Marta held the plastic carton, watching Tash's expression. In fact she had known they were running low on milk, and last night she'd sacrificed her evening hot drink for the sake of household peace.

"How did that... I mean, when..."

"We had little yesterday," Marta explained. "When I look for the milk to do my hot chocolate, there not really enough, I think–"

"Oh, of course," said Tash, nodding patronisingly. "Your hot chocolate. You use a full mug of milk for that, don't you?"

"Yes, but I –" Marta tried to explain.

"Well I suppose I'll have to get some more," Tash sighed. "I simply *can't* start the day without my skinny latte," she said, as though Marta hadn't heard the first time, or the time after that.

Marta took the hint. "I'll get it."

"Oh, *would* you?" asked Tash, suddenly all smiles again. "Only I'd have to get dressed, and my nails..."

"No problem."

Marta grabbed her purse and yanked open the front door. In fact, she was quite glad to get out. It wasn't the house that she needed to escape from; it was Tash. Tash was exhausting. The problem was that she had two personalities: the caring, easy-going, self-confident one she portrayed, and the tense and insecure one she tried to keep hidden. In living with Tash, Marta had seen snatches of the latter, and it wasn't pleasant. Like a swan, Tash was serenely beautiful but always on the cusp of turning nasty. The only way to placate her, Marta had discovered, was to play to her ego. Tell her how gorgeous she looked, how stylish. It was pathetic, really.

"Morning," sang the old man in the corner shop. He was always chirpy, presumably because he made so much money from his customers. It was extortionate – but then, the whole of London was extortionate in Marta's opinion.

She lifted the two-pint carton onto the counter. The shopkeeper thanked her. He put it in a bag, slid it back to her and thanked her again. "Seventy-five pence, please. Thank you."

Marta waited for her change, and, predictably, got thanked for taking it. She grabbed her purchase and walked out, hearing the silly little ding-dong as the door banged shut.

The English, Marta had observed, were either very polite or very rude. Back home, making a purchase would not involve fuss or pleasantries or multiple thank yous. It would just be a matter of exchanging money for goods. Here, you were as likely to be served by an acne-faced, grunting zombie as you were an over-zealous maniac with a politeness disorder.

A section of pavement had been cordoned off because of a tiny crack in a paving stone. That was another thing she'd noticed about England. You got treated like children. Everywhere you went, there were signs saying 'mind the gap', 'slippery floor', 'watch your head', as though nobody was capable of looking after themselves. In Poland, you did things at your own risk. If you stepped in dog shit, it was your fault – nobody else's. God, she missed Łomianki.

Marta nearly fell through the front door as it was thrown open by something blue wearing hair curlers.

"Did you get it? Oh, you are a *sweetie!* Thank you! Oh good – enough for my skinny latte *and* your hot chocolate!" she gave Marta a little look as if to say, *you won't make that mistake again, will you?* "Tell you what, be an absolute star and make the coffee, will you? I've got to get the timing right with these things, or my hair will fry!"

Marta nodded, adding 'manipulative' to her list of personality traits for the swan. She flicked the switch on the kettle and wandered into the lounge. Her English CV was still there – poking out from under a magazine. Clearly *Easy Living* was more interesting to Tash than Marta's list of schools and achievements.

Pouring the coffee into the frothed, steamed milk – the way Tash had taught her – Marta half-wondered whether she should consider au pair work after all.

"Oh, you've used the wrong mug," Tash exclaimed, appearing from nowhere with new, bouncy blonde curls. "Never mind," she sighed, taking the coffee from Marta. "I always have my skinny latte in a tall mug," she explained.

Marta nodded, feeling more like an au pair than ever. "Sorry."

Tash sat herself down at the kitchen table and embarked on a thorough inspection of her nails.

"Have you read my CV?" asked Marta. Now was probably not the time, she thought, but the interview was on Monday – only two days away.

"What?" Tash looked up. "Oh, er, yes. Yes I did."

"You did?" Marta was surprised; there was no evidence that the print-off had been touched.

"Yes. It's very good. The English is perfect."

"Really?"

"Yes, really!" she cried enthusiastically. "It's impeccable. You should easily get a job with that CV."

Marta smiled. Maybe Tash was more warm-hearted than she'd given her credit for. "Great!" She bounded over to the table and tugged the CV out from under the pile. This was her passport to better things. "Thank you so much, Tash!"

Tash smiled, re-inspecting her nails. "Any time."

7

"*PUSH* THE DOOR, DON'T PULL!" squawked the tinny voice through the intercom.

Marta fumbled some more with the latch, and finally found herself falling through the doorway, stubbing her toe on the step. It wasn't her finest entry.

"Um, hello," she said, looking around for the reception desk. There was foliage everywhere. Huge, exotic-looking plants leaned into the room from bath-sized pots, growing up walls and clinging to the ceiling. Behind all the greenery, bright orange panels could be seen with black and pink writing etched into them, each letter the size of a fist − presumably spelling out company mottos and mission statements. She'd seen it before, but smaller, on the Genesis website. Marta felt a hollowness in her stomach. It was all so intimidating.

"Over here," said a stern female voice. Marta changed direction and clattered over to the source of the sound. The high heels − an insistence by her mother − were making her feel gawky, and the suit jacket, which didn't quite match her trousers, was itching around the collar.

"My name is Marta Dabrowska," she told the receptionist, who sat, perfectly poised, behind a bright orange kidney shaped desk, with nothing more than a keyboard and flat-screen monitor.

"And you're here for an interview?" the woman cut in, using the minimal number of facial muscles required to speak. Her jet-black hair was secured with what looked like a skewer, her forehead pulled taut.

"Yes," Marta nodded. Was it that obvious she was an interviewee? She tried to relax, releasing some of the strain in her shoulders and neck, but then felt as though she was stooping and straightened up again. She focused on the ten-foot Genesis logo behind the receptionist's head, waiting.

"Ah, yes. You're meeting with John Rayne and Elizabeth Pardoe at ten o'clock. Take a seat–" she waved her hand towards the jungle. "I'll tell them you're here."

Marta clip-clopped across the reception area towards a pair of orange sofas that tessellated perfectly with an S-shaped glass table. She felt like a children's TV presenter going on set to talk about leaves.

Marta had woken at six this morning without an alarm. Even as her eyes had fluttered open, she'd known what day it was. She had been dreaming about the interview. This was her first one. She was applying for the position of Marketing Assistant at Genesis, a small advertising agency specialising in 'innovative campaign strategy development'. Marta wasn't fazed by the long words; that was just advertising for you. She'd done a whole degree in the subject. Of course, it would be harder when the jargon was in another language, but she'd cope. She just wished this place wasn't so… so *flawless*. If only there was a ceiling tile missing, or a leaf going brown, or a hair out of place on the receptionist's head.

"Someone's on their way down," informed the robot woman.

Marta rearranged herself on the fluorescent seat. She crossed her legs one way, then the other, and then decided that they were simply too long to cross and tried to hide them under the curvy glass table. If only her trousers matched her suit, she thought, re-living the moment this morning when Tash had passed her in the hallway. Her disdain had been so apparent, despite the winning smile. Tash had looked fantastic of course, her shiny blonde hair tied up in a ponytail, a range of brown strappy tops showing off her fake tan and a tight pencil skirt clinging to her thighs above some impossibly high stilettos. In all the days Marta had lived with the girl, she had yet to see the same garment twice. That was one of the prerequisites, presumably, of being a director's PA at Paul Smith.

In fact, Tash's extensive collection held some advantages for Marta – not least because one of the two wardrobes in Marta's room (which, between them, took up more space than her bedroom back home) was being used as an overspill, giving her free access to a vast selection of fashion accessories she could only dream of owning. Tash had given her consent, explaining that it was 'all last year's stuff'. Today, Marta had taken full advantage, spraying her wrists with some Jean Patou before slipping a Cartier watch on one hand and a selection of gold bracelets on the other.

There was a tapping sound. Striding across the leafy reception was a young woman in her mid-twenties. "Marta Dabrowska?" she barked, more stomping than stepping towards her.

Marta smiled and rose to her feet, banging her knee on the table with a thud. "Ow. Yes, is me, yes. Elizabeth Pardo?" she said, pleased with herself for remembering her interviewer's name.

The girl let out a coarse peal of laughter. "God, no!" She threw her head back. "No, Elizabeth Pardoe is a Campaign Planner. I'm just an ad assistant! I was sent down to get you, that's all. I'm Jenny."

Marta could feel herself blushing as they shook hands. Jenny was still laughing at Marta's mistake as they ascended to the seventh floor in a lift made entirely of orange-tinted mirrors. "Hah!" she chuckled to herself, shaking her head. "I don't know what Elizabeth would have thought..."

Marta had never felt less at ease. She suddenly felt desperate to run away. She didn't want to be going to the seventh floor of this orange-walled agency. She didn't want to meet this fearsome-sounding Elizabeth woman. She didn't want to see any more slim, fashionable English girls being good at their jobs. She just wanted to be back in Poland, where everyone spoke her language, where she was the best, where people looked up to her.

Yesterday, sitting in the internet café just off the Kings Road, browsing through case studies on the Genesis website, Marta had felt calm and relaxed about today. She'd even felt positive about her chances of getting the job. All of a sudden, her bravado had slipped away. She didn't feel capable of anything.

"Here we are," announced Jenny, as the lift doors slid open to reveal another orange-furnished reception area, this one airier and not home to so many plants.

It was clear from her manner that Jenny didn't have time to chaperone interviewees around the seventh floor. She marched boldly down a corridor, halting abruptly outside a frosted glass door and glaring as Marta nearly slammed into her. "Easy!"

She opened the door and nodded Marta through.

"This is Marta Dabrowska," declared Jenny. Two chairs swivelled round simultaneously to face her. "Elizabeth Pardoe," she said, "and John Rayne."

Marta smiled confidently at her interviewers as they rose to their feet. The silence lengthened, and it suddenly occurred to her that a hand-shake was expected.

"Dzien – er, good day," she muttered, as her hand was gripped firmly by John Rayne's. "Nice to meet you," she added, accepting Elizabeth's weaker grasp and inwardly cursing her clumsiness.

John Rayne was in his mid thirties, Marta guessed, although his bloodshot eyes and creased skin added a few years to his age. A slender man, he wore black-rimmed glasses and a beige corduroy jacket that gave him a retro look.

Elizabeth Pardoe was nothing like as intimidating as the image of her in Marta's head. Possibly a little eccentric, if the string of what looked like ping-pong balls hanging round her neck and the matching earrings were anything to go by, her face seemed kindly enough. She was a few years older than her colleague, and, if the order of Jenny's introductions was important, more senior.

Jenny had slipped away, leaving Marta alone with her interviewers and a colourful set of swivel chairs, flip-charts and marker pens. In the corner there were even some large rubber balls – presumably alternative seats for the whacky, creative types. It was nothing like the meeting rooms she remembered from her placements in Warsaw.

"Let's talk!" cried Elizabeth, somewhat more dramatically than necessary. "Sit down, darling!" She waved at the luminous array of swivel chairs opposite.

"OK," she went on, once Marta had seated herself on a bright yellow chair that was far too high but seemingly impossible to adjust. She half-slouched to compensate. "Now we've seen your CV, and we've seen a lot of other CVs, too. But there's only one position here." She paused, and pushed herself away from the table, rolling backwards on the chair's casters. "The thing is, we need to fill it with someone good."

Elizabeth Pardoe suddenly pushed off with her feet and spun

round several times on her swivel chair. Marta watched as the woman faced her once, twice, three times, and then came to an instant halt, flinging her feet on the ground and staring at Marta. Marta decided that she was either completely insane or testing her. She nodded.

"The job title is Marketing Assistant," the woman continued, tapping two of her over-sized beads together. They even sounded like ping-pong balls. "I'll be honest with you, darling. The role is low-level. The successful applicant will not be contributing to the creative process for key accounts at Genesis. He or she may not even contribute to smaller campaigns. His or her role is to be the office dog's body – you know?" She cocked her head, checking that Marta understood. Marta had no idea, but she nodded assertively. She would ask Tash about office dogs later.

"But that is not to say that the applicant should not have a full knowledge of what we do at Genesis, and how we go about our business. This role is for people with integrity, insight, experience, and most importantly, *ambition*. We want people who can *go on* to run campaigns, even if they're taping parcels together and fetching sandwiches at first. OK?"

Marta nodded. This was *so* not what she had expected. It seemed beneath her and over her head, all at once. And this Elizabeth woman appeared to be bonkers.

"Now, John has some questions." She nodded for John to begin.

"Yeah. Right. OK." John pinched the bridge of his nose then stretched the skin around his eyes. "So, Marta. Your CV." He slid one copy along the table for his colleague to see, and leaned forward to look at his own. Elizabeth ignored hers and sat bolt upright, staring straight ahead at the wall behind Marta's left shoulder.

"Firstly, your university. Forgive me, but I've never heard of it."

"Szkoła Główna Handlowa w Warszawie," Marta told him. "It is the best place to do studying of marketing in the whole of Poland."

"OK. And is it…" John paused while he tried to find the right words. "Is it *good?* I mean, we can only measure against what we know: Cambridge, Oxford, Manchester and so on… how does it compare to these?"

If Tash's boyfriend was to be believed, SGH didn't come close to

29

any of the UK universities in terms of quality. But Marta was doubtful of Jack's rationale, and reluctant to express his opinions in this interview. The problem was, *she didn't know*. There was no direct comparison between English and Polish institutions, or if there was, she didn't have proof. All she knew was that she had worked bloody hard to get into SGH, and competition for places was stiffer there than anywhere else in the country.

"It's the best in Poland. That is all to say." Marta shrugged. "Many people very brilliant at marketing come from Szkoła Główna Handlowa."

"Such as whom?" asked Elizabeth, from behind closed eyes.

Shit. She'd walked into that one. Marta thought quickly. Surely it was better to offer a name, even an unheard of name, than nothing at all? "Benedykt Luczak," replied Marta. Benedykt was her first ever boyfriend. He'd gone on to become a forklift truck driver.

"I'm not familiar with his work," stated Elizabeth, her eyes still shut. "John, are you?"

"I'm not, no, but I'm sure over in Poland…" John was looking down Marta's CV. "Again, I'm afraid I'm not familiar with these companies you list as your placements."

Marta began to offer explanations for each of the four firms listed – most of them advertising agencies like this one (only not at all like this one). She was becoming increasingly distracted by Elizabeth's movements. The Campaign Planner was lifting her arms like a bird in flight, only very, very slowly.

"I work for six weeks at Young & Rubicam," Marta explained, keeping track of the woman out of the corner of her eye whilst addressing John, who seemed oblivious to his colleague's behaviour. "It form part of the big global company, WPP."

John's eyes lit up at this. "Oh, of course! I knew it rang a bell. They're the ones that did the first TV ad, aren't they?"

Marta had no idea. The truth was, she'd spent her six week placement opening and sorting post. "Yes! TV, yes!" she cried. Elizabeth was now holding very still, her arms out wide. It wasn't a test, Marta decided. The woman was simply mad.

"OK, Marta, talk me through a campaign you've worked on. Preferably a multi-channel campaign," demanded John.

Shit, again. Marta had never actually worked on a campaign. She had, however, looked on the Genesis website the day before, where there were plenty of examples of multi-channel campaigns. If she could just switch a few of the names to Polish ones, invent a few details, change the client details...

"I was involved in multimedia campaign for Polish sports clothing brand..." Away she went. John seemed to be buying it, and Marta was soon lost in her own fabrications. It was going brilliantly, she thought. Until, that was, Elizabeth Pardoe came to.

"Darling! What on earth is this?" screeched the woman, looking at Marta's CV for the first time.

"Your English, darling! It's appalling!"

Marta frowned, presuming that this was some sort of joke – although it had to be said, Elizabeth's face did not appear jovial. Her CV had been checked by Tash, who had said it was fine. 'Impeccable' was the word she had used.

"'I like be ambitious and to find new and different ways to doing things,'" read Elizabeth, distastefully. "Darling, I simply can't have that. I can't. Not even for an office junior. No." She shook her head, in case there was any doubt.

Marta was flummoxed. Her CV was impeccable – Tash had said so!

"Darling, my four year-old daughter could write a better CV," she added, as though on a new mission to reduce Marta to tears.

"Er, do we have your contact details, Marta?" John asked tactfully.

"They're not even on her CV! Only Polish ones. You do *have* a place to stay in England, don't you, darling?"

Marta was determined not to show her real feelings, which were a mixture of rage, hatred, shame and despair. This woman was *not* going to get to her. "Yes," she replied, hearing a wobble in her own voice. How could she have been stupid enough not to update her CV with her UK address? And how could Tash not have spotted that, too?

"Or a mobile number? Or email?" suggested John, quietly. Another omission, she realised.

"I can give to you my London address," Marta told them, reaching down and then realising that she hadn't transferred the scrap of paper from her old tatty handbag into Tash's. She couldn't remember the postcode.

"I will call you with my new number," she said, knowing that she never would.

"Thanks for coming in, darling."

"Do call, won't you?" said John, obviously trying to make her feel better. Marta just felt like crying. What a waste of time – both her time and theirs.

"I will. Thanks, yes." Marta grabbed her borrowed handbag and fled the technicolour boardroom before the tears started.

8

THE MAN IN FRONT OF HER stamped his feet in the cold, and others started doing the same. They were huddling like penguins. Marta zipped her jacket up to her chin and scrunched her gloved hands into fists. It felt like home – not just because of the overcast skies and the biting wind, but because of the rows of people wrapped up in fur coats and hats, almost all of them Polish.

Marta tried to guess how many were here. The queue snaked all the way back to the road, densely packed and confined by cordons. Between two and five thousand, she estimated, and every one of them was under the age of thirty. No wonder businesses were shutting down back in Poland; the entire workforce was here.

There was a noise from the front of the queue. Standing on tip-toes, Marta could just make out the scene up ahead. The main doors were opening. Around her, people started jostling for position.

It was with trepidation rather than excitement that Marta trudged forwards with everyone else. The *Polski Express* ad had caught her eye with the phrase, 'Good work in all sectors', but then she'd read the rest of the advertisement. 'No skills or experience required!' screamed one line. 'Jobs for non-English speakers!' Looking around at her companions only compounded Marta's suspicions that this recruitment 'fair' would almost certainly have none of the jobs she was looking for – but then, after her experience with Genesis, she thought, maybe she was being over-ambitious.

"Excuse me! D'you speak English? D'you have a couple of minutes?" yelled a woman outside the entrance, trying to poke a microphone into the faces of passing Poles. Behind her were a couple of journalists with notepads and a cameraman waiting for the woman to get a catch.

Marta dodged the microphone and barged on, head down. She felt humiliated, like a caged animal. It was as though they were all on parade in a circus put on for the benefit of middle-class Brits. She could see the headlines now: *Poles Queue Hungrily for Plumbing Jobs. Service Sector Swells as EU Grows.* She knew how the English saw Polish migrants: as hard-working, unskilled labourers. That was it. As far as they were concerned, Poles didn't have careers; they had jobs. There was no way she was gratifying that woman with a quote.

Suddenly, Marta was inside a massive, echoing hall – like a school gym, only ten times the size. Coloured strip-lights burned holes in her retina as she stared up at the giant banners suspended from the rafters, each hanging above a company stall. The stalls – literally hundreds of them – were neatly arranged all over the room like blocks in the computer game Tetris. It was overwhelming.

"Jobs caring for the elderly!" cried a young woman, in Polish. She leaned out from behind her stall and thrust a leaflet into Marta's hand. "No English required!"

"Bar work! Catering and kitchen support!" screamed another woman, this time in English. She had an extra-long stall, and a whole team of people behind it. "Are you interested in kitchen support work?" asked the woman, catching Marta's interest in the banner, which read 'Wetherspoons'.

"Kitchen support? What's that?"

The woman smiled efficiently and handed Marta a flyer in Polish. A glance at the pictures answered Marta's question. 'Kitchen support' was washing up. Marta walked on.

"We only employ Eastern Europeans," Marta heard one guy explain to a meat-head covered in tattoos. "Most are Czech, some Lithuanian, but more and more we're recruiting Poles." The banner brandished a silhouette of a JCB.

Marta came to the end of the aisle and headed for the next, picking up pace to make it harder for recruiters to engage her in conversation. How interesting it would be, she thought, if everyone had filled out a form with their qualifications on their way in today.

The findings would shock most of the exhibitors. There were probably enough degrees and diplomas in here to run a small city – but the Wetherspoon woman didn't care about that, and nor did anyone else. They just wanted a reliable source of 'kitchen support'.

"Improve your English on the job!" claimed a hospitality company specialising in corporate functions. Yeah, right. No doubt there were endless opportunities to improve one's English doing 'kitchen support' with a crew made up entirely of Eastern Europeans, thought Marta, storming to the end of the next aisle.

The recruitment fair was not doing great things for her mood. As far as she could tell, the whole event was an excuse for British companies to get together and exploit the Polish migrant community. Marta was willing to bet that none of these firms offered more than the UK minimum wage, which, decent as it was over here, didn't do justice to the skills and experience that so many of these workers had. It was like a slave market, only with slaves who were willingly selling themselves. It made her so angry.

"The work is challenging, yes," one recruiter admitted to a girl about Marta's age. Marta slowed down and took in the details. *BirdsEye,* said the banner. Next to it was a picture of a frozen fish. It was the first time today she'd heard language she was used to hearing in the context of careers: *challenging.*

"Sometimes you may be on a twelve-hour shift, and you'll be working in a food chiller for up to ten hours of that."

Marta's heart sank. She skipped the last two aisles and headed for the exit. There were only so many insults she could take in one day.

"Leaflet?" asked a young man, in Polish. He was loitering by the door, apparently not associated with any particular stall, although he had more flyers than any of the stallholders. There was something about him – maybe his ruffled, sandy hair, maybe his eyes – that made Marta stop and smile. She took a leaflet.

"What's it for?" she asked in Polish.

"Here – leaflets," he said, pointing at the one she'd just taken.

Marta frowned. "I know, but what's it advertising?"

"Jobs in leaflets,"

"But what type of jobs?" Marta asked, wondering whether the guy was just stupid. Then she realised. The leaflets were advertising jobs handing out leaflets. "Oh, right. Thanks," she said, starting to walk on. She wouldn't throw it away right now – she'd wait until she was out of sight of the guy with the lovely smile.

"Goodbye," he said, meeting her eye.

"'Bye," replied Marta, lingering briefly but not sure how to extend their conversation. Eventually, the awkwardness got too much. With a sheepish grin and a final glance at his cute, messy hair, Marta left the hall.

9

MARTA SQUEEZED THROUGH the immovable mass of bodies and jumped off the bus, just as the doors were closing. According to the map she had borrowed from Tash, Bayswater was right near the big park. She had twenty minutes to kill.

The sky was a pure, monochrome white, and the trees were still dripping from the overnight rain. Of the few people dotted about the park, Marta seemed to be the only one who didn't have either a dog or a Lycra running outfit. A girl sped past wearing pink mini-shorts and a matching strap on her upper arm, from which protruded several gadgets. That was something Marta had noticed about London. Everybody, it seemed, owned a pair of white headphones.

Seeing the joggers reminded Marta of home. Back in Łomianki, running had been the only means of getting properly warm. She could have run that six-mile route round the village with her eyes shut. Marta missed the cold. She missed the unique combination of sweat on her forehead and sleet on her hair. It was almost tempting to break into a jog, thinking about it. But she didn't. She couldn't. It wasn't just that she was wearing the wrong shoes – a pair of office heels, borrowed from Tash – it was her mood. She couldn't run when she felt like this.

It was fifteen days now since she'd arrived in England. Fifteen days of searching for work, and not a single offer. She felt like a failure. It wasn't even as though she'd been aiming too high, either. After the Genesis fiasco and a couple more morale-crushing interviews, Marta had lowered her expectations and applied for jobs as office assistant, secretarial clerk, shop staff – she'd even gone for a job in a Polish bagel shop.

Marta had been turned down for being too quiet, too brash, too keen, too Polish-centric on her knowledge of brands. She couldn't win. English companies only wanted to hire people who'd lived English lives and attained English qualifications. It was simpler for them – less risky, less of an unknown. Marta's qualifications may as well have come from Mars, for all they cared. It was impossible for her to break in.

What upset her most was the fact that a Western European would probably have succeeded where she had failed. An Ecole Centrale graduate would have had no problems explaining her qualifications and foreign experience. French was fine. Polish wasn't. She made a decision. If she didn't get today's job, that was it. She was heading back to Łomianki.

"You want good Indian curry?"

"Chinese takeaway for you?"

"Cheap hotel?"

The leaflets were thrust at her as she barged down Bayswater, heading for number eighty-four. Usually she would have fended them off, but not today. Not when she knew that her only hope of staying in the country was to become one of them. She could hardly believe it herself. She was signing up to be one of these poor, miserable people who spent their lives being rejected and abused by strangers. The idea repulsed her.

The street could have been in another country, were it not for the black cabs hooting their way down the middle of it. Sweet, sickly incense burned from open shop fronts and the air was alive with the sound of bartering in fifty languages. Faces were black, white and every shade of brown – more diverse than you'd ever see in Poland. Marta liked it. It was a far cry from the silent, well-kept streets of Kensington.

Number eighty-four was sandwiched between a newsagent and a tattoo parlour. The door looked as though it had once been white, but years of weathering, graffiti and grime had turned it brown. There were four buzzers, none of them labelled. Marta pressed the top one and waited.

She was staring at the intercom box, waiting to speak, when suddenly a noise broke out above her.

"WHAT D'YOU WANT?"

Marta looked up. A large man face was peering down at her from three floors up, revealing a mat of dark underarm hair as he held open the window.

"I'm Marta. Here to do interview," she explained.

"WHAT?"

"I'm Marta–"

"I CAN'T HEAR A WORD. JUST COME ON UP. FOURTH FLOOR." The window banged shut.

The door started making a mechanical wheezing sound. Marta pushed on it. As she started to climb the stairs, it dawned on her that this place, with its peeling paint, splintered floors and broken banisters wasn't all that different to places she'd been to in Warsaw. When she was doing her first placement, Marta had applied through an agency that was based in a building very much like this – only colder. She'd had to sit a test in a room at the top where she felt sure the ink would freeze before it left the pen. Sadly, there would be no test today.

Finally Marta reached the summit, and stood for a few seconds to catch her breath. She was getting unfit. In the last two weeks, she'd been so busy applying for jobs that she hadn't granted herself time to exercise. Running had felt like a luxury she couldn't afford.

"Come in!" yelled the same voice that had shouted at her through the window.

When she had glimpsed the man's head and armpit from below, Marta had only seen a fraction of Barry Roffey. His body, a vast, oozing mass, appeared to have been poured into the old office chair – a foam-filled relic that was surely too flimsy to support his weight.

His office, if that was the right word, consisted of boxes – hundreds of boxes – piled up around an L-shaped scrap of threadbare carpet. In the corner of it sat Barry, behind a mountain of papers.

"Hello. My name is Marta. I am here to do interview," she explained.

"To do *interview?*" asked Barry, chuckling into his many chins. "That's one way of putting it, luvvie."

Marta stepped forward, offering her CV. "I don't think I sent this–"

"Wha's that then?" Barry screwed up his fat face and moved it closer to the piece of paper.

"My CV." Marta had been careful to amend this version, adding her UK contact details, perfecting the sentences and rearranging to be more like the examples she'd found online.

Barry leaned back in his chair. It creaked ominously. "Did you fill out a form for me?"

Marta nodded.

"Where is it?"

"I sent back straight away to you."

"Right." Barry looked at the hummocks of paper that formed an undulating surface on his desk. Dislodging just one of the sheets was likely to cause an avalanche. "Tell ya what, just do another one," he suggested, reaching backwards to one of the piles on the floor.

Marta dutifully filled out the required information: name, age, nationality, availability, day/night preferences. There were some tick-boxes at the end that Marta found slightly peculiar, such as criminal record, history of violence and religion, but she placed her ticks and returned the form.

"Oh good – you're Polish."

Marta raised her eyebrows.

"Well, I don't get no jip from the Poles – not usually. None of that bloody turban nonsense, or beards." He snorted. "Not, obviously, implyin' that you'd 'ave a beard. Hah! But the public don't take leaflets from Pakis and what-not. Now, when can you start?"

Marta looked at the man in disbelief. Was he talking about Asian people?

"I, er…"

"You've put on your form 'now', so how 'bout Monday?"

Marta nodded keenly, hiding her disgust. "Great."

"You come 'ere at eight a.m., yeah? You take your box of flyers, you go to the zone I tell ya – *no moving out of your zone, alright?* – and you give 'em away. Eight a.m. to eight p.m., with one hour for lunch. You run out, you come back for more. You get rid of your load, OK? No funny business – no binning, no pairing up, no copping off early. You're there to give leaflets out. We've got people checking, OK?"

Marta nodded, although she doubted the fact that Barry Roffey had 'people checking', and she knew for sure that he wouldn't be out there in person patrolling the streets.

"How much—"

"I'm comin' to that," he barked. "You'll do Monday to Saturday, same every day, until I say so. If you're planning to bugger off back to Poland, tell me. If you're sick, tell me. I've got a phone, so use it. You pull too many sickies, you're out of a job."

Marta nodded again.

"I pay you fifty quid a day, nothing if you're sick or caught messin' about. End of the week, there'll be an envelope here for you with three hundred quid, if it's a full week. OK?"

Some quick mental arithmetic told Marta that she would be getting just under five pounds per hour – nearly thirty złoty. That was more than she'd earn in marketing back home. She was earning a better wage standing around on pavements than she would be in Warsaw using her brain!

It was raining when Marta emerged at street level. Merchants were pulling sheets over their wares and pulling stalls under cover. The smell of pipe smoke was more potent than ever. Marta made a detour down Bayswater, breathing in the damp, fumy air and thinking.

She was still thinking ten minutes later when she barged her way onto the bus. How, after all the effort she had put in at school, at university, on all her placements, had she ended up here? This wasn't her dream: standing on a crowded street trying to shove flyers into the hands of Londoners, her knuckles white with cold. It wasn't what she'd worked for.

OK, so the money was good, but Marta wanted a *proper* job. A job in an office where she used what she'd learnt at the Szkoła. A job where they valued her creative mind, where she was able to use her intelligence. She had seen the recruitment websites: slick, glossy, full of promise. They were crammed with exciting jobs in all sectors for all types of people – all types of *English* people. Some even specified which universities applicants had to have come from. Oxford and Cambridge were the clear favourites. Lucky Tash and her cronies.

The bus squealed to a halt at some traffic lights. Rubbing a patch in the steamed-up window, Marta realised they were on Brompton Road – one stop from her house. She leaned forward and pressed the button. Still thinking about her demeaning experience with Barry Roffey, she stepped off the bus and stumbled home, hoping Tash wouldn't be back yet.

"Hi! How was your day?! Got a job yet?" sung the familiar voice from the kitchen. Tash was back.

"Hello," replied Marta, wondering if it would be considered rude to go straight to her bedroom. She really didn't want to face the inquisition about her pathetic new job.

"Want a cup of tea?" asked Tash, peeping out from the kitchen looking exceedingly smug. She had changed into yet another outfit, Marta noticed: soft pink trousers and a tight hooded top that revealed a band of perfectly tanned stomach.

Marta felt obliged to be sociable. "Yes. Thank you."

"So, any luck today?" she asked again.

Marta forced herself into a faux good mood. "Actually yes! Not a great job, but at least I will earn money. Three hundred pounds a week!"

"That's great news! Well done!" cried Tash, clasping her hands together. Then she paused, frowning. "A – a week?"

"Yes!"

"Right. Er, good. What is the job?"

Marta shrugged. "Oh, paperwork mainly," she said, trying not to lie.

"Paperwork? Is that all they told you? How very vague!"

God, she was irritating. The one time Tash proffered some semblance of interest in Marta's life, it was to ridicule her new career.

"Oh, I don't know yet. Some sort of transactions." Again, not entirely lying.

"Is it in a nice office, like you wanted?" Tash probed. Marta began to wonder whether she'd been followed out this afternoon.

"It's in a beautiful office," Marta lied. "I have my own desk, and a small plant, like this–" she sized up her imaginary pot plant in her hands – "and the people are lovely. Is near Victoria," she added, for a touch of credibility.

"Well, that's *excellent*, Marta," Tash exclaimed, handing over a cup of tea and chinking her own against it. "Here's to your new job in paperwork!"

10

TASH WAS LOOKING AT her in the mirror, barely disguising her contempt. "Are you sure you don't want to borrow a jacket?" she asked.

Marta looked down at the turquoise coat. She loved Anka's gift. "I'm fine, thank you."

Tash finished straightening her perfectly straight hair, and pouted critically at her reflection. Marta wondered whether she should have made more effort. It was her first night out in London. She was wearing a plain black top and jeans – the ripped ends hiding a pair of grubby trainers – and only a dusting of makeup. How much trouble did English girls go to?

"I think there's some jewellery and stuff in that cupboard in your room," Tash said pointedly. "Feel free to use it." Marta took the hint and went back to improve herself.

She held up a string of blue beads against her neck. The thing about Tash, thought Marta, rifling through the trinkets like a child in a dressing up box, was that she actually had no idea how fortunate she was. She lived in this beautiful world where everything was new, fashionable, pristine – where money wasn't something one needed to think about – and she assumed everyone else lived there too. The other day she had stepped over a homeless man wrapped in a blanket outside the supermarket, ensuring her suede knee-high boots remained immaculate and exclaiming, "Why don't they just get jobs? I'd rather sit in an office all day than lie on the pavement!" *If only he had the option of sitting in an office*, thought Marta. She wondered what Tash's parents were like. Mama would know. Maybe she's ask about Penelope and Henry.

"Wow," uttered Tash, clearly impressed with the transformation. "You look gorgeous." Marta had gone overboard with the makeup – accentuating her ice-blue eyes with mascara and bringing out her cheekbones with blusher. The trainers had been replaced by dainty high heels – another find from the second wardrobe – making her long legs look even longer. She actually felt ready for a night out.

It hadn't been Marta's idea to come along tonight. It hadn't been Tash's either – in fact, Marta suspected that Tash would have preferred not to have her Polish housemate tagging along. The inspiration had been Plum's – the horsy-faced girl with the awful laugh. "You *must* come to Blushes on Saturday," she had exclaimed. "It's Jeremy's birthday!"

"Ready?" asked Tash, giving herself one last glance in the mirror.

"Ready." Marta smiled. They set off for King's Road.

Their strides were in sync as they clip-clopped down Draycott Avenue. Marta could imagine how they looked to passers-by: two young, attractive English girls on their way to a bar or restaurant. They probably looked like friends, she thought. That was almost the truth. Sometimes, when Tash was in a good mood and when they found a subject they could both talk about, Marta actually felt as though they *were* friends – but not friends like Marta and Anka, of course.

Marta couldn't imagine getting close to Tash – or in fact any of the English girls she'd met – like she was close to Anka. Their personalities were too different. English girls were complicated. They had hidden agendas. They kept things from one another. They faked their emotions the whole time so it was impossible to tell how they were really feeling. At least, that's what she'd seen in Tash's clan. Perhaps that was unrepresentative.

"Who will be there?" asked Marta. She was more apprehensive than she was letting on. Even though Tash was her pseudo friend, Marta wasn't convinced she would stick around when the likes of Jack and Plum started to vie for her attention. And there would probably be lots of people like Jeremy, who, despite Marta's best efforts, just didn't seem to have any time for her. Suddenly, the image of a bar full of young men like Jeremy, sitting in a row looking down their oversized noses and mispronouncing their 'r's popped into her mind. God, tonight was going to be awful.

"Jeremy, obviously, and Jack will be along later," Tash replied. "Who else d'you know... oh, Plum, obviously. Oh!" she cried, as if suddenly remembering something. "Holly! You'll get to meet Holly!"

Marta waited for an explanation.

"You'll get on well with Holly, I can tell. She went to a state school, you know."

Marta frowned. "What's—"

"Oh, sorry. A state school – a comprehensive. In England, there are two types of school: private, and state. In state schools, you don't have to pay."

What was puzzling Marta wasn't the two-tier UK education structure (which mama had already explained to her) but the reason for Tash dropping this fact into the description of her friend – as though there was nothing more interesting to say about the girl than the type of school she had attended.

"I know Holly from Cambridge – we shared a set in our second year. She's very... different to most of my friends."

Marta couldn't help thinking this was a good thing. She allowed Tash to guide her sharp left.

"The second year room ballot is random, and if you come too far down, you end up sharing." She skirted round a group of young men in pink shirts. "I was devastated when I found out, but as it happens, I was lucky."

Marta was intrigued and amused. She could picture Tash's face when she found out that for the first time in her life, she wouldn't be residing in her own huge bedroom with en suite bathroom and double bed. Marta wondered whether she really would get on with Holly. If she had shared a 'set' (whatever that was) with Tash for a year, she would have to be either extremely tolerant or extremely annoying.

The pavement narrowed, and it became more difficult to navigate through the stream of evening revellers. Middle-aged women with well-dyed hair flaunted fur coats and diamond earrings, whilst their partners wore starched trousers and polo shirts – some of them even sporting bow-ties. Marta was glad of Tash's gaudy jewellery and the shoes that were giving her blisters.

"Here we are," announced Tash, slowing to a halt outside what looked like an expensive café. Laughter and discourse spilt through the open door and an orange glow lit up the pavement. They slipped inside, weaving between twenty-somethings — all of whom were incredibly attractive.

"He's booked out the downstairs," Tash explained, picking her way down the wrought iron steps. Marta followed with considerably more difficulty. Every time her heel landed, it got lodged in a gap, trapping her foot and requiring her to push off from the flimsy curved banister. She hadn't even set eyes on her audience yet.

The sight that greeted her instilled instant fear in Marta. Worse than the worry of having nobody to talk to, worse than the embarrassment of coming downstairs, worse even than the thought of a hundred Jeremys looking down their enormous noses at her was the fear of *spending money*.

The tables were arranged in a T-shape, each place laid for a five-course meal, with four knives per person and three wine glasses. Napkins were arranged like bouquets in the middle of each setting, and every person got a little parcel wrapped up in fine silver gauze. 'Drinks and nibbles,' Plum had said — not a full wedding breakfast! Marta tried to estimate how much she would end up paying. She had set aside twelve pounds for tonight.

"Tash! Marta!" someone shrieked. "You're just in time!" There was a painfully loud hoot of laughter. It was Plum.

Marta was ushered into the corner to make way for a procession of smartly dressed waiters — one carrying a small pipe organ made of cake, one shielding the candle flames, one brandishing plates, forks and a gigantic knife, and one following behind gormlessly. Suddenly, the room was filled with the harmonious tones of what Marta could only describe as a cathedral choir.

"Har-py bath-day to yooooou," they sang, "Har-py bath-day to yoooou", now with tenors and sopranos adding their own parts. "Har-py bath-day dear Jer-a-meeeee—" everybody paused while someone finished an elaborate descant cadenza —"Har-py bath-day to yoooou!"

There was a magnanimous roar and a clamour of applause that would have been audible at street-level. "Hip-hip!" yelled someone, above the din. "Hooray!" came the unanimous response. "Hip-hip!" "Hooray!" "And one for lark, hip-hip!" "Hooray!"

More roaring, more whooping and clapping. Marta just stood in the corner, staring. She couldn't help it. Had they *rehearsed* for this? Was this normal? Did they always put on such an elaborate performance for someone's birthday? Jeremy was beaming like a little boy – peering down at the organ-shaped cake and deciding where to make the first cut. "Gosh! It's got pedals and everything! I say! Splendid!"

"Weird time to eat cake," muttered a girl standing nearby. Marta looked at her. She was tall, like Marta, with a freckly face and brown hair tied up in a pony tail. She didn't seem to be talking to anyone in particular, so Marta braved a reply.

"Before dinner, you mean?"

"Yeah. Guess it's just so Jezza's choral chums can stuff their faces before they bugger off to entertain the Queen or whatever."

The girl snorted and reached down for her drink – a pint of beer, Marta noticed. Marta smiled. She hadn't seen anyone drink beer since she'd arrived. Tash's friends all favoured spirits and fancy cocktails.

"The Queen?" echoed Marta, quite perplexed but not afraid to ask. There was something disarming about the girl: a frankness, a straightforwardness that reminded Marta of Anka. Tash's gang were all so phoney, but this girl was different.

"Well I dunno what they're off to do, but it's usually some poncy concert in the Royal Albert Hall or whatever. That's why they're all dressed up." She nodded at the nearest one – a tall, lanky fellow in black tie. Crumbs were shooting out from between his teeth as he guffawed into his piece of cake.

"Are they… a choir?" asked Marta.

"Oh – I thought you knew them! They're Jeremy's 'muso' mates. He was the organ scholar at our college, and now he plays for the London Philharmonic Choir. These guys all sing in it – hence the heavenly voices just now."

Marta nodded. That made sense. She could see Jeremy behind a church organ.

"Sorry – I don't think we've met," said the girl. "I'm Holly."

Marta smiled. So this was Holly. "Yes. Hi. I am Marta – I living with Tash."

"Oh right! You're the Polish girl? Tash told us about you coming over!"

Marta smiled nervously. She wondered what else Tash had said. "How are you settling in?"

Before Marta could answer, a hush fell on the room, prompted by an insistent fork-on-glass chime.

"Ladies… and gentlemen!" bellowed Jeremy.

"*Oh God, not another song,*" muttered Holly under her breath.

"Thank you, everyone, for coming along tonight. It means a great deal to me, and I'm particularly honoured to have received what must be the most melodious birthday mantra ever heard in the borough of Kensington and Chelsea."

There was a patter of applause and a ripple of laughter around the room.

"Now we have to say farewell to the Philharmonia boys—" a collection of boos, sighs and 'aaaah's – some more genuine than others – "but for the rest of you, please sit down!"

Marta looked around for Tash, and saw her sliding elegantly into a seat between Jeremy and Jack, who had just arrived. There were no spaces anywhere near her.

"Shall we squeeze in here?" asked Holly.

Marta shrugged and took her seat, inwardly jumping up and down with joy: she had made a friend.

Her joy quickly turned to misery when she remembered about the five-course meal. "Oh – am not eating," she explained hastily, shifting into a gap between laid places. "Am not very much hungry."

Holly frowned. "You serious? You're not taking Jezza up on his free dinner offer? God, I've been starving myself for days – this is gonna be a feast!"

"Free dinner offer?" asked Marta. Surely he wasn't paying for this himself? There were at least twenty people down here!

"Yeah. Jezza's minted. He doesn't care."

"Mint?"

"Minted. Mega-rich."

"Oh." Marta hesitated, shifting along a little so she was half-sitting in a proper place.

"Didn't you realise?" asked Holly. "Oh no – and now you've gone and stuffed yourself so you can't take full advantage! Bummer."

"I, er… I might be able to eat maybe one course…"

Holly smiled. "Come on. Budge up. You've got some serious eating to do."

Over the multiple courses, Marta learned a lot from Holly. She was given a brief history of all Tash's friends, including a synopsis of who fancied whom (Plum and virtually every male around the table) and who had slept with whom (ditto). There were stories from their university days, some of which Marta found hard to believe – although somehow she did believe them – like the one about Jack climbing onto the college roof to re-enact the balcony scene from Romeo and Juliet via Holly's window whom he was stalking at the time, falling off, breaking his collar bone and then going to Tash's room for sympathy, upon which they snogged and started going out. Marta was also rather shocked by the fact that Tash was reigning champion of the 'Great Quad Race' – a naked run around the main quadrangle after the college 'Annual Feast Night', but perhaps Tash had been different at university.

The coffee cups came out, and Holly suddenly looked at her watch. "Shit – I've gotta go. Said I'd be at my mate's do by ten. Hey – here's my card. Give us a shout if you ever get bored of horsy-talk and sherry parties. My mobile number's on the back."

Marta took the card. "Thanks."

"Oh and good luck," Holly added quietly, nodding in Tash's direction. "She's not the easiest person to live with."

Marta watched Holly bound up the stairs and turned over the card in her hand. Embossed in blue on the thick, textured cream were the words, "Holly Banks, Associate, ANDERTON CONSULTANTS". Wow. Even Marta had heard of them. They were one of the 'big five' that Jack talked about. Holly was a management consultant.

11

BAYSWATER FELT DIFFERENT at this time of day. The air was cold and stale, the pavements clear, all the stalls shut away behind rusty, graffiti-scrawled shutters. The rustle of money changing hands had been replaced by the monotonous murmur of commuters on their way to work.

Marta was not wearing a suit. She was dressed in jeans, several T-shirts and her Malina Q jacket. On her feet were her tatty but comfortable trainers. She had a long day ahead of her.

"IT'S OPEN!" yelled Barry's distinctive voice as she rang the bell.

Her journey up the stairs was hampered by the large number of people coming the other way, each carrying a huge box against their chest. Marta took refuge in the corners of the staircase, letting people pass and then scampering up to the next waiting spot. The box carriers were mainly men, she noted, most of them her age or a little older. From the grunts of conversation she overheard, there were a number of Eastern Europeans and a few Russians. She'd come to the right place, she thought wryly.

"YOU GONNA STAND THERE ALL DAY?" shouted Barry from inside his 'office'. Marta had been waiting for the last person to pass with his box, but he seemed to be struggling just inside the door. She entered, timidly.

"'Ere you go," he barked, nodding at a box slightly smaller than the ones she had seen others carrying. Marta wondered whether he'd moved from his chair since she'd last seen him.

"And, if I... If I run out?"

Barry let out a grunt of laughter. "Oh, ya won't run out, believe me. You've only got 'alf there!" He motioned to another identical box on the floor.

Marta carefully lowered herself with the first box and loaded up with the second. Surely this was more than the others had been given?

"Eight 'til eight, OK, with an hour for lunch. Your pass is in the box. That's for if anyone questions you bein' there. Now, 'ere's your zone."

Marta staggered over and perched her load on the edge of his desk. She watched as he highlighted a wobbly circle on a photocopied map of central London.

"That's where you cover, right?" The area included Farringdon tube station and a grid of streets around it. Marta nodded, then realised with horror that the 'zone' included the street where Genesis was located.

"Fine," Marta uttered, straining to pick up her load again. She was wondering how she was supposed to get the boxes to her allocated 'zone', and how, once she got there, she was going to keep them with her as she wandered around. This was the first time she'd thought about the logistics.

As Marta turned, she found herself almost slamming straight into the other guy, who had been mending a tear in his box and was slowly staggering out.

"Przepraszam!" she gasped apologetically.

The guy took a step back, allowing her through. "Polka?" he asked, smiling.

Marta waited until she was outside Barry's office before she replied. She nearly gasped. The guy had sandy hair that was messy and slightly too long, and his eyes – beautiful eyes – were hazel. It was the guy from the recruitment fair.

"It's you," said Marta.

"Yes," he replied, grinning. "Dominik."

"Hi. Again, I mean. I'm Marta." They laughed nervously, unable to shake hands because of their boxes. Marta went first down the stairs.

"Is this your first day?" Dominik called down to her.

"Yes. You?"

"Huh. Not exactly. My third month."

"Really?" Marta was shocked. Surely nobody stayed in this job for long? She certainly didn't intend to.

"Is it OK?" she asked, squeezing past another girl on the stairway. It was a silly question, but she wanted to keep the conversation going. She still had adrenaline rushing round her bloodstream from meeting the guy.

"It's a job," he said, skirting her question. "What's your zone?"

They were nearly at the bottom of the stairs now and Marta was already worrying about never seeing Dominik again. "Farringdon."

"Oh, that's not far from mine – I'm Holborn."

Marta had no idea about London geography, but she was happy to take Dominik's word for it. They eased themselves through the exit and stood, hoisting their loads into more comfortable positions. Marta's arms were hurting.

"Don't you have transport?"

"N–no," Marta replied uncertainly.

"God, that Barry is such a dick. He didn't mention it at all?"

"No." Now Marta was really worried. Was she supposed to have a car? She didn't even have a driving licence, and couldn't imagine trying to get to grips with London traffic and driving on the left. Not to mention the cost of owning a car.

"Oh, well I guess you'll manage. You gonna go by tube?"

Marta nodded. "Was planning to."

Dominik paused for a second, staring at the ground, balancing his load on a bollard and rubbing his forehead. "Hmm."

Marta waited hopefully. He glanced up at her, then back at the ground. Perhaps he liked her, thought Marta. The idea of a Polish friend in London suddenly appealed more than anything – particularly a cute, Polish friend like Dominik.

"OK. Here's what we'll do – if you want to, that is. I've got my scooter–" Dominik pointed with his foot at an ancient, rusty machine – "so I'll load it up with your leaflets as well as mine, then I'll meet you at Farringdon. If you get the tube from Bayswater, we'll probably arrive at the same time."

Marta nodded gratefully. She wondered what the catch was here. Dominik was cute *and* nice. "Yes please."

"Oh, and here's my number in case we somehow don't hook up." Dominik pulled out a leaflet from his stash and scribbled on it.

"Thanks." She looked at the leaflet. It was an advert for some sort of dieting service.

"God, you've got a big wad here," he noted, heaving her second batch onto the rickety carrier. "You want me to lose half these on the way?"

He was smiling, but Marta couldn't tell whether he was joking. Did people bin some of their leaflets? Probably, but she remembered Barry's words from last week: *I pay you nothing if you're caught messin' about.* "I'll manage," she told Dominik.

He laughed. "Chill out – I was joking." Then he lowered his voice. "Although seriously, you're not gonna get through all these, so I suggest you leave some with me. We can always meet up if you run out."

Yes please, thought Marta, liking the idea of meeting up with Dominik. "OK then. See you at Farringdon?"

"See you there."

Marta headed for the tube station carrying nothing but Dominik's leaflet. Things felt better, all of a sudden. She had a job (of sorts) that paid reasonable money, she had a place to live, a few English friends, and now, she had Dominik. Well, she had Dominik's phone number, at least.

He was waiting for her outside the station, his hair even more ruffled from the scooter ride. "Cześć."

Marta returned his cheeky grin. She felt fourteen again. "Thanks so much."

"You know what you're doing?"

Marta pulled a face. "Er, giving out leaflets?"

"Yeah, sorry. It's just that Fat Barry didn't seem to have given you much direction, that's all."

She shrugged with fake confidence. "How hard can it be?"

Dominik gave her a sardonic smile. They both knew he'd already rescued her once today. "OK smarty-pants. You're on your own." He handed her one of her boxes. "Gimme a shout if you get through that lot – I'm just up the road."

Marta laughed as he kicked his machine into life. "Half an hour, I tell you!"

He shook his head, still smiling as he swung the scooter in a sharp U-turn and disappeared up a side street.

Marta was on a high. She didn't even mind the fact that she would be spending the next ten hours standing on the street handing out pieces of paper to people who didn't want them. She had made a friend. A gorgeous, funny, smart Polish friend, who was expecting her to call sometime today. She took care to fold up his leaflet and stuff it into her wallet in case she gave it away with the others.

Distributing flyers wasn't that bad, Marta decided, after a trial five minutes. There was a knack to it. You just had to smile at everyone and not take rejection personally. People were more likely to take a leaflet from someone being proactive than someone who looked as though this was their last hope of a job.

It was interesting, the way different people reacted. There were the insecure young men in suits who half-smiled and looked as though they wanted to take one but weren't quite brave enough, there were the hoity-toity women who couldn't even bare to crack a smile, there were those who took one out of obligation (mainly women) and then there were the men who enjoyed the fact that Marta was catching their eye, and took one because it made them feel special. After half an hour, Marta could predict who would take one and who wouldn't.

By eleven o'clock, the novelty of grinning maniacally at hundreds of strangers, leaping in and out of their paths and seeing the pavement papered with leaflets had worn off. Marta had got through about a fifth of a box – *one* box – which, by her calculations, meant that she'd need eighteen more hours to get rid of her entire assignment. It was madness. She wondered how much wastage there was in this industry. Surely the other people working for Barry couldn't be *much* better than her? So did they all cheat, and tip half their load away at the end of each day? Probably.

Marta moved around in the area, wandering up Cowcross Street and finding herself in some sort of market with pictures of men in white coats hanging up meat. There was so much of London she had yet to explore; it was just a pity she was confined to her 'zone'.

She returned to her patch for the lunchtime rush and managed to give away more in that hour than she had done all morning. The smell of bacon drifted out of a small English pub, and Marta realised she was starving. She delved into her pocket and pulled out the phone Tash had lent her.

"Dominik?"

"Hey, is that Marta?"

"Yeah – how's it going in Holborn?"

"Slow, man. You got through your box?"

"Half," she replied, trying to hide the pride in her voice.

"Wow. No cheating?"

"No cheating."

"I'm impressed. You fancy a celebratory sandwich?"

"That's why I was calling."

"I'll be down right away. Oh, and I've got something for you."

Marta paused. "Something for me?"

"Yup – I'll see you by the station in five minutes."

Marta tucked the phone away, unable to keep the smile off her face. Life had suddenly become fun.

12

"WHERE SHALL WE HEAD FIRST? Monsoon? Austique? Marosa? Oh you would *so love* the accessories in Marosa – they're made by Emma Hanbury! Austique is good too, but more for lingerie. Mind you, they always have some gorgeous dresses."

Tash prattled on about various other designer outlets on King's Road, oblivious to Marta's bored silence. Marta had no idea what she was talking about, and no intention of shopping in any of the places she'd mentioned. Marta had known it was a stupid idea for Tash to come along, but Tash had insisted. She was convinced she could help Marta find the perfect gifts for her family and Anka.

Unfortunately, Tash didn't quite understand the budget constraints Marta had in mind. When Marta had picked up her first pay packet – a brown envelope containing fifteen £20 notes – it had felt as though she'd hit jackpot. She had the equivalent of nearly 2,000 złoty in her pocket. But once she'd paid Tash for her three weeks' rent, put by enough for bus tickets and food and kept some aside for emergencies, she had found herself clutching just £35 – surely not enough to buy one gift, let alone three? London prices were absurd.

"Oh, Karen Millen!" cooed Tash, as they turned onto the main high street. Without even a cautionary glance for traffic, she danced across the road, pulling Marta by the hand. "Is your friend into fashion? She would adore this belt I saw in here the other day."

"Er…" Marta hesitated. Anka loved her fashion, but not the sort of fashion that would bankrupt her best friend. "I have not much money to spend," she explained.

"Well, it's always worth a look, isn't it?" Tash replied flippantly, pulling a small dress off its rail and hooking the hanger over her neck. "What d'you think?"

It became clear to Marta that this trip wasn't about Anka, or mama or tata or anyone else for whom she might have bought presents back in Poland. It was about Tash. Tash viewed spending money as a hobby, a leisure activity – not a functional exercise. Marta could see from the way her eyes scanned the racks of clothes and her fingers brushed the fabrics, this was what Tash lived for. No wonder she worked at Paul Smith.

"I think here is not a good shop," she told Tash, wondering how to explain the money issue. "I don't want to spend–"

"Oh, don't think about prices at this stage! You'll never get anything if you do that. Take a look around, pick out anything that you think you might want – or your friend might want, try it on, *then* decide whether you can really afford it. That's what I do."

Marta nodded patiently. Tash wasn't getting it. To her, affordability was just a hypothetical concept; she could afford anything. For her, the constraint was just her conscience, not her bank balance.

For a while, Marta played along. She tried to be more like Tash, flitting about the shop, grabbing handfuls of garments, flinging them over her arm and dashing into the changing rooms. The problem was, Marta wasn't like Tash. She didn't shop for fun, she shopped for a purpose, and she didn't enjoy trying on hundreds of beautiful tops she'd never be able to buy.

"Tash, I might go to other shops now," she said, employing some English tact.

"Oh no! Don't you like Karen Millen?"

Marta sighed. How could she make Tash understand? "Problem is, I have not much money. I don't–"

"Oh, I've got *just* the thing! You're right – clothes are too expensive. They're probably too bulky to send, too. Let's go across the road – there's an Accessorize. That's probably more up your street. None of their stuff lasts more than two months, but at least it looks nice to begin with. It's great for gifts."

Before Marta could respond, she found herself being ushered out of the shop, her armful of expensive garments prised from her and dumped on a nearby shop assistant.

"Look at this – it's a treasure trove!" remarked Tash, gleefully admiring the shop's interior. It was true; the whole place sparkled. Every wall was densely packed with bracelets, necklaces, rings and hair clips, arranged in blocks of colour around the shop.

Marta headed for the emerald section, picking out a pair of dangly earrings she knew Anka would love. There was a matching pendant on a silver cord, too. Marta flipped over the price tag. Her heart sank. Fourteen pounds – just for the pendant. The earrings were twelve pounds fifty. If she bought either one, that would use up her entire allowance. She could imagine the disappointment on her best friend's face, unwrapping the measly jewel that looked, frankly, not unlike the ones you could get in a Polish market for 12 złoty. She returned the jewellery to the rack.

"What about this?" Tash asked excitedly.

Marta turned to find her fingering the most garish collection of jewels she had ever seen. It looked like some sort of triangular doily made out of fluorescent, sparkling beads. "What... is it?" asked Marta.

It's a choker – well, necklace," said Tash. "Isn't it incredible?"

Marta nodded warily. "Incredible."

"And it's only twenty-five pounds!"

"Oh," replied Marta, deadpan. She couldn't believe anyone would actually pay for it. "Am thinking it is not really Anka's style."

Tash raised her eyebrows. "Huh."

Marta had another go at splitting off from her housemate. "Look, Tash, am very sorry but am not on the mood for this. I think I might–"

"Oh no! You poor thing – I *hate* not being in the mood for shopping. I know exactly what you want–"

"Tash, I–"

"No really – I get this too sometimes. What you need is a chai tea latte and a slice of low-fat lemon cake, and I have *just* the place to go for it! Come to think of it, that's what I fancy. Come on – we're going to the Bluebird!"

The Bluebird, it turned out, was a vast, white-washed building set back from the road behind a row of pillars. In front of it, sheltered by ornate glass parasols with heated stems, sat some Kensington locals, all immaculately dressed and sipping exotic-looking drinks.

"Is it warm enough to sit out, d'you think?" asked Tash, not pausing for a response. "No, let's head inside. It's nicer in there anyway."

Marta felt awkward as soon as she set foot on the polished floor. She hated places where they rushed up to take your coat, called you 'ma'am' and asked repeatedly if everything was alright.

"We'll go into the lounge," said Tash, leading the way across the wooden floor into a sun-drenched conservatory. She headed straight for a pair of cream armchairs either side of a block of what looked like marble.

Needless to say, they drank chai tea latte – a strange, sickly drink – and ate low-fat lemon cake. Tash extolled the virtues of living in Kensington, with its marvellous array of shops and parks, and its wonderful mix of people. Marta wasn't sure that 'mix' was the best word to describe the well-dressed young mothers pushing deluxe baby-wagons, the beautiful twenty-somethings wearing angora and the smart looking couples trailing miniature versions of themselves on reigns. The only foreign accents she'd heard belonged to rich tourists.

"So, how's your new job?" asked Tash, surprising Marta with the selflessness of the question.

"Good."

"Any nice men in your office?" she probed, raising a perfectly plucked eyebrow.

"Um," Marta felt herself smiling. He may not have been in her office, but Dominik certainly was nice.

"Ooh, there is! How exciting! What's his name? What does he do?" Tash waved her fork around like a small child.

"He's called Dominik – he does, er, similar things to me."

"So, tell me more!"

Marta shrugged. She was starting to get irritated with Tash's persistent questioning and false enthusiasm. It was obvious she didn't really care about Marta's life – she just wanted gossip, something to talk about.

Tash tutted. "OK, fine." She sulked for a moment, but not for long. "So, let's decide what you're going to buy!"

Marta sighed. There was only one way to tell Tash, she decided: bluntly.

"Tash, you don't understand. I have little money here. I will get more, as I do more work, but for now I must be careful. I can only spend thirty-five pounds on presents today. That is all I have."

Tash frowned. "OK. Well, that's fine. We'll just have to re-think our shops a little. I mean, you can still get a nice box of cosmetics for thirty-five pounds... or maybe a top, or–"

"No, Tash!" Marta said, her voice raised. She just couldn't bear hearing any more stupid suggestions from her rich housemate.

There was instant silence. Tash was glaring at her with wide eyes. Clearly nobody ever shouted at Tash.

"Sorry," muttered Marta. "But you still don't see."

To her horror, Marta found that tears were welling up behind her eyes. If she blinked, they would start streaming out. All of a sudden, she felt like a failure. It might have been the persistent reminders from Tash that she was poor, or maybe the realisation that she was living in a world where she didn't belong – she didn't know. All she knew was that she wanted to be back in Poland.

"I have thirty-five pounds *all together*," she explained. The tears flooded her vision and started rolling down her nose. "That's the problem."

Tash screwed up her face. "All together?" she repeated, perplexed about either Marta's poverty or her tears. "Oh, right."

Marta accepted the tissue that Tash was holding out. She felt so ashamed. Ashamed to be crying, ashamed to be sitting in this fancy place that was too posh for her, ashamed not to have got a proper job. She had come over here with the intention of making money – enough money for herself *and* for her family back home – and somehow she was struggling even to make ends meet for herself. It was so embarrassing. Back in Poland, everyone talked of the salaries being five times higher, but they never talked about the expense of living in London, which was a lot more than five times higher.

Tash looked at her. "You know, maybe this isn't the time to go shopping." She glanced up at a passing waiter and motioned for the bill. "Perhaps you should wait until next week."

Marta nodded, pressing the tissue into the corners of her eyes. Tash was being surprisingly intuitive.

"D'you know what I'd do? I'd go back to the house, run myself a nice bath and *relax*. Don't get worked up about silly things like shopping! Ooh – here's the bill. There are some lovely new bath salts in the cupboard." She reached into her handbag. "I might just stay out a little longer – Emma Hanbury has just brought out a new range. She has these *adorable* little wrap-around tops."

Marta nodded. She wondered whether Tash really cared, or whether the run-a-bath suggestion was simply a way of relieving herself of a Polish cry-baby while she continued to shop. Tash hadn't exactly displayed selfless tendencies in the past – that was for sure.

"Oh, d'you know what, I've got no cash! Would you mind?"

For a moment, Marta thought she must have misunderstood. Tash was asking her to pay?

"Only I don't think they take card here," Tash explained apologetically.

Marta looked down at the bill. Eleven pounds sixty. That was a third of her gift budget. "Um, well…"

"Thanks, hun."

Marta slowly laid down her twenty pound note.

"*Don't forget to tip,*" Tash advised in a whisper, as the waiter approached.

Marta nodded, feeling the tears starting to well up again.

"Right! I'm off – and you're going back for a lovely hot bath!" Tash declared.

"See you later," Marta managed, her voice breaking on the last word. She wandered out of the Bluebird feeling as low as she had ever felt. One thing had become apparent: she *had* to get another job.

13

THE MARIJUANA hit Marta's lungs like a sharp drag on a spliff. Suddenly, she was back in Łomianki, floating up and down on the park see-saw with Anka, enjoying the night rain on her face.

She returned to the present with a gasp as a hooded man stepped into her path from the shadows. He reached for something in his pocket, blocking her way. Marta's breath shortened. She started to panic.

"Weed?" said the man, leaning very close and sending a blast of the stuff straight up her nose.

Marta shook her head and walked on, careful not to make eye contact. The dealer retreated. Marta's heart was still beating double speed when she spotted another obstacle up ahead: a bunch of youths on bikes. She navigated round them, stubbornly ignoring the one who followed her, asking how much she charged. Her whole body was shaking. She was beginning to understand why North Acton was a cheap place to live.

Finally, she turned into St Leonards Road. The houses were small and terraced, behind them expanses of industrial wasteland and blocks of flats. A streetlamp shone down on the peeling paintwork of number twelve. There was a soggy mattress leaning against the front window.

"Hey!" Dom smiled, standing back from the door. He was wearing casual, low-hanging trousers and an old blue T-shirt that hugged his upper body. Marta tried not to look at his chest. He obviously worked out. "Come in!"

Maybe she should have made less effort, thought Marta, suddenly feeling over-dressed. After her experiences with Tash's friends, she had taken to borrowing her housemate's heels and applying full makeup for every occasion. Perhaps dinner in North Acton didn't warrant curled eyelashes.

"You look… lovely," Dominik said, glancing away bashfully as Marta caught him eyeing her up and down.

"Nice place," she commented, although all she had seen of it was a badly-wallpapered hallway and a wonky lampshade.

"No, it's not." Dominik glanced over his shoulder. "I'm going to apologise now for the state of it. There's seven of us here – it's a bit of a mess."

"*Seven?*" asked Marta, looking around. The house couldn't possibly have had more than three bedrooms.

"Yeah. The lounge is the Croats' room–" Dominik pointed towards the small room at the front of the house. Marta poked her head in as they passed. The dirty brown carpet seemed to pervade throughout, as did the floral wallpaper. Two scruffy-looking men occupied the space in front of the TV, thumbs manically working two games consols.

"That's Yishai and Uzoma in there. Think the others are out. Yeah, we've got two Israelis, one Iranian, two Croats, one Nigerian and me. Quite a mixed bunch."

Marta followed him into the room at the back, which, beneath the layers of grime and debris, was a kitchen.

"Oh – before I forget. This thing I've got for you."

Marta watched expectantly as he reached into a shoebox on the small kitchen table. She'd been wondering what this mystery gift could be; he hadn't given it to her last week because it needed 'fixing up a bit'.

"Here."

To begin with, Marta didn't know what it was. It looked like a palm-sized lump of plastic with tyre marks across one side and deep scratches on the other.

"Sorry about those – I thought I could file it down but I couldn't. Think it got run over."

Then Marta saw the headphones.

"Is it a music player?" she asked, just to be sure.

Dominik smiled. "It's an iPod. The most expensive one they've got out at the moment. Some city boy must've dropped it on his way into work. I picked it up in Holborn."

Marta turned the little gadget around in her hands. It was so small, but she could tell that it did great things; half of one side was a silvery screen.

"Turn it on."

Marta fumbled for a bit, then let Dominik do it for her. The device suddenly lit up like a television.

"Oh wow! It's amazing!"

Dominik laughed. "You haven't heard it play." He plugged the jack into the socket and gently inserted one headphone into Marta's ear, the other into his own. Suddenly, an eighties rock band was hammering out a bass line inside her head.

It stopped as quickly as it started. "Ah, yes, sorry," said Dominik. "That's the only problem with having a stolen MP3 player. The music that comes with it."

Marta shrugged. For her, the best part wasn't the sound quality or the whizzy controls; it was the fact that Dominik had given it to her.

"But... don't *you* want it?" she asked.

Dominik shook his head. "I've got one. A crap version – not an Apple – but I'm happy with it. This one's yours, scars and all."

Marta fiddled with the buttons on the front, which made the little display flash in all sorts of colours. She'd work it out later.

"Oh, and you're not stuck with those songs," Dominik told her. "We've got tons here on this old PC–" He motioned to an upright computer in the corner of the kitchen. "Yishai works cleaning offices, and they were getting rid of their old IT at the last place he worked. They didn't wipe the hard drive before they handed it over, so there's over six thousand tunes on that thing."

"Six *thousand*?"

Dominik smiled. "Yeah, and a load of fancy graphics software, should you ever turn to design. We've got the printers and everything. So, presumably you don't have a computer at your place?"

Marta shook her head. Somehow she couldn't imagine Tash risking her fingernails on a keyboard.

"Well, when you get bored of these songs, you'll have to come round here for a refill," he said.

Marta nodded, secretly rather excited about the open invitation to Dominik's house.

"And I have to apologise for the food, too – it's only soup."

Marta shrugged. "Potato soup?" she asked hopefully. She was missing her mother's homemade cooking.

"Actually, yes," said Dominik, lifting the lid on the huge pan simmering on the dirty stove. The smell brought back instant memories of home.

Marta perched timidly on the wooden chair, avoiding the gooey line along one edge. The house was a health hazard, but she didn't mind. At least it was cosy. The windows were steaming up and a familiar fug was forming. She felt relaxed here. It was a relief, frankly, to be anywhere other than Tash's mansion. The South Kensington place was vast and luxurious, but somehow it made her feel claustrophobic. She lived in fear of drinking from the wrong glass or spilling something on the lamb's wool carpet.

Dominik seemed even more at home in a T-shirt and apron than he was out and about on his scooter. He moved confidently about the kitchen, stirring, tasting, grabbing, wiping and inspecting thoroughly before use – much to Marta's relief. He looked like a proper chef.

"You should try getting work in a kitchen," she suggested as he set down the bowls on the rickety table. It smelled exactly like mama's.

Dominik smiled wryly. "I have done. And failed. D'you want salt? There's some in already–" He offered her a small grimy pot. "Believe me, I've tried getting work in just about everything. I got turned down for the chef job – even the chef's *assistant* job – for having the 'wrong background in food'. Fuckers. As if English meals are harder to cook than Polish ones. They offered me dish-washing work, but that paid even worse than this flyering shit."

Over soup and a bottle of wine, they talked about various career options Dominik had explored since coming to England. He had studied finance at the Jagiellonian University in Krakow – one of the best in the country – and had planned to get a job as an investment banker or fund manager over here. It was ludicrous – and somewhat depressing – to think that after three months, the best he could achieve was Barry's leaflet enterprise. After a while, Marta stopped asking, "But what about …? Have you tried …?" Dominik had tried everything. It had been knock-back after knock-back, and it was clearly getting to him.

"That was delicious," she said gratefully, mopping up the last of her soup with a hunk of stale bread.

"Not exactly gourmet," he said apologetically. "I've got some brownies though, for dessert."

"Homemade?"

Dominik smiled. "Yes – but not by me. Yishai's girlfriend made them. Oh – hello."

The two housemates who'd been in the lounge wandered into the kitchen. One of them – Yishai, Marta presumed – headed for the vat of soup on the stove and ran a finger around the inside.

"Mmm," he nodded appreciatively. "Not bad, Dom." His accent was Arabic.

"Have some if you like. We're done." Dominik turned to Marta. "Shall we move into the lounge?"

Marta nodded, trying not to laugh. In Tash's place, the lounge was this enormous front room with heavy drapes, leather sofas and the thick-pile rug. Here, it was like a teenager's bedroom.

"Sorry – I'll just move this stuff," said Dominik, shifting a plate of bolognaise and what looked like the insides of a computer from the tatty sofa. They sat on the lumpy cushions, the tin of chocolate brownies between them, bottle of wine on the floor.

It was so nice to be talking Polish again. Marta had been so busy getting to grips with London life, with the language, the people, the pace, she hadn't had time to think about home. London was so different to Łomianki. Everything here was instant and on-tap. People didn't catch your eye or nod 'good morning'. Everyone queued even when they didn't need to. Somehow, being here with Dom, she could feel herself escaping back to her old life. She felt as though Dom had been a part of it for years – although, of course, she wanted to get to know him more. There was no need to articulate her anxieties, because he understood. He was in the same situation himself, and, unlike her rich, stuck-up housemate, he was sensitive. Marta felt as though she'd found a refuge here in Acton.

"There must be a way for us to get proper jobs," Marta declared, biting into a brownie. She couldn't bear the thought that they'd be stuck working for Barry all their lives.

"If you discover it, let me know," replied Dominik.

Marta shook her head. She refused to give up like Dominik.

"Seriously, Marta," Dominik went on. "They don't *want* to employ us. Only in menial jobs, like sweeping streets and wiping toilets. I'm never going to use my finance over here. My qualifications mean jack-shit to these guys. They can't even pronounce the name of my uni."

Marta was silent. She didn't want to hear Dominik's reasoning. After more wine, the conversation moved onto lighter matters. They talked about home, about friends, about family, pets, sports – at one point Marta even found herself talking about politics. It turned out their birthdays were a day apart, although Dominik was one year older. He had also played football at Jagiellonian with someone she knew from school.

"You working tomorrow?" asked Dominik, suddenly.

Marta glanced at her watch. "It's eleven o'clock! Yes, I am. I'd better go."

"You don't have to," he said, smiling.

Marta couldn't tell what he meant. "I – I should. It's late."

"I'll walk you to the station."

"You don't–"

"No, seriously Marta – this isn't South Kensington. There's a murder every week in Acton."

Marta obliged, secretly pleased with the outcome.

"You're lucky to live with such nice people," Marta commented as they walked down the dimly lit street. Their hands weren't quite touching, but almost.

Dominik smiled. "Yeah, we get on alright. Probably 'cause none of us speak the same language."

"But at least you're... on the same wavelength," said Marta. "Living the same lives."

"Huh. Yep, all stuck in crap jobs and unable to pay more than fifty quid rent a week. Not sure if that's necessarily a good thing."

Marta laughed. She'd give anything for a housemate who understood – someone who knew what it was like to come to another country with nothing.

They stopped just inside the station and stood, quite close, facing each other.

"Well, see you at Barry's, I guess," he said.

"Thanks for tonight," replied Marta, unable to express how she really felt. She wasn't just thanking Dom for the soup and brownies. Maybe it was the wine, but she really wanted to kiss him.

Dominik leaned forward and pecked her lightly on the cheek. He smelt lovely.

"Goodnight Marta."

She smiled, pulling away. "Goodnight."

14

"WATCH YA BACK!" yelled the white van driver through his passenger window.

Marta came to a wobbly halt and pulled the ancient bicycle off the road, yanking her headphones out. The van pulled away with a plume of blue smoke that quickly engulfed her. She had never been great at cycling, even on the quiet roads around Łomianki, but here... here she was risking her life with every pedal.

The bike was an old one that one of Dominik's housemates' friends had 'found'. It was probably stolen like the iPod, she thought, but at this point her desperation outweighed her conscience, and she was just grateful for any old rusty junk they could find for her. She had felt guilty with Dominik making a detour each day via her zone to drop off her stack of leaflets, and this had seemed like the best alternative.

Today she was stationed in Chancery Lane. She'd never been here before, but Dominik had warned her. "You'll feel like scum," he'd said. "Everyone's wearing pinstriped suits and they'll look right through you – if you're lucky. One guy actually pushed me away with his umbrella." Marta wasn't looking forward to it.

Setting her box down on the pavement, Marta chained her wheel to the railing using a padlock that was probably worth more than the bike, and reached for her first wad. It was just gone eight o'clock, and already she was beginning to see what Dominik had meant.

Suits, briefcases and smart shoes rushed past in a blur. Everyone was on a mission. Alone, they marched, staring straight ahead. They all looked so serious. Perhaps this was what happened to people in positions of responsibility. Perhaps, if Dominik succeeded in getting a job in finance, this would be what he'd become.

"No thank you," said a prim lady in a lilac suit – the first to actually catch Marta's eye. A young man shook his head at her without opening his mouth, and another barged into her wrist with the side of his body as though she didn't exist. Nobody wanted a leaflet.

It had become standard practice for Marta to take a wad home with her each night, and place them in the community recycling bins on the way home. Usually there weren't too many, but today she had a feeling there might be a full box. She may as well pack up now, if it weren't for Barry's 'people' patrolling the streets identifying slackers.

The fact that these suited clones would only look straight ahead made Marta's job more difficult. Whereas in other locations, just standing in the way with her arm out usually resulted in a few leaflets disappearing, here, it was clear that an enhanced technique was required.

Marta adopted her friendliest expression and looked into the stream of zombies. There were one or two faces that looked capable of breaking into a smile, so she focused on these. When they got close, she leapt into their field of vision, brandishing a leaflet and saying "Free gym?" The approach was marginally more successful than just standing there.

It was nearly nine o'clock when Marta returned for her second wad. She stationed herself for the next stint, not really expecting much demand. She nearly jumped out of her skin. From somewhere nearby came a piercing noise like a donkey braying.

"Hueeeeh! Hueeeeh!"

Marta recognised the noise immediately. She looked up. Yes, sure enough, strutting towards her in a tight brown suit, was Tash's friend, Plum.

Just in time, Marta rolled up the leaflets and stuffed them into her pocket. Plum was with another woman – similarly dressed and in equally high heels. It was too late for Marta to move out of the way. She froze, looking at the ground, vaguely hoping that Plum might somehow not notice her bright turquoise jacket.

"Marta! Hi!"

Marta looked up feigning complete surprise, and switched on a smile. "Oh Plum! Hello!"

"What on earth are you doing here?" asked Plum, eyes wide open as though this was the most exciting thing that had happened all week.

"I'm... I'm..." Marta frantically tried to think of a reason for being here. She had told Tash her offices were near Victoria. "I'm shopping," she said, finally.

Plum frowned. "In Chancery Lane? At this time? What a strange choice!" She let out a whoop of laughter.

"Shopping for... gloves," Marta explained, spotting a shop selling mountaineering and outdoor equipment.

"Hah! I would have thought you'd have good gloves already, being Polish!" Plum turned to her friend. "Marta's Polish," she said.

"*Really?*" exclaimed the girl. "I say!"

"Sorry – I didn't introduce you," said Plum. "Fi, this is Marta. Marta, Fi. Fi's another trainee at Freshfields."

Marta nodded. Freshfields sounded like some sort of organic supermarket, although somehow it seemed unlikely that Plum and Fi were training to be checkout girls.

"Well, we'd better let you go and buy your gloves!" said Plum, overdoing the enthusiasm. Marta wondered whether she had distanced herself sufficiently from her box of leaflets. "Have a lovely day, won't you – I'll see you at the dinner party!"

The women strode off, and Marta hesitantly made her way towards the shop selling gloves. *Dinner party.* Hideous words. Marta was dreading next Friday. Tash had decided, in her role as social butterfly, that it was high time everybody got together and 'had a jolly good piss-up'. This, naturally, would mean ten couples plus Marta sitting bolt upright around the oak table drinking sickly liqueurs and talking about people she didn't know.

Marta's heart was still racing from the encounter with Plum. She hated lying, but sometimes there was no other way. Hopefully Plum was too self-absorbed to contemplate the possibility that Marta was here on anything other than a glove-buying mission, but maybe not. She was conniving, that girl. Marta had seen the way she caught Jack's eye when Tash wasn't looking. There was more to her than a braying Freshfields checkout girl.

71

Marta extracted her roll of leaflets and tried to flatten them with her palm. *Primera Sport*, screamed the gaudy heading in blue and yellow. *New health & fitness centre. One month's free membership.* She flipped the top one over. There was a map showing where the gym would be. It was near Holborn – just up the road.

From the other pocket, Marta pulled out the photocopied sketch that marked out her 'zone'. It appeared that she wasn't allowed to veer more than two hundred metres from Chancery Lane tube station. She wondered if anyone was covering the area where the gym would actually be, and if not, whether she could sneak up there for a bit.

Marta understood marketing. She'd learnt on her course that for any campaign, ninety percent of the advertising was ineffective; it was just that nobody knew which ten percent was working. Giving out leaflets to the wrong type of people in the wrong area, thought Marta, was surely part of the wasted ninety percent. She felt useless, standing in the middle of the pavement being dodged by commuters who were either too fat to care about gyms or too thin to need one.

It wasn't far to Holborn. Marta wheeled her bike along on the edge of the pavement, the nearly-full box balanced on the back. Barry couldn't complain just because she was using her initiative, could he? She was simply striving for a more targeted marketing campaign, that was all.

As she passed the shop selling gloves, something occurred to Marta. The men in suits weren't interested in taking her flyers, because they weren't the right type. They didn't care about the free month's membership. But *some* people around here were into health and fitness, as this shop proved; it was just a question of finding them. She parked her bike and grabbed a handful of leaflets.

"Hi," Marta beamed at the shop assistant, a gawky young woman with ginger hair and an awkward smile. "Could you help me, perhaps?"

The girl gave a little shrug and laughed nervously. "I'll try!"

"I have these leaflets, which are all on subject of new gym nearby, and I thought…" Marta trailed off, suitably deferential and English, "it would be great if you keep these, perhaps on the desk just here–" she placed the stack next to the cash register – "so that customers get free membership."

The redhead nodded like a little sparrow. "Oh, of course! Er... why not?"

"Thanks!" cried Marta, walking purposefully out of the shop before the girl's supervisor appeared. She could hardly believe how easy it was. She'd just offloaded a fifth of her day's assignment.

There were other outlets on the way up to Holborn. Marta left leaflets in two more outdoor clothing stores, a cycling shop and even a couple of cafés. It was easy. She couldn't understand why she hadn't thought of it before. There was even a huge gym fairly close to the site of the one she was advertising, so Marta spent a good half-hour catching people on their way to and from fitness classes, almost exhausting her stack of flyers.

"Hi!" she said, embarking on her now-familiar routine in a small running shop just off the main street. Somehow, she could tell that this one would be trickier than the others. It was clearly the owner she was addressing: a short, bespectacled man with suspicious eyes. "Could you help me—"

"Not if you're trying to sell me something," he snapped aggressively.

"Oh, I'm not," replied Marta. She was already realising this was a bad idea. "I just was thinking if you'd like to put—"

"Gimme one of them things," he demanded, wrenching one from her hand. "Fucking flyers. You know, I get enough of these things through the door at home. I bin the lot of 'em, you know. An' that's what I'll do with these."

"Oh, OK – I'm sorry." Marta started edging towards the door. Unfortunately, she couldn't retrieve the flyer that the man was still angrily waving at her.

"You got a licence for this, anyway?" he shouted, as Marta backed out and left the door to slam. She didn't think it was wise to engage the man in any more conversation – if that was the word.

"Fucking immigrants!" he yelled through the glass. "Why don't you just piss off back to your country?"

Marta took hold of her bike and ran. It was time to head back to Chancery Lane. She'd used enough initiative for the day.

73

15

"COME ALONG, MARTA! Guests are arriving!"

The words were innocuous enough, but Marta knew what they meant. She was in trouble. Tash had taken her aside earlier and explained that it would be 'nice if we could both be around for meeting and greeting – you know.' Yes, Marta knew. She knew what her role was tonight. Fetching drinks, taking coats, serving food… whatever else the host had in mind.

She abandoned the print-off of Anka's email and left her half-finished response on the bed. It was silly, she knew, replying to an email using pen and paper, but time in an internet café cost money, and that was something she needed to conserve.

"Marta? Where are you? Tom and Rosie are here!" cried Tash, her voice sounding a little more strained.

"Coming, yes," replied Marta, cringing at her reflection as she yanked open her bedroom door. She was dressed, on Tash's insistence, in one of the items hanging in the spare wardrobe: a red cocktail dress made from flimsy material – and very little of it. The low-cut design revealed more of her cleavage than Marta ever dared show, and the hem barely came half-way down her thighs. She crept down the stairs, tugging frantically at the bottom of the tiny dress and hoping her breasts would stay in.

"Oh, there you are. Could you–"

"Wow!"

"He-*llo*."

"Marta, you look *incredible!*" exclaimed Plum, throwing her hands up dramatically as Jack turned and let out a low wolf-whistle. Six faces were staring up at her.

Tash whacked her boyfriend in the stomach. "Doesn't she just? It's an Emma Hanbury, you know. Last season's, and slightly too tight – but never mind. Now Marta, would you just take Plum's coat? And – oh! Jeremy's here!"

Tash clattered over to the front door, her shrieks echoing around the marble atrium. Marta dutifully dealt with coats, feeling more self-conscious than ever. Too tight? That's not what Tash had said earlier. She had proclaimed it a 'perfect fit'.

It was a relief, ten minutes later, jackets hung, drinks poured and nibbles distributed, when Marta entered the lounge to find a familiar face in the crowd. Bare of makeup yet prettier than all those with their well-blushered cheekbones, Holly's face smiled back at hers. She was dressed, rebelliously, in jeans.

"How's things?" Holly mouthed, so that only Marta could see. Before Marta could respond, Tash jumped in.

"You two have met, haven't you? Now Holly, there's one more person on his way, and I think you'd really – ooh! Here he is!" she cried as the doorbell chimed. "Marta, would you…?"

Marta turned silently and slipped out of the room, glad to escape the ogling stares of Jeremy and Jack and the envious glares of Plum. She was beginning to wonder whether this outfit she'd been squeezed into was all part of Tash's plan to isolate her.

It was a strange sight that greeted Marta. Standing before her – beneath her, in fact – on the doorstep was a stocky, ginger-haired fellow in a pinstriped suit. His eyes were just about level with her chest.

"Hi," Marta said simply, stepping back to encourage him in and away from her breasts.

"Good *evening*," he replied, not moving, his eyes roaming hungrily up and down Marta's body. "And what a fine way to be welcomed, if I may say. Are you Holly, by any chance?"

"No. Marta. Come in," she instructed, slipping behind the open door to put an end to the staring. Something dawned on her. This guy had been invited along as Holly's mystery date. Tash had taken it upon herself to match up this ruddy-faced, ginger buffoon – not that she knew much about him, but appearances like this didn't usually deceive – with Holly. Marta recoiled at the thought. Poor girl, she had no idea what was coming.

75

"I'm Hugh," announced the short man, casually tossing his coat on top of the Indian Bamboo display as he strode through the hallway. Marta made a mental note to remove it before Tash saw.

"Hello, hello!" cried Hugh, clapping his hands together and rubbing them eagerly as he entered the lounge. He had a swagger that had clearly been cultivated to imply that something huge hung between his legs. A polite murmur rippled throughout the room, but it became evident that nobody knew who he was.

"Oh, Hugh! Hi!" cried Tash, emerging from the kitchen and flinging herself upon him. "Let me introduce you! This is Holly," she said, with a meaningful smile, steering him in a quarter-circle, "and this is Jeremy, Plum, Jack obviously, Tom-and-Rosie."

Tom-and-Rosie was in fact two separate beings who were attached at the shoulder and hip, both of them draped in expensive-looking black fabrics.

"Nice to meet you," they chimed simultaneously.

"Oh, and that's Marta. Marta, will you get one more gin and tonic for Hugh? Let's move through to the dining room." Tash skipped out, beckoning the guests to follow.

It was beginning to concern Marta that Tash might have fixed her up too with some grotesque young man like Hugh. A quick glance at the laid table, however, allayed her fears. There was no extra place next to hers – in fact, it turned out that Marta's *was* the extra place. Squeezed like a child's seat on the corner of the mahogany table was a kitchen bar stool, aligned with a miniature set of cutlery. The ludicrously high stool was for her.

"Hugh, you're at the end, opposite Holly," Tash said pointedly, "and Tom-and-Rosie, you're up this end with me. Plum, you're between Holly and Jack, and Jeremy – oh, you're there."

Jeremy was already seated at the head of the table, pouring red wine into one of the many glasses in front of him. Awkwardly, Marta slipped into the space between Jeremy and Hugh, lifting her left buttock just enough to perch on the black leather stool. She felt like a tennis umpire overseeing a very small game.

"Ooh, hello," remarked the ginger-haired fop, staring straight up Marta's dress then craning his neck to share the joke. Marta locked her knees together, desperately trying to pull some material over her lap.

"No, don't do that," said Hugh. "I like a nice view." He snorted. Marta couldn't bring herself to smile.

"So, what is it you do, Hugh?" asked Holly, loudly, clearly sensing Marta's distress.

"I'm an equity sales trader," he replied, turning his attention to Holly. "I work at Goldmans – that's how I know Jack."

Holly nodded. "How *interesting,*" she said, with what may have been a hint of sarcasm.

"Do you know Wod White?" asked Jeremy, topping up his wine glass.

"Sorry – who?"

"Wod. Woderwick White. Works in Equity Sales – joined last year, same as you."

Hugh's frown deepened, then suddenly turned into a look of jubilant recognition. "Oh! Rod! Yes, Rod Wright – I know the fellow! Sits two desks away from me! How d'you know Rod?"

It turned out that Jeremy played golf with Wod. The guys spent a good ten minutes discussing what a 'splendid chap' he was and how he had a ruddy good swing. Holly and Marta were cut out of the conversation, but that suited them fine. Holly seemed happy to eavesdrop on the conversation between Tom-and-Rosie and Plum, and Marta had her hands full obeying sign-language instructions from Tash.

"*Get the starters,*" mouthed the host, carving out an imaginary plate in the air and pointing towards the kitchen. Marta eased herself from the stool and snuck off to fetch the first course.

The preparation for this evening hadn't been too arduous – neither for Marta nor for Tash. The food had arrived at two o'clock in a van with pictures of fruit all over the sides. Inside the plastic bags were plastic containers, and once you lifted the lids off the plastic containers, you had a full dinner party, all laid out and ready to eat. Tash had instructed Marta to transfer the portions onto proper plates and to hide the packaging, then she'd explained about the last-minute re-heating, and that was it, basically. The rest of the day – well, Tash's day, at least – had been spent applying face-masks and fake tan.

"YOU LOSE!" roared Hugh, pointing at Marta as she hopped off her stool at the end of the starters to collect the plates. "Jack was thumb-master and you didn't notice!"

Marta looked at the red-head blankly. He seemed to be accusing her of something, but she had no idea what, and no idea why he and most of the other guests were grinning at her like that.

Holly leant forward. "It's a drinking game," she explained apologetically. "You have to look out for certain things happening all through the meal. Jack was thumb-master, which means that whenever he puts his thumb on the edge of the table – like this–" she nodded at her own, and then everybody else's, which, Marta realised, were all gripping the edge of the table, "you have to copy. The last person to do it has to down their drink."

Marta nodded. "OK," she said slowly, aware that all eyes were on her, but unsure about what to do. What was this crazy game? Was it even a game? They all seemed to take it so seriously. And now what was she supposed to do? Were they waiting for her to do something, or did they just want her to collect their plates?

"Drink!" echoed Jack, leaning across the table to top up her already-full glass of red wine.

"Show us what Eastern Europeans can do!" added Hugh, grinning up at her.

It seemed that they wanted her to drink her wine – all in one go. Marta didn't like red wine. She didn't really like wine at all. Beer she could drink all night, and spirits, well, she'd practically been brought up on them, but wine… ugh. She had managed to consume two glasses tonight – under Hugh's instruction – and felt quite queasy already.

"She'll see it off really quickly, I bet," squeaked the excitable Plum, as though she were watching a freak show.

Marta couldn't help thinking of parties back home, with Anka and the other girls. They'd got drunk then, too, on vodka mainly, but only because they'd wanted to. There had been no obligatory drinking. There had been one particular night when Anka had suggested they meet at the bakery after work. They'd ended up drinking, singing and laughing until three in the morning, when the bread ovens finally cooled down. Then Anka had created a sledge out of baking trays which they'd used to traverse the icy market square, back and forth. *That* had been fun. Marta grabbed the stem of her wine glass.

She tipped her head back. At first, she took extra-large mouthfuls to get it down quickly, but the tannin flavour hit her taste buds and suddenly there was no way she could swallow it. The vile liquid filled every cavity: her mouth, her throat, even her nose, and yet there was still more in the glass – heavy, viscous and intoxicating.

It's fruit juice, Marta told herself, gulping down another slug of the stuff. She was aware of the reaction from the guests. They were shouting words of encouragement at her – aggressive encouragement – and it was clear that giving up was not an option.

"Finally," jeered Jeremy, as Marta placed the empty glass back on the table. Her stomach was heaving and her head felt heavy and light at the same time. The room was moving: the walls billowing out then retreating, the table wobbling about beneath her. Marta clung to it, waiting for the moment to pass.

Tom-and-Rosie let out a patter of applause and Plum squawked something stupid about Eastern Europeans. Marta reached for a nearby water glass and took a gulp.

"*You OK?*" mouthed Holly, catching her eye. Marta nodded.

"Let's hope we can trust her with the plates!" squeaked Tash, provoking a ripple of laughter around the table. Feeling steadier, Marta pushed back her stool and started gathering the near sets of cutlery.

There was a loud metallic 'clang' followed by a shattering sound, and then silence. Marta looked back. Her stool lay horizontal on the polished slate floor, the selection of glass shards around it not quite hiding the jagged crack in the tile.

"Evidently not," muttered Hugh, grimacing stupidly around the table.

"Whoops," added Plum, exchanging sly looks with Tash's boyfriend.

"I'll give you a hand," Holly whispered, following Marta out to the kitchen.

The physical damage didn't take long to repair. With Holly's help, the pieces of glass were swept up, the area covered with a plastic bag (nominally to stop people cutting themselves; in fact to delay Tash's reaction to the broken tile) and the main courses delivered as serenely as was possible. Marta's pride would take longer to mend.

"Brilliant! Sausages!" announced Hugh, eyeing the dainty meat garnishes on the side of each plate. Marta watched Tash flinch at the reference. She too had made the mistake of calling them sausages earlier.

"Mini chorizo fingers," the host corrected.

"Well, OK then… that means we can play a whole new game: Pass the Mini Chorizo Finger!"

Marta watched in horror as Hugh slowly pushed the sausage into his mouth, then brought most of it out again, gripping the very tip with his teeth. Then he leaned towards her, the meat still trapped between his fat lips, and waggled it in front of her mouth.

What was this game? And why did they have to play games over dinner? Were posh people not able to amuse themselves by making conversation? The laughter was deafening. Plum seemed to be caught up in a fit of hysterics. "Take it from him!" yelled someone. "Take the finger!"

Hesitantly, Marta opened her mouth and accepted the greasy sausage, biting only the end, as lightly as she dared. Hugh was looking into her eyes, very intensely. Marta had never been so close to any man so obnoxious. She was still feeling slightly ill from the wine, and then there was the smell of garlic, either from the meat or from the red-head's mouth. Just as Marta thought she might vomit, slowly, his gaze still locked onto hers, Hugh pulled away, leaving the sausage dangling from Marta's lips.

It became apparent that Marta was expected to pass on the oily finger to the person on her right. Unfortunately, this was Jeremy. Bracing herself, she turned in her seat and focused hard on the end of the sausage. She was determined not to look at the giant nose looming on her horizon.

Plum's whooping was getting louder and Hugh was making comments under his breath that Marta didn't understand but took to be dirty. Jeremy's nose was eclipsing everything in her field of vision except the small stretch of meat.

Suddenly, the thought that she was locking tongues with the guy – albeit via a mini chorizo finger – became too disgusting to bear, and Marta pulled backwards, releasing her grip.

It turned out that Jeremy hadn't fully secured his grip on the meat, and before Marta had even licked the salt off her lips, the sausage came tumbling down between them, bounced off her leg and onto the floor.

"Hah! Only three people!"

"Drink!"

"More wine!"

Marta's glass was being topped up to the brim with wine – this time white. The sight of it made her feel sick.

"I can't," she said, shaking her head.

"No such word!"

"I thought Poles could handle their drink!"

"Lightweight!"

The insults were coming thick and fast but they didn't change her mind. She stood up, wobbled, grabbed onto the table, and promptly sat down again. The whole room was fluid. The oil paintings were changing shape and the carpet kept rising up to meet her. Slowly, Marta stood up again, picking her way via pieces of furniture towards the door.

"I go lie down. Feel funny," she explained.

There were raised eyebrows behind her back, she felt sure, but Marta didn't care. She didn't need to impress them, and she didn't want to play their strange games.

In the safety of her bedroom, with a litre of water and a slice of chleb inside her, things felt better again. Marta leaned against her sink, staring at her reflection and trying to work out whether she was actually swaying or whether it was her eyes. The little red dress had worked its way up as she'd climbed the stairs, and now hardly covered her buttocks. She looked like a stripper, thought Marta, drunkenly wondering how much strippers got paid in this country, and whether they really did have to strip completely, and whether she'd... Her bedroom door was creaking open.

"Hello?" called Marta, knowing who it would be. Holly was the only person down there who cared about her. Well – Tash cared in the sense that she no longer had a waitress to bring in the desserts, but that would only concern her later.

Marta came out of the bathroom. She jumped. It wasn't Holly. And it wasn't Tash either.

"Hi."

Jack was standing in the doorway. He had very muscular arms, thought Marta, distracted from the question of what he was doing in her bedroom.

"Just wanted to check you were OK," he said, moving towards her. "They gave you a pretty hard time down there."

Marta nodded, suddenly remembering the fact that the flimsy dress had ridden up to her waist.

"No, don't do that," said Jack, as she pulled the fabric down over her thighs. He was smiling. "Leave it. You look gorgeous."

Marta froze. Jack had his arm around her waist. He was stroking her hair, gently, telling her not to worry – that it didn't matter what had happened downstairs. In other circumstances, she might have enjoyed being taken into the arms of one of the most handsome guys she'd ever met. She might have relished breathing in the scent of his aftershave. She might have allowed him to move his hand down, over her shoulder, onto her breast, and to gently touch her nipple, all the while reassuring her in that deep, authoritative voice. But not when the handsome guy was Tash's boyfriend.

Marta pulled away, stepping backwards towards the bed. She suddenly felt weak. Jack was using his full strength to hold her. With one hand cupping her breast, the other firmly round her waist, he kept Marta close to him, allowing them to move backwards, but not to separate.

"No, Jack!" whispered Marta, too afraid to speak out. Her bedroom door was half-open.

Marta twisted round in his grip, but Jack moved with her, pulling her off balance and sending the pair of them tumbling onto the bed.

"Oh, it's like that, is it?" asked Jack, smiling down on her as he pinned her arms to the bed. His body was hot and heavy on top of her. "God Marta, you're beautiful."

"Jack, please–" Marta writhed on the bed but her struggles were futile.

"Shhhh," he coaxed, pulling away slightly. "Don't worry."

His breath smelt of wine. He was drunk.

"Marta, I need to st- tell you something," he slurred. He looked like a drunk Calvin Klein model. "I want you," he whispered, lowering himself upon her. "Not Tash. I want you."

Marta lay still for a second. *He wanted her?*

Suddenly, Jack's lips were touching hers, gently at first and then with more force. His tongue entered her mouth. Under different circumstances, it could have been fantastic. As it was, it was stressful and slightly painful as her hair was pinned tight to the bed by Jack's arm. It could only have lasted a few seconds, but it seemed like longer. Her mind was racing. How could this be happening? What was Jack doing? How far would he take it? Could she escape? Did she want to?

It stopped as quickly as it had started. They both heard it: the sound of footsteps on the stairs. Marta's heart started pounding. Jack quickly rolled off her and over the side of the bed. There was no sound from the upstairs landing, but then, there wouldn't be; the floor was carpeted.

She could hear Jack's stifled breathing and nothing else. The silence from outside her bedroom was making her nervous. Marta rearranged herself on the bed, smoothing down the rumpled duvet and running her fingers through her knotted hair. Her dress was all twisted round, revealing her pants and part of her bra.

"How are you feeling Marta?" chirped a voice out of nowhere. In walked Plum, her eyes boring straight into Marta's with a very unconvincing smile.

"Er, good. No, not good. Too much wine." Marta pulled a silly face.

"Mmm. Yes. It's amazing what wine can make people do, isn't it? Anyway, I'm sure you'll be fine. I'll leave you *alone*. See you downstairs in a bit when you're feeling better."

16

"NO THANKS,"

"I'm in a rush."

"Fuck off out of my way!"

Some parts of London, Marta had learned, were better than others for handing out leaflets. Oxford Street was one of the worst. The crowds were so thick that oncoming pedestrians had no way of knowing whose hand it was offering the leaflet, and most of them couldn't read English anyway.

A Japanese tourist grinned back at her through the lens of a camera, pausing briefly to frame his shot of her desperate face and then moving on, ignoring her offer of two-for-one at participating opticians. Marta wanted to scream. For nearly three hours she'd paced Oxford Street, dodging, chasing, waving, smiling – and a hundred leaflets was all she'd managed to shift.

Her patience boiled over. Sod it, she thought. There had to be a better way. She barged forwards, against the flow of shoppers, heading down a side street and away from Oxford Street. Her mother's words were ringing in her ears: 'When you come to a problem you can't solve in an hour, spend the next hour doing something else.' Well, she'd spent too long on this one already.

"CHEAP INTERNET. 50p/HOUR" read the sign, held up by a guy who was about as animated as a corpse. Marta followed the arrow and slipped through the narrow doorway.

Slinging her leaflet-filled rucksack onto the counter, she fished out a fifty pence piece and followed the man's vague nod towards the terminal in the corner. There was something comforting about internet cafés, she thought, weaving between the broken swivel chairs and wooden desks. It soothed her, the gentle tap of fingers on keys, the muted hum of concentration.

Today's frustration could not be entirely attributed to the reluctance of tourists to take her leaflets, thought Marta, waiting for the machine to recognise her password. In fact, the growing, burning sensation was nothing to do with her job. It was to do with Saturday night. Two and a half days had passed and nobody had said a word. She was finding it increasingly difficult to keep it inside her. There was a danger that if she didn't say something soon, it would come out accidentally – in front of the wrong person.

The email she'd drafted in response to Anka's last one was still in her wallet, folded and unopened. Somehow, tales of standing on street corners holding flyers and meeting sweet guys who shared flats with Croats in Acton paled into insignificance compared with recent events. Well, near-insignificance, anyway. Dom featured in the revised version – his home-made soup, his scooter, his smile – but he was no longer the main thrust of the email.

Two and a half days. Two and a half days of turmoil, of remembering his words, his touch, of trying to forget it, of maintaining her sweet, pleasant relationship with Tash, of saying nothing when all she wanted to do was pour it out to someone.

'I have so many unanswered questions, Anka,' she typed, her fingers flitting about the keyboard like a deranged pianist's. 'Like why did he pounce on me like that? Was it just a drunken accident? Does he even remember it, do you think? What will happen when we next see each other? (Which we will, I'm sure, as Tash has him round nearly every day – although not for the last few days, which worries me!) How much did Plum see? Will she tell Tash? Has she already told her? Is that why Jack hasn't been round? Could anything happen between Jack and me? Do I even want it to? He is SO attractive (I know I said that before, but honestly, you've never seen anything like it) and self-assured – and it's not just his looks, it's the way he is. Manly. In control. I think he does like me, but… OH ANKA I JUST DON'T KNOW!!!'

It felt so good to let it all out – like coming to the surface and finally breathing after spending too long under water. The response would not be instant, of course, but at least the problem was out now. Marta had shared her dirty secret. And although Anka was hundreds of miles away, confined to the shop floor of the Łomianki bakery, leading a life that bore no resemblance to hers, she'd understand. She'd write back.

The sleeves on her beautiful turquoise jacket were getting grubby, she noticed, jiggling the mouse and pressing Send. There was a lump in her throat as she watched the screen change. *Sent to Anka Kowalczyk*, it said. Suddenly her old life – her friends, her village, her home – seemed so far away, both in distance and in time.

Shaking herself, Marta emptied her inbox of junk, logged off and bent down for her rucksack. As she did so, her mobile phone vibrated in her pocket. She frowned. The display began +48. Poland.

"*Słucham?*" whispered Marta, hurrying out of the café with a brief nod at the dozy guy behind the desk.

"Marta? It's me!" Loud, excitable and Polish, Marta recognised the voice in an instant.

"Anka! What a coincidence – I just emailed you!" cried Marta, leaning her rucksack against a wall and perching on it, half-focusing on the feet of passers-by.

"I know you did, silly! I'm online. I haven't finished reading it, but I just had to call. Wow, Marta, your life is *so exciting!*"

Marta smiled. The sound of Anka's voice brought back the lump in her throat. Virtually everything in Marta's life, now and in the past, instilled boisterous enthusiasm in her best friend. Perhaps it was because Anka maintained such a narrow, risk-free existence herself. Maybe Marta was doing all the things Anka wanted to do but wasn't quite brave enough to try.

"So, this guy! More information, please! What happened that night? And I want to hear more about the Polish leaflet man. He sounds cute. Oh, Marta, your life is like a soap opera! So ridiculous!"

"Ridiculous is the right word," Marta replied. "It's not *that* exciting. But anyway, how are *you?* What's going on in your world? How are things in Łomianki?"

"Oh, shut up about that – you know the answers! I am fine, nothing is going on in my world, and things in Łomianki are exactly the same as when you left us, except that everyone is two months older, and everything happens a little slower, on average, now that you're not here."

Marta grinned to herself. "I don't believe you. Has nothing changed at all? What about the mural on the side of the church hall? Is that finished? Weren't they going to put in some traffic bollards on the entrance to–"

"Marta! I don't give a shit about murals or bollards! Tell me about your men!"

Marta laughed. "Well, you got the email, so you know about Dom – that's the one with the nice smile and sandy hair that really needs a bit of a cut, but he gets away with it because of his eyes, which are kind of hazel and quite unusual, for a Pole, and he goes everywhere on this rusty old scooter, and–"

"Enough! He sounds lovely."

"He is," Marta replied thoughtfully. Dom was lovely.

"And the other one? The one that nearly *raped* you?"

"Anka! I wouldn't go that far. It–"

"Well, he would have, by the sounds of it!"

"No he wouldn't. Well… I don't know. But the thing is, I really don't know if he likes me, or whether it was just the wine talking, and I can't even work out whether I like him, or whether he's just so attractive that I'm just blinded by that, or… oh, I don't know. I'm confused."

"No shit."

"And anyway," Marta added, "I shouldn't even be considering going anywhere near him, because of Tash."

"What? Tash? The rich bitch who can't brush her own hair without your help? What has she got to do with it? What right does *she* have to dictate–"

"She's going out with Jack. Didn't you read my email?"

"Wh– er, what?" The line went quiet. "Um… Must've missed that bit. Right. Er, well that changes things slightly."

"Slightly."

"So, to clarify," Anka said slowly, after a pause to digest the information, "your housemate's boyfriend came onto you at your housemate's dinner party, and your housemate's friend *may* have caught you two at it on your bed – but you don't know for sure."

"We weren't 'at it'! I didn't have any say in the–"

"Ah, so it *was* nearly rape then, was it? If you had no say in it?"

Marta grunted, defeated. It was true, Jack had been pretty rough with her. Not rough in an unpleasant way – well, OK, maybe it would have been unpleasant had Plum not appeared on the landing – she didn't know. Maybe she was making excuses for him. She was confused.

"So," Anka went on, "you are having trouble deciding between two men, one–"

"I'm not deciding between them! I just needed to tell–"

"Marta, you *are* deciding between them. Or, if you're not, then you should be. It's not good to get involved with more than one. So, option one is Polish Leaflet Man with the scruffy hair, nice smile, cute eyes, good sense of humour, and, from what I can tell, a soft-spot for you, and option two is English Cheat with the chiselled looks, arrogance, aggression, possible alcohol problem and girlfriend – oh, who happens to be your housemate and effective landlord. Tough decision, Marta. Very tough."

Marta snorted and remained silent. She wanted to fight back, but couldn't think of a point worth making. For all her anxieties, Anka knew how to construct an argument.

"OK, you're right," she said, finally.

"I know. Shit – I'd better go. The bagels are due out. So just promise me this, OK? You won't have anything more to do with the stupid English guy, except to smile politely when he comes round to see his girlfriend."

Marta smiled. "OK. I won't."

"Promise?"

"Promise. Thanks Anka."

"No worries. I like a good drama – but only when it's got a happy ending. So nothing more to do with him. Nothing," she warned. "I know his type."

Marta was doubtful of that – she'd never met anyone in her twenty-two years in Poland who came close to him in looks or personality – but she agreed all the same.

"Miss you, Marta. We all do."

Marta's throat was clogging up again. "Miss you too. Bye," she managed, hearing the clatter of the bagel rescue operation before the line went dead.

She tucked the phone away in her pocket, dusting herself down and hauling the rucksack onto her back. As she did so, the phone bleeped. Marta pulled it out again. A message.

Hi Marta, Jack
here. I'm sorry.
Call if U want2.
J

Marta stared at the text. She read it four times, trying to work out what it meant, and what to do in response. Anka's words were still echoing around in her head. Nothing more to do with him. Nothing. She re-read the SMS one more time, then pressed the delete button and locked the keypad.

17

"HELLO?" Marta said timidly. The number on the display was a London one she didn't recognise.

"D'you want the good news or the bad?" asked a gruff male voice.

"Uh, sorry… I…" Marta stammered, wondering whether it was simply a wrong number.

"I said, GOOD OR BAD," the man bawled down the line, instantly conjuring an image of his face: Barry Roffey. Her boss.

"Um, good," Marta replied, feeling her hand shaking against her ear. Why was Mr Roffey calling her now, at the end of her shift on a Tuesday?

"Well the good news is that you're getting paid early this week. Like now. In my office. Quick as you can. Get ya skinny little arse over 'ere. By my reckoning, that should be fifteen minutes, if you're where you're supposed to be, which you're probably not. I'll tell ya the bad news when you get over 'ere."

"Oh, um, yes–" Marta realised she was stammering into a dead line.

It had crossed her mind earlier to pop into a couple of sports stores she'd frequented the previous week and try to offload a few more leaflets with them. Surely contact lenses were essential eyewear for serious sportsmen? They would welcome a two-for-one offer from participating opticians. However, the tone of Mr Roffey's voice indicated that the priority for Marta was to get to his office, not to distribute the rest of her load. She would find a suitable skip on the way to Queensway and dump them in there, taped up in the plastic bag – the same routine she went through at the end of each day.

It worried her that she'd been summoned to her boss' office part-way through the week. Pay day was Saturday; surely any news or instructions he had for her could wait until then. Barry's tone of voice was disturbing, too.

There was a litter bin opposite the Hyde Park gates that served her purpose, enabling Marta to climb the dirty stairs with a near-empty rucksack – not entirely empty, so as to avoid suspicion.

Barry Roffey was talking to someone inside his office. As she raised her hand to knock on the door, she faltered. He was talking into his phone. "I understand, yes, she shouldn't have done that... Yes, no I know, she's on her way as we speak... Oh, she'll certainly get that, I can assure you... Well, not working for me, that's for sure..."

Marta's knuckles drifted away from the door. The snatches of conversation worried her. Were they referring to her? Had she done something wrong? Was Barry referring to something she'd done? Surely not. Marta was probably one of his most productive workers – Dom reckoned so, anyway. Marta was mid-thought when she heard a loud crash – the phone being slammed down – and then a groan of what sounded like constipation but could have been exasperation. Marta seized the moment.

"COME IN!" growled her boss.

Barry Roffey was a deep purple colour. Reclined in his rickety chair, his rolls of fat hanging out through the gaps and his arms dangling by his sides, his neck and face were visibly pulsating. Poor heart, was Marta's first thought on seeing him. *Oh shit,* was her next.

"Marta Da-brow-ski," he snarled, watching as she inched carefully across the cluttered room. Marta glanced at his face and decided it would be unwise to correct him on his pronunciation of her surname. "What THE FUCK do you think you've been doing?"

"Sorry. What do you mean?"

"WHAT DO I MEAN?" Barry leant forward, causing the chair to creak ominously. "What I MEAN, you skinny little Polish imp, is that you've been dumping leaflets ILLEGALLY!"

Marta could feel the blood pumping round her head. This was it. This was the end of her first job in England. And all because someone had found a few leaflets in a skip somewhere – probably not more than twenty – and somehow, God only knew how, they'd traced it back to her.

"It was very few—"

"VERY FEW!" Barry paused for a second, lowering his voice. "I have had no less than four complaints about you, Marta Dabrenka. FOUR! You've made enemies all over London, as far as I can tell, and that's enemies of the COMPANY. *My* company."

Marta frowned. Four complaints? This didn't make sense. She had been careful about dumping the unused leaflets – never leaving them in the same place twice, always wrapping them, taking care not to be seen…

"Did I tell ya to go wanderin' into shops, into leisure centres, into cafés and bully junior staff into taking your leaflets? Did I? Did I tell you to spend your time millin' around stores and dropping piles of the things on their counters? NO! I FUCKING WELL DID NOT!"

Marta's frown deepened. So this was what it was about. It wasn't the end-of-day dumping, it was her efforts to be innovative. Her attempts at targeted marketing.

"I did not do bullying—" Marta couldn't summon her English fast enough.

"Don't fuckin' argue with me." Barry stared at her, exhaling noisily through blocked nostrils. "I'm the one who's fending' off the fuckin' complaints. I've 'ad people threatenin' to close me down, I 'ave. CLOSE ME DOWN!"

"But the workers, they tell me…" Marta's voice petered out.

Barry Roffey was shaking his head, slowly, angrily. "I've sacked people for being lazy. I've sacked 'em for cheatin', for stealin' – even for rollin' up spliffs with me leaflets an' smokin' 'em. But NEVER 'ave I got rid of someone for fuckin' TRESSPASSIN' IN SHOPS AN' FORCIN' LEAFLETS ON—"

"I did not force on any people," she explained. "I just thought it to be enterprising to—"

"I DON'T FUCKIN' PAY YOU TO BE ENTERPRISING!" Barry exploded, then fell quiet, his laboured breathing the only sound in the room.

"Take this," he said finally. "It's ya last two days' pay. More than you deserve, but I'm a decent guy like that. Take it and fuck off out of my office. And DON'T COME BACK."

Marta snatched the envelope and marched out, as instructed. She was still shaking, but now with rage, not nerves. She'd been sacked. Sacked from one of the most basic jobs in the world. Sacked for trying to employ some common sense. Marta wasn't sure whether to feel proud or ashamed. Or simply scared about being unemployed again.

The journey through Queensway, across the park and through Kensington passed in a blur, her thoughts blotting out everything else. How had this happened? Mr Roffey had sacked her because he'd had complaints. But why had the store managers complained? What was wrong with a bit of cross-selling? She'd only tried it in places where the leaflets were appropriate for the types of customer, and never against the will of the shop staff. There were so many rules in this country! In Poland, nobody would lose their job over something like this.

By the time she reached the flame-lit entrance to 14 Egerton Square, Marta's temper had lessened a little. Part of the blame, she acknowledged, lay with her – for misinterpreting the terms of her contract, for being too bold. She had forgotten that things happened differently in London. Everything was regulated. That was why they didn't have any snack-bars in the street, why there were no flower stalls in Leicester Square, why even the buskers had to stand in silly 'zones' under ground. There were rules about everything. Maybe it would take some time to adjust.

Putting her key in the lock, Marta was almost ready to accept the fact that she'd lost her job through her own doing, and to get on with the next task: finding a new one. But something distracted her as she turned the key.

There was something at the bottom of the stone steps leading up to the front door – something that wasn't usually there. An ornament, or a box of some kind. She had already passed it and ignored it, but now she looked back, realising what it was. In the half-light, she could just make out the familiar red stripe along its length. Yes, there was no doubt – it was mama's old suitcase.

Mystified, Marta opened the door to shed light on the case, dumping her jacket in the hallway. Her investigation was brought to an abrupt halt by an ear-splitting scream that could probably have been heard back in Queensway.

"YOU LITTLE BITCH!" screeched the voice, coming from

inside the house and getting louder. Marta leapt backwards, half-tripped down the steps and landed with her foot in a flower pot, dangerously close to one of the flames.

The tall, slender silhouette of Tash, clad in a tight-fitting evening dress and heels, appeared like an apparition in the doorway. "I CAN'T BELIEVE YOU HAVE THE AUDACITY TO EVEN COME *NEAR* THIS HOUSE, YOU SCRAWNY LITTLE PEASANT! JUST FUCK OFF BACK TO YOUR COUNTRY AND DON'T COME BACK!"

Marta stumbled away from the flame, mentally preparing for a chase but not making a move yet. In those heels, Tash wasn't going anywhere fast, and Marta felt confident she could outrun her if it came to it. *Scrawny little peasant?* Marta's English wasn't perfect, but she knew how insulting that was. She looked up, feeling a mixture of anger and humiliation. For a moment, Tash appeared to be frozen rigid at the top of the stairs, her eyes boring into Marta's like acid. Her cheeks were swollen and streaked, Marta noticed. She could guess what had happened. Plum had told Tash what she'd seen on Saturday night.

Or, Marta reflected, perhaps Plum had disclosed what she *hadn't* seen on Saturday night. Plum had no scruples. That was evident from the way she flirted with Jack. It would be just her style, thought Marta, to embellish for her own personal gain – either to get into Tash's good books or to get into Jack's pants. There was no time to think through the possibilities.

"Tash, please believe me that I did not want anything–"

"SHUT UP AND FUCK OFF. I'VE CLEARED YOUR ROOM. DON'T *EVER* COME BACK."

"Please–" The door slammed shut, and Marta heard the bolt being drawn across.

For several seconds, she stood, staring up at the huge front door, waiting, hoping, for something to happen. Nothing did. Marta bent down and picked up her battered suitcase. This was it. She'd been told to fuck off – not for the first time that day – and it seemed that she had no option but to do just that.

18

THE RAIN HAMMERED against the café window, almost rivalling Aretha Franklin who was wailing from the tinny stereo behind the bar. Marta watched the droplets run down the outside of the steamed-up glass, glowing red in the tail lights of a passing car.

She looked up. The waitress was blinking at her with a slightly frightened expression. Marta stopped blowing bubbles in her milk and let the straw slither out of her mouth.

"You want order food?" she asked. Her accent was Polish.

Marta shook her head. She considered responding in their native tongue and striking up a conversation. Maybe the girl could help find her a home? And a job too, perhaps? It was an option. But not an attractive one. No, Marta hadn't come to England to beg. "No thanks," she replied in her best English. She would get through this on her own.

Drinking through a straw always helped her to think. Marta had had some of her best brainwaves whilst gnawing on something. And so, chewing hard on the flimsy plastic and slurping up the lukewarm milk, she went through the issues on her mind.

She had nowhere to live. It was raining outside, it was dark, the café closed in twenty minutes, and Marta had no home to go to. Living with Tash had been difficult, to say the least, but it had been warm and spacious – and cheap, compared to what she knew of London hotels. Hell, it had been more than that. She'd had an en suite bathroom and her own TV. She'd taken it all for granted, and now she was homeless. The more she dwelt on this, the more attractive the option of striking up a conversation with the waitress became.

She had no source of income. That was another concern. It had taken her more than a fortnight to get the job with Barry Roffey, and now she was back to square one, with a blank English CV and no chance of a reference from her last employer. The brown envelope in her wallet contained three days' salary, so in total, Marta had just under three hundred English pounds. That wouldn't last long.

The priority, Marta knew, was to find somewhere to go tonight. There was only one place Marta could think of. One place where she'd feel welcome, where she might get a home-cooked meal, and where there were so many people sleeping on the floor that one more wouldn't make any difference. She pulled out her phone.

"Hi, it's me, Marta," she gabbled the instant he picked up.

The line went dead.

"Hello? Dom? Hello?"

Marta stared for a second at the dormant handset. She'd been cut off. She redialled and waited while it rang. Brrrr, brrrr. She listened impatiently to the monotonous ring tone, trying to keep her temper under control. Brrrr, brrrr. She lost count of the number of rings. Brrrr, brrrr. Eventually, Dom's voicemail interrupted, and then his message – first in Polish, then English.

"Leave me a message and I'll call you back. Keep it short please. Whatever they say, length does matter."

"Hi Dom, it's me. Marta. Not sure what happened there, but could you call me back? It's quite urgent. In fact, very urgent. I mean, well, what I really need is a place to stay tonight. Maybe a few nights. Er, anyway. Long story. I've had a bit of a bad day. Um… yeah. Could you call me as soon as you get this? Thanks. Bye."

Marta ended the call and checked her balance. £2.29. Tash had lent her the phone with a whole load of call credit included, but it was running out fast. Marta had no way of topping it up herself as the contract belonged to Tash, so in effect, it would soon be useless. Still, at least she still had the phone. It was a wonder Tash hadn't snatched it from her on the doorstep.

Marta slurped up the last of her milk and tried not to think about Tash's outburst. She'd been upset. She was a sensitive girl, too – and insecure. Poor thing, it was probably a very reasonable reaction to whatever Plum had told her, which – oh hell, that wasn't true. Let's face it, she hated them both. She hated them all: Tash, Plum, Jack, Tom-and-Rosie… the whole lot of those snobbish, stuck-up rich kids.

Marta checked her watch and thought about calling Dom again. Perhaps he was on the tube. Maybe he'd gone into a tunnel before. Or maybe he'd had another call waiting and taken that. She picked up the sticky menu and gazed, unseeing, at its text. Down, up. Down, up. Absent-mindedly, she picked the straw from her glass and started chewing. Something was troubling her.

If they'd been cut off by bad reception, then why had Dom's phone rung perfectly clearly when she'd called back, only seconds later? And if they *had* been cut off by bad reception, why hadn't Dom called her back? He hadn't called back even after her frantic voicemail message, which, by now, he must have picked up. Didn't he want to help her?

Marta redialled Dom's number. There had to be a rational explanation. Maybe she could just go round to his place? A housemate might be in and take pity on her. There was still the possibility that he hadn't received her voicemail, or that he'd lost his phone and couldn't call, or that he'd been kidnapped and… no. These were ludicrous thoughts.

The familiar ring started up again. Brrrr, brrrr. Brrrr, br – and that was it. All of a sudden, half way through a ring, Dom's voicemail cut in. Marta ended the call quickly, but not quickly enough to prevent 20p being wiped from her balance.

She slumped back against the plastic, foam-filled seat. Marta knew what it meant when a call went to voicemail part-way through a ring. It meant that the recipient had pressed 'Reject'. Dom had rejected her. He didn't want to help.

Marta pondered this odd behaviour. The last time she'd seen Dom, he'd been his usual cheeky self; dodging death on his scooter, carrying her leaflets into town, laughing and joking about how much he hated his job. They'd had a coffee before starting work, and he'd suggested meeting up again sometime for a meal. Why would he reject her like that?

Marta jumped as her phone started vibrating in her hand. It was a message. A message from Dom.

DON'T EVER CALL
AGAIN. OK?

Marta frowned, scrolling down to the bottom and back up again. What? He was cutting her out of life? Marta re-read the text, wondering whether Dom was joking, or whether there was some hidden meaning between the lines. She sat for some time, holding the phone in her hand, thinking. There was only one conclusion she could draw: Dom never wanted to speak to her again.

The waitress approached timidly, her body language telling Marta what she already knew.

"We close now," she whispered apologetically.

Marta nodded. She dropped the semi-masticated straw in the glass and handed it over. Aretha Franklin's backing girls were silenced mid-chorus, and suddenly the only sound was the pounding rain on the window. The waitress flicked the main lights, casting a guilty glance in Marta's direction. Perhaps she understood, thought Marta. Perhaps she too had been in this situation and recognised the look on Marta's face.

What now? Suddenly, Marta felt incredibly lonely. She was sitting in a closed, dark, café in a strange city with nobody – not even Dom, her one friend, or so she'd thought – to call on. Where could she go? Who could she ask for help? There was no one. All the people she trusted were six hundred miles away. She was on her own. Her bottom lip began to tremble, and tears started to build up behind her eyes.

"EVERYBODY OUT!" yelled a fearsome looking woman with dyed red hair, presumably the Polish girl's boss. There was nobody else in the café. It really was time to go. But where to?

The tears were flowing. Marta hauled her suitcase out from under the table and rose to her feet. Everything she owned was crammed into that old leather box. Or at least, she hoped everything she owned was in there. It somewhat depended on Tash's state of mind when she'd packed it, which, thought Marta, might mean that she was now the owner of a load of old linen or something. Sniffing miserably, she lugged whatever it was through the café door.

The rain lashed down on her face, soaking her skin almost immediately. It was then, as she tried to manoeuvre herself under a newsagent's awning and felt a large droplet run down the back of her neck, that Marta realised something. She'd left her jacket at Tash's.

Suddenly, she was sobbing. Anka had given her that jacket. She had spent half her month's earnings on the beautiful thing, and now it was sitting in Tash's hallway – or maybe in her dustbin. Marta would probably never see it again. What would Anka say?

That wasn't the only reason for the tears. The other reason, of course, was Dom. He had deserted her. He had seemed so kind, so keen, so… so bloody perfect in every way. She'd really started to fall for Dom – and she needed him, too. But he'd turned his back on her. It was almost beyond belief. He'd asked her to dinner two days ago, for God's sake. Something must have happened for him to have changed his mind. Marta wiped a hand across her wet face, trying to pull her emotions together. Everything just seemed so bleak now. She had nothing to live for in England.

It wasn't sensible, but Marta decided to use up her remaining credit on a phone call to Poland. She needed to pour everything out to Anka. Her real friend. Standing in the shop doorway, shivering, Marta pulled out her phone.

She started to dial and then stopped. No. She couldn't spend her last £2.09 on an emotional conversation with Anka. It would upset Anka, which would upset Marta even more, and then they'd both be in floods of tears and no closer to solving her problems. Despite her mood, despite everything, she had to think rationally or she knew she'd regret it later.

Marta's fingers were numb, and it took a while to work the stiff latch on the suitcase. Eventually, the lock slid open. Leaving only a small opening for her wrist, she reached inside. To her relief, she found herself touching the familiar fabrics of her belongings – not dirty linen after all. She felt her way through the mess, finally recognising the furry lining of her hooded top and pulling it out.

She reached back inside, slipping her hand into the secret lining. Phew. Her stash of money was still there, in its old sock. She counted it. Three hundred and twenty pounds, including this week's pay. That was nearly two thousand złoty. In Poland, that would be enough to live on for months – even staying in a decent hotel. But here, Marta knew, it was nothing. Some youth hostels charged £20 per night, according to Dom – not that she knew where to find one. If she went to Heathrow, thought Marta, and found a cheap flight, maybe sleeping in the airport for one or two nights… Oh dear, she was already budgeting for her air fare home.

This wasn't the right attitude, Marta decided, wiping a sleeve across her wet forehead. She couldn't return to Poland after only two months. That would make her a failure. Two months, and she'd only just broken even, once you factored in the air fare and the £100 that tata had given her – which Marta was determined to pay back. She had intended to come over to England and start a career. She wanted to make her parents proud, not embarrassed. She couldn't face sloping off home with her tail between her legs, explaining to everyone that England had proved too much for her.

At least she had a good grasp of the language, thought Marta, brightening slightly at the thought of the waitress who could hardly speak English. *She* had a job. She was getting by. If she and thousands like her could do it, then Marta could too.

Suddenly, inspiration struck. There *was* someone else she knew over here. Someone who spoke no English, but someone who might be able to help her. He'd certainly seemed friendly enough on the bus, and she knew he had somewhere to stay...

Marta pulled out her wallet and rummaged among the notes and receipts. There it was: the torn-off piece of cigarette packet with the phone number of Lukasz' friend.

"Uh, yeah?" someone slurred in Polish, when the phone was finally picked up. There was a lot of noise in the background – shouting, shrieking and loud garage music.

"Hi!" shouted Marta. "I'm a friend of Lu–"

"You the girl wi'the dope, yeah?"

"What? No!" Marta yelled, her voice being drowned out by a whale-like noise at the other end. "Hello?" she screamed. "I'm a friend of Lukasz. Is Lukasz there?"

There was a clattering sound as though the receiver had been dropped on a hard tiled floor, then another whooping noise. After some more clattering, the guy's voice came on again. "What?"

"IS LUKASZ THERE?" asked Marta. The guy was off his head.

"Who? Where's the drugs?"

Marta sighed impatiently. This was costing her money. "I NEED TO SPEAK TO LUKASZ. IS HE THERE?"

"Lukasz has the dope?"

Marta nearly put the phone down, but as she pulled it from her ear, another idea struck.

"OK, I have the drugs," she told him. "WHERE IS YOUR HOUSE?"

"Hah! Drugs' up, everyone! It's here!" There was a roaring sound at the other end.

"WHERE IS YOUR HOUSE?"

"London!" replied the guy, laughing like a hyena. The rest of the pack were doing the same in the background.

"WHERE EXACTLY?" asked Marta, starting to get desperate now. This loser was her only hope for finding a dry floor to sleep on tonight.

"Tell Lukasz t'get here with the drugs, OK?" slurred the guy, giggling. Then there was a sharp 'ding', a bubbling noise, and then silence. He must have dropped the phone in his drink.

£1.69. That was all she had left. She hadn't got any closer to finding a home for the night. In desperation, she scrolled through her messages, wondering whether somehow there was a trace of the one Jack had sent her. Of course there wasn't. She had deleted it. Not that she'd relished the idea of begging to Jack – the root of all her problems. He probably would have been only too happy to help by providing her with a bed to sleep in – *his* bed. No. Despite the cold, Marta was glad she didn't have the temptation of knowing his number.

Marta stared into the darkness. She wanted Dom more than ever. Why had he pushed her away? The only explanation she could think of was that somehow, Tash had got hold of his number and sunk her claws into him – lying about Marta, out of spite. It seemed unlikely, given that the two had never met, but that was all she could come up with. In which case… in which case she had to go and explain the truth.

Tucking the piece of cigarette packet back in her wallet and coaxing it shut, Marta prepared to make the journey to Acton. It was a bold move, and she wasn't looking forward to the confrontation, but it was her only option.

Her wallet wouldn't shut properly. There was something inside that didn't quite fit in the notes section with all the other bits of paper and junk. She pulled it out, folded it in two and stuffed it back in, yanking the zip shut. And then she opened it again. Her heart started pounding as she realised what it was that had been sticking out. It was Holly Banks' business card.

With a shaking hand, Marta punched the numbers into her phone.

19

STEPPING OUT OF THE BATH, Marta rubbed herself dry with the rough green towel. There was a stain in the corner that she was trying to avoid, and the towel had a musty smell as though it had been put away damp. She thought back to the soft, fluffy white ones that had hung from the heated rails in her private bathroom and smiled. The smelly towel didn't matter, and nor did the brown marks in the bath, or the blobs of toothpaste all over the sink.

After just twenty minutes, Marta felt more at home than she had done in the whole two months she'd spent at Tash's. In fact, she'd started to feel more at home even before she'd been shown to the peeling front door with its mound of junk mail. The moment she'd stepped onto Kilburn High Road and been handed a card saying 'Cheap phone calls to Eastern Europe', her mood had brightened.

The streets had been bustling even at nine o'clock at night – and not with the type of people that filled the Kensington pavements. There were no super-slim women with push-chairs, no dolled-up rich kids with straight, whitened teeth, no city slickers in pinstripes. These were real people: men spilling out of betting shops, single mothers smacking rampant toddlers, drunkards singing, babies screaming… Marta liked it.

"Time for a drink?" asked Holly, as Marta crept into the kitchen wearing a borrowed tracksuit. Her own clothes were tumbling round and round in the dryer, her suitcase having proved to be about as waterproof as a flannel.

"Yes please."

Holly peered into a cupboard and then withdrew, looking

unconvinced. "OK. Looks like Rich has drunk most of my stash, so it's beer or beer, I'm afraid. D'you drink beer? I could do tea or–"

"Beer is good," Marta said gratefully. Actually, a cold beer was exactly what she needed. "Who is Rich?"

"Oh – he's my flatmate. One of them. There's two: him and Tina. Both friends from uni. Oh, and don't worry – not from the same bunch as Tash and that lot. Rich was an engineer with me, and Tina I know from hockey."

Marta nodded. She accepted her beer and looked around the tiny kitchen. The whole house was small, but then this was probably typical for normal Londoners earning normal salaries.

"So," said Holly, sitting down at the mini kitchen table and kicking out a chair for Marta. "Not a good day then?"

Marta smiled. She cracked open her beer and took a swig straight from the can. *This* was how drinks were supposed to be served – not with ice and a twist of organic lime. She shook her head.

"So, you were half-way through telling me about Jack the Twat. What happened after Plum caught you two together?"

"Nothing. Nothing, Holly. So I think, 'is OK. I don't need to worry'. Nobody know what happened, and Plum, she will not say anything."

"And then what?"

"Well, then I get home today – no, wait. I forget something. He send me a text message."

"Who, Jack?"

"Yes. It says, 'Sorry, call if you want,' or something like this. I forget as I throw away message as soon as it arrived. I don't want nothing to do with Jack."

Holly gulped down her beer, nodding. "Damn right. He's more of a bastard than I thought. Very good looking, but what a git."

"So then I get home today, and Tash, she has put all my things in a suitcase and leave in the garden, and I go inside, and she come out from somewhere, nearly push me down the steps, and she stare at me, saying, 'Get out and fuck off back to Poland, you peasant girl,' or something like this. She was *scary*, Holly. Very scary. I wanted to explain, but couldn't. She shut the door."

Holly snorted. "She called you *what?*"

"I wanted tell her it wasn't my fault, it was Jack – her boyfriend – but she don't listen. She was upset. I look at her face, and it was red, like she was crying, you know?"

Holly nodded. "I suspect that Plum might have employed a little artistic licence when recounting what she'd seen to Tash. She's a bitch. I never liked Plum."

"But you are all friends from the university?"

Holly shook her head. "I wasn't friends with the Kensington posse. But I ended up seeing lots of them when Tash and I shared a room. On her own, Tash was alright. She was needy and insecure, and she had to be the centre of attention the whole time, but deep down, she was a nice girl. Well, that's what I thought. I may have got that wrong. I only hung out with that lot out of necessity. My real friends were people like Tina and Rich."

"I don't understand them," Marta admitted. "They are so *complicated*."

Holly nodded. "Too rich for their own good."

Marta took another sip and thought about the Kensington 'posse'. Maybe their wealth did have something to do with it. Perhaps that was why Marta had never fitted in – would never fit in. All their lives, they'd had people to do things for them: nannies to care for them, parents to drive them around, teachers to school them through their exams, daddy to pay for things. Mama had always said that it was healthy to experience some hardship in life – some situations where you had to 'get your hands dirty' or suffer. For Tash's gang, hardship was being told by the waiter that their dish had run out and that they'd have to pick again.

There was a noise as though someone was trying to break the latch on the front door.

"That's Rich," Holly explained calmly. "His key doesn't work very well. Sometimes it takes him a good five minutes to get in." She took another swig of beer and grinned. The scratching noise continued.

Finally, there was a heavy thud, followed by a grunt and the sound of the door slamming. Holly leaned back in her chair and poked her head round the doorway. "Hi!"

Rich was tall. That was the first thing Marta noticed. The second thing was his smile. Rich had one of those faces that fell naturally into a smile. He had light blond hair, freckly cheeks and uncommonly blue eyes that, Marta observed, tended to focus on Holly.

"Meet my flatmate, Rich. He's a defected engineer, like me—"

"Defective?" Rich interrupted. "I was perfectly good!"

"Defect-ed," Holly replied. "He's doing a teacher training course – I know, poor kids. Rich, this is Marta. We're rescuing her from the evil clutches of Tash Gordon. She'll be staying on our lounge floor for a bit – hope that's OK."

"Awesome. Hi. Nice to meet you." Rich bounded over and shook Marta's hand. "Welcome to the cess pit."

Marta frowned, still smiling. She didn't know what a sex pit was, but it sounded rude.

"He means it's a dump. Which it is," Holly explained. "You probably noticed that."

Marta smiled, relieved that it wasn't so rude. "You never see my place back in Poland."

"By the way, Rich, I see you've devoured our drinks cupboard with the exception of the dubious liqueur with no label," Holly commented.

Rich pulled a face. "Ah, yes. That was the guys this weekend. Er, sorry. I'll replenish it right away. Well, soon. At some point. In the meantime, I guess there's no chance of a beer, is there?"

Holly rolled her eyes and reached backwards, yanking the fridge door open. "Just this once," she muttered.

Rich tore open his can, ruffling Holly's hair over-zealously and pulling out a seat next to hers. Yes, thought Marta, Rich fancied Holly. It was less clear whether the converse was true. If she had to guess, she thought, watching Holly brush the hair off her pretty face, she would say that Holly was oblivious to her flatmate's affections.

"So, what d'you do, Marta?" asked Rich, wrenching his gaze off Holly for just long enough to pose the question.

Marta faltered. This was the part she hadn't yet told Holly.

"I…"

She didn't know what to say. The truthful answer would be 'nothing'. She no longer had a job, and in career terms, she never really had one in the first place.

"You work in marketing, don't you?" prompted Holly.

Marta exhaled uncomfortably. "Well, I would like to. But today I lost my job."

"How careless," remarked Rich, tucking into his beer. "Where did you last see it?"

"Shut up Rich. What d'you mean?"

"Well, I had this job. And today, the boss he call me into his office and he say, 'you causing too much trouble, so you must leave.' So now I have no job."

Marta was beginning to feel upset, just telling them. Maybe alcohol on an empty stomach hadn't been such a good idea. Her bottom lip was beginning to tremble. She knew what the next question would be, and she didn't want to answer it.

"Trouble? What were you doing?" asked Holly.

This was it. This was where Marta had to explain that the last few weeks of her life had been spent standing on street corners handing out pieces of paper.

"I... well..." Marta collected herself together. She was going to have to tell them. "My job was leaflets," she said. "It was giving out leaflets. Silly job, I know. But I couldn't get any better. I looked, and I get rejected. My English is not perfect, so cannot do marketing here, they tell me. So I give out leaflets, you know?"

Holly nodded. Rich was squinting into his beer can as though something unexpected was floating inside it.

"So anyway, these leaflets, they for all kinds of things. Sometimes gyms memberships, sometimes phone calls, sometimes banks... all sorts. So when I give out these things, I start to think, 'I know, why don't I put these leaflets in clever places, where the right people will see them?' You know, like leaflets for gyms in sports shops, and leaflets for opticians in old-people coffee shops, this sort of thing."

Holly nodded. "Makes sense."

"So, problem is, these places, not all of them like me putting the leaflets. Some get angry. And they contact the advertising firm, and they contact Mr Roffey, my boss, and he contact me, and bang! My job is gone, 'cause I am trouble-maker."

Holly was looking at her with a puzzled expression.

"He fired you because you were putting some thought into his clients' marketing strategies?"

Marta shrugged. "Guess so."

"Well the guy's an idiot then! What a dick. He doesn't deserve to have you on his payroll."

Marta laughed dryly.

"That guy clearly wouldn't recognise good marketing if it came up and walloped him in the face," Holly went on, slamming her beer can down on the table. "I think it's a good thing you're not working there any more."

Holly was right, in a way, thought Marta. but she hadn't recognised the crucial point: the point that Marta no longer had a source of income.

"Tell you what," said Holly, looking intently into Marta's eyes. "I've got a few ideas about where you might wanna work. Places that *value* initiative instead of sapping it out of you."

Marta's head shot up. "You do?"

Holly nodded vaguely, looking into space.

Rich leaned towards Marta. "She's having a brainwave," he said confidingly.

Before the brainwave could materialise, however, there was another sound at the front door – this time more of a battering noise, as though someone were ramming a large object against it.

"Tina," both Holly and Rich declared simultaneously.

"She's drunk," added Rich, leaning sideways to get a view of the small hallway. Then he jerked back to the table. "*And not alone,*" he added in a whisper.

Marta sat quietly, watching Rich watching Holly who was watching the door, which was in danger of being bashed off its hinges.

Eventually, after an extra-loud thump and a little squeal, there was silence.

"*Now she's instructing the guy to go into her room,*" whispered Holly, tilting back on her chair at quite an extreme angle. "*Ooh, and now she's lurching this way.*" She swung back to the table and gulped down some beer.

"Oh, hi Tina!" cried Holly, with mock surprise that was lost on the poor drunk girl as she staggered across the kitchen towards the tap.

Tina was a striking black girl whose legs might have rivalled Marta's in length; it was difficult to tell, as Tina was far from vertical. Her eyes shone out from her dark complexion, wandering all over the place but still retaining a defiant beauty. She was dressed in a tight-fitting suit and impressive high heels.

"Hello! Ooh, hi. You don't live here." Tina tottered back to the kitchen table, spilling most of her water along the way.

"Well observed," said Rich, shaking the droplets off his shoe.

"Actually, she does," replied Holly. "She's staying on our floor for a bit. Marta, meet Tina. Tina's a professional piss-head and part-time trader at JC Morley."

"Nice-t'meet you," slurred Tina, tripping over her own foot and landing in Rich's lap. "Ooh. Hello."

Rich extracted his flatmate and propelled her towards the door. "I think you'd better get back to your room, hadn't you?" He gave her a meaningful smile.

"Hmm. Yeah, well goodnight everyone. Goodnight Martha – hic – Marta!"

They all waited until the footsteps had disappeared inside Tina's bedroom, and then burst out laughing.

"Well, that's Tina. I think that just about sums her up, don't you?" said Holly.

"I'd say so. I think her professional objective this year is to sleep her way around the equities trading floor. I guess next year she'll switch to bonds."

Marta laughed. "She seems nice."

"She's lovely." He nodded. "It's just a pity she needs wankers in pinstriped suits to tell her that."

"C'mon Rich," said Holly, rolling her eyes. "She's only having fun."

"Sorry. I guess it's just that I've got the room next to hers." He rose to his feet. "Which is where I'm heading. G'night all. Sleep well. Thanks for the beer."

Rich disappeared with a final glance in Holly's direction. She didn't seem to notice. Draining her can, she crushed it in one hand and turned to Marta.

"You look knackered. Wanna go to bed?"

Marta nodded. She felt exhausted, all of a sudden. They left the cans in the pile that was accumulating on the kitchen table and crept into the lounge.

Lying on the sofabed beneath Holly's sheets and a hairy eiderdown, Marta let her eyes fall shut. Almost immediately, she slipped into a semi-lucid state that was somewhere between awake and asleep. She was stranded, alone, in a desert-like place, watching as a stream of friends and acquaintances passed her, ignoring her cries for help. Then, just as a flock of mad people on trucks arrived, waving, there was a creaking noise. A shaft of light fell across her eyes.

"I was thinking, Marta," she heard, as she hauled her mind back to reality. Holly was standing in her pyjamas in the doorway, glass of water in hand. "I know it's easy for me to say, because I grew up in this country and I went to a uni that everyone recognises, and I'll probably never have a problem getting work… but I think you'll do fine here, and you don't need to push yourself so hard right now. I know you've got to earn money, and you want a career, and someday you'll do something spectacular and take over the world, but you've got plenty of time. You can slow down a bit."

Marta tried to drag her brain back into gear.

"At least," Holly added, "that's what people tell me. Not that I listen to a word of it. I'm the same as you. Impatient. Just thought I'd pass it on though. G'night."

20

IT WAS STRANGE, talking into the microphone on Holly's computer and hearing her mother's voice coming through speakers.

"I'm good! Things are really great," she lied. There was no other way with mama; she would be booking herself on the next flight to London if Marta even hinted that something was wrong.

"Are you calling me from inside a tin can?"

Marta laughed. "I'm using Skype, on a computer," she explained, careful not to let slip whose computer. As far as her mother knew, she was still living happily in Egerton Square, using Tash's borrowed phone.

"Using sky? What are you talking about?"

"Skype. It's a way of making phone calls through the internet. It costs hardly anything, and if you were able to get online we could call each other for free."

Her mother tutted. "Calls through the internet? Whatever next? We've only just got used to these cordless telephones! Oh – that reminds me. I popped into the bakery yesterday. Your friend Anka has a phone that's so small I thought it might get lost in her ear!"

Marta smiled. "How is she?"

"She seems well. Said you had a nice chat the other day. Told me all about your new life… I think 'crazy and wild' was the term she used, which concerned me slightly. You are taking care, aren't you? Eating well and getting enough sleep?"

"I'm fine," Marta assured her, hoping that Anka hadn't mentioned anything specific to her mother – like the fact that she'd been set upon by her hostess' drunk boyfriend and consequently kicked out. Sweet and exuberant though she was, Anka was not known for her tact.

"...I know you don't cook properly for yourself," her mother went on, "but you must make sure you get enough vitamins. English food is so bad – they process all the nutrients out and replace them with salt..."

She prattled on about essential minerals for a bit and then dropped the question Marta had been dreading.

"How is Tash?"

Marta hesitated. She had meant to tell her mother about the eviction. Mama was open-minded, sensible, understanding. But she was also a worrier. The idea that Marta was now living with a near-stranger would probably horrify her, especially if she knew that her old housemate, the daughter of mama's friend, was no longer speaking to her except via curt text messages to Holly.

"She's fine!" replied Marta enthusiastically. "We get on so well."

"Oh, good! I was going to write to her parents this week – just to thank them for putting you up in their house and lending their daughter, so to speak. Maybe I should send Tash something, too? D'you think she'd like a little Polish gift? Maybe some Łomianki pottery?"

"Er, maybe," Marta jumped in, panicking slightly. The answer was no, Tash would *not* like a Polish gift of any kind, and was quite likely to come round and stab Marta with any Łomianki pottery that she received in the post. "I'm not sure, mama. She has quite fussy taste. Maybe wait until I next come to visit, and I can pick out something I know she'll like?"

"Yes, OK. Good idea. I'll write to Penelope and Henry and leave the gift for now. What's the house like? Is it very big? I think Penelope said there was a grand piano! Do you play it?"

"Um, no. It's... well, it's grand. I mean, everything in the house is grand – not just the piano. To tell the truth, I've been too scared to lift the lid on the keys – it must be worth thousands. Everything is worth thousands, mama. It's mad. There are *flames* either side of the front door – like in the old English films where the men in tights ride up to the estate on horseback!"

"Oh, how wonderful. You must take some pictures! Will you send me some photos?" she asked, as Marta panicked some more. "And of you and Tash? I'd really like that. My daughter in London," she mused, with pride in her voice. Marta hoped she'd forget about the photos. "That's a shame about the piano. Maybe you could play it sometime when Tash isn't in – you were so good when you were little!"

Marta didn't bother arguing. The truth was, she had never been good at playing the piano. Nobody in her family was musical, but mama herself was tone-deaf, so never realised.

"Your sister played so beautifully in the school concert two weeks ago," she went on. "She was accompanying Tomek. His violin-playing hasn't improved much since you left, to be honest – he still sounds like a squeaky door – but the accompaniment was lovely. Oh, and I saw Beatrycze's mother in the interval – d'you remember Beatrycze?"

"Of course. We were in the same class."

"Well she went off to London too – I'm sure you remember. According to her mother, she's happily married to an Englishman – a doctor, I think she said. But that's nonsense, of course. Everyone knows she went off with that older man and disappeared. Poor girl – and poor family, too. I think her mother was rather envious when I told her about you finding a proper job so quickly. How's that going?"

Marta cringed, staring into the screensaver on Holly's computer. 'WORK!' in a chunky 3D font was bouncing around the screen. How ironic. Now was her chance to come clean. One step at a time, though. Today she'd explain to her mother about the job. She'd tell her about the house thing some other time.

"Well, the thing is, the work wasn't quite what I'd expected, to tell the truth."

"What d'you mean? And why are you talking in the past tense like that? Aren't you there any more?"

"Er, no. I, um, I left. A few days ago."

"Oh," mama replied. In just one syllable she managed to convey such disappointment. "Why did you leave? Wasn't it challenging enough? What exactly were you doing there, anyway?"

"Um, I was…" Marta couldn't bear it. She could *not* tell her mother the truth. "Well, it was paperwork-based. And yes, you're right – it wasn't challenging enough. The work was dull, and I wasn't using anything I'd learnt on my course."

"Oh dear," her mother replied. "And was there no opportunity for progression? No way of 'climbing the ladder'? I know how impatient you can be, Marta. You didn't leave too soon, did you?"

Marta nearly laughed. "Don't worry, mama. I haven't thrown away an opportunity. It was never going to be a good career move, working there. It was just a job. I'll find something else – something more worthwhile."

"I'm sure you will," said mama, sounding more confident. "You know what's best. You'll get yourself another job in no time."

There was a pause while Marta considered telling her mother the whole story: about Barry, about getting sacked, about the futility of looking for 'career jobs' in England. Before she could though, mama was off again.

"No time at all, I'm sure. There aren't many people who came top of their year at Szkoła Główna Handlowa!"

Marta tried to let the comment pass, but couldn't. Her mother just didn't understand. "It's not that simple, mama."

"What d'you mean?"

"Well, it's all very well coming top of my year, but I came top of my year in an institution that nobody here has ever heard of. For all they know, SGH could be some ten-man cult in the middle of the Polish countryside."

"Don't be ridiculous! Everyone has heard of SGH."

"No they haven't, mama. Over here, people can only name two places in Poland: Warsaw and Krakow. I can't get a job on the basis of my qualifications."

"Well, I'm sure you can get one on the basis of your skills – and your personality. Just as you did for the last one."

Marta mumbled sounds of agreement to appease her mother. The problem was, her skills weren't recognised over here either. English employers seemed to be under the impression that Poles didn't really have skills (except plumbing skills, of course); they just had a good 'work ethic'. And as for getting by on her personality... well, judging by what Marta had experienced so far in her interviews, personalities were actively discouraged in the UK workplace.

"How is tata?" she asked, changing the subject.

"Oh, he's good," her mother replied.

Marta waited. She couldn't be sure whether it was latent concern from the last subject of conversation or whether it was something else, but mama's response sounded hollow.

"Is he still being screwed over by Polkomtel?" she asked, when her mother still didn't expand.

"N–no. Well, yes – in fact, they're having a bit of a restructure in the cabling department, and his job has shifted slightly."

Marta wondered whether her own lying had been as transparent as her mother's. "What d'you mean, 'shifted'?"

"Well, your father has been moved to another department – temporarily, they say. The thing is, Polkomtel is under new management. His new bosses are German, and they seem to be rather… ruthless."

"Mama, are you saying tata might lose his job?"

"No!" she replied quickly. Too quickly. "No, some of his colleagues might, but he'll keep his job – just a different one. You don't need to worry about it. He's fine. Happy as ever in his new role!"

The sudden frivolity in her voice worried Marta. Mama wasn't a frivolous woman. "You will let me know if anything changes, won't you?"

"Of course! Yes, of course I will. Oh, that reminds me – he's asked me to find some super-strength indigestion tablets. God knows where I'll get them from."

"What?"

"Oh, don't worry. I'll find some. He's started getting terrible indigestion. I blame the water. They're fiddling with the supplies and adding all sorts of nasties… It never tastes the way–"

"Mama, since when has tata been getting indigestion? Has he been to the doctor about it?"

"No! Of course not! Why would he go–"

"Because it might not be indigestion! He should see the doctor! I mean, what if it was…" Marta hesitated. Her medical knowledge was limited. "Something worse?"

"Marta, I think you take after me. Stop worrying! You've got enough going on in your life without getting worked up over tata's ailments."

"OK. But you will make him go to the doctor if it doesn't get better, won't you?"

"Of course I will," replied mama unconvincingly.

"And you will tell me what's happening over there, too? Let me know about the Polkomtel restructuring thing – and anything else?"

"Yes! Ooh, in fact here's some news: they're shutting down the leisure centre on the way into Warsaw. Caused a bit of an uproar when they first announced it, but I can see why they did it… Not enough young people around to keep it going. I mean, it's only us oldies left over here now. What would we want with a helter-skelter swimming pool like that?"

"Oldies? Mama, you're fifty-three! That's not old."

"It's not young, either. Really, it's getting worse. There's nobody of working age to fill the positions, so they're cutting all the jobs. It's only Anka and others like her who don't have the nerve to move on… they're all that's left. I saw Benedykt the other day – your first boyfriend. Remember him?"

"Of course." Marta remembered him well. Going behind the science block with Benedykt had been the only reason she'd ever missed a class in school. "He's trying to become Mayor of Łomianki isn't he?"

"Not any more. He's moving to London. Maybe you'll see him around," mama said pointedly.

"Hopefully not," she replied. The last time she'd met Benedykt, he'd been sporting a pair of fake glasses and a neatly trimmed beard, holding a clipboard and flirting with middle-aged women.

"Oh?" said her mother. "Does that mean there might be someone else on the scene?"

"No, it means that Benedykt has turned into a bit of a knob since going into politics."

"Oh," replied mama, sounding peeved.

Marta was quiet for a few seconds. She was thinking about the guy she had thought was 'on the scene'.

"Well, I'm sure you're making lots of new friends," declared mama. "And your English must be near-perfect now!"

"I guess so, yeah!" agreed Marta, injecting some enthusiasm into her voice.

"I'm so proud, Marta. It does make me happy to hear about your new life in England. You know, not many people have done as well as you."

Marta felt a wave of guilt wash over her.

"I should go. Ewa has piano practice at the church in ten minutes. I'm sure you have things to be getting on with, too."

"Oh yes – plenty of 'crazy and wild' things."

"Oh, Marta, don't," her mother chided. "You take care of yourself, won't you?"

"'Course I will. And you take care of tata, yeah?"

"We'll be fine. 'Bye Marta."

"Bye!"

"Don't forget the vitam–"

Marta had already pressed the red button.

21

THE BRIGHT SPARKS INTERVIEW was not going well. It had been doomed from the start – ever since she'd run over the recruitment specialist's foot with her wheely chair and knocked a pile of folders onto the floor.

"So tell me about your last placement – if you could call it that. You seem to have worked there for… what – four, five weeks?"

"This wasn't career job," Marta explained. "Was just a little job to get me money for paying rent in London."

"OK," said the woman, slowly. Her red hair was scraped back over her head, her flesh pulled tight so as to give no indication of her age. "And you plan to go into marketing with no UK experience other than this 'little job'?"

Marta nodded. "I have the experience, but in Poland. Have done good work in–"

"I'm sure you have, I'm sure you have," the woman said patronisingly. "But you do understand that our clients – those companies with whom we might place you – expect a very high calibre individual from this agency, and so it is our duty to ensure that every one of our 'sparks' – that's what we call them – have the skills, qualifications and *relevant experience* to equip them for a very challenging workload?"

Marta nodded sullenly. She just wanted to leave. There was no way they were going to hire her as one of their 'sparks', so she might as well stop wasting everybody's time. To be honest, she felt a bit cross with Holly for suggesting she apply. Clearly, inequality was as rife here as everywhere else: they weren't willing to hire someone with a Polish background. She was too much of an unknown.

"Now you graduated from the Sko – Skol – Shoo –"

"Szkoła Główna Handlowa w Warszawie."

"Yes, er, there. Could you tell me a little bit about your course? About the university?"

Marta opened her mouth to talk, but was silenced by the sound of the door opening behind her.

"Ah, Laura!" cried the MD, losing interest in Marta momentarily. "Come in! I was just explaining to Martha here—"

"Marta," she interjected.

"I beg your pardon?"

"Marta. Is my name."

"Yes, I know. Sit down, Laura – try to avoid the mess over there. That's our client folders all over the floor. Yes, I was just explaining to Martha how important it is for our 'sparks' to have sufficient experience in their sector before being sent out to clients."

Laura, a slim, pretty blonde in a tight pencil skirt, pulled up a chair and flashed a business-like smile at Marta. She was probably only a few years out of university herself, but she clearly knew what was what.

"Imperative," she agreed, nodding. "Our reputation rests on the excellence of our sparks."

Marta nodded again, her patience draining away. Why was she sitting here with these hateful women?

"Good news, though!" chirruped young Laura. "Your tests have been marked, and your scores have come through as 'high' in every section!"

A small flame of excitement flickered in Marta's despondent soul. The tests she had sat half an hour ago had been easy – just basic mathematics and common sense – but perhaps not everybody found them so simple.

"You're the first person since I started working here to score full marks in numerical reasoning," Laura told her, beaming.

Marta beamed back, equally falsely.

"Well that's excellent, Marta," said the MD encouragingly. Marta took it as a positive sign that the woman had finally learnt her name. "Well done."

"Have you done any tests like this before?" asked Laura.

"No. But they quite easy, like problems you get in school," Marta replied. Perhaps they thought she'd cheated.

"Polish school," said the MD with raised eyebrows, looking meaningfully at her subordinate. Marta's hatred for the woman grew.

"Oh yes," said Laura, turning back to Marta. "When did you come over to England?"

Here we go, thought Marta. Another inquisition about how little experience she had in UK marketing. "Two months ago."

Laura nodded. "Okaaaay," she said, glancing sideways at her boss. "And you haven't worked here in any other capacity, have you? Any shop work? Any au pairing?"

Marta sighed. "No. Have not." She couldn't keep the resentment out of her voice.

"Because you see, the thing is, Marta, you can't really expect to leap straight into a career over here with no demonstrable capabilities."

"I have them," said Marta defensively. "Just not in this country."

"Mmm, yes," said Laura, looking again at her boss. "Relevant experience is very important, and I'm afraid to say, I don't think your placements over in Poland will carry much weight with potential employers here."

"Then how do I get relevant experience?" asked Marta, plain angry now. She didn't care about working for Bright Sparks any more – she just wanted to prove her point.

"Well, that's the difficulty, I agree," replied Laura, looking flustered.

"I cannot get experience anywhere because I do not have experience," Marta went on. "Is crazy! I just want experience – not lots of money or anything like this... Just some time in good English company, but nobody give me that chance!"

The woman leaned forward across her desk and looked Marta in the eye. She paused for a second, then spoke, slowly. "I hear what you're saying, Marta. It's not easy for people like you." She pursed her lips, still looking right at her. "Now. We have over a hundred clients on our books – nearly half of them marketing firms or others that would suit your skill set."

Marta nodded, waiting for the 'but'.

"But we operate on a need-to-hire basis here, which means that we can only assign sparks to projects as and when the requests come in from clients. Even for our best sparks, sometimes it takes months to find them work – and that might only be a fortnight's placement. Our clients are highly selective, and very demanding."

The woman paused, smiling at Laura who nodded subserviently.

"You have an added disadvantage," the woman went on, "in that you've never really worked over here. We have over five hundred sparks on our books, and we assign projects on the basis of track record. Let me advise you, Marta. Sign up to a number of agencies – not just Bright Sparks – and *badger* them. Be persistent."

Marta nodded again, wondering where badgers came into the plan. This was surely the most patronising woman she had ever met.

"Something will come up, I'm sure. You're a smart girl, Marta – as your test results show. We have your details on file. We'll call you if anything suitable comes up."

22

THE MUSIC WAS HEAVY ROCK: loud, angry and disharmonious, with a tuneless chant that consisted mainly of the word 'fuck'. It wasn't ideal for running to, but it suited Marta's mood. She pounded down Kilburn High Road, oblivious to the honking horns and pedestrians in her way.

Running was Marta's way of venting frustration. Back home, she'd taken it up as a way of getting warm in the winter months, but today there was no need for that. She simply needed to run off her rage.

She turned down a road that looked as though it led to the park. Memorising a route from Holly's map had proved impossible as all the street names looked the same, but it didn't matter. Right now, she didn't care where she ended up.

Her life was a disaster. She had come to England to start a career, to elevate herself, to help her parents, and she had ended up with this: no job, no home and no friends – apart from Holly and her mates, and they were only trying to be charitable.

Marta picked up speed, taking advantage of the empty pavement and tail wind. Her chest was starting to ache now. She'd heard nothing from Bright Sparks of course – or from the four other agencies she'd applied to in the last week. She didn't expect to hear from them. Nobody wanted to hire a girl with a Polish degree.

The rock music beat its way to a dramatic end, and an old man started crooning about birds falling in love. Marta pressed fast-forward. She was beginning to wish she'd taken the opportunity to change the play list before Dom had turned nasty on her.

If only she hadn't been born Polish, she thought sullenly as Eminem started rapping in her ears. How different things might have been if she'd been sent to an English school, obtained English qualifications, absorbed English culture. Maybe she would had gone to Cambridge, like Holly. Or anywhere – any English university would be better than bloody SGH.

The road opened up and Marta found herself nipping between vans and trucks on a fume-filled, six-lane junction. Was it this hard for everyone who came to England? Did they all meet the same brick walls trying to fit in?

The answer, she knew, was no. Not everybody found it this hard, because not everybody tried to fit in – not properly. Other Poles over here were content to waste their university degrees being brick-layers, au pairs and odd-job men. There were qualified neurosurgeons driving fork-lift trucks around warehouses and nuclear physicists cleaning tube station toilets. Marta wasn't prepared to do that.

Her stride fell in time with the music, Eminem's chant keeping her running faster than she'd usually go. *I've been chewed up and spat out and booed off stage…* Her lungs were hurting with every breath, but it was a satisfying pain that proved she was pushing herself. *All the pain inside amplified by the fact that I can't get by with my nine to five…* It was so frustrating. It felt as though there were so many opportunities in London, so much going on, such freedom… but it was all passing her by. Marta couldn't get a piece of it. The opportunities were too hard to grab. The job market here was like the vodka market back home: clean and open on the outside, impenetrable underneath.

A pair of workmen in yellow vests looked up from their newspapers and whistled appreciatively. Marta passed them and smiled. Crazy men. Crazy, lazy men. English labourers never did any labour. And why were they whistling at a sweaty girl in old shorts and an unflattering sports bra?

Perhaps it was the music, or the warm, spring-like air, or simply the fact that she was out here, bounding along roads she'd never seen before in an exciting new country, but something lifted inside her. The whole city was full of crazy people, she decided, thinking of the over-polite newsagent, the women queuing outside the post office and the little boys in miniature suits on the King's Road. It was a crazy city, but she liked that. She wanted to stay in this place – not just to make money, but to make her mark. That was why she'd come over.

There was already one Pole who'd made his mark, thought Marta, looking across the road at the evidence. It stood out from everything else in the parade of shops, not just because of its size but because of the slick window display in various shades of green.

Michael Marks had come over with nothing. He was a Jewish refugee who came over to escape persecution in Poland. Marta had read his biography. He'd set up his store with a five pound loan from someone he didn't even know – someone who had seen his potential and had faith in his idea. A market stall was all it was, to begin with, but it grew. It grew and grew so that soon there wasn't a single person in the country who hadn't heard of Marks and Spencer.

If he could do it, thought Marta, then so could she. It was just a question of finding that person who would see her potential. Of all the recruiters she'd met in the last week, surely one of them would take that risk?

A Queen song came on, and Marta found herself flying down a wide, tree-lined avenue with strips of sunlight streaking the path. *And the world… I'll turn it inside out, yeah…* It didn't matter about finding a job – not for now, anyway. Holly was right. She didn't need to push herself so hard. Something would come along. It didn't matter that Dom had turned out to be a fickle bastard. Holly and Tina and Rich were her friends, and thanks to them, she had a place to stay. *I'm burning through the sky, yeah…* She could make things work over here. Nothing was impossible. It just took patience. Suddenly, her earlier despondency seemed like a distant memory; all that mattered now was the future.

A man on rollerblades came powering towards her. He was built like an athlete with chocolate brown skin and white teeth. Marta smiled back at him. Perhaps she'd meet a new man over here. Perhaps she'd find a job after all. Perhaps she'd think of a way of making her mark over here. Marta ran on, fuelled by a newfound energy. Tonight, suddenly anything seemed possible.

It was almost by accident that she found her way home. Turning into what she thought was a side street that led to West Hampstead, Marta realised she was already on Kilburn High Road, just down from

Holly's flat. She walked the last few metres, stretching her over-worked muscles and shaking her limbs.

"Cześć," said a voice as she burst through the front door.

Marta looked up. Walking towards her through the kitchen with a drink in his hand, was Dom.

"You been avoiding me?" he asked in Polish, grinning as though nothing was amiss.

Marta stared, her mind burning with hate and lust all at once. She didn't know what to ask first. "Wh – what are you doing here? *Me* avoiding *you?* Where – how did you find me?"

Dom laughed. "Slow down… How I found you is a bloody long story. After you ignored my voicemails and texts, I went and asked Barry–"

"Wait – what? What voicemails? What texts?"

"The ones I left at various points this week, on your–"

Marta groaned. "If you left them this week then that's why I didn't get them. Tash kicked me out and demanded the phone back. But while we're on the subject of–"

"I heard about that. I went round–"

"You went round?" Marta asked, horrified. "To Tash's? You could've been killed!"

Dom smiled. "I took that risk. Well, actually, I didn't know about the risk. But anyway, she didn't kill me; quite the opposite. She tried to flirt with me."

Marta cringed. "Eugh. I bet she did. But listen Dom, I need to know about the text you sent me. What the fuck was that about?"

"Which one?"

"The one you sent on the night I got kicked out! After you'd ignored all my calls and my frantic answerphone message – the one that told me not to call you ever again!"

Dom frowned. "I didn't send you a text saying that."

"What?"

"Some bastard nicked my phone two weeks ago. I think it was the same night you got kicked out. So…what, they sent you a message?"

Marta nodded, the relief flooding her body. "Told me never to call you again," she explained.

Dom looked really upset. "Right," he said, nodding. "Nice."

"Mmm. I did think it was a bit weird. You didn't have to do too much to get this address from Tash, I hope?"

Dom pulled a face. "Nearly. She's an animal, isn't she? Is she on heat or what?"

"She's newly single I think. That's my fault, apparently."

"Ah. That would explain what she called you."

Marta waited for Dom to expand. A smirk was creeping up his face.

"What? What did she call me?"

"D'you mean before or after the treble gin-and-tonic?"

"Urgh. You didn't, did you?"

"'Course I did. It was free booze and I was going on out afterwards. Besides, she wouldn't have given me your address otherwise. Ugly trollop, by the way. That's what she called you. Twice."

Marta opened her mouth to shriek an obscenity about Tash, but as she did so, her phone – her new, unsophisticated phone that only had four options for ringtones – started playing its silly jingle at full volume from inside her bag.

"Is that Marta Da-brow-ska?" asked a woman in clipped English.

"Yes," she replied, mouthing *sorry* to Dom, who was starting to head for the door. Marta moved round to block his way.

"My name is Caroline, and I'm calling from a firm called Bread and Butter, a London-based agency that specialises in sourcing catering and waiting services for corporate events…"

Marta pulled the phone away from her ear just for long enough to whisper, "Don't go – won't be long!" Dom was scribbling something on a notepad by the door.

"…which is where we got your details," the woman went on. "Now I know you applied initially for office work, but we wondered how you might like to try…"

Dom tore off the sheet and handed it to her. *Call me,* it said, then a number. He slipped backwards through the door with a grin. Marta wished she hadn't taken the call.

"Hang on–" she hissed, covering the mouthpiece with her hand. It was too late. Dom was half way across the road.

"…We wondered whether you'd be interested in doing some work for us!"

Marta watched Dom fling himself onto the scooter and kick it into life. "When?" she asked, wondering what type of work they were talking about.

"Saturday night. It's a corporate function. A dinner in Soho Square. You'd work six 'til two and get seventy-five pounds. Just ordinary table service. Nothing special."

Marta was still high from her run, and from the realisation that Dom was back in her life. She looked at the scrap of paper. Things were looking better already. She had no idea what the work entailed, but clearly here was an opportunity, and she was going to seize it.

"Why not?" she said. "Sounds good!"

23

FOLDING NAPKINS. That was Marta's first task. It equalled her previous job in terms of intellectual stimulation, but at least it didn't involve such public humiliation. At least here she was providing pieces of paper that people wanted – but that wasn't much consolation. It was still a shitty job.

"Your apron's skew-whiff," chided the stroppy, middle-aged woman who seemed to be in charge. Marta obediently yanked the waistband round on the monstrous garment. "And hurry up!" the fat woman added, looking over her shoulder. "You should be done w'napkins and onto wine by now!"

Marta upped the pace of her folding. *Skew what?* She felt like a robot on a production line: Lift, shake, fold, arrange, fiddle until it looked more or less right relative to the ridiculous number of forks on the table. Not that a robot would be dressed in such a frumpy outfit, she thought. The skirt was designed for someone twice her width and half her height, and the shirt… well, it looked more like a tent than a shirt.

A cold draught swirled through the marquee, setting table cloths flapping and flower displays wobbling on their stands. Six men in black T-shirts appeared at the entrance, holding up pieces of marquee fabric and looking perplexed.

Folding her last serviette and nudging it gently into position, Marta picked up her empty box and headed back to the servants' quarters – or 'hub', as they were supposed to call it.

Unfortunately, the men in T-shirts were wrestling with a large plastic banner right in front of the entrance. Marta watched, unimpressed. They had to be English, she thought, noting the fact that four out of the six men were standing around with their hands on their hips.

Marta coughed. They looked over, glancing down at her legs and making no effort to move out of her way.

"Wha' was that about getting things laid, Jay?" yelled the guy holding the end of the banner to one of the stationary men. The others all roared with laughter, their eyes flitting between the joke teller's and Marta's.

Marta waited expressionlessly, focusing on the text as the guys tried to establish which way up the banner was supposed to go. WELCOME TO THE 200TH ANNUAL CAMBRIDGE ALUMNI DINNER, Marta read as it was hoisted into position upside down. Beneath the words was a man-sized crest in red and yellow that she recognised from Tash's framed photographs. The event was clearly some sort of commemorative feast for those studying aluminium at Cambridge University.

The clowns finally realised that they were erecting the banner across the doorway and shuffled sideways. There was another comment that Marta didn't understand and more raucous laughter as she finally slipped through the gap.

"You on wine?" asked a girl, pointing accusingly at the mound of brown boxes in the corner.

Marta nodded timidly. "Opening bottles, you mean?"

"Yeah," the girl snapped. "You better hurry up. They all need to be done for after the champagne's run out, innit."

Marta nodded again and reached down for the first box.

The 'crew', as they were called, consisted of a dozen young girls from somewhere called Essex and about twenty Eastern Europeans, very few of whom spoke any English. The former did not mix with the latter, as Marta soon learnt.

"So the event is for who?" she asked, twisting the corkscrew into her umpteenth bottle. "Cambridge people?"

"Whassat?" said the blonde who was perched on the champagne rack composing a text message.

"Who is it for, this night?"

There was no reply. Marta glanced up at the girl, who was staring into the colour screen on her phone, pressing buttons with utmost concentration. Finally, she looked up. "Uh?"

"What is this night? Is for Cambridge people, but in London?"

After several seconds of silence, Marta looked up from her bottle-opening. The girl was scowling unpleasantly at her as though she'd just let out a tremendous fart. Before Marta could start to explain herself, another English girl wandered over.

"Whassup?" she said to the blonde.

Out of the corner of her eye, Marta watched as the blonde nodded in her direction then, making no effort to lower her voice, muttered, "Fucking foreign girl – trying to start on me."

"Fuckin'hell," replied the other girl. "We 'ad enough o'that last week. Let's go an' hide in the loos. I've got some fags. Can't be doin' with these freaks."

The two girls hurried off. Marta tried to focus on pulling the corks, not on what she'd just heard. They were just mean, silly English girls who hadn't grown up yet. She shouldn't take offence.

Strangely, after all those weeks of standing on street corners, being rejected by passers-by, Marta still found it hard not to take the girl's comment personally. She *did* take offence. All she'd asked for was an answer to her question. She hadn't been 'starting on' her; she'd been making conversation. Being sociable. Surely they did that over here? It wasn't just a Polish thing?

Marta could feel her face glowing red. She felt embarrassed, even though she'd done nothing wrong. It was the way they'd reacted – clamming up and rushing away as though she had leprosy or something. What was wrong with her? Did she have some sort of weird mannerism? Or did the girls just have something against foreigners? Marta's thoughts were interrupted by a Polish voice.

"Need a hand?"

A dark-haired Polish girl with a pale complexion not dissimilar to her own was leaning on the champagne rack where the blonde had been.

"I was giving out drinks, but I've been demoted," she explained. "The fat boss told me to help out back here."

Marta smiled gratefully. "I don't think they like us," she said.

The brunette raised an eyebrow. "Of course they don't. We bring their wages down, don't we? Pass me that bottle opener."

"You'll get blisters," Marta warned, showing the girl her sore, red palm. "You mean they get paid less?"

"Less than they used to, yeah. The English girls got nearly forty złoty an hour before we came along. Now they get whatever we get. It's no wonder they hate us."

Together, they worked through the mountain of boxes. They were silent for the most part, but it was a companionable silence, broken only by the onset of a commotion in the middle of the 'hub'. The fat woman was dragging two girls across the hessian matting by their ears, causing quite a lot of loud squealing.

"Get offa me! I'll fuckin' sue! Let goa me!" screamed one, whilst the other just made yelping noises like a little dog.

"I'll get offa you when you've explained what you was doin' back there," replied the overweight mistress. Finally, she let go of the girls' ears and they both squirmed backwards.

"Aw! OK!" cried the more vocal of the two, whom Marta recognised as the blonde from earlier.

"Was you smokin' in the portaloos?" demanded the woman.

"No!" said the girls together, both equally unconvincing.

"Are you tryin' to lose your jobs, girls?" asked the red-faced woman, suddenly noticing that all her staff were standing around, staring. "Get back to work, all of you!"

"No, we ain't," replied the blonde sulkily.

"Then whose are these?" she asked, waving a packet of cigarettes in their faces. Marta watched surreptitiously as she opened her next bottle.

"Hers," snapped the girl, pointing – and for this, Marta looked up – straight at Marta.

Before Marta could start to defend herself, the other girl leapt to the attack. "Yeah, they're hers. We was just flushin' 'em down the loo, innit."

Marta was shaking her head, horrified. "They not mine cigarettes, I promise!" she said. "I don't have no–"

"Shut up!" barked the woman. "I've had enough. You're all lying, far as I can tell, so just get back to work. You two, what was you on, before?"

The two English girls faltered for a moment, then the blonde pointed at the stack of unopened bottles. "Openin' them."

The woman sighed. "Well get back to it, OK? We ain't got no time to waste. You—" she pointed at Marta. "Dunno what you're doin' there. Start puttin' garnishes on them plates and take 'em out."

The canvas quarters were quiet for thirty seconds while everyone watched the ferocious woman storm out. The only sounds were the sizzle and chatter from the kitchen and the muted hum of a string quartet in the main marquee. Marta crept over to the table of plates, still reeling from her ordeal. Did English girls have no morals?

It was with trepidation that Marta set foot on the uneven marquee floor, her arms both stacked precariously with plates. It had taken three girls and several minutes to load her up and for Marta to learn how to walk with the things, and she hadn't even practised unloading.

There were hundreds of people in the marquee, all dressed extremely smartly – black bow ties for men, long, shimmering dresses for women. Marta scanned the room, counting the ornate table decorations. There were twenty, which meant that there were two hundred and forty guests. She crept slowly towards her designated table.

As she hovered uncertainly between the elbows of two men, feeling the top plate start to slip, one of the guys noticed the lettuce leaf fall onto the table and graciously relieved her of the sliding plate, freeing up her right hand and averting a catastrophe. Marta thanked the man, who smiled back, his kindly face pitted and wrinkled with age.

The man motioned for his companion to move his elbow so that Marta could guide the next plate in, and, hey presto, another one was unloaded. She moved round the table, stooping down between two finely dressed ladies with white hair that had been dyed yellowy-blonde. This waitressing thing really wasn't so hard after all.

It was as Marta unloaded her final plate that disaster struck.

"My goodness! It's Marta!" cried a voice that she instantly recognised but couldn't quite place.

Marta looked down at the guest who had spoken. Even before she had seen the whole face, she knew who it was. That nose was recognisable anywhere.

"Jeremy!" she cried, trying to mask her dismay. "What... why... why you here at this dinner? Are you an aluminium student?"

Somehow, Jeremy managed to look down on her, despite being a good few feet lower down than Marta. He was frowning. After several seconds, in which Marta could feel the eyes of every guest around the table boring into her baggy, unflattering uniform, Jeremy started to smile.

"Aluminium," he said, his eyes full of mirth. "Ha! Alumni, aluminium. I'd never thought of that! Oh dear me..." He chuckled to himself, exchanging glances with some of his companions, who started to smile.

"Is it funny? Why you laughing?" Marta asked, not enjoying the situation at all.

"Oh dear me," Jeremy muttered, still guffawing with his chums. "Alumni means 'of the establishment'. It means ex-attendee, or ex-student − of Cambridge in this instance. Nothing to do with aluminium!"

Marta nodded, seeing her mistake. It really wasn't *that* funny, she thought, trying not to make eye contact with Jeremy or his friends. There were worse mistakes she could have made.

"Marta comes from Poland," Jeremy explained to the table, when he'd finally got over his chortling.

There was a chorus of 'oooh's and 'ahah's from everyone around the table. The man next to Jeremy, a stout, middle-aged fellow with lots of chins and no hair, leaned back in his chair and looked up at Marta. "Good for you!" he exclaimed, patting her backside approvingly. "Need more like you in this country, we do. Hard working folk who don't mind getting their hands dirty! Splendid! Good for you."

It was time to leave, Marta decided. There would be no more waitress service for table eighteen − not by her, anyway. She muttered something about bread rolls and hastened back to the hub.

Marta stood, staring at the tessalating plates on the table. Her mind was not on the job. It was on how to escape from the job without forfeiting her seventy-five pounds' pay. She slipped off to find the portaloos.

Sitting on the flipped-down toilet seat, her head resting in her palms, Marta felt her phone vibrate in her saddlebag-like skirt pocket. She had three text messages.

From: Holly Banks
PS meant to say, he may b
on the rebound…
he's like that!

Marta frowned, and read the previous message, hoping that would shed some light on the matter.

From: 07839 921347
Hi Marta, Have been trying
desperately 2get in touch! T
wouldn't tell me where you'd
gone but I just met Holly.
Am SO sorry for everything.
Please let me make it up
to you.
Call me. Jack x

Marta's frown intensified. Jack? Trying desperately to get in touch with her? Marta doubted it. And Holly was probably right. He'd been dumped by Tash, so he was looking elsewhere. She checked the first message.

From: Holly Banks
Hi M, word of warning:
just saw Jack Templeton-Cooper
in a bar. I gave him yr new
no. He insisted – not sure
why. Suggest u ignore the
tosser. C U later! Hx

Marta smiled wryly. Thank God for Holly, she thought. In her current state of mind, trapped in a plastic toilet cubicle, skiving from a job that involved being ridiculed by rich buffoons in bow-ties, she might have been tempted to give Jack a call. But Holly was right. He was a tosser. A tosser on the rebound. She unlocked the flimsy, carpeted door and returned to the hub in search of someone who'd swap roles with her.

24

"WHAT DID YOU DO?" asked Dom, mopping up the coffee that Marta had spilt on the plastic table cloth.

"Hid in the kitchens," she replied. "I had to. All the jobs seemed to involve going into the marquee and I couldn't run the risk of serving table eighteen again. I told the chefs I'd been sent to the kitchens to help. They gave me odd jobs to do – pouring gravy, squirting cream, you know… I think they felt sorry for me."

"You were squirting cream 'til two in the morning?"

"Pretty much. Sometimes I disappeared to the toilets. They had these weird caravan-things with toilets inside – but posh caravans with wallpaper and little boxes of tissues and posies of flowers everywhere."

Dom pulled a face. "Sounds odd. Will you work for them again?"

Marta hesitated. At two o'clock in the morning on Sunday, she had vowed to herself that she'd never again stoop as low as she had done that night. Even without the Jeremy incident, it would have been embarrassing. Degrading. But now, when faced with the choice of Bread and Butter Catering or being out of work again, she felt less certain. Marta shrugged.

Dom nodded, staring into his cup. They were sitting in the Polskie Delikatesy in Acton. It was a shop really, but it had a couple of tiny tables by the window and they served the full range of Polish snacks.

"Oh my God!" exclaimed Marta, noticing something through the window. "Is that a Polish newsagent?"

Dom looked at her. "Calm down. Yeah. That's where I get my paper each Sunday on the way here. Everything's a week out of date, of course, but it's in the right language. They're as friendly in there as they are in here. I love it."

Marta shook her head. "Like a corner of Warsaw," she said. "Is this your little Sunday routine, then?"

Dom smiled sheepishly. "Yes," he said, blushing. "I know. I know it's sad. But I miss home. I come here on a Sunday and I get greeted in Polish, I get served in Polish, I read the news in Polish… It makes a break from the other six days. Oh, thanks—" Dom leaned back as the pretty young waitress slid a plate of jabłecznik onto the table between their cups. "My favourite − thanks!"

The petite waitress smiled at Dom and slipped away.

"That's Dominika," he explained, blushing again. "She's the daughter of the owners. Sweet girl. Always gives me some sort of freebie − ever since she learned we were both called Dom."

"Ever since she started fancying you," Marta teased.

"Bullshit," he said defensively.

"True!" she replied in the same tone.

Dom rolled his eyes. They both knew Marta was right. But really, you could hardly blame the waitress.

There was an awkward silence. Dom took a bite of the jabłecznik. Marta did the same.

"I'm jealous, Dom," Marta mused, after several minutes.

"Why, because Dominika fancies me?" asked Dom, grinning.

"Oh − no," said Marta, whose thoughts had moved on from the little waitress. "Because you live in a place like this − where you can get kabenosy and chleb and kiszone ogórki five minutes away from your house!"

Dom shrugged. "Acton has its downside," he said. "Like the chances of getting your phone wrenched out of your hand by a bunch of kids on bikes…" He smiled wryly. "Anyway, isn't Kilburn just the same?"

"No," Marta shook her head. "It has a few Polish shops, but it's not like this. Kilburn's for Irish and black people."

Dom nodded vaguely, his gaze shifting to the group of young men who were congregating on the pavement opposite. They were Polish, thought Marta. She could tell by the week-old stubble and the hollow faces. Before she could say anything, Dom started banging on the window.

"*What are you doing?*" she hissed. She didn't want to be part of a Sunday morning brawl.

"It's Mariusz and that – they're my mates."

"Your mates?" she echoed, watching as some of the guys raised a hand in mock salute.

"Yeah, I met them a few months ago. They live near here."

"What are they doing?" asked Marta. They looked as though they were waiting for a bus, but there wasn't a bus stop anywhere near.

"What does it look like they're doing?" asked Dom, as though she were stupid.

"Well, waiting. But I don't know what for. They won't get a bus standing there."

"Wrong," replied Dom, picking at the jabłecznik crumbs and downing the remains of his coffee.

Marta frowned at him. "What? You have to stand at a bus stop to get a bus – same as in our country!"

Dom smiled, clearly sensing her frustration. "Not this sort of bus," he said. "Watch."

They continued to stare at the bunch of guys, who stood, hands in pockets, barely moving. After a couple of minutes, they stirred. A battered old hatchback pulled up alongside two parked cars .

"They're not all getting into that thing, are they?" asked Marta.

Dom just grinned, still watching.

Marta's bewilderment grew as one by one, the men disappeared inside the car. By the time the sixth and final one levered himself into the back, the vehicle was visibly rocking from side to side. Eventually, the door was hauled shut and the car pulled sluggishly away.

"What are they doing?" asked Marta.

"Going to work," Dom replied. "Have you never seen that before?"

Marta shook her head. She'd seen groups of young men lurking randomly on street corners, but she'd never stopped to wonder why.

"I joined them once," Dom told her. "Never again though – unless I lose the leafleting job."

"Where did they take you?" asked Marta, still shocked.

Dom laughed. "It wasn't as though they were holding me hostage – I did *ask* to go. We went to a building site just north of Ealing. Half an hour away. It was random labour – nothing hard. The money was OK, but not as good as Barry's."

"You spent half an hour in the back of a car with five other men?" asked Marta, wide-eyed. "Five fat men, like them?"

He nodded. "I wouldn't do it again. They kept farting. Thought it was funny. Mariusz was driving. I didn't know any of the others at that point. They were all older – most of them drunk. I was squeezed in at the end with some guy's arse in my face. He'd been eating onions all day, and Jesus, it showed."

Marta tried to keep a straight face. "Stick with the leaflets for now," she advised. They looked at each other and both burst out laughing.

Marta tried to finish her drink but kept erupting in fresh giggles whenever her lips met the cup. Finally, she managed to banish all thoughts of onion-flavoured farts from her mind and gulped it down.

"Have you ever been to the Wailing Wall?" asked Dom.

"The what?"

Dom shook his head disapprovingly. "Don't you know anything about this city? Do you know where Hammersmith is?"

Marta hesitated. "I've seen it on the tube map…"

"Well it's near here," said Dom, rolling his eyes. "You can walk from Acton. I can't believe you've never been to Hammersmith – it's the Polish capital of England!"

"I've spent too much time hanging out with Cambridge graduates," Marta admitted.

"Well, if you think Acton's like home, you should see Hammersmith. The Wailing Wall is like a home to half the Poles here – it's the reason most of them came over!"

"What *is* it?"

"Well, it started off as a newsagent window," Dom explained. "You know – a place where you can put cards offering services, or asking for work. But then they ran out of room in the window, so they extended it halfway along the street. Honestly, Marta, you should go. It's a real sight. Requests for plumbers, builders, cleaners and au pairs – well, actually it's more for prostitutes now, disguised as masseuses and escorts."

"Oh really?" she said. "And why are you telling me this, exactly?"

"I didn't mean—" Dom trailed off, embarrassed.

"I'm joking. I didn't really think you were suggesting I pimp myself out. Although, being unemployed…"

"Marta, don't!" cried Dom, sounding genuinely concerned.

Marta laughed. "I wouldn't, silly. A school friend did that and disappeared. But I might pop down to the Wailing Wall and have a look. Sounds interesting."

Dom nodded. "Worth a trip. That's how I originally found Barry's. Although…" He paused, looking pensive. "I wouldn't hold your breath for a great salary – unless you go for the masseuse option, that is. The English people have got wise to it now, and they only offer what they can get away with, which is usually shit."

Marta nodded. That seemed to be what was happening. Poles were earning themselves a reputation as England's low cost workforce.

"Shall we go?"

"Yeah, let's."

"I'll walk you to the tube," offered Dom. "I've got half an hour to kill before the Croats wake up and challenge me to a wrestling match on the Nintendo Wii."

Marta didn't object. She emptied her wallet on the table and left enough to cover the bill while Dom left a hefty tip for the waitress. "I'll get the next one," he said. "Maybe I'll have a real job by then."

Marta stopped, half in, half out of the café. "Have you applied for something?"

"Don't get excited. I won't get it. It's with TFL – Transport for London. Driving tube trains."

"Oh." Marta couldn't hide the disappointment in her voice. "Why?"

Dom frowned. "What d'you mean, why? Because I have to get out of this dead-end leaflet job?"

"But I mean, why another crappy menial job?"

For a fleeting moment, Marta thought she saw a flash of irritation cross Dom's face. "Because it's good money. It'd be shifts, and the night work is really good pay."

"But…" Marta didn't want to antagonise him, but she just couldn't keep her opinions to herself. "Shifts driving underground trains, Dom? You're a finance graduate! You went to Jagiellonian

University! I mean, I know we're only young and I know I sometimes aim too high and set myself up for a fall, and our English isn't perfect, but… don't you want a proper career here?"

Dom sighed, sounding more resigned than cross. "Of course I *want* a career. I'm just realistic about my prospects of getting one. I've been here for nearly a year now, Marta. Believe me, I've tried."

Marta said nothing. It was so frustrating to hear him say this. She couldn't bear it. There *had* to be a way of getting somewhere in England, and surely it didn't involve driving trains in dark, smoky tunnels or serving dinners to condescending Englishmen?

They walked on to the sound of passing cars and tooting of horns.

"Maybe you could work your way up within TFL," she suggested quietly. "Maybe you could get yourself into the finance department, and get promoted and one day become CFO of Transport for London!"

Dom was smiling. Marta realised her suggestion had been delivered with slightly too much enthusiasm.

"And maybe not!" replied Dom, mimicking her tone just as she had done earlier.

Marta nodded. "OK." She was still secretly hopeful that there was another way. They had reached the tube station, but Marta didn't want to leave. "Hey, what's in the bag?" she asked, just to prolong their conversation.

Dom looked down at the lumpy plastic bag in his hand. "Oh – my sister's birthday present. She's twenty-one next week. I thought it would fit in a post box, but it didn't."

"What is it?"

Dom looked down guiltily. "Well, I know it's cheap, but… well, it's recordings of Radio 1. She's mad on it. There's about twenty CDs in here – every breakfast show and drivetime for the last two months. I've personalised the inlays, though."

"Don't be like that – it's a great idea! I'd love a present like that."

"Really? Oh good. I was worried I'd come across as tight. Or skint, which would not please my parents. Hey, you might even get to meet my sister. She wants to come over and stay in a couple of weeks, if she can get a cheap flight – although that's not looking likely at the moment."

"That would be good," Marta nodded. It was Anka's birthday in less than a month. How nice it would be to get her to come over to London too – how nice, but how impossible. Anka would never be able to afford the flight, and Marta wouldn't be able to help her out – not at this rate. God, she *had* to find a new job.

"So, see you around, I guess."

They were standing quite close. In her imagination, Dom was reaching out and slowly wrapping his arm around her waist, drawing her closer, pulling her lips onto his… In reality, he was just standing there, looking at her.

"Bye," he said quietly, still not moving away or reaching down for his bag. Marta looked into his hazel eyes, then down at the ground.

And then it happened. Marta felt him move closer, so his chest was touching hers. She could feel the heat of his body through his T-shirt. This was not their usual goodbye. One hand slipped around her waist, just as it had in her daydream, while the other slid lightly up her back and into her hair.

Marta felt herself stumbling up against him. This was it – it really was happening. She felt Dom's lips touching hers, just lightly – then he pulled away, but only to smile at her. Then he kissed her again, firmly, urgently, his tongue gently exploring her mouth.

"Bye," said Marta, finally, when Dom's hand fell away, reluctantly, from her waist.

"Bye."

Marta laughed softly. "Should stop saying bye, really, and just go."

"Mmm," Dom agreed, releasing his fingers from her hair and stepping away as though he didn't really want to. "Yeah. Bye."

Marta felt like a teenager with a crush. "See you next week some time?"

Dom nodded. "I'll call you."

Marta turned to enter the station, grinning.

"Oh, and Marta?" called Dom, as though he'd forgotten something.

Marta looked back.

"Bye!"

25

"PINTS ALL ROUND?" asked Holly, looking around at her flatmates.

There were nods of agreement from Marta and Rich. "With chasers!" cried Tina.

Holly cringed. "It is a school night, T. We're not all hardcore traders like you."

Tina rolled her eyes in disgust but didn't push the point. They were sitting in the corner of their local, The Good Ship, one of the more classy establishments on Kilburn High Road. This meant simply that the chances of being held at knife-point by a crazed homeless man were lower here than elsewhere. There had been a reason for them arranging to come out drinking en masse this evening, but now that the night was upon them, no one could remember what it was.

It was Tuesday, two days after Marta's kiss with Dom, and she was still on a high. She hadn't told anyone in case nothing came of it, but it was becoming increasingly evident from the tone of his text messages that something *was* likely to come of it. Marta pulled out her phone and planted it subtly in her lap beneath the splintery table.

The silly phone could only hold twenty messages at one time, so she had to be selective about which ones she saved. She re-examined the latest one.

> Don't tease me, M –
> I wdn't object 2 seeing
> u in waitress outfit,
> although... have u

considered career as
nurse? Mmm. Dinner
Fri? Dx

"What are you doing down there?" demanded Tina, testing out the sturdiness of the little stool on which her tiny buttocks were perched.

"Nothing," Marta replied quickly. She was just scrolling down to Dom's previous message.

"Who are you texting with that massive grin on your face?" Tina asked suspiciously.

"Nobody," said Marta, wondering how she could explain her smirk. "I wasn't doing texting, I was just…"

Rich leaned over and peered into her lap. "I think she was just thinking about upgrading her Fisher Price phone," he said, "to a yoghurt pot and string."

"Hey, excuse me, mister!" cried Marta, grateful for the distraction. "It is very good phone thank you and well suiting to my needs. It is 'doing the job', as you say!" She'd been learning English phrases from Holly and was pleased to have slipped one into conversation so smoothly.

"I reckon it's you that's been 'doing the job', Miss Dabrowska," replied Tina, raising an eyebrow. "Look at that grin she's trying to hide, Rich – look!"

Marta was beginning to get to know her flatmates. On several occasions, she had ended up cooking for Tina and Rich when they got back from work. It was a way of paying them back for the rent-free accommodation. Rich was easy to work out: he was honest, kind and quietly confident. He knew what he wanted (Holly), and he was patient enough to wait for it. Tina was more complicated. On the outside, she was loud, crude and flippant. She was shallow, only caring about her next date, her next shag. But that wasn't all. She was shrewd and sharp, too. Very sharp. Tina understood people – in some cases, better than they understood themselves.

"Doing the job? What you mean by that?" asked Marta, playing innocent but aware that Tina was seeing straight through it.

"You know exactly what I mean, honey," Tina replied, shaking her head. Then, without warning, her slender brown arm reached across the table like a snake's tongue and snatched up the brick-like phone.

"Hah! Let me see…"

Marta watched in horror as Tina's dark, beady eyes scanned the text message on the screen.

"It's in Polish," Tina declared, disappointed. "What does it mean?"

Marta shrugged. "Nothing much."

"Ah, so it's dirty, is it?"

Marta took her phone back. "No," she lied. The message referred to squirting cream until two in the morning and was laden with innuendo. Marta could feel the blood rushing to her face. "It's about… stupid stuff. Nothing."

"What's about nothing?" asked Holly, returning from the bar with her fingers stretched painfully around four pints.

"A message from D-kiss-kiss to Marta that makes her blush when she reads it," replied Tina. "Who's D-kiss-kiss?"

With Holly's input, it emerged that the mystery man was the guy who had come to the house to find her two weeks before. Tina rushed to declare her approval. "He was cute!" she exclaimed.

"And he'd even braved Tash's to find you," added Holly.

"So, have you shagged him?" asked Tina expectantly.

"Tina!"

"What?"

"You can't just ask—"

"Why not?" Tina frowned. "So, have you, Marta?"

Marta shook her head, overwhelmed. "No! Stop!"

"Yes, stop," echoed Rich, speaking for the first time. "Tina, some people don't start their relationships by sleeping together."

There was a swift exchange of looks between Holly and Rich that didn't go unnoticed by Marta or indeed Tina, who was pretending to focus on sliding the beers around the table.

"We are not boyfriends and girlfriends," said Marta, by way of a final explanation. "We only friends, but on Saturday we realise we maybe like each other more than that, and… we kissed." She looked down at her drink, and added sheepishly, "Was nice."

Both Tina and Holly nodded, slowly. Everyone was grinning – even Marta. It felt good to be sharing the news about Dom – even if it was with English girls who didn't really understand. Things were different in England. Girls did things in a different order. Here, they would meet a guy, go on a date and get drunk with him, have their first kiss, sleep with him (all in one night, if Tina was anything to go by), and then start to get to know him. It was all wrong. Back in Poland, you got to know people before you had sex with them. At least, that was how things were in Łomianki. Perhaps she was just old-fashioned.

"So when are you next seeing each other?" asked Tina.

"Friday. We go to dinner I think."

"Very nice," Tina replied. "Has he got his own place?"

Marta shook her head. "He's Polish. 'Course not. He share with six other."

"Oh crap," replied Tina. "Does that mean we all have to avoid the lounge on Friday night?"

It took a couple of seconds for Marta to realise what Tina was saying, but then she caught on. "No!" she cried, embarrassed. "Can I have my phone back, please?"

Tina tutted and returned the brick. "By the way, you know you've got a voicemail on there, don't you?"

Marta frowned as Tina pointed at the funny symbol on the pixelated display.

"Really? That's what it mean?" Marta had been wondering since lunchtime why there was a picture of a bowtie in the corner of her screen. She retrieved the phone and pressed a selection of buttons that eventually put her through.

"*Welcome to the voicemail message centre for oh, seven, nine–*"

"BAW-BAW-BAW-BAW-   OOOOH,   SIX   DEAD HEDGEHOGS IN A ROW!" yelled a tuneless voice over a PA system, blotting out all other sounds.

"What the fuck…!" screamed Tina.

"Open mike night," shouted Holly back, nodding towards the back of the pub, where, on a sunken stage, four gothic teens in leathers were throwing their heads around beneath bright coloured lights.

Marta abandoned her phone call and looked at her flatmates for an answer.

146

"Down our drinks and then leave?" suggested Holly, above the din.

As they were deliberating over whether their ear drums could withstand a moment more of the torture, the barman solved their conundrum and turned down the amp.

"Thank the fucking Lord," said Tina, as the foursome continued to jump about on the stage, seemingly oblivious to the snub.

Holly attempted to placate her flatmate, who was in danger of leaping over to the band and wrenching the mike from the lead 'singer'. Marta tried again to retrieve her voicemail.

"*Welcome to the voicemail message centre for—*"

"But that's not 'music', is it? Nobody wants to be subjected to that noise as they sit here, innocently drinking their pints, do they?"

"*You have one new message.*"

"It's open mike, Tina – that's the whole point. It's to give bands a chance to perform live when they can't get booked for proper gigs."

"Yeah but there's a *reason* these guys don't get booked for proper gigs, isn't there? THEY'RE SHIT."

"*Hi, this is a message for Marta Da-brow-ska,*" Marta heard, pressing her head against the earpiece to make out the message above Tina's rant. "*It's Laura here, from BrightSparks.*" Marta's heart started thumping. She thought back to the terrible interview where she'd damaged both the director's foot and her self esteem in the space of about two minutes. "*I wonder if you could call me back about some potential work we have for you. It's an Assistant Analyst position in a strategic marketing consultancy near Holborn. Two weeks' work, starting next week, so the sooner you can call me back the better. My number is oh two oh seven...*"

"Aghhhh!" screamed Marta, drowning out Tina's argument about why tuneless rockers should be banned from Kilburn pubs. "They find me a job! Is the agency you told me about, Holly – they want me to work in strategic marketing consulting place for two weeks!"

Marta's flatmates turned to her, realising the significance of the news.

"That's awesome!" cried Holly.

"Congratulations!" yelled Tina.

"Great stuff. Well, at least I think it's great stuff. What consultancy is it?" asked Rich. "Not Andertons I hope?"

Marta shrugged uncertainly, noting with interest the look that passed between Holly and Rich at the mention of Holly's employer. "Something in Holborn – I have to call them back. Oh–" she gasped as something occurred to her. "You think it's too late? You think they might give job to someone else when I didn't call back? Oh no! Am an idiot! Should have guessed it was voicemail – oh no!"

Rich shook his head. "Stop worrying, Marta. They'll give you time to call back. Just make sure it's first thing tomorrow. So, what's the role? What will you be doing in the way of market-based strategising?"

Holly whacked him. "Shut up Rich."

"No, really, I just wondered what–"

Holly silenced him with a look. "It's not all corporate jargon and bullshit, you know."

He raised an eyebrow, as though they were continuing an old conversation that nobody else knew about. "Is it not? So you're defending your profession all of a sudden?"

Holly glared at him as if to say, 'not now, Rich'. They had clearly been talking about Holly's career.

"Anyway, when does the job start?" asked Tina brightly. "Assuming they haven't given it to someone else, that is."

Marta smiled nervously. "Next week." Her stomach was already starting to feel queasy. Rich's words had sparked fears about how she was going to cope in the world of business jargon – *foreign* business jargon. If he, a UK graduate, couldn't understand it, how was she going to manage?

"I bet you can't wait," said Tina, possibly sensing her nerves. "From canapé waitress to strategy consultant in one fell swoop – woo hoo! This deserves a toast!"

Marta frowned, envisaging a celebratory slice of wholemeal. Tina was holding up her pint of beer, so Marta obligingly did the same.

"To Marta's new career!" Tina yelled, to the sound of the leather-clad headbangers.

"To Marta's new career!" repeated Holly and Rich.

Marta watched as her glass was buffeted in all directions by the other three. She didn't feel brave enough to celebrate her 'new career' on the basis of one unreturned phone call – not yet, but she did have a good feeling about this opportunity.

"It's only two weeks of work," she said, "but I will impress them. I will make them want me for longer. When I put a foot through the door, as you say—" Marta paused for her flatmates to appreciate her use of colloquial English – "they will ask me for full-time job! And I will have proper salary and I will pay you proper rent! I promise, it will happen very soon!"

Marta could feel a familiar sense of determination burning inside her. This was her first real opportunity in England, and she wasn't going to let it slip away. There would be no more desperate searches for poorly-paid menial jobs. She looked around at her flatmates triumphantly. They were all looking away. On closer inspection, they appeared to be laughing.

"What?" asked Marta.

Tina's shoulders were shaking, her head bowed as she struggled to restrain herself. Holly was trying to confine her giggles to her pint glass. Rich leaned forward.

"I'm not sure putting your foot *through* their door is the sort of entrance they're looking for," he said.

Marta looked at him. "I got it wrong? The phrase?"

Rich gave her a quick, surreptitious nod. "You get a foot in the door – you don't put your foot through it."

"Well I'm gonna go and put a foot through the bar," declared Tina. "And this time I'm getting chasers!"

Marta laughed – she couldn't help it. These English people had such silly, meaningless phrases. And when was the toast coming? Was Tina getting that from the bar too? Marta tipped back her glass and drained it, slamming it down on the table like people did over here. She sat back in the rickety wooden chair. At last, she was beginning to feel welcome. Soon, she'd be earning her money the way English people did too – in a graduate job. She couldn't wait.

26

"JUST TELL ME, DOM – I hate secrets."

Dom smiled cryptically. "You'll have to wait and see, won't you?"

They were crawling through the Friday night traffic in a taxi – a taxi that was already costing Dom twelve pounds and they'd barely left Kilburn. Marta stole a glance at her fellow passenger. He'd had his hair cut for the first time since she'd met him, and he was wearing a shirt. He looked slick, yet at the same time over-dressed – like a footballer wearing a suit. Marta began to wonder whether the evening would warrant something smarter than the short black skirt and knee-high boots. Although… if Dom's expression ten minutes earlier had been anything to go by, she'd made the right decision.

"I've got some news," said Dom, his brown eyes dancing with excitement.

Marta looked at him. She knew instantly what it was. There was only one thing it could've been. He'd got the tube-driving job. She was pleased, in a way, if not surprised. The only surprise was that Dom hadn't expected it himself.

"Well? Tell me! Then I'll tell you mine," she said. Dom's eyes were wandering – consciously or not, she couldn't tell – up and down her bare legs. She waited for them to roam up to her face. In fact, she was dying to tell Dom her news, but it was difficult to know how. This was their first date – if you could call it that – and she didn't want to monopolise it. She'd called the agency first thing Wednesday, having convinced herself overnight that they'd given the job to someone else, but miraculously, they hadn't. They gave her the details of the two-week placement and told her to start the next week.

"No – let's wait until we get there," said Dom.

Marta nodded reluctantly.

Dom looked at her for a second, clearly trying to work out what her news might be before forcing himself to look out of the window.

Marta did the same, watching the pound shops, internet cafés and all-you-can-eat-for-a-fiver buffets slide past as they chugged down Kilburn High Road. She was thinking about Dom's new job. He was planning to spend eight hours a day under ground. Eight hours, in a dark, polluted tunnel, his only contact with mankind through a one-way intercom, and then only to instruct passengers to move away from the doors. And then there were the suicide jumpers... The thought of ramming into a leaping figure at forty miles per hour, seeing the blood drip down your windscreen as you pulled into the station...

"Dom," "Marta," they said at exactly the same time.

"Go on."

"No – you go on."

"I just wanted to ask about your news," she said.

"Me too – bloody stupid idea waiting 'til we got there! Tell me yours."

"No – you first."

"OK," said Dom, needing little persuasion. "I've got a new job."

"Brilliant!" replied Marta, trying to sound enthused. "The tube driving one?"

Dom shook his head, smiling. "No. I took your advice and made a few applications. It's been a busy week."

"So...?"

"Well, I've finally got a job where I'll be using my brain."

"Really?" asked Marta, genuinely excited. "What is it?"

"I'm going to be financial assistant in a small law firm in Holborn."

"Holborn?"

"Yeah, why?"

"That's where I'll be working!" cried Marta. "Well, for two weeks, at least. I've got a placement through Holly's agency – a real job, in strategic marketing!"

Dom slid sideways in the cab and, quite unexpectedly, kissed her. Before Marta knew what was happening, it was over and Dom was back in his seat. "Of course you have. I knew you would."

Their mini celebration was thwarted by the cab driver ramming open his hatch and asking Dom for directions. They were somewhere near Hyde Park, noted Marta, and seemed to be heading for Kensington.

"We're not going to Tash's for dinner, are we?" she asked with mock anxiety.

Dom gasped. "You've ruined the surprise!" he replied, failing to hold the distressed expression. "Anywhere here on the left is good," he told the driver.

Marta hopped out, surveying her surroundings as Dom handed over what must have been a day's salary to the cabbie. They appeared to be in a residential street somewhere near Knightsbridge.

"Where are we?" she asked.

Dom just took her hand, grinning, and led her across the road towards an unobtrusive brick building on the end of a row of houses, much like all the others with the exception of the long glass windows and hanging baskets. Above the door was a quaint hanging sign saying *Wodka*.

Marta said nothing. She had asked enough questions already, and she was rather enjoying the experience of holding hands with Dom.

"It's a restaurant!" she exclaimed, as they were ushered through the curtain doorway by a middle-aged woman in a spotty dress. "Oh wow... a Polish restaurant!"

They were shown to their table by the polka-dot woman, who bustled off to shout at one of the many young Polish girls who were flitting between the tables.

"I didn't even know there were Polish restaurants in London," said Marta, marvelling at the setup. The restaurant was small and split into two halves – one with heavy oak panelling and dark velvet drapes, the other, where Marta and Dom were seated, bright and airy with white floor tiles and colourful oil paintings.

"It used to be the Kensington Palace dairy," explained Dom. "A guy called Jan Woroniecki opened it twenty years ago, and it's been in Polish hands ever since."

"Amazing!" exclaimed Marta as a dog trotted under their table.

"Chodź tutaj!" screamed the woman in charge, sending the mongrel scampering to the back of the restaurant via a small piece of cheese on the floor.

"Just like at home!" said Marta, remembering the restaurant in Łomianki where the resident dog had got so fat that it no longer fitted between the tables – it just lay on the doormat, opening and shutting its jaws.

The waitress took their drinks order in their own language.

"How did you know we were Polish?" asked Marta. "Is everyone?"

The waitress smiled. "Not everyone, no. We get mainly tourists, and some English, of course. After working here for two years, I can tell where they're from. American, Italian, Polish... I usually know when they walk through the door." She shrugged. "Don't ask me how."

Marta nodded. She understood. It was the way people walked, the way they dressed, their demeanour. They watched her weave expertly through the maze of tables and chairs, stepping over the sulking dog.

"Here," said Dom, opening Marta's menu in front of her. Gołąbki, leniwe, kaszanka... all her favourite dishes. It was just like being in Poland – except, of course, for the clientele.

It was impossible not to stare at the next table along. An elderly man with thin wisps of white hair scraped over his head was shakily dipping his bread into the soup of a busty young woman wearing sheer tights and hotpants. Marta grimaced and forced herself to look away. She wondered whether the girl was Polish. She was Eastern European; that was for sure.

The darker half of the restaurant was filled mainly with one long, candlelit table occupied by a group of young Poles – she could tell they were Poles from the regular cries of "Na zdrowie!" and chinking of glasses. They were loud, but not loud in an English way. There were no cries of "Drink, drink!", no standing on chairs, no swift exits to the toilets. They were just having fun – Polish fun.

The waitress returned with two ice-cold Żywiecs and helped them narrow down the impossibly long list of delicacies. The beer was dry and strong, the way beer should be – not like the watery stuff they pumped out in pubs over here.

"Proper chleb," Dom remarked, tucking into the bread. "It's even better than the stuff I get on Sundays."

"You're such an old man," Marta teased. In fact, Dom looked anything but an old man, his sporty physique visible through the freshly ironed shirt.

"I just like to do things my own way," he said. "You know, Yishai from my house goes over to Israel with an empty suitcase every two months. He comes back with it full – full of home-cooked food."

"Hasn't he found an Israeli café in Acton for his Sunday mornings?" asked Marta, tucking into the stuffed cabbage leaves that had appeared in front of her.

"He's looked," Dom told her. "But they're all Polish delis and oily spoon cafés. And he doesn't eat pork. Honestly, English cooking sucks."

Marta laughed. "My flatmate Holly has a rule for her cooking: she says any meal must take less time to prepare than it takes to eat."

"What? That's ridiculous!"

Marta shrugged. "She's English. She's a busy person. No time to cook."

"What does she live on?"

"Sandwiches, mainly."

Dom shook his head, reaching across the table and swiping a mouthful straight off Marta's fork. "Crazy English," he said, grinning as he chomped on her food.

"Cheeky bastard."

The restaurant started to fill up, as did Marta, although the wine was washing everything down nicely. Twilight turned to darkness outside, and the converted dairy started to look more like a restaurant. An old-fashioned street lamp outside was just starting to come on, casting a flickering glow on Dom's sandy hair through the window. His eyes, Marta noticed, kept making detours to her cleavage when he looked at her face during conversation. She didn't mind. She too was trying to imagine what his chest would look like without the shirt.

Their conversation was interrupted by the sound of a shrill English voice on a nearby table.

"Go, lab, key," the woman was articulating to the waitress, a timid girl who could have been the younger sister of the one serving them. She was lifting her shoulders apologetically and trying to catch a glimpse of the woman's menu.

"GO-LAB-KEY!" repeated the woman, who was dining with a man of a similar age – mid forties – and of equally impatient disposition. They were both staring at the girl as though she were completely stupid.

Marta smiled and leaned over. She was drunk, she realised, almost toppling sideways but grabbing onto the table just in time.

"She can't understand you because you're not saying it right. It's ga-lob-ka, not go-lab-key. And you should not be so rude – it is you who make the mistake."

Marta turned back to her meal and chopped up the last few pieces of sausage meat. She could feel Dom's eyes upon her, and, she suspected, quite a few more from around the restaurant. A hush had fallen on the place. She continued to chop, unabashed.

"What?" said Marta, looking up a moment later when the atmosphere had resumed but Dom was still looking at her. "Well there's no point in being English about it, is there?" she said. "The woman was being rude; someone had to tell her."

Dom nodded, smiling. Marta looked up again. This time she met his gaze and held it. His smile faded gently and his brown eyes were just staring into hers. It was as though he wanted to say something. She watched him, hardly daring to move, but then the moment seemed to pass and Dom's eyes darted to the floor.

"So, new job," he said, reverting to an old conversation and still managing to sound smooth. "Does this mean I'll never get to see you in that attractive waitress uniform you told me about?"

Marta glared at him with mock menace. "Don't even joke," she said. "I'm not donning that whale outfit for anybody – not even you."

Dom pretended to sulk, but his act was interrupted by the waitress asking about desserts.

"I can't," Marta told her, genuinely upset that she hadn't left room for kolaches with cream. Dom apologised for the both of them and asked for the bill.

"Fancy finding a bar halfway between yours and mine?" he asked, having handed over a wad of banknotes that must have come straight from his last brown envelope.

Marta looked at her watch and did a double-take.

"Wow, is it really–"

155

She grabbed onto the back of her chair as she almost fell into the table. She hadn't stood up for a while, and the wine had gone to her head. "Shit. Whoops."

Re-orientating herself, Marta realised that the piece of furniture propping her up was not actually a piece of furniture after all. It was Dom's arm.

"Thanks," she said, feeling less wobbly and more embarrassed. She could feel the heat of his arm around her waist, and it was a relief to find that she could still feel it as she moved across the restaurant. The team of waitresses said a friendly goodbye, insisting on filling Dom's pockets with sweets and giving them each a shot of fluorescent yellow liqueur – despite Marta's state.

It was Dom's idea to get another cab. "Live like Londoners," was all he said when he saw Marta's bemused expression. "We'll be earning real London salaries soon – stop worrying."

Marta had had too much wine to worry. Dom was right. Soon they'd be earning proper money. They were moving up in the world.

The taxi swung right onto Knightsbridge, sending Marta slithering across the plastic seats and into Dom's lap. She clambered off, tugging her clothes back into place and wishing for a moment that she'd opted for a longer skirt.

"Sorry," she said, twisting round and pushing the locks of hair off her face. Her legs were still somehow entwined in his.

"No worries," he said, grinning. Marta flailed some more, then realised why she was finding it so hard to right herself. Dom had her trapped around the waist. She stopped struggling. Dom loosened his grip, allowing her to wriggle round so that she was effectively lying across him. Her head was on his shoulder. She could feel it move as he lowered his arm.

Marta looked up at his face. His eyes were roaming up and down her body, hungrily. She raised her head and let Dom slide a hand into her hair, lifting her, drawing her closer. She could smell his body. She breathed it in, running a hand over his shirt sleeve, feeling the bulge of his muscles underneath.

"We're not going to a bar, are we?" he murmured, touching her lips gently with his and brushing a strand of hair off her forehead.

Marta could feel her breathing become quicker, more shallow.

She shook her head and allowed Dom's lips back onto hers. Then she realised: *they had nowhere to go.* Despite her state, Marta was alert enough to remember the conversation Tina had started in the pub three days earlier. She didn't have her own bedroom, and surely Dom shared his with a dozen Eastern Europeans.

"But–"

Dom silenced her protests with his lips, and Marta was lost again. Her skin tingled where his fingers touched her face. The kissing was more passionate now. Like magnetism, there was something pulling them together.

"WHERE EXAC'LY D'YOU WANNA GO IN ACTON?" demanded the driver, suddenly.

Marta sat up, yanking the skirt down from her waist and trying to look like a respectable passenger. Gosh, she really was behaving like an English girl!

"St Leonards Road," Dom replied calmly, simultaneously pulling Marta back into his lap. "Just off Victoria Road."

Unfortunately, Marta couldn't help behaving like an English girl. It was Dom's fault – he was irresistible. They pulled up to number twelve, and Dom, like a true English gentleman, paid the driver and helped Marta out.

"But Dom," Marta protested, envisaging a lounge full of Croats playing Nintendo Wii at full volume and a bedroom full of friendly Nigerians. Dom continued to lead her to the front door.

The house was unexpectedly empty.

"*Where is everyone?*" whispered Marta, half-expecting the music to re-start and the crowd to jump out at them from the kitchen.

"*Away!*" Dom whispered back, walking backwards and pulling her close to his body as he kicked the front door shut. Then, in a normal voice, but softly: "There's some Czech national holiday this week and the Israelis have decided that now is a good time to visit their hometown near Gaza. Not sure where Uzoma is, but he stays out late most nights."

Dom had hardly finished his sentence before Marta felt his lips back on hers. He took a step back, his chest still tight against hers, drawing her into a part of the house she'd never seen before. They seemed to be under the stairs in a small room with a sloping ceiling that stretched all the way down to the floor. It was like a cupboard, but a very cosy cupboard with everything a guy could possibly need: airbed, stereo, laptop, dartboard and mini bar.

It was difficult to say how they got from being vertical in the doorway to being horizontal on the bed, drinking shots of limoncello off each other's chests.

"Marta, I'm worried about your top," Dom told her, pouring another shot and putting it down on the ledge that served as the bar. "I don't want it getting wet," he said, smiling.

"Mmm," said Marta, moving closer. "What should we do about that?"

Dom ran a finger lightly down the side of her top, next to her arm, veering casually over her breast on the way. Marta caught her breath. His hand moved effortlessly underneath the top, travelling up on her bare skin, drawing patterns around her erect nipple. She waited, enjoying the anticipation but strangely desperate for Dom to remove her top.

The next thing she knew, Marta was lying on the bed in her bra and skirt, feeling the sticky limoncello trickle out from between her breasts. Dom's tongue moved up, over her neck and onto her mouth once more. She could taste the sickly alcohol on his lips.

"Marta, I'm worried about your skirt," said Dom, pressing her against the bed with his body and running a hand down to her waist.

Marta smiled, pushing him sideways so that she was on top. "And what about your shirt?" she asked, starting to unbutton it.

It seemed a shame that a body like Dom's spent most of its time hidden away under T-shirts. Marta straddled him, half naked, just looking at his chest and his arms. They were tanned, like his face, and it was obvious he spent a lot of his time doing weights.

What happened next was a blur; there was a flurry of clothes flying off, of bodies pressing against one another, of rolling and sliding, of frenzied kissing and suddenly they were naked, their bodies slippery with a mixture of limoncello and sweat.

"Marta," Dom murmured as he rolled on top of her.

If he'd meant to say more, he didn't. Marta pulled him onto her and wrapped her legs around him. He slipped inside her. Despite Marta's efforts to remain Polish tonight, despite her intentions to avoid following in her nymphomaniac flatmate's footsteps, she couldn't. He was in her, around her and on top of her, rock hard, groaning. She was panting, feeling the heat of his body every time he moved towards her.

They rolled over. She was on top of him, her breasts pressing up against his chest, her legs locked around his. Suddenly she too was groaning, her whole body on fire. Their bodies shuddered as they came, both of them, then collapsed, exhausted, as one.

27

MARTA'S EYES FLUTTERED OPEN, and then closed again. She was awake, but only just. Her body felt heavy and tired, and at the same time... sticky. Very strange. Marta ran her tongue round the inside of her mouth. It tasted of mouldy onions with a hint of lemon. Her head was throbbing.

There was a funny noise coming from outside the window: a warbling – no, a cooing. That was it: pigeons cooing. How odd. Marta allowed herself a quick squint at the world through half-closed eyes. The room seemed to be the wrong colour. In fact, everything was wrong: the light, the sounds, the smell...

Marta's eyes opened. *She was in Dom's bedroom.* And – the memories flooded back – she had slept with Dom last night. Oh God, she'd slept with Dom. She was lying with him, naked, in his bed. Her mind filled with questions. Was this bad? Should she have held back? What would Dom think? Did it mean anything? Would it happen again? God, she hoped so.

She turned her head, very gently. A tuft of sandy hair was poking out from under the duvet next to her, and Marta could just make out his long, dark eyelashes in the shadows. Even first thing in the morning, Dom was cute. Marta watched him quietly, listening to the soft, steady purr of his breathing. Her right leg was in between his, so she couldn't move – not that she wanted to.

"Marta," Dom uttered, shifting towards her, eyes still shut.

Marta wriggled closer, aligning her body with his under the covers. He reached out and pulled her towards him, his eyes still shut but breaking into a smile. Then Dom was on top of her, looking straight into her eyes – sleepily but lustfully. She lay back, feeling

Dom's erection digging into her groin. He rearranged the locks of sticky hair around her face. "Gorgeous," he said, lowering himself so that he was almost inside her.

The moment was shattered by the sound of a high-pitched ringtone. They tried to ignore it, rubbing against one another, kissing.

The ringing went on.

"Is that yours?" asked Dom, reluctantly raising himself from her body.

Marta realised that it was in fact hers; she just hadn't recognised the silly ringtone. "Yes."

"Want to answer it?" he asked, propping himself up on one elbow and letting Marta touch his bicep.

"No."

Finally, there was peace. Dom rolled onto one side and started touching Marta on her inside thigh. She was feeling weak. His hand slid masterfully up her leg, but then just as she thought she couldn't take any more, it stopped. Dom looked at her. "It's ringing again."

Dom was right. The phone – wherever it was in the jumble of belongings all over the room – was bleeping away.

"Hello?" she said, perched on the end of the bed and wondering who would be calling her from a withheld number at nine o'clock on a Saturday.

"Marta, it's me."

She recognised the voice, but it sounded strained. "Holly?"

"Yeah – I'm sorry it's so early. I didn't wake you, did I?"

Marta looked round at Dom, who was sitting behind her on the bed, his legs wrapped around her waist, his penis hard against her back. "No – I was awake," she said, removing Dom's hand from where it was wandering.

"Oh good. Only I'm trying to get hold of Tina, and she's not picking up. I just wondered whether she was in the house?"

"Um…" Marta shuddered as Dom started nibbling her ear and neck. "I don't know…"

Holly tutted. "Might've known. She's not back from wherever she was last night, is she? Dirty stop-out."

Marta felt a pinch of guilt. There was something wrong though, thought Marta. Holly sounded quite worked up. "Are you OK?"

Holly sighed. "Well, no, not really. I've been in the office since eight o'clock yesterday morning and I've still got fuck-loads to do before our deadline at two today – God knows why the deadline is two o'clock on a Saturday – and there's no way I'll be able to make today's hockey match, which I'm supposed to be captaining."

"You been in the office since twenty-five hours?" Marta asked, incredulously. Surely it wasn't possible to stay awake, *working*, for that long?

"Yeah, and counting." Holly sounded really unhappy. Marta couldn't imagine what Holly was doing at Anderton's, but whatever it was, it seemed wrong that she was doing it all through her weekend.

"Look, if Tina makes a reappearance, can you tell her I'm desperate to get hold of her? She'll have to stand in as captain for today, and we'll need to find a sub for me… fuck knows who we're gonna get at this short – oh my God, hang on…"

"What?"

"Marta. You run, don't you?"

Marta had lost the thread of the conversation around the part where Dom reached a particularly sensitive part of her body. "I run?" she repeated, feeling very hot all of a sudden.

"Yes – you run, don't you? You do sport… you could stand in for me!"

"In this game… hockey? You mean I play?" Marta asked, struggling to stay in control. She should have told Dom to stop but she couldn't.

"Yes! Brilliant! OK, Marta, when Tina comes back, just ask her to sort you out with kit and stuff. She knows where everything is. Oh and tell her she's captain. Match starts at one, and you're meeting in the changing rooms at half twelve. Good luck!"

In other circumstances, Marta would have objected. She had never played this mad game where they run around with wooden sticks and wear plastic blocks in their mouths, and she never wanted to. But the phone went dead before she could think of an argument, and actually, she wasn't sure she was capable of arguing – or in fact doing anything, in her current state.

28

"OK! POTHITHIONS!" yelled Tina, removing the purple thing from her mouth and spitting a gobful of phlegm on the astroturf. "Defence, sort yourselves out at the back, with Jen sweeping. Chelsea Ladies have got some really good strikers, so you'll need to hang back. Vic and Sam on the wings, me up front... who else? Em, where d'you play?"

Tina looked quite imposing, standing there in her tight purple skirt and Kilburn Ladies top, her long, skinny thighs disappearing into thick padded shins and mean-looking boots. She was one of the only girls on the team who managed to look stunning, as well as scary. Most, it had to be said, were rather butch.

"Marta, where d'you wanna play?"

Suddenly, everyone was looking at her. Marta shrugged at her flatmate, who was no longer the carefree piss-head she knew. She'd turned all bossy and organised.

"OK, you can play up front with me. Guys, for those of you who haven't met Marta, she's our flatmate and she's standing in for Holly today. She's pretty fast, but her ball skills may be a bit rusty."

Marta didn't catch everything Tina said, but she got the gist. It seemed that she was leaving out one vitally important fact: that she'd never played hockey before.

"Tina, I want to explain that I will be very rubbish as—"

"Marta, you'll be great," Tina said quickly. "You've got nothing to worry about."

Marta had everything to worry about. Like the fact that these balls they were whacking around were very, very hard. And the fact

163

that nobody had told her where she should stand on the giant pitch or what she should do when she was there. And the likelihood of her team mates with bandanas and muscular legs passing the ball to her and watching her mess it up. And of course, the fact that she was still drunk from last night and frankly, had other things on her mind.

The brief lesson she'd had from Tina on the tube would have to suffice, Marta realised, seeing the other girls migrate to the green expanse of fake grass. She shoved the plastic block into her mouth, readjusted the flappy skirt and jogged onto the pitch with everyone else. This would be an excellent learning experience, she told herself.

Marta trotted over to the spot where Tina was pointing and waited for the game to begin. Directly opposite her was a frightening looking girl with red hair and big thighs who was grunting like a tribesman at her team mates. The Chelsea Ladies looked pretty fearsome in their slinky yellow and brown. Marta watched the middle of the pitch, where Tina and her opponent were bent over the ball, poised for action. A small man in black and white hovered next to them, whistle in mouth.

The most peculiar thing happened next. The girls in the middle started bashing their sticks against one another's, directly above the ball – as if performing some sort of ritual. Then all hell broke loose. One of them hit the ball, which went zooming towards the opposition and stopped by a girl in yellow, who whacked it in the other direction. The ball flew at high speed between yellow and purple players, always hovering just above the incredibly smooth surface. Marta, meanwhile, ran randomly up and down her part of the pitch wondering what she should be doing.

Then it happened. Marta made contact with the ball. Not necessarily in the way she had intended, but she made contact nonetheless. After a good deal of whizzing about, the ball shot off the pitch and came to a halt at the perimeter fencing. Marta was the closest player, so she took it upon herself to fetch it. This was when she learnt how difficult it was to push a small, heavy object along with a spindly piece of wood. It was like trying to rescue an insect from the surface of a swimming pool using a broom handle.

"You take it!" yelled Tina, when Marta had finally coaxed the ball back onto the pitch.

Marta shook her head, shrugging. What did she mean, 'take it'? Take it where?

One of her team mates pointed to the line that marked the edge of the pitch. "Take it from there," she said. Marta hesitated. She was confused. The girl seemed to be implying that she should put the ball back on the line – which, in Marta's vocabulary, was 'put it' – quite the opposite of 'take it'.

Finally, Tina came to the rescue. "I'll take it!" she shouted, running over wielding her stick and brandishing a row of purple teeth. "You go down the line!"

Marta gratefully relinquished the ball, wondering which line she was supposed to be going down. There was more jargon involved in hockey than in marketing.

From that point onwards, Marta opted to loiter in the free space near the goal where the ball rarely went. There was a lower risk of getting in the way out here, and there was, she imagined, a remote chance that she could help guide the ball between the posts.

Her ploy didn't work for long. After only a few minutes, several purple team members started shouting in her direction, waving their arms. Marta moved back into the danger zone and tried to work out what they were saying.

"Marta! Marta!" she heard. It was strange, because she didn't think anybody had listened to Tina's introduction. "Marta!"

Her team mates were pointing at the red-haired girl, who was powering up and down the pitch, doing a rather good job of catching the ball on her stick and bulldozing through the Kilburn defence.

It occurred to Marta, after quite a lot of squinting and shrugging, that they weren't saying her name after all. They were screaming "Mark her!" At least, that's what it sounded like.

Mark her? What, did they mean she was to hit the big girl with her stick and leave a mark on her skin? Marta grimaced. She hadn't seen anyone else marking members of the opposition.

"Mark that girl!" screeched the girl with pigtails, sounding desperate.

No, Marta decided. Whatever they wanted, she was not going to resort to violence in this game. She felt sure that 'marking' the opposition was not allowed, and that if the little man in black and white saw her... well, she might get the whole team into trouble.

Finally, the whistle blew and Marta's ordeal was over. Her limbs were still in working order, her face was in tact, and she hadn't scored any own goals for the opposition. It was a job well done, she thought proudly.

"Awesome!" cried Tina as the girls gathered round on the side of the pitch. She was holding out a clear plastic bag full of what looked like slices of orange. "This is good, everyone. We should feel really proud. Chelsea Ladies are second in the league, and they've won every game this season."

There were nods of agreement accompanied by a slurping sound. Marta was wondering whether she should apologise openly or just wait until the tube journey home.

"In the second half, we need to be more aggressive," said Tina.

Marta stared at her. *Second half? Surely she had misunderstood. They were only half way?*

Marta's fears were confirmed as the pep talk progressed. They were about to go back onto the pitch.

"Marta, you need to mark more closely – your player's bloody good so stick tight," Tina instructed.

Marta nodded obediently. Stick tight. Mark closely. Aha. That was preferable to whacking the redhead with her stick.

"And let's push up! We can win this. Let's go!" yelled Tina, shoving her block into her mouth and tossing the orange peel onto the ground.

For Marta, the second half consisted of an exhausting game of follow-my-leader, with the redhead as perpetual leader. She was, considering her stocky build, remarkably fit and she didn't seem to like Marta tagging along. There were times – like the time when the girl stopped to retie her shoelace and Marta crouched down next to her – when Marta wondered whether she was taking this 'marking' thing too far, but, if the purpose of the task was to exclude the girl from the game by trotting along next to her, well, she was doing very well.

Something exciting happened just after the referee said, "Two minutes". Tina stopped the ball with her stick and cleverly weaved it past lots of the yellow players, almost all the way to the goal. As she lifted her stick to bash it past the goal keeper, one of the yellow girls whipped it out from under her and sent the ball rushing towards the redhead, i.e. towards Marta.

Marta tried to intercept the ball but of course, failed, leaving it to bounce off the redhead's stick and off the end of the pitch.

"Well left!" shouted one of the purple players as she went to retrieve the ball. "Short corner. Well done Marta!"

Marta had no idea what she had done, or not done, but it seemed that half of her team were assembling in some sort of semi-circle around the goal, while half of the yellow team were loitering inside the goal looking angry. The little man was ordering some of Marta's team back to the other end of the pitch. Marta waited for further instruction, but everybody seemed too busy planning their own strategy.

"Tina...?" said Marta, quietly.

Tina glanced sideways, then back to the girl with the ball, who was crouching on the back line like a cat waiting to pounce.

"Just try and get a goal!" she said quickly, making some sort of secret hand gesture to the girl with the ball.

It all happened too quickly. Marta was vaguely aware of the ball being hit before she felt a pang all the way up her right arm and heard a faint 'thud', followed by an ear-splitting scream all around her. She thought she also heard the sound of the whistle beneath all the screams, but maybe not.

"What happen?" she asked, as Tina came running towards her, stick raised above her head.

"We fucking won! That's what happened! And you helped the goal in!"

Marta frowned. How strange. And how frustrating that she hadn't seen it. "Really?"

"Yes! You're our hero! Well, strictly speaking that girl on the opposition who pushed the ball in is our hero, but you did fucking brilliantly!"

There was a flurry of hand-shaking, hair-ruffling and – more alarmingly – bum-slapping as the girls trampled happily off the pitch. It seemed that Marta's earlier clumsiness had been forgotten or forgiven, and some of the girls, Marta noted as they pushed open the doors to the Chelsea clubhouse bar, were even mistakenly talking about 'Marta's next match'. She knew it wasn't warranted, but the praise felt… well, it felt nice, and Marta found it hard to lift the grin from her face.

"Am not staying for very long," she explained to the girl with pigtails who was sliding a huge jug of frothy purple drink towards her.

"Why the hell not?" the girl demanded. "This is the most important part of the match!" She poured Marta a pint of the stuff and moved onto the next girl's.

The truth was, Marta needed to go back to bed. She needed to sober up, sleep, eat, drink water and reflect on the last twenty-four hours. Everything had happened so quickly she hadn't had a chance to think. And getting drunk with English girls in a noisy sports bar was not going to give her that chance.

Marta sipped her purple drink. It was disgusting. Sickly and sour at the same time – like blackcurrent mixed with urine. She swallowed it, wiping her mouth and wandering off towards the toilets.

She was making her way back to the hockey girls through the sweaty bar, trying to think up a credible reason for leaving so early that didn't involve Dom, when someone tapped her on the shoulder.

"Hey. Marta?"

She recognised his voice instantly and shuddered. What was he doing here?

"Hi," she said blankly, turning to face him. There, in the middle of the bar, dressed in a casual rugby shirt and surrounded by sweaty, brutish lads, was Jack Templeton-Cooper.

"So, you're playing for the Kilburn Ladies now?" he asked. His hair was still wet from the shower.

Marta shrugged, looking over at her team mates. "Just today. Holly couldn't play."

"Did you win? What a coincidence you're down here the same day as us… I can't believe it!"

She nodded, deadpan. "We won, yes." Marta couldn't believe that Jack had been such a temptation before. Of course, he was gorgeous – his chiselled features and rugby build were a draw for any girl – but he was so arrogant. And boring.

"Well done." Jack smiled, moving closer so that only she could hear above the din. "Listen Marta, about my text message." He looked down at the floor as though finding it difficult to find the words, although Marta had a feeling it was all an act. "I really am sorry. I'm sorry about everything – including going out with Tash in the first place, but that's another story – I just… I just want to make it up to you. To apologise."

Marta frowned. His words were probably supposed to tug at her heartstrings, to contain some deeper meaning, but they left her cold. She wasn't thinking about Jack's corny words. She was thinking about her night with Dom.

"You must've gone through hell when Tash, er, when she suggested you leave, and it was all my fault. I just wish I'd been there for you. You should've called me, Marta."

There were plenty of things she could have said – most of them rude – but Marta couldn't be bothered. "I'm fine," she said simply.

"Well," said Jack, looking genuinely stumped by her lack of interest. "Just call me if you fancy that dinner. The offer is an open one. You've got my number."

"No I haven't," replied Marta.

"Oh right," said Jack calmly, reaching into his back pocket. He really did have thick skin, she marvelled. "Well, here's my card anyway. Like I said, the offer's open."

Marta took the card, flashed him a false smile and brushed past to collect her things.

29

"YOU CAN GO ON UP," informed the receptionist. "First floor. Just ask for David Lyle."

Marta stepped into the lift, checking her suited reflection in the mirrored walls. She looked nervous. In the short ride up she tried to compose herself, trying out different facial expressions and postures. None of them made her look any more relaxed.

"Ah, hello!" cried a squeaky male voice almost as soon as the lift doors opened. Marta stepped into the lobby – a strange experience due to the large number of shapes in various shades of yellow and green that were suspended from the ceiling – towards the short, smiling man. He was wearing, rather surprisingly, a flowery shirt and jeans. Marta instantly felt over-dressed.

"Marta Dabadabaduda, or some such unpronounceable name, I presume?" he said, embracing her with a firm handshake and silly grin.

"Da-brov-ska," she said politely.

"Excellent, well, come on through. I'm David Lyle. Like the sugar – ahahahaha! I'm Managing Director here. Welcome to Stratisvision."

Marta followed the little man through a swipe card-only door and into a huge open plan office. The theme from the lobby extended throughout the office.

"Bet you can't guess our corporate colours!" he joked as he led her through a hanging green foam archway that seemed to serve no purpose other than to take up space. Marta tried not to look too nosy as she glanced around the room. It was buzzing with activity: phones ringing, printers whirring, people rushing from desk to desk. It looked

170

so intense – but so silly, with all these coloured shapes. And she was definitely over-dressed, judging by the glimpses she'd caught of leather boots, tight jeans and big tassely belts.

"My office," he announced, holding open the door of an all-glass room in the middle. There was a band of opaqueness at shoulder height (nearer head-height for David Lyle) that prevented people from looking in.

"Sit, sit!" he commanded, motioning to the colourful chairs around the oval table. "So! You're here with us for what... two weeks?"

Marta nodded.

"And very nice it is to have you, too. So, d'you know what we do here at Stratisvision?"

Marta nodded again. She had studied the website on Holly's computer. "Help clients solve marketing problems in strategic and pragmatic ways."

David drew back his head in mock surprise. "*Very* good. So, you've done your homework then. But let's just talk for a moment about *what we do*. Because the answer you gave is good, but it doesn't give any indication of what we stand for. What we're like, as a company."

Marta noticed a string of beads around the director's neck, like the sort that a beach bum might wear.

"We make love to our clients!" cried the man, banging the table with his palm and looking at Marta. "Ha. Not literally, of course. Well... unless of course you want to. And let me tell you, sex is positively encouraged in this firm. Positively encouraged." The director gave her a lingering look. Marta wished she'd opted for trousers, not skirt.

"No, we make love to our clients, *metaphorically*," he said. "We are passionate about our clients. We get close to them. We understand their problems. We know what keeps them awake at night. And that's the important thing. Whatever you end up working on here, remember that: make love to the client."

Marta gave a nervous laugh, then realised he was deadly serious.

"Moving on!" cried David, clapping his hands and wandering over to a bookshelf that was stacked mainly with origami animals in yellow and green. "Take this," he said, plucking out a slim booklet and tossing it onto the table. "That tells you everything you need to know about us."

Marta flicked through it politely. It was full of swirly patterns and colourful pictures, with occasional words written in huge, chunky fonts. "Thanks," she said uncertainly.

"Now you're probably wondering what on earth you'll be doing here for two weeks, hmm?"

Marta was actually wondering what on earth David Lyle had on his feet; his shoes looked like leather flippers. She nodded anyway.

"Well, the fact is, I don't know. But I do know that we're bloody busy right now, and there's no shortage of work! I expect someone will grab you the minute you sit down, so be prepared for that."

"OK."

"Not that you're likely to be work-shy... being Polish!"

Marta gritted her teeth. She felt like a goldfish in a tank, being taunted. Finally, David pushed open the door.

"Kim! Kat! Nik!" he called. "Would one of you show our lovely Polish temp around the office?" He turned back to Marta and lowered his voice. "Never can tell the difference between them," he said.

A Barbie-like figure approached David's office. Kat had white-blonde hair like an albino, but dark, tanned skin. Her beauty was marred only by her sour expression.

"OK, let's go," said Kat, brusquely, marching off towards one end of the office. "This is Patricia Catermol's office? But she's not around? She's the CEO?"

Marta trotted to keep up with the girl. For some reason, Kat's voice seemed to lift at the end of each statement, as though she were asking a question.

"You'll hardly ever see Patricia, she's so busy? You've met David, and this is Joan, Peter, Charlotte, Dean..." the list went on. Marta forgot every name as soon as she heard it; all English names sounded the same anyway – especially when stated in Kat's questioning way.

"...this is me? And that's Nik and Kim?" finished Kat, strutting back to where they'd started.

"Thanks," replied Marta, feeling a bit lost as Kat returned to her seat and got back to whatever she'd been doing.

Eventually, one of the other slim, pretty girls – Kim or Nik – looked up and said, "You can sit anywhere – we hot desk."

Marta nodded, none the wiser. Did she have to find a hot desk? How would she know which ones were hot? Was she supposed to go round all the spare ones, feeling the temperature of each? What a stupid idea. Marta wandered to the next block of kidney-shaped desks and stopped at an empty one opposite a young guy – the only one who had smiled at her when she'd been paraded round.

"I can sit here?" she asked.

"You can seat anywhere – ee's hot desking," replied the guy. Hot desk-*ing*, noted Marta. His speech sounded funny. Maybe he was foreign, she thought hopefully. He looked foreign – dark eyes, dark eyebrows and hairy chin, all slightly askew as though his face had been fitted together in a rush.

"Thanks."

Marta sat down and rattled the mouse. Everything in this office was shiny and new – most of it yellow or green – including the huge flat screens on each desk that looked like televisions.

Ten minutes later, she was still sitting there. She had read – if that was the right word – the colourful Stratisvision booklet four times, and followed every link on the Stratisvision website. Marta was bored.

There were two other people on the curvy desk besides Marta and the guy with the wonky features. One was a middle-aged woman with short mousy hair and a scowl, the other was a man in his thirties who looked like Superman: good-looking in an American way with a square jaw, black-rimmed glasses and a serious expression as though he really was busy trying to save the world. Everyone was staring at their screens. Marta seemed to have picked the one desk that was exempt from the frenzied activity.

A full thirty minutes later, just as Marta was considering marching back into David Lyle's office and demanding to know the whereabouts of this so-called deluge of work, the wonky-faced guy popped his head up.

"You smoke?" he asked.

Marta smiled. Today, she would be a smoker. If inhaling a bit of nicotine was what it would take to penetrate this mysterious consultancy and lift her chances of a job offer anywhere above zero, then she would take the health risk. Marta nodded.

"Come with me. I show you smokers' corner," he said, revealing another crooked smile.

The first drag was a surprisingly pleasant experience, considering she hadn't smoked for nearly eight years. Marta breathed deeply, letting the chemicals fill her lungs. Doing nothing was remarkably stressful.

The guy's name, it transpired, was Carl, and he was Italian. As it happened – much to Marta's delight – he had started at Stratisvision in the same way as her: as a temporary assistant analyst. He spoke softly but was open and frank.

"You don't know anyone at all?"

Marta shook her head. "Apart from David Lyle who tell me about having sex with clients and Kat who ignore me," she explained.

Carl nearly choked on his cigarette. "Oh dear," he laughed. "Not a good start. So, a summary?"

Marta exhaled. "Yes please."

"Kat and Nik and Kim. They are all the same: fashionable girls who spend most days on Facebook on the internet. They do the 'fun' projects," he explained, scratching quotations in the air. "Like the Topshop re-brand and the Olympic campaign."

Marta smiled.

"Neil is their same level, but he only does spreadsheets, I think." He took a last drag on his cigarette and stubbed it out on the metal grate. "On our desk, there is Joan and Dean. Joan I hope you will never work for. She is... how do you say... manic depressive. Dean, he is very senior, even though only thirty-one. Do not joke around with heem!"

She nodded. "So, I choose a good place to sit, then?"

"Then there is Charlotte – the one who does the marching around the office. She is an *angry woman*. I hope also that you never work for her. You know the one?"

Marta shook her head.

"She is the one with the beeg, fuzzy hair."

"OK. Anyone else to know?"

Carl tucked the cigarettes away in his pocket, squinting in

thought. "No, I don't think so. These are the main ones. Oh – I forgot the most important! Patricia. The CEO. She is also scary, but mad. She is not here much. But the reason that Kat is here? She is Patricia's niece."

Marta smiled knowingly as they headed back to the office. It was nice of Carl to share his knowledge. She wondered how he had picked it up in the first place.

"One more thing!" said Marta, just before Carl swiped his card at the door. She had been in two minds about whether to ask him. "I have no work. Should I ask someone?"

Carl laughed, shaking his head. "Marta, if you have no work, this is a good thing. You do not say anything. They are paying for you to do nothing. Wait a bit, and the work will come – for sure, but until then, just enjoy the quiet!"

They re-entered the office, ignoring the customary scowls from the staunch non-smokers.

'Enjoying the quiet' was harder than it sounded for someone like Marta. Even as she sat down at her desk she could feel the irritation beginning to burn inside her. She picked up the booklet and flicked through it again, despite knowing every page off by heart. Her foot started jiggling under the table. She moved the mouse. The website was still there, bold and colourful. She hated having nothing to do.

Suddenly, the noise level picked in the office behind her. It sounded as though an elephant was charging through it with someone very noisy on top. The floor was actually shaking.

"Not that section! Yes, I'm talking about the segmentation… The brand egg – we need to rethink. I'm going to get someone working on that today…"

Marta turned round. Careering towards her was not in fact an elephant. It was a woman with a large amount of brown, fuzzy hair and a very loud voice. She was on the phone.

"That's what I'm going to do!" she said, pausing as she approached Marta's desk. Then, without warning, she flipped shut her phone and looked down at Marta.

"Hi, I'm Charlotte," she said brusquely. "I believe you're here to help. I'm working on a project for PopsCo and we need an extra pair of hands. Now, write this down: natural, fresh, authentic – are you writing this? Good – authentic, real and healthy. Got that? Right. I need a moo ball in A1 for each. Have them on my desk end of play today. Good girl."

The woman paused briefly to check that Marta had scribbled something down, then rushed off. Marta let out the breath she'd been holding. What was a *moo ball?*

For a moment, Marta stared at the back of the booklet where she had jotted the random words down. *Natural, fresh, authentic, real, healthy.* What did it mean? There was only one thing she could think of to do.

"Carl!" she whispered.

"Oh dear," he replied, quietly. "You are working for Charlotte…"

Marta pulled a face. "Had no choice! What is a moo ball?"

Carl stared at her, then suddenly burst out laughing.

"What?"

He looked up and laughed again. Finally he replied. "Ees not a 'moo ball' – ees a 'mood board'!"

"Oh, right," said Marta, still confused. "And what is that?"

Slowly, Carl explained the concept of a 'mood board': a collection of images that represent a mood or state, stuck onto a piece of cardboard. Not very complicated, really.

"And where I get the pictures from?" asked Marta, not quite believing that her first task was this simple.

Carl looked at her with a glint in his eye. "Have you ever used Google?"

Marta smiled, embarrassed, and turned to her computer screen. She looked up a few seconds later.

"Thanks," she whispered.

He smiled. "No problemo."

30

"OK, SO WHAT DO I COOK TONIGHT? And where is Holly?" asked Marta. "She never come home any more."

Rich smiled wryly across the kitchen table. "She won't be back before midnight. She texted me earlier."

Marta screwed up her nose. "She spend all her life in that office," she said, getting up and peering into the fridge. "Just you and me, then. You like the meat pie thing I did last week?"

Rich looked up at her, as though he'd only just registered she was talking. He seemed preoccupied.

"Sorry – yeah. I loved it. Best thing I've had in ages. But hey, Marta, don't feel obliged to cook, will you? I can do us some pasta or something. I really don't mind."

Marta shrugged. "If I not paying the rent, I should pay in some way. And anyway, I don't like your English food. It is…" Marta struggled for the word. "Blank."

Rich frowned. "Do you mean 'bland'?"

Marta thought for a second. "Yes, I mean bland."

"OK then. Suit yourself. I'm more than happy to eat whatever you cook."

Marta set about preparing the dinner – her little brother's favourite dish. Rich sat slumped at the kitchen table, flicking over the pages of one of Tina's magazines. He wasn't even pretending to read the articles.

"What is your problem?" she asked as she pummelled the lumps of meat.

Rich shook his head and looked at Marta. "Marta, in this country,

177

if you ask that question it generally means you want to pick a fight with someone."

Marta took in this nugget, unimpressed yet again with the English way of doing things. Why couldn't they be direct about anything?

"It's not so much my problem, anyway. It's Holly's," explained Rich. "I'm worried about her."

Marta nodded, feeling around in the fridge for vegetables that weren't mouldy. "She works hard," said Marta.

Rich lurched forward as the fridge door swung shut, catching it just in time to grab a beer from the door. "Ta. Yeah, she works hard, but I don't think that's the problem," he said, cracking open the can. "Holly has always worked hard. That's the way she is. That's why she got a first when all the other engineers got two-ones."

"What did you get?" asked Marta, intrigued about this part of their lives. It was amazing to think that while she had been living at home in Łomianki, travelling in to the Szkoła every day and coming home to her family, Holly, Tina and Rich had been living in one of those ancient stone colleges in Cambridge, with courtyards and fountains and butlers. It sounded such fun.

"Two-one," Rich replied sheepishly. "I wasn't prepared to put in the hours during our final year. Holly was."

Marta started stripping the old, yellow strands from the outside of a leek, hoping to find something edible inside.

"So, what is Holly's problem, if it not the hard working?" Marta was intrigued about how much thought Rich had put into this. It certainly wasn't typical flatmate concern.

Rich took a swig of beer and shrugged. "I dunno exactly. She just hasn't been herself for the last few months – ever since she really got into her job. She's uptight."

"Up *tights*?"

"Uptight. Tense, stressed," he explained.

Marta nodded. That was certainly true. Holly used to be the life and soul of every event – she told the funny stories, she played the practical jokes, she made people laugh. Now, she just went to bed.

"I just don't think the City is right for her," declared Rich. He was quite perceptive, for a guy.

"You mean London?" asked Marta, horrified at the thought of Holly moving away.

"No – I mean 'the city'," he said. "You know – the square mile."

Marta frowned. "Square mile?"

"Oh, sorry. Um… the 'square mile' is the area around Moorgate and Bank where all the investment banks and law firms are based. It used to be a geographical thing, but a lot of firms have moved away to other parts of London, and now it's just a terminology thing. 'The city' represents high pressure jobs, basically.

"Is Holly's job high pressure?" asked Marta. She had a feeling it was, but she'd never stopped to think about what Holly did.

Rich lifted his shoulders slightly. "I guess." He took another swig. "She never really talks about it. Only to moan, and she doesn't like doing that so… I dunno."

Marta chucked the leek in the bin, having peeled off every rotten layer and been left with a soggy stump.

"She only ever wanted one thing at uni," mused Rich, swilling the remains of his beer around in the can. "To be the best. At everything. Hockey, music, dancing, engineering… I think that's why she went into consultancy. It wasn't because she wanted to do it; it was because that's what all the best people were doing. She wanted to be classed a success."

Marta chopped up the remaining vegetables and dropped them into the pan. She was feeling a little uncomfortable hearing Rich delve so deeply into Holly's psyche, but at the same time she was fascinated. This 'square mile' thing sounded awful – like a prisoner of war camp, or worse, Oświęcim. People went there with great intentions, hoping to make a difference, do great things, and came out demoralised, flattened, unfulfilled.

Rich was right. Holly was driven by success. That was why she'd got a place in one of the most prestigious firms in the world, and that was why she spent so many days and nights in the office. Surely the long hours weren't *expected* of her, were they? She just wanted to succeed. To do well. Marta knew how that felt.

"She's got such drive," Rich went on. "When she decides to go for something, she'll put everything she's got into it. It was the same all through uni. That's why she's wearing herself out in this job – because she can't do anything badly."

Marta left the food to simmer and joined Rich at the kitchen table, setting down two more cans of beer. There was a question she was dying to ask him – in fact, she'd been dying to ask him since the day she moved in.

"Rich, are you in love with Holly?"

Suddenly, the can fell away from his lips. He stared at Marta. "What?!" The smile disappeared quickly. "What are you talking about?"

Marta didn't back down, despite Rich's reaction. "Well, I just wondered. You care so much for her. I think you love her."

Richard's eyes flitted down to the floor and darted about uncertainly. He looked flushed. "We're... we're mates. We're just friends. I mean... we know each other really well, and... I dunno. We're just mates."

Marta nodded. Rich still wasn't looking her in the eye.

"OK," she said. "I only wondered."

"Yeah well, now you know." Rich yanked open his second beer with unnecessary force. Like a frustrated teenager, thought Marta. He couldn't talk about his feelings. English people were like that: up tights.

"Now I know," said Marta, nodding. "You want sauce with your meat pie?"

31

MARTA DIDN'T SO MUCH HEAR the woman's approach as feel it. The footsteps reverberated around the office, desks wobbling and screensavers dissolving in her wake.

"Something else for you," she said, leaning forwards on the desk and giving Marta an unpleasant view of her swinging breasts. "It's for the CSD beverage project I mentioned. I need a deck of presidents in above-the-line media – probably fifty to sixty presidents in all, one president per slide. Each slide should contain – write this down – the brand, the campaign, dates, outcome and stats where you can get hold of them. OK?"

Marta nodded confidently. "Fine." She had no idea what the woman was on about, but Marta was beginning to realise that Charlotte wasn't the sort of person to spare time for explanations.

"Email them to me by lunchtime tomorrow," she instructed. Then she was gone, storming through the office like a tornado.

A deck of presidents. Like, the President of the United States, she wondered? Marta stared at the notes she had made, wondering where she was going to find sixty presidents and wondering how this all fitted in with CSD beverages, whatever they were.

A full minute later, Marta was still staring at the notes, frowning. The instructions were no clearer now than when Charlotte had barked them at her.

"You OK?" said a voice. It was Carl, espresso in hand.

"No," she said, more despairingly than she'd intended.

"No panic. What's up?"

Marta sighed. "This," she said, pointing at her own scribbles. "It make no sense, and Charlotte need it by tomorrow lunch."

Carl squinted at the page, which contained a messy combination of English and Polish. "I can't read it. What does it say?"

"I have to find fifty to sixty presidents. Then I put each president on a page, and write about–" she checked her notes – "brand, campaign, dates, outcome and stats where I can get a hold on them."

Carl was looking at her as though she were mad. "Presidents?" he asked. "Are you sure she said that?"

Marta nodded. "Fifty to sixty presidents, she said."

"You are sure she didn't say 'precedents'?"

Marta thought for a moment. What was this word? "Perhaps."

Carl nodded. "I think it's more likely she meant precedents. You know? Examples of things that have happened before?"

Marta began to smile. Yes, this made more sense. It did seem odd that Charlotte had asked for a list of presidents.

"You know what, Marta, you may be 'in luck', as they say."

Marta watched as he sat down and started clicking his mouse.

"Excellente," he said, finally. "You are in luck!"

Marta got up from her chair and skipped round to his side of the desk. He was opening up a presentation.

"I did this for David two months ago, but he never looked at it," said Carl. "It is a set of brand and campaign precedents in the soft drinks market. Take a look."

Marta scrolled down the presentation with growing excitement. "Carl, this is exactly the thing I have to do! Can I use this? Are you sure?"

Carl shrugged. "Well, you probably shouldn't claim that you deed eat, but yes – I don't see why you can't use eat. Be nice to know that my efforts weren't entirely wasted."

Marta was beside herself with gratitude. "You can send me this?" she asked. "And of course, I will tell Charlotte that you did it," she added.

Carl smiled, crookedly. "Perhaps say that I *helped* with it. That way we both get some credit."

Marta nodded. "OK. Thanks!"

"Pret, or somewhere original?" asked Dom, pulling away from their embrace.

Marta glanced around, grabbing his hand. "Here," she said, turning them both in a quarter-circle and leading the way down a side street off High Holborn.

Dom was wearing a suit again. His crisp white shirt still had the creases from being in the packet. He looked almost like a grownup businessman, thought Marta, only a bit too cute.

"Where are you taking me?"

Marta smiled. "No idea. Let's explore."

They found a small café on Red Lion Street that was filled with workmen in hard hats and lawyers with briefcases.

"So, how is it?" asked Marta as they sat down.

"You first – how's yours?"

Marta pulled a face. "Variable," she said. "There are some nice people, some boring people, some nasty people and at least one dickhead. The work is fine, but only after the guy opposite has explained everything."

"Guy opposite?" said Dom, raising an eyebrow. "You haven't met a new one already, have you?"

Marta smiled, running a hand up Dom's thigh under the table. "Not like that," she replied. "Carl is nice. He's Italian. And he's got a funny face, like this." She pulled hers into a peculiar shape.

"Oh good." Dom leaned back as a skinny young waitress came over.

"Have you chosen?" she asked, in Polish. Marta smiled. It happened so often now – in shops, in bars, in stations – she no longer got excited. They gave their orders and thanked the girl in Polish.

"She's probably got a degree in nuclear physics," said Marta, cynically.

Dom tutted. "Don't make assumptions; she might enjoy working here."

Marta looked back at the girl, who was miserably reaching for pieces of cheese behind the counter. "Does she look as though she's enjoying it?" she asked. "Anyway, how about you? What's your new job like?"

Dom extracted a toothpick from the grubby plastic container and started idly cleaning his nails. "Well…" He winced as he poked the splint straight into his flesh. "It's harder than I'd imagined," he said.

"What d'you mean?"

"Well, bear in mind I've only ever worked in finance during my summers at uni and on a six month placement. The accounts I saw then were in perfect shape, and everything pretty-much ran itself."

"So what's the difference here?"

Dom frowned. "Well, the accounts are in a mess, and the previous guy was incompetent – that much is obvious just from looking at his filing system – but as well as that… oh, I don't know. I just get the feeling there's something weird about this company. They seem to do things in strange ways. I think it's going to take quite a while to get their accounts in order."

"But that's a challenge," Marta pointed out with a glint in her eye. "That's a good thing, isn't it? You wouldn't get that driving tube trains down tunnels."

Dom smiled. "No, yeah I guess you're right." The smile slowly turned into a misty, pensive expression. It was only when the food arrived that his smile returned.

"Aren't you supposed to be a financial assistant?" asked Marta, through a mouthful of tuna. "That sort of implies that you're assisting someone – not doing it on your own."

Dom nodded, waiting for the strands of stringy cheese to break off between his mouth and the panini. "Yeah, that's the theory. That's what I'm being paid to do. But the new 'financial controller' has yet to materialise, and I'm beginning to wonder whether he or she exists at all."

Marta chewed thoughtfully for a moment. "That is weird. Have you asked about it?"

"Yeah, and I've been given a different answer every time. One guy told me he was serving his notice period elsewhere, one said he was on holiday, and one guy just looked at me blankly. I tell you, it's odd."

Marta nodded. "Especially for a law firm. They do everything by the book."

Dom smiled. "Except their book-keeping."

They finished their sandwiches and drank their tea – the Polish way, with lemon, not milk. Then Marta looked up at the clock. Her legs were wrapped around Dom's under the table, and his hand was playing with the inside of her thigh. She didn't want to move.

"Back to it?" asked Dom, finally. He pulled a face as though he wasn't keen either.

Reluctantly, they rose to their feet, leaving a generous tip. What Marta really wanted to leave were the contact details for the Bright Sparks agency, but she knew that was a stupid idea. The girl might have other career aspirations – she might even have another job already. Perhaps she was a law student, or a ballerina, or an artist – maybe waitressing was just a way of earning extra cash.

"Meet again later this week?" asked Dom.

Marta allowed herself to be pulled close, her arms hugging his back. She could feel Dom's breath on her hair. God, if only they didn't have to go back to their offices. "Depends on work, but hopefully."

32

MARTA FOLLOWED HER COLLEAGUES through the wooden doorway, ducking beneath the low-hanging beam. The place looked funny enough from the outside with its black walls, little windows and colourful plants sticking out of the roof – but it was even stranger inside.

It took a few seconds for her eyes to adjust to the darkness. Ye Olde Cheshire Cheese was like an old stone dungeon – only warmer and slightly more homely. Weak rays of light trickled through the dirty windows on the street side and an orange glow emanated from the bar. It was a true English pub, thought Marta.

"This way! Follow me!" instructed David Lyle, the only person short enough not to have to bend over.

They trooped down some wooden stairs that reminded Marta of the ladder she'd had on her bunk bed as a kid. Some of her colleagues had to actually slide down the last few steps to avoid knocking themselves out on the ceiling.

"Here we are," announced David, clapping his hands gleefully at the sight of the Reserved signs on the tables. "Let's get the bar going!"

Marta looked around in awe. The room – if you could call it that – was no bigger than Holly's bedroom, yet crammed into it were a dozen small cast iron tables with miniature seats around the edges and even smaller foot-high stools, as though the bar staff had been expecting a group of school children. How on earth were all the employees of Stratisvision going to fit in here?

"What's everyone drinking? Beer? Wine? I'll get a mixture," said David. "In separate glasses – don't you worry," he added, looking at the nearest person, who happened to be Marta. She gave an obliging smile.

The director disappeared down some more steps as the room filled up with sweaty bodies. Marta looked around for someone to talk to.

"Bloody awful client," declared Charlotte to a group of senior-looking consultants Marta didn't recognise. She moved further into the throng.

"Paris Hilton has *so* had surgery," said Kim to a group of similarly shallow girls. Marta jostled her way to the edge of the group, hoping to make eye contact with one of them. "Apparently she's had her legs lengthened," said one girl. Marta joined in with the looks of disbelief. None of them noticed her. "They break your bones and put bits of plastic in before they heal," the girl went on. The circle remained closed. Marta sidled into the corner of the room.

"No point in trying to win another contract from them," moaned Joan. "They don't have the budget." Marta wondered whether she ever had anything positive to say.

Just as she was debating going over to talk to the office geek, Neil, she heard the boss' jovial tones once again. "Coming through!" he cried, brandishing above his head a large tray of drinks. He'd managed to spill almost half the contents on his way over.

"Ciao," said a voice right next to her ear. "Looks like I made perfect time!"

Marta smiled. Carl was standing beside her, watching the procession of bar staff follow in David's wake with more drinks and a bucket and mop.

It occurred to Marta that Carl was standing very close – closer than necessary, despite the cramped conditions. He had become quite familiar with her over the last few weeks, she realised with a sinking feeling. It was distinctly possible that the wonky-faced Italian fancied Marta.

"You want a drink? My round," he offered, winking. "What would you like?"

Marta opted for beer, feeling a mixture of dread and guilt descend upon her. She had to tell Carl about Dom, quickly.

"Na zdrowie," said Carl, returning with two pints. "I learned that today."

Marta smiled awkwardly, holding up her drink. "Na zdrowie. And who taught you that? Google, perhaps?"

Carl grinned. "Of course. My best friend."

There was a difficult pause. Marta was desperately trying to work out a way of weaving Dom's name into conversation.

"Bad idea, these drinks," said Carl, eventually.

"Why?"

Carl shrugged. "Look. It just gives the cliques a chance to grow stronger and isolates the loners even more." He nodded at the closely-packed colleagues. It was true. The 'cool' gang – Nik, Kat, Kim and the rest – were clustered in the middle sipping wine, looking beautiful, their heads close together as though they were bitching about people nearby. Neil was sitting alone on one of the tiny stools, making patterns in the condensation on his glass.

"I guess." Marta nodded. *My boyfriend thinks... My boyfriend always says...* no.

"David's idea, of course. He thinks it's good for team morale. He is wrong. He would do better to give everyone money for drinks and let them go spend it anywhere they like. Then they would thank him. We could go to a bar far away from this crowd, and actually enjoy the drinks."

Marta agreed, nervously. She couldn't tell whether Carl was implying *they* could go to a bar on their own or whether he was speaking hypothetically. She hoped the latter.

"Any minute now," he said, "he'll jump up onto one of those seats and start waving his arms about – I warn you."

Marta frowned, but even as she did so, a clearing was forming at the back of the group and people were starting to shuffle away from it.

"Ladies and gents! Good evening!" cried the director from his elevated position on one of the rickety stools. "Shuddup!" he added when everybody ignored him. Slowly, the hubbub died to a murmur.

"It's good to see so many of you down here this evening – good to see that the free drinks bribe still works." He paused to wait for the laughter, which never came. "Anyway, yes, so it's been a good month. A *very* good month. We've won lots of new business – some would say more than we can handle. And I know we've been working our little socks off as a result."

"*Some* people have," whispered Carl quietly. "Others have been playing golf."

Marta nodded, wishing he didn't have his mouth quite so close to her ear.

"And to that end, we've had a very profitable May," announced David, reaching down with his right arm and clicking his fingers. Someone perceptively passed him his pint. "We put over five hundred K in the bank this month – wham, bam, thank you mam – and it's looking like June will be another big month for Stratisvision."

The man took a large gulp of beer and held the glass down at his side, waiting impatiently for someone to take it.

"Now, for those of you thinking, 'bloody hell, when's the work gonna end?!'," he said, putting on a frighteningly high-pitched voice, "the answer is 'soon'. And by that, I don't mean we're gonna lose all our contracts – God forbid – I mean we're gonna make some hires."

Marta felt Carl nudge her in the ribs. Was David Lyle talking about hiring her?

"We're advertising for analysts and assistant analysts as we speak, and for those of you who don't know, we've already got a temp in to help the consultants – Marta? Where is Marta, our lovely Pole?"

Marta could feel every set of eyes in the room turn to her as she reluctantly lifted her hand.

"Hi," she said, smiling around at the faces.

"Whether or not there'll be Pole dancing later remains to be seen," said David, "as is always the way at these end-of-month drinks, I'm sure," he added, snorting at his own joke. A few sharp breaths were drawn around the room – the most notable by Charlotte, who stood in the corner, eyes fixed coldly on the speaker.

"Well, that's all I'm going to say," finished David, not showing any signs of embarrassment. "It's been a bumper month, so let's get bumper pissed!"

He hopped off his stool, landing almost on top of poor Neil.

"So," said Carl, raising an eyebrow. "You got the moment of fame."

Marta took a small step back. He was definitely flirting.

"There's always someone he picks on," explained Carl, moving forward to close the gap between them. "Usually a girl," he added.

Marta lifted her glass and drained it. She was drinking unusually quickly this evening. Carl noticed and rushed to catch up.

"Another?"

Marta nodded, watching as he barged keenly through the crowds to fetch the pints. She *had* to tell him about Dom.

He returned with two fresh beers and an over-zealous expression. "They're talking about you over there. I didn't know you lived in Kensington!"

Marta frowned. "I don't now – I used to. Who is talking about me?"

"The girls." He nodded to where Kat and her cronies were huddled, heads close, voices muted. "I live near there – Shepherd's Bush."

Marta frowned. Her geography of London was good enough to know that Shepherd's Bush was not very near Kensington – or at least, not near in terms of house prices. She was more concerned with the fact that Kat's gang seemed to be talking about where she had lived. How did they know about that? What were they saying?

Before Marta could probe any further, a rotund figure crept into her field of vision, promising to curtail any conversations about the office bitch's intelligence.

"Marta!" cried David. "There you are! I hope I didn't embarrass you just now."

Only yourself, thought Marta, smiling sweetly at the director as she noticed Carl slip away into the darkness. Wise move, she thought enviously.

"I've been hearing great things about you!" he said, peering into her face. "Great things."

Marta looked up, waiting for him to expand. Carl, she noticed, had been cornered by Neil and was reluctantly entering into a conversation – probably about Excel or trigonometry.

"You've been doing some excellent work, I hear," David went on. Marta wondered whether he really had heard anything at all, or whether he was just bullshitting. "For… for all sorts of people."

He was bullshitting. Marta had only worked for one person since she'd arrived, and that was Charlotte. It seemed unlikely that she would have taken the time to extol Marta's virtues to David Lyle – she barely allowed herself time to breathe.

"Good," said Marta. "It is very interesting work."

David beamed at her. "That's what I like to hear! An interested Pole. An interested, hard-working Pole!"

Marta managed to muster a smile, despite the fact that the director had started gyrating in front of her and was revealing a white band of flab around his waist every time he lifted his arms. "Bit of dancing, later…?" he muttered between breaths.

Thankfully, moments later he noticed that most of his beer had sloshed onto the floor (again), and bounded off to get a fresh one.

Marta turned round. Towering above her was Dean, the guy who had sat on her desk for her first few days.

"Hi," he said, smiling like Clark Kent. "So, how are you finding Stratisvision?"

He would be devastatingly handsome, thought Marta, if he just loosened up a bit.

"Good, thank you. Very interesting work," she parroted, remembering what Carl had told her on her first day. Dean was young, but very senior – possibly even a director, she thought, not able to recall his exact title.

"That's good to hear," he said, deadpan. *Chill out,* Marta wanted to scream. She wondered whether she was being vetted as a potential 'new hire'. It was possible. Surely the decision-making would not be left to David Lyle?

The conversation was sputtering to a halt – possibly because Marta wasn't thinking of enough insightful observations, but frankly she didn't have the energy. It was hard work, this 'small talk'. After a while, you just ran out of things to say – earlier with some than with others. That was something she'd noticed about English people. Too many of them took life too seriously. So intent on being a 'winner' in life – because they did seem convinced that life was one long competition, some of them – they forgot how to actually live it. Dean had probably never broken a rule in all his thirty-something years.

It became clear that Dean's attention was divided between their assessment of the B2B utility sector's branding achievements and something going on elsewhere in the room.

"Quite, quite," he said, nodding vaguely. "A highly competitive market. Will you excuse me – I must catch Charlotte before she leaves."

With a twitch of his lips that was probably Dean's idea of a smile, he rushed off, ducking as he swung up the stairs in pursuit of the disappearing bouffant.

Marta took a swig of beer, looking around the room. She wasn't sure if she wanted to find Carl or not. Telling him about Dom was proving harder than expected, but then… she didn't have anyone else to talk to.

A waitress was touring the crowded room with a tray of what looked like fried worms. Marta watched as David Lyle took a handful and tipped his head back, throwing the things down his throat. She ventured towards the waitress, mainly for something to do.

They weren't fried worms, it transpired. Marta took a tentative bite, and decided that it was… batter. Battered batter. She subtly dropped her handful on the floor and washed out her mouth with beer, stopping by a group of consultants that included Joan the manic depressive.

Nobody noticed her. Marta shifted sideways and saw Carl, perched next to Neil on a stool, desperately trying to catch her attention with a 'rescue me' look. Marta deliberately misread the signal and waved back cheerily, moving out of sight. She raised the glass to her lips and then stopped herself. She was feeling quite woozy. This was not the occasion for getting drunk – no matter what David might say.

The toilets were tucked away behind the stairs, amidst more low-hanging beams and archways. Of course, there was a queue. There was always a queue. English girls seemed to take twice as long to pee as Polish girls. Marta pulled out her phone, on the offchance that Dom had replied. She had two unread messages – one Polish, one English.

Hi sexy, of course I do.
Can't do 2moro, but
Sun? Not sure I can
wait 2 whole days tho…
Dxx

Hi gorgeous. We still
haven't gone for that
dinner. Let me know
when & where – I'll
take u anywhere. J

Marta stared at the handset. She couldn't quite believe what she was reading. Jack was still going on about that dinner they were never going to have. Didn't he understand rejection? Marta read it one last time and pressed delete. Maybe he'd never been turned down, she thought. That was possible. He was very attractive, and charming. And if he hadn't completely screwed everything up as he had done, he would seem like a really decent guy. Well… maybe.

Marta re-opened the message from Dom. Her heart still jumped every time she saw Dxx. She wanted to be with him now. She wanted to see that cute smile, watch his lovely brown eyes dance around as he talked… Oh, if only she didn't have to stay in this strange English pub with these hideous people. If only this wasn't her biggest chance yet to secure herself a proper job in England.

"You gonna go?" asked a girl, poking her in the back. Marta practically fell into the cubicle.

When she emerged, a familiar figure was standing in her way, leaning into the mirror above the sink. Marta had eyed up the knee-high suede boots and tight jeans on the way into work that morning.

"Excuse me," said Marta. "Can I wash…"

"Sorry," Kat replied, flicking her white-blonde mane and smiling apologetically. The smile quickly vanished. "Oh. Hi Marta."

"Hi! How are you?" Maybe it was the alcohol, but Marta felt more determined than ever to hold a conversation with the girl. Apart from anything else, she wanted to know what they'd been saying about her earlier.

"Good, thanks," she said flatly, perfecting her lashes with a finger. "A bit drunk."

Marta nodded, shaking the water off her hands and deliberately timing her exit to coincide with Kat's. *A bit drunk.* Three words – that was a start.

"Me too! I think it is David's plan," said Marta, following her closely through the toilets and back into the pub.

"That'd be right," muttered Kat, dipping her head as she re-entered the Stratisvision reserved area. Marta darted round to her side. She was going to get into a conversation with these girls if it killed her.

"I have never… shagged in a taxi," said one girl, looking around at the faces and lingering pointedly on Kat's.

Kat's mouth turned up on one side in a half-smile. "Oh, very good," she said sulkily. Hand me my wine."

Marta watched as the yellow liquid disappeared down Kat's throat. There was a murmur of appreciation as she drained the last drop and held out her empty glass to the group. Someone took it and headed off to the drinks table for a refill.

"We're playing 'I have never'?" Kat explained to Marta.

Marta nodded. She remembered Tash and the others sitting round that polished oak table, cackling as they caught each other out in this game.

"Girls, you all know Marta, don't you?" Kat asked the group, as though referring to herpes.

There were nods and fake smiles from all the girls. Marta smiled back, wondering how long it took these girls to put their faces on in the mornings – they looked as though they'd been airbrushed on.

"OK, your go," said Kat. Everyone looked at Marta.

"I have never…" *understood why English girls have to play silly games to have fun instead of just talking and joking like everyone else,* Marta considered. "Kissed a girl – on lips," she said finally.

A surprising number of girls in the group raised their glasses.

"I'm bored with this game?" declared Kat. She glanced at Marta as though it were she who had dampened the excitement. Perhaps girls always kissed on the lips in this country. Those in mid-chug lowered their glasses, clearly relieved.

None of the girls had actually been enjoying the game, observed Marta – except Kat, perhaps, with her vindictive streak. Remarkably, though, they probably would have continued to play it for as long as their leader dictated. They really didn't seem to have minds of their own, she marvelled. Marta wondered what they would do if Kat was to leave the company. Would they find their way into the office each morning? Hmm. Life without Kat, mused Marta. It would certainly make Stratisvision a more enjoyable place to work.

It came as something of a surprise when the girl on Marta's right suddenly turned to her with a smile.

"So, how's your first week been?" she asked. Marta vaguely recognised her as one of the graphics girls from the far side of the office. She was pretty in a feline way, with upward-slanting eyes and jet-black hair that flowed like liquid down her back.

"OK," replied Marta, wary of the fact that the CEO's niece was standing beside her.

"You're working for Charlotte, aren't you?" asked the girl.

Marta nodded, pulling a face that could have meant anything. She guessed that Charlotte probably wasn't a big hit with the 'cool' gang.

"Bad luck, eh. How's it going?"

Marta shrugged. "She is a demanding woman," she said, not quite ready to open up.

"That's one way of putting it. Workaholic loony is another. Seriously, if she hasn't bitten your ear off in a violent rage yet then you must be doing something right."

Marta smiled. Perhaps this girl was nice after all. Perhaps they were all nice, in fact – they just got nasty when removed from their little clique. Or maybe they were all just drunk.

"I think she liked the work I did," Marta told her. "But I had some help," she confessed, suddenly wanting to tell someone.

"Who from?"

"Carl."

"Oh yeah?" asked the girl, raising an eyebrow. "The Italian stallion's been helping you out, has he?"

Marta rushed to explain. Clearly rumours were already flying round the office about them. "He just give me a presentation he did," she said. "Then I give it to Charlotte, and try to say that it is Carl's work, but she never listen. She just take it and think that I did it."

"Huh." The girl looked at Marta, her cat-like eyes squinting hard. Suddenly Marta regretted confiding in her. "So you took credit for Carl's work, did you?" she asked.

Marta opened her mouth to explain, but the girl's face said it all.

"Looks like you *have* learnt something in your first week," she said, smiling coldly – or conspiringly – Marta couldn't tell. "Well done."

Marta had one last go at explaining, but she found herself talking to the girl's slick, black hair. The circle had closed. Marta was on her own again.

33

DOM WASN'T AT HOME. Marta peeled back the soggy mattress and squinted into the front room, but she already knew he wasn't there. A dark-skinned foot stuck out from beneath a pile of bedding on one of the sofas – maybe a Nigerian foot, or Croatian or Israeli – but it wasn't Dom's. His housemates spent Sunday mornings in a semi-comatose state on their living room floor, but not Dom.

There was only one place he could be. Marta let the mattress spring back to the window and let herself out through the rusty gate. She headed off, hoping she could remember the shortcut to the delikatesy that he'd shown her a couple of weeks before.

It was a warm morning, the first one all year that actually felt like summer – not that winter had felt particularly wintry; the temperatures had barely dipped below zero and the snow had lasted about ten minutes. Marta slowed down, enjoying the heat of the sun on her back and the twittering of birds on the telegraph wires. Even North Acton, crumbling and graffitied though it was, looked nice this morning. Well – sort of. Marta stepped over a puddle of dried vomit on the pavement. Nothing could dampen her mood today.

All the parts of her life were finally slotting into place. She had a job – admittedly only a short-term one, but that would change in the next few days, she'd make sure of it. She had friends and a place to stay – again, only a temporary measure but she'd soon be able to pay her way – and she had Dom. Perhaps that was why she felt so happy this morning.

Marta thought back to that miserable recruitment fair back in January. Even then, as he'd handed her that misspelt leaflet, grinning that sheepish grin of his, she'd felt the spark between them. Then when they'd collided in Barry's office on her first day, she'd felt it again. Standing at junctions trying to thrust flyers into reluctant hands, there had only been one thing that had brought some excitement to her day: the prospect of lunch or coffee with Dom.

It was madness, really. Not Marta's style at all. She didn't go soft like some of her friends did when it came to men. She never had done. She'd had plenty of relationships back in Poland – most of them light-hearted flings, but a couple more serious. She and Piotr had lasted nearly three years. Tall, sporty and extremely good-looking, Piotr had also been sensitive – probably more aware of Marta's needs than she was herself. He was a qualified doctor, too, with a good job in Wrocław. To everybody in Marta's life – Marta's mother's included – Piotr could do no wrong. He was 'the one'.

Except that Marta didn't need 'a one'. She had never allowed herself to rely on others. She was strong. Independent. She had split up with Piotr as soon as she'd made up her mind to come to England, and, although she'd never told anyone this – not even Anka, who had helped her to make the decision – the break-up hadn't really hurt her. The only pain was caused by the awful knowledge that Piotr was beside himself over the split. For him, it was the worst thing that could have happened, and that in itself had been suffering enough for Marta. But that was all.

She didn't need anyone else. Marta had come to this conclusion before she'd left Poland. She was strong enough on her own. But now she'd met Dom... Well, he was different. But then again... oh dear. The rational and emotional parts of Marta's brain were thrashing against one other. It wasn't that she needed him – she just wanted him. The whole bloody time.

The red and white bunting above the Polskie Delikatesy fluttered into view as she rounded the corner and Marta found her step quickening. She could just about make out the movement of people inside, although it was difficult to see anything clearly because of the sun's reflection on the glass.

Marta's attention was diverted for a moment to a stunning young blonde strutting along the pavement up ahead. Marta wasn't the only one watching the girl's boobs bounce up and down in the flimsy top that revealed a glimpse of flesh above the microscopic skirt. A couple of lads on BMX bikes were wheeling their way towards her and an old man was pretending to adjust his cap across the road. If it hadn't been for the fact that they were in Acton, and the fact that the girl was carrying a tatty brown bag that was at odds with the rest of her flawless appearance, Marta would have assumed her to be a prostitute.

The girl hesitated outside the delikatesy, looking up at its colourful name and then down at something in her hand. Marta wondered whether she was in fact a prostitute, meeting a client on a very low-grade job. Maybe she was Polish, thought Marta sadly, thinking of those cards Dom told her about on the 'Wailing Wall'. After one more glance at the name, the girl cautiously pushed open the café door. Marta watched as she slipped inside, her silver high heels catching the light as she climbed the small step. She was too refined to be a hooker, wasn't she? Marta walked on. Maybe she'd find out when she got there. Maybe she should stop being so nosy. Mama had always said she asked too many questions.

It was only as Marta skipped across the road that she looked up again at the delikatesy. What she saw made her stop, right there, in the middle of Victoria Road. A horrible, sickly feeling engulfed her. She didn't want to believe what her eyes were seeing. *Dom was kissing the girl.*

Marta moved, zombie-like, to the edge of the road, vaguely aware of the risk of being hit by a car. She couldn't take her eyes off the scene in the café. Dom had got up from his seat by the window – the seat he'd been sitting in two weeks previously when he and Marta had shared jabłecznik before their first kiss – and was standing, embracing the girl.

It was no ordinary greeting. Marta stared, horrified but transfixed as her world fell apart before her. Their faces were so close – they were kissing, pulling away to exchange words and smiles, then kissing again, arms all over each other. Marta moved into the doorway of the next door building, half realising that she might be spotted but not really knowing whether this would be a good or a bad thing. She hadn't thought anything through yet. All she knew was that Dom was kissing another girl.

Finally, the pair sat down – the blonde taking Marta's seat from before. She ran a hand through Dom's hair affectionately. Dom leaned forwards, grinning, and touched her face in some way – Marta couldn't see how. The waitress came over and Dom flirted a little, the way he had done before, then restored his full attention to the blonde.

Marta felt physically sick. The questions were tumbling around in her head, but there were no answers yet – only a huge, hideous realisation screaming out at her: Dom was a cheat.

With a final glance at the giggling couple, Marta turned her back. Unseeing, she picked a route back to North Acton that didn't involve walking past the café window. She hadn't noticed before, but her eyes had been filling up with tears. Now her cheeks were sopping wet and she could barely see a thing. Marta didn't care. She didn't want to see. Right now, she didn't care if she walked out in front of a London bus. Any physical pain would be better than this.

How could he? Who was she? Were there others? Was Marta just one of many in Dom's string of 'special' girls? Did she mean anything to him at all? Were they all just conquests? Was he really like that? How long did he think this could last? How could she have made such a huge, *huge* mistake about someone's personality?

The questions kept coming, but still no answers. Horrific scenes kept running through her imagination: Dom saying goodbye to Marta after their first kiss and going to meet the blonde. Dom sleeping with the blonde in the same bed, in the same way that he had done with Marta – maybe only hours later. Dom meeting Marta for coffee then whizzing off on his scooter to meet the next girl. Dom putting crumbs of ciasto into the blonde's beautiful mouth, then kissing her... Marta tortured herself with the images.

By the time she reached the tube station, a small amount of reason had crept into Marta's thinking. She had no idea who the girl was, or whether there were others like her, or whether Dom really felt anything for any of them. She didn't know and didn't care. At least, that's what she was telling herself. Her biggest mistake, she realised, was to let Dom into her life – to spend time with him, to open up to him, to open her fucking *legs* to him. That had been her mistake. She had broken her own rules and gone soft on a guy.

This was why Marta never got too involved, she thought, wiping a bare arm across one eye and then the other. Her vision cleared a little and a watery impression of the eastbound tube platform came into view. The deeper you got, the further you had to swim to the surface when it all fell apart. Marta took a deep, shaky breath and slowly exhaled, feeling the emotions settle inside her.

The train rattled to a halt on the platform and Marta stepped inside. She was strong, independent. She didn't need Dominik. She'd get by without him. In fact, she was already doing fine on her own.

34

"DOES THAT SOUND OK, HUN?" asked Kat, smiling down at her through perfectly curled lashes.

Marta nodded, although it sounded anything but OK. It sounded very confusing. "Just a question," she said, choosing her words carefully so as not to appear stupid. "Where are these informations, exactly? Do I find them on the internet?"

Kat pouted at herself in the mirrored office window. She no longer appeared to be listening. "Yeah, and the places I told you about? Datamonitor, Keynote, Mintel, Forrester... you know?"

Marta nodded and ducked as the blonde ponytail flicked round in her face. The Barbie-like figure strutted off towards the cluster of desks that the cool gang had chosen to occupy today. Marta sighed and leant back in her chair, lifting her notepad with little enthusiasm. *Datamonitor, Keynote, Mintel, Forrester...* no, she didn't know. What were these things? How could she find out without exposing her ignorance – and without asking Carl? Could she really be bothered?

She stayed there, slumped in her seat, staring at the jumble of words in front of her. She wasn't thinking about the words. She wasn't thinking about the task Kat had set her, or the difficulties of working for a stuck-up bitch who had something against you and who seemed determined to see you fail despite calling you 'hun'. She wasn't even thinking about the fact that Charlotte had set her a deadline of three p.m. today for something else – an equally demanding and mystifying task. She was thinking about Dom.

All morning, she'd been trying to put him out of her mind. She had made a concerted effort, despite the lack of sleep, despite the freshness of yesterday's revelation, to focus on one thing: the presentation. She was doing her best to think about brand synergies and partnerships in the carbonated soft drinks market, but her brain kept making the wrong connections. PopsCo, retailers who sold cold drinks, cafés, that café in Acton, that horrible scene with the blonde… Every time, she would stop herself, put her brain back on track, and find exactly the same thing happening again.

She really didn't have time to daydream. What with Charlotte's presentation and now Kat's cryptic demands, she had an almost impossible task ahead of her. She should have felt proud that so many people were giving her work, and eager to get it all done. She was becoming a valued member of the team, an asset. It was exactly what she had been striving for. But somehow, she didn't feel valued. She just felt miserable.

It was silly, she knew. They hadn't even been 'together' for more than a couple of weeks. Nothing changed in that time, did it? She was still the same independent girl she had always been. Dom was still just a guy she'd met – someone she could forget just as easily. She had a job, and that was still her priority. She had a life to lead, and Dom had his. They were no longer linked. It was just a question of putting that period behind her – of getting on with the future.

Except it wasn't that easy. Oh, God, if *only* things hadn't changed in the last few weeks. If only she could get on with her life as it had been before Dom stepped into it. If only she could clear him and all his memories from her mind, erasing the time when he'd handed her that leaflet, the time when they'd collided in Barry's office, the time he'd cooked her soup, the time he'd kissed her, held her close, stroked her hair… And it didn't help that he was still texting her. Marta pulled her phone towards her again, tears building up behind her eyes.

Hey sexy, fancy lunch
2day? I have 2tell u
something. Where were
u yest? Missed u! Dxx

Talk about mixed messages. *Hey sexy, I have to dump you.* Nice. Unless, of course, he wasn't going to tell her about the blonde. Perhaps he thought he could keep his dirty little secret, and he was planning to tell her something else. *Missed u?* Yeah right. That was exactly how it had looked yesterday as he'd wrapped his arms around that little bimbo's waist. Marta sent the phone skidding across the desk. She wouldn't be meeting any lying cheats for lunch today.

It was an hour later and the presentation had barely changed. Marta stared at the words in front of her. Teen Preferences for Unorthodox CSD Brands. Apart from the title, the slide was blank. Marta was thinking about how Dom might have looked as a teenager. Similar to how he did now, she thought: scruffy, cute, always smiling. Marta cursed silently and forced herself to consider the slide's content. *Damn him*, she thought, typing the first bullet-point on the slide. He was still messing things up for her even now he was out of her life.

"What's that?" asked Kat, appearing from nowhere and frowning at Marta's screen.

"Oh, is something for Charlotte," Marta explained, expecting an outburst regarding her prioritisation.

"Oh, right," Kat said simply. She leaned closer, pushing her pert bottom into the gangway just as Dean walked past.

"It's for PopsCo," Marta explained needlessly. There was a PopsCo logo on every page.

"Right," Kat nodded, straightening up and checking her reflection in the window. "You know, you don't need to write proper sentences when you do presentations like that? Note-form will do. I've worked for Charlotte a lot – that's what she likes. It's the content she wants – not the sentences? When d'you think you'll be able to start on my work, by the way?"

Marta stared for a second, gobsmacked. Kat was *being nice*. "Er, after three o'clock. I will finish Charlotte's before then."

Kat nodded, straightened her silky top and flounced off.

By some miracle – or maybe as a consequence of the hint that Kat had given her – Marta *did* finish Charlotte's work before three o'clock. At two forty-five, she flicked through the slides one last time, closed the file and pressed Send. The presentation was rough, but crammed with content. Marta felt pleased with herself.

Even though her office was at least four blocks from Dom's and there was no way he'd be eating his lunch at three o'clock, Marta couldn't bear to risk running into him. She dashed into the nearest shop and grabbed the cheapest roll she could find, almost knocking over the guy in the flowery shirt who was joking with someone just inside the door. Looking back, she realised with dismay that the holidaymaker was in fact her boss. Luckily David Lyle was busy high-fiving the café owner.

Kat's task was proving harder than she had imagined. After nearly an hour, all Marta had managed to do was ascertain that the strange names in her notebook – Mintel, Keynote and so on – were research agencies, and according to Google, they charged up to $5,000 per report. In some cases, parts of the reports were available to view online, but always the boring parts, or the parts with no data. Surely Kat hadn't intended for Marta to buy any reports like this? And if she had, why hadn't she mentioned it?

Marta stared at the screen, quietly drumming her nails on the desk. She had two options. One, ask Carl. Two, ask Kat. Option one was the easiest, but Marta was desperately trying to avoid the onset of more rumours about the 'Italian Stallion' and her. Besides, he had already done her a huge favour; she didn't want to be any more indebted to him. Option two was unappealing as it involved entering the 'cool zone' and exposing her vulnerability to everyone within earshot. After a few seconds' deliberation, Marta rose from her seat.

They were laughing at something as Marta approached. Kim and Nik were making comments and provoking the others to turn round in their seats, upon which they would collapse in fits of giggles. Kat was trying to keep a straight face but failed every time her eyes met anyone else's. As Marta got closer, she realised what it was: they were laughing at her.

Marta continued towards them, determined not to let it show that she'd noticed or cared. One of the girls leaned sideways and whispered something to Nik, who looked down at Marta's shoes and expelled a snort of laughter. There were more suppressed giggles and fleeting glances in her direction.

Marta walked on, eyes straight ahead. She should have anticipated it, really. She knew that she didn't dress well enough for this place. She hadn't bought any clothes since arriving in England, apart from a belt to replace the one that had broken around her suitcase – and that had been a cheap, thin belt, not the fashionable type that these girls wore around their hip-slung jeans. And her old brown shoes – well, they were pretty fashionless even by Polish standards.

"Hi," she said, trying to sound confident despite the eruptions of giggles around the table.

"How are you getting on, hun?" asked Kat, patronisingly. There were a couple more snorts of laughter.

"I need some help," Marta said quietly.

"You need some help?" repeated Kat, loud enough for most of the office to hear. "What d'you mean?"

Marta explained her predicament regarding the reports and Kat started nodding understandingly.

"OK," said Kat, glancing quickly at the other girls and catching a raised eyebrow from Kim as though they were sharing a private joke. "Here's what you need to do." She exchanged looks with another girl across the table. "You need to ask our research person for help. She's that woman in the spare office at the end?" Kat pointed towards the glass-walled office next to David Lyle's. Inside was the woman with the orange tan whom Marta had seen flitting about the office all day. She was wearing a bizarre green cardigan that went all the way down to the ground and a hair clip like a tiara.

"Research person?" she repeated, confused as to why Kat hadn't mentioned this before.

"Yup, that's her. Just go in and tell her what you want."

Marta nodded. It all seemed too easy. "So I just... go ask her for all the informations?"

Kim looked up. "Make sure you're clear about what you want," she advised. "You've got to be firm or she'll get it wrong."

Marta frowned. They were suddenly being all nice again. The earlier joke about her clothes appeared to have been forgotten, and the girls were all studiously staring at their screens again.

"OK," said Marta. "Thanks." She consulted her notes quickly to remind herself of exactly what she required, and headed off to meet the research woman.

Her gentle knock was ignored. Marta knocked again and walked in.

"Excuse me, but I need you to get some informations," she said. The woman barely moved. Perhaps she was slightly deaf, thought Marta.

Suddenly, an overly-tanned face was staring at Marta, blinking. "I'm sorry? What?"

"I need some information," corrected Marta, hoping her grammatical mistake had not been picked up on. "Some research, please."

The woman was staring at her as though she were asking for a frogspawn cocktail. "Have we met?"

Marta took an apologetic step towards her, holding out her hand. "No, sorry. Marta."

"Patricia," said the woman, still frowning. "And what exactly did you say you wanted?"

Marta froze. Something had just clicked in her mind. *Patricia*. She recognised that name. Then she realised. This was not a research person who spent her time fetching reports by Keynote and Datamonitor. This was Patricia Catermol, Stratisvision CEO.

"I just... um, I think... I just wanted to introduce myself," Marta mumbled unconvincingly. Then, with more confidence, "And to say that I am very much enjoying working here. Nice to meet you."

Patricia was still frowning, but no longer incredulously – just curiously. "OK, well, nice to meet you, Martha."

"Marta," she corrected, switching on a smile and leaving the room.

Her heart was still pumping madly as she sat on the flipped-down toilet seat and stared at the ends of her scuffed brown shoes. What an ordeal. What a cruel, unnecessary ordeal. She had pulled it off, thanks to some quick thinking and a bit of luck, but only just. It was unbelievable that anyone would be vindictive enough to play a trick like that – to someone who had done them no harm, too. What was up with those girls? They really didn't seem to like her.

Marta went the long way back to her desk, avoiding the inevitable ridicule from Kat and the gang. There was only one way of getting this work done – and she *was* going to get it done, even though she was full of loathing for the girl who had asked for it. She'd have to ask Carl.

"Have you looked on the V-drive?" he asked, looking at her as though it were the most obvious thing in the world. "She did... tell you about the V-drive, didn't she?"

Marta frowned. V-drive?

Carl rolled his eyes and indicated for her to look over his

shoulder. "See? Here – all the reports are filed by agency name, alphabetically. We subscribe to most – Datamonitor, Euromonitor, Findnote, Geobrand…"

Marta stared, nodding grimly at the evidence before her. They were determined to make a failure of her.

"Thanks Carl," she said, regretting her earlier coldness when he'd wished her good morning.

"No problemo," he said. "The V-drive," he added, looking up at her and making a gesture with his fingers and tongue that she hoped was not supposed to be seductive. "Always remember the V-drive."

Marta nodded awkwardly and hastened away. Shit. He was going all creepy on her. She had to get him to back off – but carefully, because she needed him. Oh God. Why was everything so complicated?

Her phone was ringing when she approached her desk.

"Hello?" she gabbled, just in time.

"Cześć!"

Oh no. She had finally managed to banish him from her mind, and now he was here, in her ear, chirpy as ever. A weird mixture of emotions ran through Marta's mind. Was it possible to hate someone and desperately want them at the same time?

"Listen, Dom–"

"Can you talk? I've got to tell you something, Marta."

Marta started to rise from her seat. She didn't want her colleagues to hear her being dumped. As she did so, she sensed a presence behind her. She turned. Her face fell.

"I can't talk," she said, hoping Charlotte didn't understand Polish. She was blocking Marta's way, arms crossed, nostrils flaring.

"But Marta, I've got to–"

"I've gotta go," she said, cutting him off.

Charlotte was looking at her with an expression Marta had never seen before. Her face was one big snarl. "I got your presentation," she said, coldly.

Marta just nodded. Several people on neighbouring desks were pricking up their ears.

"Now Marta, I know English isn't your first language, but I'm afraid this just *won't do!*" She slammed down a print-off of Marta's work. "It's like an analyst's subconscious ramblings. It's thoughts… notes! The slides are barely intelligible – let alone sufficient for us to show to the Head of Marketing at PopsCo. How are we supposed to convince them with this?" She rifled through the pages and stopped at one of the later ones. "'Underground/niche brands popular when not deliberate, e.g. teens.' What on earth is that supposed to mean? It's just... gobbledegook!"

"I was told–"

"I'm afraid you need to buck up your ideas, Marta," said Charlotte sternly. Marta noticed David pop his head out from inside his fishbowl office to see what the noise was about. "We don't make exceptions for nationality here."

Marta sank back into her chair. She felt despondent and a little embarrassed, but most of all, she felt incensed. Clearly Charlotte did not like her presentations in note form after all. Kat had tricked her again. Was there no limit to how low that girl would stoop? Angrily, Marta opened up a browser and logged onto hotmail. She was in no mood to complete the assignment for the heartless blonde bitch – not now. Later, for sure. She wasn't going to fall into yet another trap by failing to do her work, but right now, she wasn't in the mood. She needed to calm down.

Hi Marta!

We have finally connected to this internet you've been telling us all about! See – I have my own email address. I'm rather slow at typing so I won't write much but your sister is getting very quick so she'll be in touch soon I'm sure.

We are all well here. I hope you're still enjoying your job and eating enough vegetables.

All our love,

Mama x

PS What did you buy Anka for her birthday? We are dying to know!

Marta closed her eyes and buried her head in her hands. She couldn't believe she'd forgotten. Yesterday was the second of May. Her best friend's birthday.

35

"AND THEN I FORGET ANKA'S BIRTHDAY!" finished Marta, letting her head fall forwards onto the kitchen table.

Tina leaned over and extracted two cans from the fridge. "Who's Anka?"

Marta shook her head at the beer that was sliding towards her. "My best friend, in Łomianki. Her birthday was yesterday. I never miss it, ever, in my life since I was five!"

Tina pulled a face as though she couldn't see what all the fuss was about, pushing the can back towards Marta's head.

Marta sighed, ignoring it. "God, I messed everything up."

Tina frowned. "No you didn't. From what you've told me, it's other people who've messed things up for you." She cracked open both cans and took a huge swig. "Apart from the birthday thing, which was your fuck-up."

Marta rolled her head sideways to face Tina. "Thanks."

She could feel Tina's jet black eyes on her, frowning. Marta didn't care what she thought. Too many shitty things had happened today for Marta to care about anything. At some point, she knew, she'd have to start trying to rectify it all – call Anka, send something over, make a last-ditch attempt to impress her colleagues at Stratisvision, speak to Dom for the very last time… but for now, she just felt like wallowing in her own self-pity.

"Why do they hate me?"

"Who? The girls in your office?"

"Yes! I did nothing to them – nothing! But they hate me."

Tina sighed and met her eye. "D'you know the word 'prejudice'?"

Marta nodded. At school she had watched a film called Pride and Prejudice in English lessons. She remembered the puffy skirts and men in cravats. Elizabeth had been *prejudiced* against Mr Darcy because he had seemed like a snob. Marta wondered how this related to her.

"They don't like you because you're different."

Marta shrugged, still slumped over the table. "Everybody is different."

"Well, some people don't like that." Tina kicked her gently. "You should count yourself lucky – at least people only start discriminating once you've opened your mouth. They judge me as soon as I walk through the door."

Marta looked up, briefly emerging from her sulk to consider what her flatmate was saying. To her, Tina was a bossy, smart, fun-loving girl. Marta had never imagined that anyone would see her differently. But they did – of course they did. For the first time, Marta wondered what it would be like to be Tina. In some people's eyes, she wasn't a bossy, smart, fun-loving girl. She was a black girl – just as Marta was a Polish girl. Maybe Tina was right about Kat and that lot. Maybe they were *prejudiced*.

"Y'know what?" said Tina, eventually. "You need a night out. You need to forget about what's-his-face and those pathetic little bitches from work. Come on, let's—"

"I don't want a night out," Marta protested, pushing the beer away from her once and for all and collapsing again. "Am not in the mood."

A night out with Tina really was the last thing she wanted. The world seemed gloomy and dark. Everything was awful. The idea of sharing her evening with people who saw the world as rosy and full of promise… well, it didn't appeal. She didn't want to don a false smile and drink pints with rich, English boys. She wanted to dwell on the crapness of now.

"Shut up and stop feeling sorry for yourself," said Tina, ripping open the beer and pushing it so forcefully towards Marta that she had to sit up to avoid getting covered in froth. "Now drink!"

Marta looked at her flatmate. She was back in hockey captain mode. Drinking the beer was not an option; it was a requirement. Obediently, Marta took a small slurp.

"Now, you can stop worrying about your friend. I'll get something couriered to her from work tomorrow morning – it'll reach her by noon. What's she like? Does she like clothes? Sport? Fashion? Films? Beastiality—"

"Fashion," Marta interrupted, reluctantly engaging in the conversation. "She loves English fashion – magazines, clothes… these sort of things."

"Well that's easy then. My desk secretary has shit-loads of magazines that she doesn't read, and I can use up some of the Accessorize vouchers I've had for yonks and never planned to spend. Sorted. Now, let's go and change."

"Tina…" Marta moaned, pleading with tired eyes.

"Stop whinging. I've felt like you do before, and I know the cure." She smiled. "It's a good shag."

Marta looked at her, horrified.

"And failing that," Tina added, "it's a good night out on the piss. Oh, in fact…" Her eyes lit up. "Brilliant. Some of the lads are out tonight celebrating a massive trade that went our way. I nearly joined them but then I realised that Shanksy, the guy who – oh never mind. It's a good group. And, oh my God, I just realised. Bufty! You are SO gonna love Bufty – I can just tell!"

"What is Bufty?" asked Marta, not the least bit convinced about going out with Tina and 'the lads'.

"*Who* is Bufty. He's the most incredibly fit, sweet, intelligent, good-looking guy on the planet. He trades derivatives on the next desk next to me. You'll love him. Now come on!"

Marta found herself being hoisted upwards, her arm above her head. For a couple of seconds, she was dangling from Tina's grasp and then she was up, being dragged towards the stairs by her skinny flatmate.

Against her will, Marta found herself knocking back the rest of the can of lager as Tina held her hostage in her walk-in wardrobe, picking out ridiculous things for them to wear.

"Nothing too sexy," she muttered, holding a black cocktail dress up to Marta's shoulders. "Most people will've come straight from work. Hmm. How about these? Ooh, perfect."

The girls stepped out of the taxi beneath a vast building made of concrete and glass, both dressed in tight, pinstriped trousers and tops that surely could never be worn in an office. Marta was doubtful about this 'city chic' look that Tina insisted they go for, but she'd had little say in the red push-up bodice thing from which her breasts were trying to escape.

"We'll have to walk from here," Tina explained. "Cabs are only free to and from the office."

Marta nodded, wondering how Tina would justify a journey to the office at half past eight at night. The walk was not a long one. Jamies was a slick-looking bar surrounded by a sea of dark-suited bodies. It was clearly the JC Morley local. There must have been a hundred people standing outside – nearly all of them men. No wonder Tina loved her job.

"They'll be inside," announced Tina, walking quickly but saucily towards the entrance. Heads were turning. Marta was finding it difficult to avoid locking eyes with the pink-shirted guys as she followed her friend through the throng of beer drinkers.

"There they are!"

Elbows out, they made their way through the bar. There was something odd about the clientele, thought Marta, looking around. Maybe it was the lighting, but… no, it wasn't. It was simply that they were all extremely attractive. Aside from the odd pint-swilling fifty year old, every one of the revellers was aged between twenty and thirty-five, and almost without exception, they were incredibly good-looking. The men, who outnumbered the women by about ten to one, were chiselled, tanned and well-built – if sometimes a little stocky. The women were slim, elegant and perfectly proportioned.

"Hey – look who's here!" cried a large, bear-like man, emerging from a group of young men. "Where did you come from?"

Tina didn't seem to mind or even notice the quick grope of her backside as the man guided her into the thick of the crowd. She simply grabbed Marta's arm and, keeping her close, yelled, "Guys, this is Marta! She's my flatmate and she's come along to get pissed with us!"

There was a roar of general approval followed by an abrupt stampede towards the girls.

"Champagne?"

"Cocktail?"

"What're you drinkin'? I'll get it."

Marta wasn't sure what she'd ended up asking for but she allowed the blond, shiny-faced youngster to go and fetch it.

"That's Dish," explained the bear-like man. "He's the one that did the big trade today, so drinks're on him."

Marta nodded, trying to relax as she lost herself in sweaty suits. She was losing Tina in the crowd.

In another situation, it might have felt good being plied with expensive alcohol by a selection of suave, single young men. They were lovely to look at, and seemed very keen to engage in conversation. But as she'd told Tina before, she just wasn't in the mood.

"Champagne," announced the blond guy, returning with two over-sized flutes and a fresh bottle. Expertly, he popped off the cork and filled the glasses above everybody's heads without spilling a drop. He was obviously well practised.

"I'm Ben, by the way," he said. "But they call me Dish."

Marta nodded. He was probably her age – early twenties – but he had the cockiness of a middle-aged salesman.

"Nice to meet you," she said, opting not to ask him about his nickname, which she felt sure he was waiting for her to do. She glanced back at Tina who had disappeared in a frenzy of roaring and jeering. It seemed that Marta was on her own for the night.

"Oh, and this is James," added Dish, making room for another trader. Marta turned round. She tried not to stare as she shook his hand. She couldn't take her eyes off his face. The man was beautiful. His skin was dusky and his eyes, though ice blue like hers, were slanted in a way that suggested he had some oriental genes.

"Or Bufty," he added, as though slightly embarrassed. "That's what they call me."

Marta nearly said something, then forced the champagne to her lips. So *this* was Bufty.

Flattering though it was to be eyed up, chatted up and entertained with such intensity, it felt awkward being the centre of attention in a crowd of strangers. After her first glass – which, she realised, was the equivalent of three normal-sized champagne flutes, Marta slipped off to the Ladies.

Her reflection stared back at her – tired, confused and barely recognisable beneath Tina's makeup. She could leave now if she wanted. It was probably the best thing to do. Tina wouldn't mind. Let's face it, she hadn't brought Marta here for purely selfless reasons. Come to think of it, Tina probably wouldn't even notice her go.

One more drink, she decided. That would be all. Leaving now would be rude. But only one. A hangover was the last thing she needed in the office tomorrow.

Waiting to be noticed on the fringes of the group, Marta started to have second thoughts. Maybe she should leave now. She had nothing in common with these rich, champagne-drinking traders apart from their colleague, whose house she happened to be living in. She didn't want them to feel obliged to talk to her. She didn't want to be force-fed alcohol. Yes, perhaps she would leave after all.

"So, Tina mentioned you were Polish," said someone, emerging at her side with a fresh glass of champagne. It was Bufty. She nodded, averting her gaze from the mesmerising blue eyes.

"Me too. Well – one quarter," he added sheepishly.

"Oh! Mowisz po polsku?" asked Marta, excited about the prospect of common ground and the chance to talk Polish.

Bufty smiled. "Sorry – no idea what you just said. My grandmother never taught her children Polish, so my mum never knew any. Bit of a waste really, as Polish is becoming the second language over here, isn't it?"

Marta laughed. "We're everywhere."

Bufty puckered his lip. "Well, I dunno about that. There aren't too many on the trading floor."

"Yet," added Marta, grinning. "We won't be working in bagel shops and building sites for ever, you know."

"Maybe," he replied vaguely. Marta waited for him to expand, but he didn't. She wondered whether Tina was right about the *prejudice* thing. Surely Bufty wasn't *prejudiced*?

"So where do you work?" he asked.

Marta told him. He nodded. Then, for some reason, she told him everything – about her search for work, the recruitment fair, her leaflet job, the agency interviews and then her current situation at Stratisvision. Bufty sipped his champagne and nodded, looking at her through half-closed eyes.

"What a shocker," he said when she'd told him about Kat and her dirty tricks. "Tell you what. You should quit. You should walk in there tomorrow, slap them round the face and walk out. That's what I'd do. You shouldn't have to put up with that crap."

Marta hesitated. Was he joking? Had he not listened to anything else she'd told him? Had he not grasped the fact that Stratisvision was her only hope of building up a half-decent CV in England, and that walking out was not an option?

"I quit my first trading job when they didn't give me the bonus they'd given the analysts the previous year," he went on. "They were offering us seventy K when it was a well-known fact that they'd paid six-figures the year before. I demanded they match it and they didn't, so I quit."

Marta nodded silently. They were talking on different levels. Marta was talking about stepping onto the employment ladder and trying desperately to hang on; this guy was talking about leaping off the ladder at the other end. Six figures? In his first year of work? That was just crazy.

She let Bufty talk. It was enlightening to hear his views on the world – well, on the workplace at least. That seemed to be his area of speciality. Salaries, promotions, bonuses, appraisals, trades, assessments and after-work drinks – he was an expert in all these things. More and more, Marta was intrigued by this place they called 'the city'. She could see its appeal – and not just the financial appeal. From what Bufty was saying, it was a special place where alpha males (and occasionally, females) got together and used their incredible intellect to do ground-breaking deals under huge amounts of pressure. Tina had obviously done well to get here.

The money seemed ludicrous, too. *Now* Marta could see why girls back in Poland aspired to come over and marry a London banker. Not that it appealed to her. No, the idea of relying on somebody else for an income – especially someone as flirtatious as Bufty – turned Marta off. And he was the nicest of the bunch. The others… well, she couldn't imagine being married to any of them. There was something about them – maybe their egos – that disagreed with her.

"…That's what we do with the new guys," he told her, finishing the tale about poor little Dish who was taped to his chair, spun round and wheeled into the boss' office to vomit.

Marta was laughing despite herself. "So mean!" she cried. "Did he got told off by the boss?"

"Told off? God no. Boss thought it was funny and ordered him to clean it up – with his bare hands."

Marta screwed up her face and listened while he started telling her about his 'induction'.

It was several glasses of champagne later when the bear-like man moved – or rather, fell – into their conversation.

"What's this, then? Bufty monopolising the pretty Pole, eh?"

Marta and Bufty stepped backwards to allow the man to right himself.

"Have you heardtheplan?" he slurred, looking at Marta whilst hanging off Bufty' shoulders. "Going to Abacus! Gonna get rat-arsed!"

"*Stay* rat-arsed," muttered Bufty under his breath, propping the guy against a nearby pillar.

Just as Marta was about to make her excuses and catch the last tube, her phone rang. She pulled it out from the tight back pocket of Tina's trousers and tried to focus on the display. God, she was drunk. She peered closer. As she did so, she suddenly found the phone being wrenched from her hands.

"Hello!" bawled the large man, frowning as he tried to make out the voice at the other end. "What, Marta?" He winked stupidly at Marta. "Oh, she's here alright. But she's… abitbusy!" Another wink, this time at the crowd that was gathering to listen. "No, I don't think she'll be freeforabit! Sorry young man. Goodbye!"

Marta retrieved her phone, to the sound of guffaws and applause from the traders. She checked the last caller, already knowing who it would be. Squinting at the handset confirmed her theory.

Well, she thought, letting her eyes wander back to Bufty's. Perhaps the trader had done her a favour. Dom wouldn't be calling her back for a bit – or perhaps for ever. That was what she wanted, wasn't it? Yes? No. Yes. Her drunk brain couldn't function properly. It felt as though she were playing poker with herself. She was bluffing, or double-bluffing, or maybe even triple-bluffing if that was a term – but she didn't know which. Maybe the guy had done her a favour.

Somehow, Marta found herself standing at the side of a small, sticky dance floor in an underground nightclub with neon lights round the bar. The place was heaving with young, suited men and a few women who had rolled up their suit skirts and undone some blouse buttons to make themselves look less smart.

The journey here had passed in a blur. They had either walked or taken a cab – she couldn't remember. It had been hard to resist the raucous cries of Tina's workmates and the softer, more persuasive tones of the blue-eyed derivatives trader. Marta wondered what time it was. Perhaps she'd still make the last tube if she left after the next drink? It was strange, but she was no longer sure she wanted to leave.

"Come on, baby!" yelled Tina, above the din of *I Will Survive* by Gloria Gaynor. Marta just had time to drain her shot and slam the empty glass down before her arm was nearly yanked out of its socket.

The dance floor was virtually empty, but that didn't matter. It gave Tina and Marta more room to perform their improvised dance routines. *I should have changed that stupid lock, I should have made you leave your key* – Tina threw Marta across the floor as though she were the key in question – *If I had known for just one second you'd be back to bother me… Go on now, go! Walk out the door!* Marta brushed herself off and joined Tina in strutting towards the only other dancers, two sweaty traders, who looked genuinely hurt as the girls simultaneously turned their backs on them. It was silly, but fun.

The song came to a triumphant end, and suddenly Tina was dragging Marta off the floor as quickly as she'd pulled her onto it.

"Let's call Holly!" she shouted. "She works near here – she might be around!"

Marta nodded enthusiastically and allowed Tina to push her towards the exit. If anyone needed a night out, it was Holly. She spent her whole life in that office of hers.

They tottered up the stairs until Tina cried jubilantly that she had some reception on her phone.

"Hello? Hey babe, is that you? Hol? It's Tina. Oh, I can't hear you!" Tina scowled madly at her handset. "CAN YOU HEAR ME?"

Marta nearly fell backwards as her flatmate lost her footing and stumbled down a couple of steps. A bouncer was coming towards them, Marta noticed as she grabbed Tina's phone.

"Holly? It's Marta! Are you there?"

"Of course I'm fucking here!" replied Holly, sounding quite cross. "I've been yelling at that deaf bint – is she drunk?"

"Yes." Marta watched as Tina saw off the bouncer with a series of hand gestures and loud explanations. "But is so good here, Holly, we want you to come too!"

"God, you're drunk too, aren't you? Where are you?"

"Place called Aba- Alpha- I forgot name. Hang on. Tina, Tina, where are–"

"No, don't bother," said Holly. "I won't make it out before it closes anyway. Have fun though. See you later."

Marta started trying to persuade her to change her mind, but she realised after a while that she was speaking into a dead line. Tina grabbed her phone back. "Is she coming out?" she asked excitedly.

Marta shook her head. Poor Holly. She sounded so unhappy. Maybe a call from her drunken flatmates was not what she needed when she was trying to get her difficult, important assignments done. What was she *doing* there, anyway? Marta tried to picture the scene: Holly bent over her desk, like Cinderella, a long list of things to do pinned up beside her by the evil boss. Who was that boss? If Marta ever got to meet him, she'd have a thing or two to say – that was for sure. Oh, poor girl. Why couldn't she come out, just this once?

The dance floor was filling up. On it, the other two traders were busy doing a flamboyant version of the Englishman's disco dance: shuffling from foot to foot, wiggling their shoulders and occasionally making wild stabs at the air with their fingers. *Up-side down you turning me, you giving love, instinctively…* Marta found herself mouthing the words as she and Tina headed towards the guys.

Dancing as a foursome didn't work for long and when the music slowed, it seemed almost natural for them to split into pairs – Tina taking the burlier, blond guy and Marta finding herself in the arms of a tall young man with a spiky quiff. It was strange, really. She'd never spoken to this person in her life and all she knew was that he worked at JC Morley with Tina, but here she was, rocking gently with him to the sound of *I am the One and Only* by Chesney Hawkes. It felt, well… quite nice, actually.

It was apparent that Tina and her guy were interested in more than just dancing. Their entwined silhouette moved closer to the disco lights and then disappeared altogether behind the speakers. Marta began to wonder whether the same would be expected of her. She was thinking about this when suddenly her man's arms weakened around her. She looked up.

The spiky-haired guy let go of her and stepped backwards, with some reluctance. Standing over her, smiling, was Bufty. He looked even more handsome now, the coloured lights reflecting off his dark, exotic skin. Marta found herself pressed up against him, looking up at his eyes. It was lovely. But again, it was weird. One minute earlier, she'd been in the same position with another man. She felt a bit like a spliff being passed around.

"Kiss me," he said softly in her ear.

Right there, in the middle of the dance floor, like teenagers at a school disco, they kissed. Marta almost laughed as she felt his tongue enter her mouth, his warm, wet lips on hers. It was ridiculous. This man, Bufty, was kissing her in front of all his colleagues and a nightclub full of people. But then, everything seemed ridiculous tonight. Maybe it was the champagne.

"Follow me," he said afterwards, leading her by the hand towards the exit. He stopped at the cloakroom and passed a ticket to the woman on the desk. "D'you have a coat?"

Marta giggled and let out a hiccup. "Don't know!"

They established that Marta had not had a jacket and that Tina's tight little top was all she'd had on all night. Bufty put his suit jacket over her shoulders and, keeping his hand round her waist underneath, led her out.

It was only when her flesh made contact with the night air that Marta realised what was happening. She was going home with a guy she didn't know. She didn't even like him, really. He was arrogant and *prejudiced*. She didn't want to go back with him or to have sex with him, which was clearly what he had in mind. She was drunk and so was he, and he probably couldn't even remember her name. He just wanted a fuck.

"We could walk, but we'll get a cab. It's only money," he said, sticking his hand out into the road.

Marta stepped sideways, wriggling free of his grip around her waist. She didn't know what to do, but she knew that she had to escape. Despite the fuzzy feeling in her brain, despite Tina's words, she knew that a good shag was not what she needed. At least, not from this good-looking stranger. There was only one man in the world she wanted right now, and even though she knew she shouldn't be thinking about him, he was there in her mind, naked and gorgeous, his sandy hair tousled, on top of her.

A taxi pulled up. The trader held open the door for her. For a moment, Marta just stood there. Then she muttered something about work the next day, thanked the guy, pulled off her shoes and ran.

36

MARTA CLICKED ON 'ACCEPT' and watched the appointment drop into her calendar. CATCH-UP, that was all it said. What was that supposed to mean? Why had David Lyle summoned her to his office at two o'clock with no more explanation than that?

All sorts of possibilities ran through Marta's tired, paranoid mind. Maybe he was going to ask her to leave. Perhaps he was going to question her over the shoddy work she had done for Charlotte. Or perhaps Kat's clan had played another trick on her and she was about to find out what it was... they'd been suspiciously quiet these last few days. Marta closed the mysterious appointment and looked at the PowerPoint slide on her screen.

The brief wasn't difficult. It basically involved rearranging numbers in boxes and changing the colours to make them look pretty. Any other week, Marta would have been screaming with boredom at the monotony of the task. Right now though, it was just about right. She had the concentration span of a minnow.

Drag, drop, format. Drag, drop, format. Marta was trying to work out why she felt so unsettled. OK, she was likely to be jobless in just over twenty-four hours' time, but that wasn't it. The agency had hinted at the prospect of more work when she'd called them yesterday, so hopefully, if Stratisvision didn't give her too harsh a review, she wouldn't be unemployed for long. The guy from Tina's office, Bufty, had apparently asked for her number on Tuesday, which was flattering, but that hadn't lifted her spirits – not that he'd called, anyway. Even the fact that her best friend had forgiven her for forgetting her birthday and was saving up to come over to London hadn't made an impact on her state of mind.

It wasn't really a question of working out the cause of her unhappiness – more of admitting the cause. She knew what it was, but she also knew that she had no way of fixing things, so it seemed pointless addressing the issue. There could be no going back to the old ways with Dom, because he wasn't the person she'd thought he was. She had to move on.

Mindlessly, Marta dragged, dropped and formatted. It was only when she came to the end of the fifty-page pack that she thought to look up at the clock. With horror, she realised it was five past two. She grabbed her notebook and launched herself into the gangway.

As she peered through the glass between the frosted panels, Marta noticed her heart pounding against the inside of her chest. Suddenly, she was nervous. Her mouth had all but dried up and she could feel her legs shaking inside her trousers. It was something to do with the realisation that Stratisvision was the only real company that had offered her work in England, and that this could be the end of it all. If she got sacked from this firm then the agency wouldn't place her anywhere else, and she'd be back to handing out leaflets.

"Entrez!" squeaked the director from within.

Marta wiped her clammy palms on her shirt and stepped inside.

"Bon journo," he said proudly, exposing a small piece of what looked like broccoli between his front teeth. Marta relaxed a little. It was difficult to feel on edge when the person in charge was David Lyle. He swivelled a full 360 degrees before wheeling his way towards the oval table in the middle of the room.

"Good morning," said Marta, noticing that her voice sounded higher than usual. Nerves did weird things to the body.

"Yep, just testing out me old linguistics," he explained, moving a wad of papers to one side. "Ooh – hang on, you're Polish. Let me see now…" He squinted up to the ceiling, where, Marta noticed, there was a sticker saying 'Upside-down thinking' in swirly letters. "No, don't know it. Bonovska Journovski?"

"Dzien dobry," Marta replied, smiling and perching in the seat opposite the director.

"Ah, of course! Jen debris!"

Marta forced a laugh, waiting for the 'catch-up' to begin. The longer David Lyle larked about, the shorter her nerves became. She was clamping her knees together under the table in case the trembling affected the furniture.

"So…" David turned to her and grinned, displaying the greenery between his teeth. It really did look like a small sprig of broccoli. "You're probably wondering why I called you in here on this fine Thursday afternoon," he said.

Marta nodded politely and hid her shaky hands in her lap.

"Well… hmm. Where to begin," he said, fiddling with the leather bracelet around his wrist. "OK. Appraisals. Now, you may or may not be aware that everyone working at Stratisvision undergoes an appraisal at the end of every piece of work – temporary or permanent, full- or part-time."

Marta shook her head, wondering what he was talking about. Suddenly, the joker had gone all serious.

"Ah, OK. Well that's probably my fault for not telling you, but anyway." Lyle leaned back and extracted a folder from a mass of paperwork on his desk. "This is you, this is."

Marta watched as he opened the dark green cover with her name on it. Inside were a lot of identical pieces of paper that looked like application forms or something.

"I've had a quick squiz at these," he said. "And, well… it seems as though you're a bit of a schizophrenic!"

Marta frowned. She didn't know what one of those was, but it didn't sound good.

"Some excellent reviews, and some er, less than excellent ones, shall we say."

Marta waited for him to explain. He clearly wasn't going to show her the pieces of paper.

"So, here's the deal. Everyone in the firm who has got to know you, through work or otherwise, is asked to fill out an appraisal form. So it looks as though you've worked for… Charlotte – quite extensively, I see – and Kat, oh and Dean. And there are personal appraisals from Carl, Kim, Nik and… Oh – and Patricia! I say."

Marta nodded patiently, wondering where this was all leading. Her hands were sweaty again. She was dying to read what these people had written about her.

"General office behaviour is the first thing," he said, flicking through the documents. "Excellent work ethic, helpful, enthusiastic, open... uncommunicative, sullen and evasive. Hmm."

It was all Marta could do to stop herself from scowling and wrenching the papers from his hands. She could guess who wrote each one of those words.

"Project skills, where applicable," he muttered. "Ooh – you've got an 'excellent' from Charlotte. That's unheard of. What was this Brand Precedents work you did for her?"

Marta felt a pang of guilt as she described Carl's presentation. Now was probably not the time to own up, she decided.

"Yet you got a 'poor' from her on this PopsCo thing."

"That was Kat!" Marta blurted out before she could stop herself.

The director was looking at her. "What d'you mean?"

"Er, that was Kat who tell me to do it wrong," explained Marta, instantly wishing she hadn't said anything. She was coming across as churlish.

He sifted through the papers. "I don't think so," he said. "The 'poor' was due to your lack of grasp of the English language."

"But–" Marta started, regretting it. "Kat advise me wrong. Doesn't matter."

Lyle nodded as though he wasn't really listening anyway. "OK, managing your time seems good – oh. Apart from one 'very poor'. How strange."

Marta nodded. It wasn't strange at all. Kat had it in for her. She'd probably done the same for all the questions.

"And similarly for quality of deliverables," noted Lyle, confirming her suspicions. "Very interesting comments on your personality," he said, lightening up for a moment. "'Bold and assertive' is one person's comment – one rather senior person, too," he said.

Marta smiled. Kat's trick, sending her into the CEO's office to embarrass herself, had backfired.

"...and yet, someone else claims you are 'moody, unpredictable and at times downright miserable'!"

Gosh, this was a horrible process. She'd had no idea she was being so closely scrutinised by those around her. If she'd known, perhaps she would have pretended to be a bit happier these last few days.

"Right," said David, suddenly slamming the folder shut and

looking at her, goggle-eyed. The buffoon was back. "So what does this all mean?"

Marta looked at him, wondering whether he expected an answer. She certainly didn't have one for him.

"It means that you're a complicated person, Ms Darawavsky!"

"Dabrowska," Marta corrected quietly. She disagreed with him, but she decided to keep quiet this time.

"But that's not always a bad thing," he went on. Marta tried to work out from his tone whether he was leading up to positive or negative news. It was impossible to say.

"Your work has been variable, just like your personality," he summarised. "That seems to be the feedback from your colleagues. But on the basis of the excellent work you did for Charlotte during your first week – and some of the other bits and bobs, I'm pleased to offer you an extension of your contract for the next six weeks, should you want it." He stared at her with raised eyebrows.

Marta's smile spread quickly across her face. Of course she wanted it. So shocked was she that David's speech had culminated in good news, she probably didn't show quite how pleased she was.

"Thank you! Yes, I would like it."

"Well, we take on all sorts here – lunatics, manic depressives, schizophrenics…" He smiled.

Marta laughed, even though his description of her was hardly fair. She felt guilty that the offer had been based so heavily on a piece of work that she hadn't actually done, but then, she'd taken the blame for a lot of things that had been someone else's fault, so maybe it all balanced out in the end. It wasn't as though Carl needed the credit, after all.

"Just remember what I told you at the start: make love to the client," he said. "That's what we do here at Stratisvision."

Marta nodded. *Make love to the client, who you'll never even get to meet.* Strange request.

"And you're on four hundred pounds a week, aren't you?" asked Lyle, scribbling something on the corner of the folder.

"Yes," replied Marta, hoping that this wasn't an honesty test. She was on three hundred pounds a week.

David Lyle looked up. "Excellent!" he said. "Well, glad to have you with us for longer!"

They both stood up and shook hands.

"Jen debris!" he cried, so passionately that the piece of broccoli shot out from between his teeth and landed on Marta's right breast.

Marta managed to ignore it for long enough to return David's smile and flee his office. She felt elated, but guilty too. It was time to go and thank Carl.

37

MD: Anka!

AK: Hey buddy, how's Londynia?

MD: Good – well, complicated. How's things in Lom?

AK: Same as ever… nothing changes. A few more people gone, that's all

MD: I got yr text – you're coming over?

AK: Hopefully! Need to check that the bakery can survive without me ☺

MD: Don't they burn all the buns when you're not there?

AK: I'm manager now – did I tell u that?

MD: Manager?! Wow – no u didn't say! CONGRATS!

AK: ☺ Don't get excited – it's only a bakery, M. I'll let u know when I can take some days off. What about your job? Any news on extending it?

MD: Well yeah… it's all a bit weird but I've got 6 more weeks there – management seems 2 like me even though half the company doesn't

AK: AWESOME – 6 more weeks! They'll definitely take u on permanently after that – well done! Company not liking u – ?!

MD: Don't ask. Long story – I'll save it for when u come over. More English girls with something against me ☹

AK: Their loss, I say. Glad u haven't found yourself a new best friend anyway!

MD: No chance

AK: Hey, am wearing those beads u sent me – everyone wants 2know where I got them!

MD: Glad u like – and sorry they were late! D'u have a webcam there?

AK: !?%★&!? In Łomianki town library? You're joking, right?

MD: Sorry, of course. Just wanted 2c u

AK: Actually I do have a pic – one mama took on my birthday – hold on…

MD: Come on! Where is this pic?

AK: Patience… This is a Polish connection, remember ☺ I'm downloading it from my email – oh, done. Here u go…

MD: Wow! Nice pic – you look like an accessories model!

AK: Yeah right – wearing 7-yr old jeans

MD: Seriously, u look gorgeous. U R wasted over there in that bakery, A.

AK: Thanks – but don't try & tempt me to Londynia!

MD: Any nice men in Lom?

AK: U R joking again, Marta… stop it

MD: So that's a no?

AK: None that have come anywhere near the bakery or town library ☹ But what about u? U getting over the two-timing bastard?

MD: Truthfully, no. God Anka, I think about him ALL THE TIME

AK: Course u do. Trick is to find someone else, take your mind off him. Apparently.

MD: That doesn't work.

AK: …speaking from experience?

MD: Well, sort of. Went out this week with mad flatmate + her trader friends. Nearly went back with one but didn't.

AK: Ooh! Exciting – what's he like?

MD: Quarter polish, actually – v good-looking. Lovely eyes.

AK: U said that about the last one. Stop judging them by their lovely eyes!

MD: Sweet, too – but way too rich

AK: TOO rich? Is that possible?

MD: Yes. Rich & arrogant – he patronised me

AK: The fool. He shd've known better

MD: Still having probs w. the Italian at work – he fancies me but I need his help!

AK: Is that a prob?

MD: Yes if he expects something in return for his help!

AK: Sounds like he wouldn't dare. Don't worry – just don't lead him on or anything.

MD: I won't!

AK: Where've u gone?

MD : Sorry – just getting my phone. Got a text… guess who from?

AK: Dom?

MD: Yes!

AK: Saying what?

MD: Hang on…

AK: Tell me!

MD: Saying: Marta, I really need to tell u something but u won't pick up yr phone. I don't know if I've done something wrong, but if I have, please tell me. I want to talk! I won't contact u again until u call me. All my love, Dxx

AK: God, does he really think u haven't worked it out?

MD: Seems so. Wish he'd just leave me alone.

AK: U gonna call him?

MD: Gah! I don't know. I want 2, but am worried I'll fall for his lies/excuses & he'll win me back.

AK: In which case, don't. He won't call u again, so it's over forever. Goodbye. Good riddance!

MD: Hmm, yeah.

AK: God Marta, u've got guys desperate for u! Don't fall for the one rotten one

MD: Yeah u're right. Should concentrate on work anyway.

AK: Exactly. By the way, u know your mum thinks u've been doing some sort of high-flying marketing job since u arrived?

MD: Agh! Yes I know, & I meant to warn u not to talk about that – did u?

AK: Didn't chat. She just went on about how proud she was ☺

MD: So embarrassing, I know. Hate lying to her but she just won't understand how hard it is here

AK: Don't blame you, M. At least u have a great job now!

MD: For next 6 weeks…

AK: Stop beating yourself up! U've made it in Londynia – u shd b proud!

MD: Like mama

AK: Not *that* proud maybe…

MD: Hold on – another text

AK: Popular girl! Another guy?

MD: AAAAAAAAARGH! Yes, another guy

AK: Who?

MD: Remember Jack, boyfriend of awful housemate?

AK: Course I do! He got u kicked out of that place, right?

MD: Yeah – he's been texting since then

AK: & u ignored him, right? What does he say?

MD: Says: Hey babe, do U play tennis? I have a court at my club this weekend – mixed doubs. I'll lend u racket etc. Looking forward 2seeing u in short white skirt… Jack x

AK: 'Babe'?! Since when?

MD: He calls me that. Split up with Tash & now thinks I'm his.

AK: Idiot! Another idiot!

MD: Yeah

AK: Marta…………..? You're not thinking of going, r u?

MD: Well I'd quite like to play tennis – haven't played since moving here

AK: HE'S NOT ASKING U TO PLAY TENNIS

MD: I know, but I cd just play & then leave

AK: Marta, I know I've never met this guy but I have a BAD FEELING about him

MD: OK – you're right. No tennis. No games.

AK: Exactly – he's a player. Shit, I gotta run – library shutting!

MD: OK kochana – thanks for advice!

AK: Don't b silly – u need it ☺

MD: Shut up – I don't

AK: Bye xx

MD: xxxxxx

38

"GREAT SHOT, MARTA! Where did that come from?"

Marta shrugged casually. Actually, she was rather proud. The ball had gone belting down the tramlines with more precision and pace than any other shot played all afternoon.

"Fifteen all."

Marta skipped into the service box and waited while her partner prepared for his serve. She was tempted to look back and watch his muscular body stretch up and blast the ball over the net – but she knew it wouldn't look very professional. When you were playing on courts like these, well… you had to try and look professional.

Disappointingly, Jack's first serve hit the net. Marta darted down to retrieve the ball and waited, praying for the second one to go over.

It did – and with incredible force. Marta watched as the girl made a valiant effort to connect with it, only to find that the serve had been loaded with spin. There was no way anyone – let alone this petite young blonde – could have reached it in time.

"Good serve!" cried the girl's partner, clapping his hand against his racket in recognition. "You're starting to warm up, aren't you?"

"Just thinking about it," replied Jack, smiling as he neatly caught the ball that was hurtling towards him. He lifted his sunglasses and wiped a hand across his forehead.

Charles was a school friend of Jack's. His girlfriend, Tiff, had only started learning tennis a year ago, but was playing a reasonable game. She'd had coaching – from someone called Mark Peachy or Patchy who was clearly a big name in tennis, although Marta had never heard of him. She had of course gasped incredulously when they'd told her.

The first fifteen minutes had been a disaster for Marta. Her shots had been wild – so wild, in fact, that one had gone sailing over the fence and into the duck pond – and as a result, she'd found herself focussing on what Jack and the others were thinking of her instead of on the game itself. The more she dwelled on this, the worse she played, until eventually she pulled herself together – but not before they'd lost four consecutive games to Charles and Tiff. They'd ended up losing the first set 3–6, but Jack didn't seem particularly angry at her for messing things up.

"Thirty-fifteen," uttered Jack as he moved back to the baseline. He still had a smile on his face, as did Marta. The score in this set was 5–1 to them, and they both knew that they were going to win it.

There was a whoosh of air as the ball shot past Marta's left ear. She stayed on her toes, watching Charles step into the shot. Suddenly, the ball was rushing towards her face. Instinctively, Marta raised her racket and ducked. Experience had taught her to keep her wrist firm, which was just as well given the impact it took.

She hadn't meant to close her eyes; it was a reflex. But the next thing she knew, the ball was dribbling slowly away from the net on the other side and Charles was reluctantly trotting towards it.

"Great volley," said Jack, grinning at her. Initially, she assumed he was being sarcastic, but his smile suggested otherwise. "Set point."

Marta stood, poised, waiting for Jack to finish the game.

The rally was a confusing blur. Jack served wide, with enough spin to send the ball into the next-door court, but somehow Tiff stuck out her arm at exactly the right angle, sending the ball looping back to Jack. He slammed it down the centre of the court, where, miraculously, Charles popped it back over, just within Marta's reach. She returned the ball to Tiff, who hit it straight back, and the same thing happened again. On and on it went, with nobody able to put the ball away once and for all.

Then Marta's impatience got the better of her. She wanted to finish the game, and she wanted to win. The ball came towards her from Charles who was at the back of the court, ready to pounce. Tiff was with him at the back, waiting to take instructions. Marta raised her racket behind her head, guided the ball in with her other hand, and then swiped. Right across the court, in line with the net. Charles and Tiff made a half-hearted attempt to move for it, but they were too late.

"Awesome shot," said Jack, jogging up to slap hands with Marta. She felt something leap inside her.

"Yah, well played," Charles agreed. "You really got your eye in by the end, didn't you?"

"End?" asked Jack, raising an eyebrow as they congregated at the net. "You mean you're not up for the deciding set?"

Charles and Tiff looked at one another. "Got to scoot, I'm afraid," said Charles. "Seeing the in-laws at three for afternoon tea." He pulled a face.

Tiff whacked him in the chest. "Stop it," she chided. "But I don't think we can, really. Sorry."

Jack shook his head in mock disappointment. "Running scared," he said. "Pathetic."

"Next time," replied Charles, holding out his hand across the net.

Jack shook it, then moved over and kissed Tiff on both cheeks. "Well played."

Marta found herself leaning forward to kiss Charles in the same way, and then Tiff, which was rather bizarre. She hadn't kissed girls like that since living with Tash. It was a posh people's thing, she decided. "Well played."

They collected the balls and waited while Jack pulled off his T-shirt and started rummaging around in his kit bag, bare-chested.

"Show-off," teased Charles, slapping Jack's sweaty, muscular back.

"Jealous," Jack replied, extracting a top and pulling it on. Marta giggled and caught Jack's eye. He was probably right. Charles' body was nothing like Jack's.

"Did you drive here?" asked Jack, heaving the bag over his shoulder.

Charles nodded. Tiff pointed towards the car park. An open-top silver Porsche Boxter was visible through a gap in the trees.

"New car?" asked Jack, slightly enviously.

"Bonus day," replied Charles with a wink.

The men admired the machine for a few seconds and then looked at one another.

"Well, thanks for the game," said Charles. "Looking forward to the re-match. Nice to meet you, Kat! See you soon!" He waved and led his girlfriend away.

Marta turned to Jack. "Why did he call me Kat?"

Jack looked as baffled as Marta. "I have absolutely *no* idea." He stared after the couple as they headed off over the perfectly manicured lawn. "No idea at all. I did introduce you at the beginning, didn't I?"

Marta nodded. Charles' slip would have passed unnoticed were it not for the strange coincidence that Kat was the name of her arch enemy.

"He's always been terrible with names. Marta, Kat, Jessica… they're all the same to Charlie. Anyway, what're you up to now?" he asked. "You don't have to shoot off, do you?"

Marta hesitated, deciding to put the whole Kat incident down to a spooky coincidence. The fact was, she *did* have to shoot off because she'd promised herself that she'd play tennis and only tennis with Jack today. But the situation wasn't as she'd imagined it. Jack wasn't trying it on at all. He hadn't made a single pass at her and somehow, it didn't seem likely that he would. And besides, she couldn't think of an excuse not to stay. Marta smiled and shook her head.

"Great. I'll show you around."

The place was incredible. Marta had guessed it might be, from the stone entranceway with its uniformed guards, the well-kept lawns and the pond behind the tennis courts – which, she now discovered, were just four of what must have been dozens of courts scattered about the acres of land that constituted Hurlingham Club.

"This is the lake, obviously," stated Jack as they walked over a quaint wooden footbridge. "Now home to one more tennis ball," he added, smiling. "And over there, where you can hear all the screaming coming from, that's the outdoor pool. It's heaving in summer."

They followed the winding path up the hill towards a huge, Georgian house. It looked a bit like Tash's mansion, only bigger. Marta looked around at the luscious lawns and the colourful flowers bordering the shrubberies. "It's like from a film," she remarked, thinking of the costume dramas she'd watched in English lessons.

"They do use it for filming occasionally," said Jack, looking at Marta and seeing Holly's racket bag on her back. "I'm so sorry – let me take that." He reached round and relieved her of it.

Usually Marta would have objected to such pointless chivalry, but here, in the grounds of such historic splendour, it seemed OK to allow the odd gallant act. And besides, her limbs felt tired walking uphill in such strong sunshine.

"Yes, they filmed something or other for Cannes a few years back, but the members didn't like it because the rest of the film turned out to be porn. I think they're a bit more picky about who uses their land now."

Marta smiled. "What's that?" she asked, pointing towards a flat patch of grass to their right that was separated from the undulating lawn by a hedge. It was so perfectly horizontal it almost looked like a lake, with statues dotted about in the middle.

"That's the croquet lawn."

"Croaky?"

"Croquet. D'you know what croquet is?"

Marta shook her head. "Sounds like a disease."

Jack laughed. "I'll show you."

They veered off the path and cut a straight line across the springy lawn. It was only as they got closer that Marta realised the statues were actually people. They were moving about, but very, very slowly. She followed Jack to a gap in the hedge.

"Croquet. See? There's a series of hoops stuck in the ground, and you have to hit a ball through them in a certain order using a rubber mallet-thing. Look – watch that one." Jack put an arm gently around Marta's shoulders and pointed with his other hand.

Marta watched as the white haired man swung the long-handled mallet between his legs, sending a ball rolling along towards one of the hoops.

"Like golf," she remarked, feeling a slight sense of disappointment as Jack's arm slipped off her shoulder.

"Golf for people who don't want to walk."

Marta nodded. "Looks like fun," she said, not wanting to offend Jack in case it was the national sport or something.

He looked at her sceptically. "It's a load of bollocks."

They laughed and turned their back on the slow-motion scene. It was strange, but Marta felt as though she was beginning to understand the quirky English customs. Yes, croaky was a load of bollocks, as Jack put it, but she could see why they played it. It fitted in with their heritage. If only Poland had such a heritage, thought

Marta. There was nothing but pain and gloom in her country's history: bloody wars, bitter land squabbles, death camps, invasions and communism. Most Poles of Marta's age would rather forget the past and move on – but they couldn't, because that would be disrespectful. England was different. It had a rich history, and people remembered the nice things, not just the sad.

"Pimms o'clock?" he asked, as they approached the side of the huge white house, where a number of parasols were pitched like over-sized daisies on the patio.

Marta looked at her watch, frowning.

"Sorry – it's a phrase. D'you fancy a drink?"

Marta smiled. Another silly English phrase. A drink was exactly what she felt like, even though it was exactly what she'd vowed to avoid. She nodded happily despite herself.

"Thanks for coming," said Jack, once the old lady had taken their order.

"Thanks for inviting me," she replied. "It was a good game."

Jack squinted down at his feet and then up again. He just couldn't help being sexy, thought Marta, wishing she hadn't noticed.

"I didn't mean just the tennis," he said. "I meant… I meant thanks for agreeing to see me. At all."

Marta shrugged as though it were no big deal, which was ridiculous because she'd been ignoring his messages for months.

"I know I fucked things up for you, Marta. I've been feeling shitty about it ever since I found out from Tash."

Marta nodded, not sure what to say.

"There's no excuse for the way I behaved on… that night," he said, pausing as the elderly woman approached their table with a tray of drinks. The jug was filled with brown liquid in which floated a rather strange selection of salad items like cucumber, strawberries and orange peel. Jack ignored it and went on. "Except to say that… well, the truth comes out when you're drunk."

Marta looked him in the eye and managed to hold his gaze. What was he saying? That his drunken fumblings that night were a representation of how he really felt? Did he really have a deep-rooted yearning to pin Marta to the bed in her underwear? Marta looked at the ground, unable to maintain eye contact any longer.

Jack paused – deliberately, she thought – still looking at Marta. He wanted her to understand. Well, she did understand; she just wasn't sure she wanted to. She wasn't sure she could fully trust a man who got drunk and tried to rape a girl in his own girlfriend's house.

"But anyway, I felt bloody awful when I found out that Tash had blamed you for the whole thing and kicked you out. Awful. I tried to tell her, you know. I really tried to explain it was me, but the stuck-up cow wouldn't listen. Never does. She just hears what she wants to hear."

Marta couldn't help smiling. "So you're not friends now?"

Jack laughed. "You could say that."

The awkwardness faded. Looking at him, Marta couldn't help feeling that Jack's motives for meeting up today weren't as suspicious as she'd first assumed; he just wanted to apologise, explain himself and clear the air between them. She wasn't sure whether he was also trying to express some other feeling towards her, but if that was the case, she thought, then she'd play dumb and pretend not to understand. Life was complicated enough already.

"Nice outfit, by the way," Jack remarked, glancing approvingly at her legs.

"Thanks," she said bashfully. It had been a team effort finding white clothes that Holly, Tina and Marta all agreed upon. Her flatmates had been all too happy to help dress her for the game at Hurlingham, on the understanding that she was meeting her 'new mystery man'. They probably wouldn't have been so obliging had they realised who the mystery man was, thought Marta, guiltily.

"So, Pimms?" offered Jack, stirring the brown concoction. As he did so, Marta's phone rang.

"Sorry," she said, pulling the phone from her pocket and accepting the glass, in which floated a chunk of apple and a clump of green leaves that looked like pond weed.

It was Dom. Marta hesitated, then pressed Reject.

"Another boyfriend?" joked Jack.

Marta laughed flippantly, tucking the phone away. "Just… someone."

"Cheers," "Na zdrowie," they said, raising their glasses. Marta threw back her head and swallowed, blocking all thoughts of Dom from her mind. She had Jack now. She didn't need any lying, cheating Polish men in her life.

It actually tasted nice: sweet and fruity, but with an alcoholic twist that made Marta feel instantly drunk. "It's so lovely here," she said, looking out at the green, rolling grass and tennis courts beyond. It was difficult to believe they were in London. "How do you join this club?"

Jack smiled wryly. "Don't hold your breath," he said. "The waiting list is about twenty years long."

"Twenty years?!" Marta spluttered, wondering whether she'd got her numbers mixed up.

Jack nodded. "They give priority to the children of members," he told her. "That's how I got in."

"Nice place for kids to learn tennis," remarked Marta, thinking of the crumbling concrete playground where she and Anka had first played. They'd had to prop up the net with pieces of wood in the middle and when it came to calling shots out they'd just used their judgement, as the lines had all worn away.

"Yeah," Jack nodded, extracting a strawberry from his drink and eating it. "So you didn't have clubs like this back home?"

Marta rolled her eyes, hoping Jack was being sarcastic. "'Course not. Everything beautiful got bombed down in the war. There were some clubs for the rich people, but not much because of communism – you know." She shrugged.

They talked for a while about Poland, about the differences between Łomianki and London and the way things were going. It was funny to hear things from Jack's point of view. He seemed to have this simplistic notion that there were two parts to society: the rich part, in which people deserved to be rich because they worked 'bloody hard', and the poor part, for which he had no sympathy because the people were all either lazy or stupid. Marta was curious to find out where the hard-working poor people fitted in, but she didn't get a chance to ask. She didn't dare ask where he thought *she* belonged.

It was clear that Jack had little idea how other people lived – even other people in his own city – but Marta could see why. He'd been brought up by rich, upper-class parents. He had mixed with others like him – both in school and at university, and now at Goldman Sachs. He'd probably never even spoken to anyone poor, except maybe when dealing with waiters or shopkeepers. As with Tash, he'd never experienced hardship. He seemed amazed by everything Marta told him.

"What *is* the minimum wage over here? I'm afraid I have no idea."

Marta smiled. "Here, is nearly one thousand pounds per month. In Poland, is only one hundred fifty pounds."

Jack pulled a face. "Blimey. How does anyone survive on a hundred and fifty pounds? I spend that much on alcohol every *week.*"

He seemed utterly shocked, and slightly guilty for being so out of touch, thought Marta. It was almost inconceivable that this was the man she had promised herself not to get involved with. Jack was witty and charming, and only a little bit flirty – not at all like the monster who had pressed himself on her in Tash's house.

"I could stay here all day," he commented, draining his glass and pushing the empties away from them. "Shame I've got to work."

Marta frowned. "Work?" It was the last thing she expected him to say. For a start, he'd just downed a pint of this sickly brown Pimm stuff.

Jack nodded unhappily. "And I know what you're thinking. I've had too much to drink. You're right. But there's an acquisition that goes public on Tuesday and I'm on the deal team."

Marta nodded. She had no idea what he did for a living, or what 'going public' meant, but it was sad that he had to do it on a Sunday, whatever it was.

"That's the thing about being a banker. You've gotta put in the hours." He shrugged. "It sucks, but it'll pay off in the end."

Marta smiled. She knew all about that. Perhaps Jack's 'end' would coincide with her 'end' and they could live a rich, happy life together.

Jack paid the bill; Marta let him. Usually she'd insist on going halves, but she had a feeling that Jack wouldn't like that. And anyway, he clearly wasn't short on cash.

"You work hard, too. I know you do," Jack said, hoisting both racket bags onto his back. "I saw that the first time I met you. You've got drive. You're ambitious."

Marta nodded, slightly surprised at Jack's comment. He was right. She was ambitious. But most people didn't see it at first – not over here, anyway. They saw a girl who was Polish.

"That was the problem with Tash," Jack went on, almost talking to himself as they wandered towards the duck pond. "All she wanted to do was buy handbags and get her nails done. So tedious. She didn't have a single ambition – except to become an It girl and quit work. Didn't even care about her stupid fashion job – except for the freebies she got from it."

Marta wasn't sure what to say. She didn't like the way Jack seemed to be comparing her with Tash.

"Anyway, that's all water under the bridge," said Jack, appearing to snap out of his reverie.

"I can see that," said Marta. Of course it was water. It was a pond, for goodness' sake.

"Oh – no, sorry," Jack smiled. "I wasn't referring to that water. It's a saying. 'Water under the bridge.' It means 'it's all in the past'."

"Oh." Marta nodded. Then she laughed. These mad English phrases made no sense at all.

"You OK going by tube?" asked Jack.

"Is the easiest way."

Jack swung the smaller bag off his shoulder and handed it to her. "Thanks for coming, again."

"Thanks for inviting me, again." Marta smiled.

There was a brief moment of uncertainty, then Jack leaned forward and kissed her on one cheek, and then the other – the posh English way.

"Would you... Would you consider meeting up again, sometime?" he asked.

Marta grinned. "I would consider it, yes."

39

"EVERYTHING OK, GIRLS?" asked David Lyle, grinning stupidly.

Marta nodded silently. Kat was busily sifting through papers on the meeting room table next to her.

In fact, everything was not OK. It was Marta's first client meeting, and she had only found out about it this morning when Kat had swanned past her desk saying, "Don't forget about the Unilight kick-off at ten!"

Helping Kat was never going to be easy, Marta decided. She'd clearly neglected to tell Marta about the meeting on purpose to make her look flustered in front of their senior colleagues – and today, they really were senior. A glance at the attendee list on the agenda told Marta that even Patricia Catermol would be present. The CEO never came to project meetings.

David Lyle started clicking his biro against the table, seemingly oblivious to the irritating noise. They were waiting for Dean to arrive with the clients – and presumably for Patricia to make an appearance, too. She'd be fashionably late, Marta predicted. She was too important to wait around for anyone.

"Ooh good – nice biscuits," exclaimed David as the small, pretty catering assistant crept in with a trolley of refreshments. He reached sideways and plucked a chocolate wafer from the plate.

Marta looked down at her blank notebook. This really was an important meeting, she thought. They never had biscuits and coffee wheeled in.

"Want one?" asked David, sending a shower of wafer crumbs across the table.

The girls shook their heads. Kat was still leafing through her papers – whatever they were. Marta's phone vibrated silently in her lap. She looked down, grateful for something to fiddle with.

> Fancy a mystery excursion
> next Sat? No need for short
> white skirt this time – unless
> U want… I'll pick U up @ 11,
> your place.
> J

Marta started to smile, then snapped shut her phone, realising that Kat was peering over her shoulder.

"Ah, hello!" cried David, looking up and brushing the crumbs from his shirt – a brightly coloured Hawaiian affair with daisies for buttons.

Dean stepped into the glass-walled meeting room, upright and professional as ever. In his wake, a large man sporting chinos and a gaudy red shirt was followed in by a small Chinese girl.

"Stefan! Good to see you!" cried David, rising to his feet and extending both hands as though greeting a long-lost brother. Clearly David owned the Unilight 'client relationship'. "You've met Dean, then? And this is Kim, er, Nik, er, Kat… and Marta. They'll be working on the innovation programme with Dean. Patricia's just on her way. And this is…?"

David stooped down and peered at the petite Chinese girl in Stefan's shadow.

"B," she said quietly.

"B?"

"Nobody able to pronounce my name," she explained. "Just call me B."

Marta smiled as she shook the girl's hand. She wasn't the only one who had issues telling people her name.

Stefan and B sat along one side of the table opposite Dean, Marta and Kat. David poured coffees and spouted nonsense from the foot of the table while everyone else shuffled their papers.

"Well," said Dean, clearly taking charge. "We may as well get started without Pa-"

"Good *morning!*" sang a warbling voice that filled the room. Patricia was draped in something that resembled an orange sari with gold jewellery to match. "Sorry I'm late," she said, rushing over to Stefan and planting a kiss on each cheek. She ignored B. "Too much to do and not enough time…"

Dean waited for the CEO to swoop into the empty chair at the head of the table, then had another go at starting the meeting.

"So, thanks for coming, everyone. I presume everybody's seen the proposal and the briefing pack I sent out yesterday?"

There were nods from all round the table. Marta frowned.

Smoothly, and so slowly that nobody else noticed, Kat slid a wad of papers sideways towards Marta. Marta took them and started surreptitiously flicking through the pages. She felt like thumping Kat under the table. Why had she waited until now to share this?

"So I think we can get things wrapped up pretty quickly today."

Wrapped up? Marta looked at Dean. She had no idea what he was talking about.

"I suggest we whiz quickly through the pack and then we can iron out any issues as we go along. It will be Kat doing a lot of the groundwork for this," he said.

Marta glanced sideways at Kat, who was smiling up at Dean. It was good, in a way, that Marta wasn't being given too much responsibility at this stage, although it was also frustrating. She was just as good as Kat, and likely to contribute an equal amount on this project. They just didn't seem to see her as a team mate.

There was a rustling noise as everyone in the room turned over the title page of the briefing pack. *Strategic marketing innovation at Unilight,* read Marta, mystified.

"I think we're all in agreement on the project objectives," said Dean, "but just to confirm: the purpose of this programme is to develop a consolidated view of our desired B2C market position in light of the changes to Unilight's core business roadmap for the current phase of innovation."

Marta stared at the words on the page.

"Yes?" asked Dean, looking around the table for agreement.

There were nods from all round the room.

"All singing from the same hymn sheet," said Stefan, grinning.

Marta was lost. The words were dancing around in front of her, long and meaningless, and now the client was talking about *hymn sheets*. She wished she'd had a chance to see this pack before the meeting.

"And this will be accomplished by the exploration of key strategic themes in the sector," Dean went on.

God, this was hard. Marta was used to marketing jargon – she'd studied it for three years – but this was something else. It wasn't just the language barrier. These people seemed to enjoy making simple things complex.

Simultaneously, they turned the page and were confronted with a diagram that looked like a mushroom on its side with lots of green boxes and yellow arrows.

"This is our preferred approach," said Dean, clearly seeing the diagram as self-explanatory. "We call it the innovation capture funnel."

Marta glanced at Stefan, who was nodding fervently, ogling the page as though it were porn. Next to him, B scribbled frantically on her copy.

"And this is the sort of thing that can be tailored to suit our needs," noted Stefan, still staring avidly at the bizarre diagram.

"Abso-*lutely*!" cried Patricia, nodding excitedly at the client. She was clearly 'making love' to him, thought Marta, wondering whether she realised that her sari-like garment was slipping off her left boob.

The page-turning continued. Marta looked at the words with everyone else and studied the weird schematics, nodding when others nodded and laughing at the client's jokes. Inside, she was drowning. The document meant nothing to her. Her head had gone under sometime around the point when Dean had talked about 'active feedback loops' and 'KPIs', and now she knew she wasn't coming up again.

"Always worth raising something up the flagpole, seeing if anyone salutes," said Stefan, in response to an enthusiastic suggestion by Patricia. "That's the great thing about distributed innovation networks."

Everybody nodded.

"Speaking of flagpoles," replied David, his eyes dancing with mirth. He was clearly about to make a joke. Marta looked down at her pack. "We've got our very own pole!"

The client looked at him, nonplussed. "Your own pole?"

"Yes! Sitting over there!" David pointed. "Marta's Polish!"

Stefan gave an unconvincing smile and nodded politely. David Lyle went on, unabashed. "Yes – shouldn't have any problems getting the work done with a Pole on the team!"

The client nodded again and flicked through the last few slides in the pack. "Well, for the research part at least, I'm hoping that B can work closely with your people. You know… many hands and all that."

Marta and B exchanged a quick, knowing smile. They were both working for idiots.

"Great," said Dean, reclaiming control. "Well, we probably don't need to go through the last few pages as it's all about the team, and you've met us now."

Marta looked at the chart that listed everyone's roles on the project. On the Stratisvision side, there were only two names: Dean and Kat. She tried not to take it personally.

"Well, thanks everyone. I guess it's just a question of getting stuck in now!" Dean slammed shut his presentation pack, indicating that the meeting was over. Others around the room did the same.

Marta caught B's eye across the table. It was a question of 'getting stuck in', but not for everyone. Stefan, Patricia, David and even Dean would probably not even attend another meeting after this one. Their presence here today was purely cosmetic – to show the other side that they were taking the strategic marketing innovation programme at Unilight seriously. They wouldn't actually be doing any work. It would be Kat, Marta and B 'getting stuck in'. That was how things happened in consultancy, Marta was beginning to realise. The higher you got, the easier your life became.

"Lovely to meet you," said Stefan, squeezing everybody's hands, one after another. "See you again."

The room quickly emptied, leaving just Dean, Kat and Marta alone with the uneaten biscuits.

"So. Four workstreams," Dean summarised. "Background research, framework development, idea generation and third party involvement. The last one can pretty-much be handed to B, as she'll know who the stakeholders are."

The girls nodded. Miraculously, Marta had jotted down the four workstreams correctly during the meeting, although she didn't know what any of them meant.

"You OK to divvy them up between you?" asked Dean.

They looked at each other and nodded again. Kat was wearing a nasty fake smile.

"Great! Well, shout if you have any problems. I'll leave you to it."

"No worries, Dean." Kat looked up at him, batting her eyelashes.

Dean looked at her for a second, then nodded curtly and marched out.

Marta stared at the four bullet-points. She was rather hoping Kat would suggest they work together on all four elements, but she knew that her chances were slim.

"I have a feeling the fourth workstream may take longer than anticipated," said Kat. "I'll take on that part."

Marta frowned. "But B will do—"

Kat was shaking her head. "No, B won't do it. They often say things like that in meetings to make it seem as though it's a joint team working together, blah blah blah, but really it's us doing the work. That's why they're paying us, right? We're the consultants?"

Marta nodded slowly. She wasn't convinced. Dean had just told them that this piece of work would be handled by B. Kat was glaring at her. "So that leaves one, two and three for you to do."

"Me?" Marta looked at Kat, eyes wide with astonishment. She was giving the rest of the work to Marta?

"What's the problem? I thought you were supposed to be good. I'm giving you the easy parts of the project. Can't you even cope with that?"

Marta stared at Kat, saying nothing. *The easy parts.* Yeah right. Marta could see what Kat was doing. She was getting Marta to do nearly all of the work, leaving the rest for B and taking on nothing herself.

"You are not doing—"

Kat sighed loudly, cutting her off. "Marta. You're an assistant analyst. I'm an analyst. That means you assist me. OK? I'm asking you to do parts one, two and three, because part four will be time-consuming and difficult. It's not much to ask. But if you think you're not up to the job, I can always tell—"

"No!" cried Marta. She knew that Kat's threat wasn't an empty one. She'd take pleasure in telling David Lyle that Marta couldn't manage.

Kat smiled. "Good. So you're happy with what you're doing?"

Marta nodded. She wasn't the least bit happy, but she knew that prolonging the conversation with Kat wouldn't make her any happier.

"You've got everything you need in that pack," Kat told her. "The deadline is a week on Thursday, so be ready to email it to me by the Wednesday before."

"OK," said Marta. She felt like crying.

Kat held the meeting room door closed for a second, preventing Marta from leaving. "You got some glowing reports, apparently. They obviously like you."

Marta said nothing.

"Just so you know, though, glowing reports don't get you everything." She yanked open the door and marched out.

40

"CONNIVING LITTLE BITCH," said Tina, shaking her head. "And she's the CEO's niece, you say?"

Marta nodded. They were propped up on the sofabed in the lounge with all the windows open, enjoying the night breeze on their faces. Tina was nursing an all-day hangover.

"Thing is," explained Marta, "I think she doesn't like me being there. She hate me, and really really want me to fail. Don't know why."

Tina reached into the bowl of popcorn that sat between them. "'Cause she's a jealous cow, that's why. So d'you think you can do it, all this work she's set you?"

Marta thought for a second. As it happened, one good thing had come out of today's events. After the meeting, she had returned to her desk and stared – literally, stared at the jargon-filled presentation that was supposed to be her guide. During the meeting, it had made no sense at all. It was just a fifty-page pile of nonsense – stupid phrases and pointless diagrams. But, after two hours of staring followed by extensive use of the online thesaurus, a few nuggets of sense had started to creep in. She was beginning to understand the task.

"Maybe," replied Marta. Then, with sudden newfound resolve, "In fact, yes. I can do it. I just need… steering. Is that the word?"

Tina smiled. "Guidance? Someone to keep you on track?"

"Yes, that. But I can't ask Kat – she will trick me."

Tina nodded. "What about the guy you mentioned – Dean?"

Marta shook her head. "Too senior. No way." Dean was so busy and important he probably wouldn't even answer questions from Kat.

"What about that little Italian helper you had?"

Marta screwed up her nose. "Carl. He is so nice, but not involved in this project. I need help on the details. It would take too long to explain him everything. And anyway," she added, "I think he like me."

"Hmm," grunted Tina through a mouthful of popcorn. "Tricky."

It was indeed tricky. Marta was starting to get quite concerned about the affections of her Italian colleague. He was so sweet, so kind and so keen to help her, but Marta couldn't help thinking there had to be an ulterior motive. She'd have to try and drop Jack's name into conversation – soon, before Carl got his hopes up too far.

There was a scratching noise at the front door followed by the sound of something heavy being dumped in the hallway.

"We're in here," called Tina.

"Fucking lock," muttered Holly, sighing heavily and collapsing in one of the lounge chairs.

"Nice to see you, too."

Holly said nothing. She shut her eyes and let her head roll backwards. She looked pale, even in the half-light.

"Hey, Holly might have an answer for you," suggested Tina, poking Marta. "She must've seen this a hundred times before at Andertons."

"Seen what?" asked Holly, lifting her head a little.

"Marta's having a shit time at work. She's got to do some sort of strategic bullshit programme all by herself."

Holly sighed again. "Hmm."

Tina frowned. "Come on Holly – you know everything!"

Holly clearly wasn't in the mood for jokes. She sat up, leaned forwards on her knees and looked at them.

"I don't have all the answers, you know. My life isn't perfect either."

"Sorry Hol, I didn't mean—"

"I know you didn't, but that's what everyone thinks," replied Holly, staring at the carpet, not at Tina. "I'm a management consultant at a Big Five firm, so I must know everything. I must be sorted. I must have everything I want – a fat salary, a work-life balance, a nice bloke... Well, it's not fucking true, is it? I'm earning the most money I've ever earned, and I'm the most miserable I've ever been."

Marta and Tina exchanged a quick glance. Marta had never seen Holly like this, and from the look on Tina's face, neither had she.

"I spend my whole life pretending to be a success, making everyone go 'ooh' when they hear the name of my firm, but I'm living a lie! I'm not a success, I'm just a fucking slave in a big firm where nobody knows my name."

"You're tired, Hol—"

"Yes, I know I'm tired!" she replied, almost shouting. "I've been in the office for about a hundred hours this week, haven't I? Of course I'm bloody tired!"

Tina nodded silently.

"I can't even begin to explain how much I hate that place," she said, her eyes wild with anger. "I hate the building with all its fancy glass doors and tinted windows, I hate the work – which isn't the least bit 'cutting edge', it's just time-consuming and dull – and I hate the people. I *hate* the people."

Marta watched Holly. She was so different to the happy-go-lucky girl she'd met at Jeremy's birthday dinner.

"People at Andertons only want one thing: to climb the fucking career ladder and earn more money. They're all so busy stabbing each other in the back they can't even remember why they're there. It's all about 'brownie points' – I can't stand it!"

"What?" Tina frowned.

"God, they'll do anything to prove they're the hardest-working person there. They drop in phrases like 'when I saw the email at midnight' and 'on my MBA'… as if the directors give a shit! They're like hamsters, running around in their silly little wheels looking smart and trying to impress people, but they don't realise the joke's on them! They'll all think they've won when they retire to their country homes in Dorset with their wives and kids who probably don't even belong to them… but they haven't won, because they haven't fucking lived!" She let out a long, unhappy sigh.

"Do I take it you're not enjoying work at the moment?" asked Tina, smiling cautiously.

Holly didn't even laugh. "I can't stand it. I can't stand dressing up in these stupid suits, being subservient to patronising idiots, not being allowed to speak out in meetings, seeing twats in my department arse-licking their way towards promotion, taking cabs everywhere, working weekends and never playing hockey… God, when was the last time I actually made it to a match?"

Tina shrugged timidly.

"It's so unrewarding," Holly went on. "I do a project, hand it over, get no thanks and then take on the next one. Then it's the same all over again. I don't even get to go to client meetings! It would just be nice to see some reward, for all my hard work."

"Well, you do. Sort of," said Tina. "In your pay cheque."

Holly groaned. "You don't get it! That's not what I want! I don't care about the pay cheque – I want more than that! I want to know what my input was for. I want some respect. I want to feel part of the business. I want–"

"You want your own business," Tina finished.

"No–" Holly faltered. "Well, maybe. But the point is, I can't stand the way it works at Andertons. But no one I know understands that! They all think I'm some sort of 'high achiever' but I feel like I'm not achieving anything! Why the hell did I go into consultancy? What was I thinking?"

Tina smiled. "Same thing everyone at Cambridge was thinking: that all the best graduates go into the city."

Holly rolled her eyes. She seemed to be calming down a bit; her outburst had obviously been cathartic.

"Maybe you should quit," Tina suggested after several minutes of silence.

Holly glared at her. "Would you?" she asked, quite intensely. "Would *you* quit? Either of you?" She looked at Marta and then back at Tina.

Marta thought about this for a moment. If she were as miserable as Holly was in her job – which she wasn't, and in fact her own problems seemed quite trivial in comparison – then would she walk out? She wasn't sure.

"If your parents called you every Sunday to see how your wonderful career was going, if you lied to them each week because you knew they'd be disappointed to hear the truth, if you'd spent your whole life hearing people tell you you'd be a 'high flyer'… would you quit?"

Marta found herself shaking her head. Suddenly she understood what Holly meant. She was in the same situation herself, coming to London. Everybody back home had such high hopes for her. They expected her to do well. It was exactly the same. Whenever mama called, she asked about Marta's job with such pride in her voice, it was impossible to let her down. Marta lied, just as Holly lied to her mum. "You can't quit, Holly."

Tina looked less certain. "But if you're really unhappy…"

Marta winced. Maybe Tina had never been in this situation. She was happy enough living her mad life trading bonds and sleeping with traders – she had never felt trapped like Holly. This 'city' thing sounded like hell, but it was a hell that people put up with because of the benefits: the money, the image. Holly didn't care about those things. Marta didn't either, but she knew that they were in the minority, thinking this way.

"Marta's right. I can't quit," declared Holly. "I'm stuck at Anderton's."

Tina wasn't convinced. "Jobs aren't for life any more. There's no stigma attached to leaving one profession and joining another."

"Except when you only stick one for six months," added Holly. "And anyway, if I don't end up doing consultancy, what *do* I do?"

Tina looked at her. "Chill out, for a start."

Holly rolled her eyes. "I don't have time to chill out. It's OK for you. You've got a life. You've got time to think. You're out of the office by five every day and in bed by ten – somebody else's, usually."

Tina gasped as though shocked by what Holly was insinuating.

"And that's the other thing," said Holly. "Men. The last time I met someone – properly, not Tina-style, I mean – was back at uni."

Marta nearly said something, but didn't dare.

"You're off bonking traders every night and Marta's got her mystery man… And meanwhile I'm holed up in a glass office with a bunch of brown-nosing nerds. How am I supposed to meet Mr Right–"

"But Holly!" Marta cried. She couldn't help herself. She had to get her to realise that Mr Right was here, living under the same roof, waiting for her. "You already found him," she said. "He–"

There was a scratching noise at the front door.

"Hello! Anyone home? Oh, I say." Rich walked into the lounge and stopped dead in front of Holly. "Sorry, do I know you?"

Holly smiled – for the first time that evening. "I lived here once," she said. "Before I got transferred to a cell block in Andertons."

Rich nodded, taking a closer look at Holly's face. "You look awful."

"Thanks," she said, smiling some more.

"Only joking." He leaned forward and messed up her hair. "There. Now you just look silly."

Holly whacked him on the backside as he leant over to grab a handful of popcorn. He lost his balance and landed half on Tina, half on Marta, his hand in the empty bowl. There was popcorn all over the sofabed.

"Hey, that's my bed!" cried Marta, grabbing a handful of corn and stuffing it into Rich's mouth. Tina did the same, leaving him grunting and unable to speak. Suddenly, everyone was laughing.

Holly rearranged her hair and stood up, kicking Rich back onto the sofabed just as he managed to haul himself up.

"Silly boy," she said, still smiling. "Right. I'm off to bed. Thanks for stopping me from slitting my wrists, guys. G'night all."

41

A STRIP OF SUNLIGHT pierced through the gap in the living room curtains, glowing red on Marta's eyelids. She turned over and buried her face in the pillow. It was the weekend, she deduced. The sun didn't get that high in the sky until ten or eleven o'clock. Her sleepy brain came to and she found herself smiling. Today was going to be fun.

She took longer than usual deciding what to wear. It didn't help that she had no idea what she'd be doing. In the end, she opted for jeans – the tightest pair she owned, with high heels and a hooded top. It didn't do to try too hard.

"You off out?" asked Holly, propping open the fridge door and slurping from a carton of orange juice. She too was wearing jeans, but she was dressed for comfort. Dressed, Marta suspected, for a day in the office.

"Seeing a friend," Marta replied. It was sort of true.

Holly looked at her, one eyebrow raised. "A friend…?"

Marta smiled sheepishly. "OK, is a man. A man friend."

Holly rolled her eyes. "You and your mystery man. When do we get to meet him?"

"Maybe soon," she replied. *Or maybe you already have.*

Holly swung her bag onto her shoulder and headed for the door. "Well, have fun. I certainly won't."

Marta pulled a sympathetic face and watched her disappear through the front door. Poor Holly. She really wasn't enjoying life at the moment. Marta wished there was something she could do to help, but she knew there wasn't. Grabbing a banana from the sideboard,

Marta followed her out, glad that she'd arranged to be picked up a few blocks from the flat.

She wasn't trying to mislead her flatmates. She didn't like lying. It was just that she suspected they wouldn't approve if they knew she was seeing – well, sort of seeing – the guy who had made her homeless in the first place.

Jack needn't have told her what he drove. It stood out from the others like a Prada bag in a Primark store. She made a beeline for the shiny black Audi TT.

"Hi," said Jack, lifting his sunglasses as Marta got in. He was wearing a pink open-necked Polo shirt and chinos that blended in with the cream upholstery.

"Hi Jack."

He kissed her, the formal way – once on each cheek. Marta tried not to take offence. In truth, she wasn't quite sure where she stood with Jack, or where she wanted to stand. Her initial reservations had been dispelled when he'd taken her to his posh country club. He certainly wasn't the womaniser she'd assumed – quite the opposite, in fact. He seemed like a genuinely nice guy, and, even though he didn't have a clue about how other people lived, he was interesting. He was also a challenge.

Marta liked a challenge. That was why she'd come over to England. Jack – he was one of the trickiest challenges she'd come across since arriving here. She couldn't work him out. He didn't give much away in terms of emotional clues. He was distant, aloof. He played his cards close to his chest – so much so that Marta sometimes wondered whether he liked her at all, other than in a physical sense, of course. Maybe this was what made him so intriguing.

"You look gorgeous," he said, eyeing up her legs and reversing expertly out of the space.

"Thanks." *So do you,* Marta wanted to say, but held back. She had a feeling Jack knew that already.

He manoeuvred the car onto Kilburn High Road, his movements as slick as the car he was driving.

"Where we going?" asked Marta, as they crawled between the endless sets of traffic lights. Pedestrians weaved between vehicles, peering into Jack's car like tourists on a safari.

Jack glanced sideways, smiling. "You'll see."

Marta pouted. She hated surprises – even nice ones.

"You'll enjoy it, I promise," he said, indicating to turn right down a side street.

Marta remained silent. She hated being told how she'd react to things even more than she hated surprises.

They weaved along residential streets, the spooky woman's voice on Jack's GPS directing him this way and that. At one point, Marta leaned sideways to see if the end destination was displayed on the screen, but Jack shook his head, smiling. "That won't tell you anything – unless you've done the knowledge."

"I have lots of knowledge," she replied, insulted by Jack's insinuation.

He laughed. "Not knowledge. *The* knowledge," he replied, calmly lifting his hands from the wheel to draw quotation marks in the air. "The test that cab drivers have to do to show they know every road in the city."

"Oh." Marta screwed up her nose, none the wiser. She decided to pretend not to care where they were going. They were weaving through grey streets bordered with crumbling terraces and blocks of flats. It reminded Marta of home. Jack pressed a button without moving his hands from the wheel, and suddenly Fat Boy Slim was blaring from the stereo.

Minutes later, the drabness gave way to leafy suburbia. The pavements widened and instead of high-rise flats there were Victorian houses, set back from the road behind well-trimmed hedges.

"What dress size are you?" asked Jack, as though this were a perfectly normal question to ask.

Marta frowned. "What?"

He pulled up to a T-junction and waited for the road to clear.

"You know – size. Like ten? Twelve?"

Marta was trying to work out why Jack might be asking her dress size, but she was drawing a blank.

"Ten, most places, but legs are always too long for clothes."

Jack nodded, smiling. He pulled out with unnecessary speed.

"Why you ask me this?"

Jack continued to smile. "You'll see."

"Hmph." Marta crossed her arms and stared into the oncoming traffic. What could Jack be plotting? Something where they'd have to change their clothes? Something that involved putting on boiler suits or protective clothing? She dreaded the thought. He wasn't planning for them to go paint-balling, was he?

"OK, I'll tell you," he said, clearly clocking her irritation. "We're going to South Ealing."

Marta had never heard of the place. "Why?"

"Well, have you heard of Julie Norman, the fashion designer?"

Marta thought for a second. "Yes! The high street shop! I have heard of."

Jack was shaking his head, smiling. "You're thinking of Jane Norman. Julie Norman is a famous designer – she makes clothes for the Beckhams."

"Oh. Right." Marta thought she remembered Tash mentioning the name, come to think of it, but she couldn't see what this had to do with her.

"Anyway, Julie Norman is a family friend of ours, and her daughter, Emily, has just set up her own line of clothing."

"So, we go to see your friend, Emily?"

"Well, yeah. She called me up the other day and asked whether I had a 'special someone' who might like a load of this season's fashion, straight off the sewing machine, so to speak. She's just opened a store in Ealing and she wants someone to try out her new stuff."

"We are going to try on her clothes?" It was flattering that he considered her to be a 'special someone', thought Marta, but she wasn't sure she liked her role as mannequin.

"Not we – you. And she means to keep, not just to try on."

Marta still didn't get it. As far as she could tell, they were going to Jack's friend's shop to buy some clothes. Questions filled her mind. Would it be expensive? Would Jack pay? What if she didn't like the style? Would she have to pretend to find everything adorable, the way English girls did? Would she be obliged to go back to this girl's shop and buy more?

"Don't look so worried," said Jack. "It's free fashion. Enjoy it."

"Oh." Marta nodded. Free. That was a relief.

Jack parked the car alongside a small common where men in

white were playing a slow game of cricket – not that cricket was ever exactly high speed. They crossed the road and followed the tree-lined pavement to a row of shops. A few had old-fashioned signs hanging over the doors in black and white. *Cream of the Crop,* said the one. *A Stitch in Time,* said another. It was all very English.

There was no rusty sign above *Emily Norman.* The exterior was minimalist and chic, as was the interior. Inside, there were mirrors on every wall, including the floor and ceiling, and the transparent clothing racks were hung sparsely with the type of garment you saw in Vogue or on the catwalk. Marta instantly thought of Anka.

There was a clattering sound that echoed across the mirrored shop, accentuating its emptiness. Marta wondered how long it had been in business – and how long it would stay in business, at this rate.

"Jack! Darling! How lovely to see you!"

A tall, buxom woman in her early thirties emerged from the back of the store. Even from a distance, Marta could sense her style: cool, suave, sophisticated. She was wearing high-heeled boots that came all the way up to her knees and a wrap-around woollen dress-top thing.

"Emily," he replied warmly, holding out his arms and waiting for her to clip-clop towards him.

"God, it's been ages, hasn't it?" the woman exclaimed, still holding Jack in her arms as though one kiss wasn't enough. Marta found herself willing him to let go of her. It wasn't that the woman was attractive – not in the conventional sense of the word – she was just… well, she seemed very sure of herself. And she clearly fancied Jack.

"I can't remember the last time," agreed Jack.

"Oh, and this is…?"

"Yes, sorry. Introductions," said Jack, stepping away from the woman at last. "Marta, this is Emily. Emily, Marta."

Emily smiled down from her stilt-like boots. She was one of those women, thought Marta, who managed to patronise you just by looking at you.

"*Lovely* to meet you, Marta. Oh, I've been so looking forward to you coming!" she cried, clasping her hands together. "I hope you like my new line – I *so* want someone to start wearing it, and – oh, look at your legs! They're model legs! You'd look incredible in one of my summer skorts-and-waistcoat outfits!"

Marta smiled back. What on earth were 'skorts'? She glanced sideways at the nearest rack of clothes. They certainly were high fashion. Most of the garments were so stylish they didn't appear to fall into conventional categories. What *was* that thing that looked like a tube with tassels? Perhaps they were next season's, she thought. What would Anka say when she told her?

Emily was still beaming. "Now, who's for coffee? There's a Starbucks just along here – I'll get. Cappuccino? Latte? I fancy a nice chai tea latte. What about you?"

Marta flinched at the words, remembering back to that fateful day's shopping with Tash. "Cup of tea, please."

"Just like a Brit!" cried Emily. "You are fitting in well. Jack tells me you're Polish?"

Marta nodded, wishing he hadn't. It would be nice if, occasionally, people just treated her as a person – not as a Pole. She could almost see what was going through Emily's mind: the questions about what Marta was doing over here, where she was working – was she an au pair? A cleaner? – and what dear Jack was doing with a mere Polish girl.

"What about you, Jack? What d'you fancy?"

Jack shook his head, waving away the question with his hand. "No, I'll get it. You girls get on with the dressing up."

Jack disappeared, leaving Marta alone with the assertive woman in the scary boots. She was excited about the prospect of walking away with an armful of new designer fashion, but at the same time, she was apprehensive. She wasn't sure why this woman – a supposedly successful fashion designer – would want her to take away half her stock.

"Here, dump your bag at the back," Emily instructed, grabbing Marta's scruffy handbag. "OK, so where shall we start? Trousers? I bet you have awful trouble getting them long enough, don't you? Let's see what we've got."

Emily strutted about the place, picking out garments as she saw fit. Any anxiety Marta had had about choosing suitable clothes were dispelled as the bossy designer marched up and down, holding clothes against her body and returning to the racks. Clearly Emily was making all the decisions.

"Let's try that lot, for starters," she said, depositing a mound of clothing in Marta's arms. "There's a changing room back here."

Marta felt like a contestant on one of those awful image makeover programmes on TV. Obediently, she took off her clothes.

By the time Jack returned from Starbucks, Marta had already tried on more pairs of trousers than she'd ever owned in her life.

"Next!" yelled Emily. Marta dutifully emerged from behind the curtain, assessing the stretch in the fabric around her hips. The trousers were low-slung, tight and slightly flared at the bottom. They were surprisingly comfortable to wear.

"Bloody hell," said Jack, looking as though he might drop the three coffees. "Incredible."

Emily rolled her eyes. "Well, it's the arse that's incredible. But the clothes do it justice, eh?"

Jack just nodded, staring. Marta ducked back into the changing room.

Half an hour later, they were onto more daring outfits. The dress that looked like a shawl was probably the most bizarre in Emily's collection – rejected on the grounds that it had to be worn without a bra and couldn't be trusted not to slip off one shoulder – alongside the chiffon skirt that turned into shorts at the bottom.

"Done?" asked Jack, addressing Marta's body, not her eyes. She was dressed in her favourite combination – if not the most adventurous: a chiffon top with a cutaway neckline and a pair of pale, tight jeans.

Emily folded the last garment and crammed it into the bulging cardboard bag. "Enjoy!" she cried, handing the bag to Marta.

Marta smiled awkwardly. She still didn't understand why the designer was happy for her to walk out with all these clothes, but she wasn't complaining. "Thank you so much," she said. "Am so happy for you letting me model these for free."

Emily looked at her blankly. She opened her mouth as if to say something, then shut it again. Then she switched on a smile. "Any time, darling!" She glanced at Jack. Then, and Marta couldn't be sure about this, but she thought Jack might have winked back at Emily.

They walked out to Jack's car, leaving Emily in her shop doorway, still basking in the success of her clothes – or the fact that she'd just pecked Jack on the cheek. Marta walked round to the passenger door, clutching her bag of clothes and thinking. Something didn't feel quite right. It was odd that Emily was giving away a large part of her collection. It wasn't as though Marta was anyone special. OK, she had longer legs than most, and the clothes did look good on her, but it wasn't as though she'd be walking around with the labels on display. How would Emily benefit?

Marta could only think of one explanation. *Jack was paying for the clothes.* Could he be? Did he feel so ashamed of Marta's dress sense, her second-hand outfits, her Polish tastes, that he was buying her a new wardrobe? Marta thought back to the looks she used to get from Tash when she put on her Malina Q jacket. Was Jack embarrassed to be going out with her as she was?

"See you again, I hope!" yelled Emily, blowing kisses in their direction.

Marta waved back. Maybe she was just being paranoid. After all, Jack's ex-girlfriend had been very glamorous, so she was probably just feeling inferior. There was probably nothing sinister to this whatsoever. She got in the car, banishing the negative thoughts from her mind. Jack had simply taken her here to help out a friend – and in so doing, he happened to have acquired for Marta a whole load of beautiful, fashionable clothes. In return, Marta would wear them with pride, telling everyone she met where they came from.

Jack opened his window and stuck his hand out as they pulled away. Then, as smoothly as he changed gear, he reached over and slid a hand onto Marta's leg.

"You look amazing," he said.

Marta smiled, and as she did so, realised something. For the first time in weeks, she hadn't thought about Dom all day. Well, until now, anyway. Ha. She was finally moving on.

42

"IT STILL HASN'T ARRIVED. How large is the file?"

Marta looked up, determined not to be flustered by Kat's tone of voice. "Is four megabytes," she said, pressing Send and hoping Kat wasn't looking at her screen. It was Thursday morning, the day of the final run-through for the presentation that had occupied most of Marta's waking hours in the last two weeks. She was supposed to have sent it to Kat last night, but by midnight it still wasn't finished, so she'd come in at six this morning to get it done. To say that the task had been stressful would have been an understatement.

"I'll check one more time. If it hasn't reached me you'll have to save it to USB. Fuck, it's nearly eight-thirty. David will be in any minute." Kat sighed dramatically and strutted back to her desk.

The office was still relatively empty, but Dean and a few others were in, quietly listening to Kat's performance and no doubt picking up on the fact that Marta had let her down. Marta turned to her Outlook calendar to find out the time of the run-through. Kat's high-heeled shoes was clacking towards her again.

"Got it," she said. "Finally."

Marta forced a smile and looked up. "Is it OK? The presentation?"

Kat shrugged. "We'll see, won't we?" She hesitated, eyeing Marta suspiciously. "Where d'you get that?"

Marta smiled innocently. "What?"

"That skirt. I've seen it before, in Vogue or something. Where d'you get it?"

Marta maintained her smile, relishing the prospect of telling the fashion guru something about fashion. "Is designer. Emily Norman."

Kat frowned, obviously unable to work out how a Polish girl could afford Emily Norman, but too proud to ask. She flicked her white-blonde hair like a girl on a shampoo advert and headed back to her desk. Marta grinned to herself. The score was two-nil to Marta. Not only had she accomplished the impossible on the presentation (it was 'just right'; Carl had told her so) but she had trumped Kat in the fashion stakes.

Marta's diary was empty. She opened up Dean's. His was crammed full of meetings, including one at nine-thirty called 'Unilight run-thru'. Kat's also contained the nine-thirty run-through. Marta frowned and pushed back her chair.

"Kat?" she said, standing over Kat's desk. Only one of her followers was in, and she was busy scrolling through photos on Facebook.

Kat raised an eyebrow in acknowledgement as she continued to compose an email.

"Am I coming to Unilight run-through at nine-thirty?"

Kat swivelled round in her chair. "No."

"Why not?"

Kat shrugged casually. "No need. It's a run-through for David and Dean."

"But you are going, yes?"

"Yes. They need someone as support, in case anything needs changing in the presentation."

"But I did the presentation," Marta argued, quietly but firmly. The girl on the desk glanced up, clearly sensing the tension.

"Don't flatter yourself," Kat told her. "You did part of the presentation, and I've slotted that into the main presentation, which I wrote. There's no need for you to be there at nine-thirty, OK? I'm sure you've got plenty of other stuff to be getting on with."

Marta nodded, wondering whether it was worth arguing. The truth was, she had written a fifty-page slide pack which formed the bulk of the presentation. Kat had added six slides at the back – six slides which B had sent over from Unilight.

"Fine. Good luck with run-through," she said, storming back to her desk.

It took a couple of minutes for Marta to calm down, and then a few more for her to start thinking rationally about what to do. The problem was, Kat would go into that meeting and take credit for all Marta's work – except, of course, the mistakes. Those would be Marta's fault.

Perhaps she would email Dean – maybe David Lyle and Patricia, too – and show them what she had done. She needed to let them know how much she'd contributed, how hard she had worked. But she couldn't do that. This was the real world, not school. She wasn't trying to become teacher's pet. But how did people get recognition when they had colleagues like Kat?

Marta was still pondering her dilemma when her seat started wobbling like a bucking bronco.

"Good morneeng," said Carl, releasing the chair and settling down opposite. "How ees the presentation?"

Marta shrugged. "OK, I suppose. Is done."

Carl nodded slowly, looking across the office. "Oh. I see. Presentation is in the meeting room and you are not. Oh dear."

Marta nodded, looking up in time to see Kat disappearing through the frosted glass doors with David Lyle and Dean in tow. She had a stack of colourful print-offs under her arm.

"No problemo for you," Carl said. "If it is good, they will remember you were involved with a good project. If it is bad, Kat will look stupid in the meeting. You have nothing to worry about."

Marta nodded reluctantly. Carl was right. She didn't need to worry. Everyone did work that went unacknowledged from time to time. She just had to try and avoid being put on projects with Kat in future.

It made a nice change, having nothing to do. The past two weeks had rushed by so quickly she'd had no time to chat, or even eat – only occasionally surfacing from PowerPoint to thank Carl for coffee or a piece of advice. He'd been a hero these last few days.

"Ees your life gonna be a beat calmer, now?" he asked, popping up from behind his monitor. Marta hesitated, distracted by an email that had arrived in her inbox.

> From: *Jack Templeton-Cooper, IBD*
> Subject: *Last night…*
> …*You looked amazing. I still feel horny now, thinking about you.*

Marta frowned, closing the email quickly in case anyone happened to be walking past with very good eye sight.

"I hope so," she said, returning Carl's smile and clicking on Reply.

From: Marta Dabrowska
But I didn't see you last night! You are getting confused with another girl... ☺

"Maybe you wheel have time for lunch away from your desk?" Carl suggested hopefully.

Marta took the hint. "Maybe. And if I do, am paying for your lunch also."

It was the least she could do, really. And Marta was keen to repay Carl for his help in as many ways as possible that weren't sexual.

"That would be nice," said Carl, glancing down Marta's top.

Jack's reply came almost instantly.

From: Jack Templeton-Cooper, IBD
You didn't see me, but I saw you. In my dream. You were wearing an incredible dress.

Marta hit reply, then wondered what to write. It was strangely exciting to know that Jack Templeton-Cooper had been dreaming about her, but she wasn't sure she wanted to engage in dirty talk over email – especially on her Stratisvision email account.

From: Marta Dabrowska
What was this dress like?

The tremors in the office indicated that Charlotte was walking through it. Marta flicked to the PowerPoint presentation and pretended to edit a slide. Thankfully, the stomping continued past her desk, only slowing as it reached Carl's.

"What's your capacity?" she barked.

Marta stared at the slide, wondering how Carl would answer a question like that. Capacity for what, she wondered? Spaghetti? Beer? Ooh – a message from Jack.

"Ees OK. Can do something for you eef you lake," Carl replied.

"Great," said Charlotte. "Come over to the end office in five minutes and I'll brief you. Drop anything else you've got on; this is a priority."

Charlotte charged off, leaving Carl to breathe a long, slow sigh. "Looks like lunch ees off," he said.

"Another day," replied Marta, not particularly bothered about lunch but feeling a mixture of pity and envy for Carl. The guy was working for Charlotte – a fate she didn't wish upon anybody – but at the same time, he was *valued*. He was looked upon as a reliable resource; someone who could be trusted with important tasks. Priority tasks. Nobody marched up to Marta and demanded she drop everything else she had on. Ooh – another email from Jack.

From: *Jack Templeton-Cooper*
PS Transparent dresses aside, what are you doing 2 weeks from now? Does a masked banquet in the Natural History Museum appeal? You'd have to put up with my colleagues for company I'm afraid, but it should be a tolerable night.

Marta nearly squeaked with excitement. She pressed Reply and tried to think of a suitably witty response. That was the thing. Jack was so clever with his words. She knew she was as sharp as he was, but it was so much harder in another language. Hmm. Something about masks, or natural history…?

"Marta, are you busy?"

Marta whirled round. She had no idea how long Dean had been standing there.

"A little," she replied, pressing Escape and discarding her email. Shit. Had Dean seen anything of their exchange?

"Could you pop into the meeting room for a minute?"

Marta nodded, trying not to look guilty. Dean seemed angry – or maybe Dean always seemed angry. He was a very serious man. Clutching her notebook and a pen, she followed him through the office.

Kat was just leaving the room as they approached, followed by

David, who was clapping her on the shoulder and saying "Great work," over and over again. Kat was beaming like a girl who'd just won Miss World. Marta avoided catching her eye.

"How did it go, the run-through?" asked Marta, once they had settled in the empty meeting room with the door shut. Dean was stretched out in the seat at the head of the table, looking scary.

"It went OK," he replied coldly.

"Any changes I need to make to my parts of the presentation?" she asked, wondering whether now would be an opportunity to explain how much she'd contributed to this assignment.

Dean screwed up his face, as though he couldn't decide how to respond.

"See, this is what I wanted to talk to you about," he said, finally.

Marta nodded brightly. He still looked very serious.

"Kat forwarded me the email you sent her this morning."

Marta nodded again. This was excellent news. I meant that Dean would know exactly what she'd done. "So you saw my parts of the presentation?"

"Mmm." Carl looked pensive, as though he were picking his words carefully. "And that's what concerns me."

Marta frowned. Didn't Dean think her work was good enough? That was impossible. Carl had checked it. He would have told her if it hadn't been up to scratch.

"A question for you, Marta." Dean looked at her sternly. "Do you really believe you gave a hundred percent in this project?"

Marta hesitated. Was this a trick? Of course she'd given a hundred percent. More than that. She'd been in the office 'til midnight last night and back in at six this morning. The past two weeks had been almost entirely devoted to this presentation.

"Yes. I believe that I give one hundred percent." She returned his stern expression.

Dean closed his eyes, as though pausing to consider something.

"Is it not good enough, my work?" asked Marta, desperate to find out why Dean's reaction was so negative. She had expected quite the opposite; secretly, she had expected praise.

"That's not for me to say," replied Dean, pushing up from the table.

Marta mirrored his actions, barely registering her own movement towards the door, or Dean's polite dismissal. She was totally preoccupied. Had she not worked hard enough? Were her standards too low? Had Carl just wanted to flatter her by saying her work was 'just right'? She didn't know. All she knew was that Dean was holding open the door in a way that suggested he wasn't at all impressed.

Marta wandered through the office, downbeat. Maybe Dean was just a perfectionist, she thought. Maybe he gave everyone that speech. Yes, that was probably it. Dean was one of those people who could never be happy. She sat down at her desk. Her phone told her that she'd missed another call from Dom. She pressed delete. At least he'd stopped leaving messages. With the thoughts tumbling around her head, Marta jiggled her mouse and started to re-draft her email to Jack.

43

"IT IS CALLED 'MAY BALL' but it happen in June?"

Holly smiled. "It's stupid, I know. I think it's always been like that. It's a Cambridge thing."

Rich nodded, adjusting his bow-tie. "Tradition."

Marta glanced sideways. Rich was handsome, she realised for the first time since she'd met him. Not that he'd ever seemed unattractive; it was just that he always looked… messy. Removed from his old trainers and low-hanging jeans, though, he scrubbed up pretty well.

Marta picked up the pace a little and turned back to take a photo. Rich darted sideways to get between Tina and Holly, reaching out and gently squeezing their bare shoulders. It was the perfect shot: the mottled pink sky bringing out the colour of Tina's fuscia dress, Holly's slinky blue halterneck contrasting with the cobbles and stonework. Marta looked at the screen until the preview disappeared. "Is beautiful."

Rich stepped forwards. "Beauty is in the eye of the beholder," he said, grabbing the camera and whisking it away.

"Eye of what?" asked Marta, but Rich was already behind the lens, composing his shot.

Marta smiled obligingly, feeling self-conscious in the body-hugging shimmery outfit they'd lent her. It wasn't that she didn't like it – the dress was divine; light blue to match her eyes – it was just that she felt out of place in such finery. This was the sort of thing celebrities wore when they walked down red carpets. It wasn't for commonplace people like Marta.

"Lovely," said Rich, passing the camera back to Holly.

They were approaching a large, stone archway that looked like something from a Harry Potter film. Above it was a carving of a fat man holding a chair leg or something and cut into the vast wooden door was a smaller one that kept swinging open to let pairs of people walk through.

"So, welcome to our college," said Tina.

Marta shook her head, smiling. It still seemed absurd that whilst she'd been living at home with mama and tata, cycling between temporary wooden huts just outside Warsaw, Tina, Holly and Rich had been learning in such palatial surroundings.

"You got the tickets?" asked Holly. Rich reached into his back pocket and waved two black envelopes in the air. Not for the first time, Marta felt a pang of guilt. The Cambridge flatmates had bought two 'double tickets', which entitled four people to attend the ball. They had insisted that Marta come with them and didn't pay on the grounds that the tickets had already been bought. She felt like a charity.

It was a strange sight that greeted them on the other side. They were entering a huge, grass courtyard bordered with ancient white buildings and flowerbeds. Snaking around the outside of the courtyard was an incredible array of coloured dresses and black and white suits. It was the prettiest queue Marta had ever seen.

It was also the most entertaining. Before they had 'gone through' (whatever that meant), they had been jumped at by a juggling fire-eater, tricked by a man with a wand and entertained by a group of young men in stripy waistcoats singing loudly whilst bobbing up and down.

"Let's go!" cried Tina, as they exchanged the tickets for small plastic wrist-bands that looked like cattle tags.

They found themselves in another courtyard, this one decorated ornately in flowers and lit up with lights that transformed the grey stone into a colourful masterpiece. It was like walking through a film set.

"Champagne?" offered a young man in an apron.

Marta took it, remembering what the others had said. *Everything's free once you're in.* It was true. The place was heavenly. They drifted along one side of the courtyard where someone was giving out shells.

"Mmm, oysters," said Rich, reaching out and grabbing enough for them all.

Marta wasn't convinced by the gooey, stringy fish-like things. They had a consistency like the inside of a tomato: impossible to chew.

"Champagne?" offered someone else. It was madness – champagne coming at her from all directions! Marta declined, admiring the bottles – literally, hundreds of bottles – that were crammed together inside what looked like a boat full of ice.

"I'm starving. Let's eat," suggested Tina, who had apparently not eaten since yesterday lunchtime in anticipation of the 'amazing grub'.

They wandered through more stone archways and over a bridge, all lit up and adorned with flowers. How much must the tickets have cost?

Authentic Chinese stir-fried noodles or pork from the enormous pig that was being roasted on a spit – that was the choice. In the end, they opted for both and sat down to eat it in front of a fairground ride, washing it down with champagne. Marta sipped hers, not wanting to drink too much in case things went blurry. She wanted to remember everything about tonight.

A photographer jumped out of the darkness and snapped Holly and Rich, obviously mistaking them for a couple. Easily done, thought Marta, smiling as the man showed them his handiwork. He had caught them mid-conversation and they were smiling into one another's eyes.

"Come on – time for dodgems," suggested Holly, turning away from the photographer with a brusque smile and hitching up her dress. Marta caught Tina's eye and grinned.

After the exhilaration of dodgems – which left Rich significantly more battered than his female flatmates despite their heels and restrictive attire – they wandered over to a grassy bank that was slowly filling up with ball-goers. Marta wasn't a big fan of fireworks, but she had a feeling these might be more impressive than those at the annual Łomianki display.

She was right. The sky was ripped apart with a deafening eruption of reds, greens and yellows, accompanied by the pop-pop-pop of a hundred explosives. They kept coming, too – lighting up Cambridge as brightly as the midday sun. There were small, silent white ones that flood-lit the air, cheeky yellow ones that weaved spirals and squeaked as they went and of course, a phenomenal outburst of colour to end the display. The crowd was in raptures.

"Jazz tent? Casino?" asked Rich, when the applause had finally died down. "Hypnotist?"

They drifted happily from marquee to marquee, sometimes venturing into the main stone building to see a show, hear some music or stop by the chocolate fountain. Marta preferred the outdoor entertainment; the tents reminded her too much of working for Bread and Butter Catering. They watched a band called the Rolling Clones – a very good copy of the band that tata used to listen to – and later on saw a guy called Jason Donovan. Marta had never heard of him, but all the girls got very excited about his act, despite the fact that he seemed drunk and only had five songs.

After a while, Tina declared an interest in getting her tarot cards read and abruptly disappeared. Marta watched her slink off, perplexed.

"She's pulled," explained Holly, nodding towards the good-looking pianist who had just finished his set. He was slipping off in the same direction as Tina. Marta smiled, shaking her head.

They returned to the main tent where a bunch of mad-looking men and women were leaping about on the stage with violins and drums. The man at the front was shouting into a microphone, saying things like, "Skip to the right!" and "Now change partners!" to a mass of sweaty ball-goers who were prancing around the tent.

Marta found herself following Holly and Rich onto the rumpled dance floor. It was harder than it looked, jumping in time with the banging drums and following orders from the man at the front. After ten minutes, she ducked out, welcoming the blast of cold air from outside and a break from her partner's armpits.

Separated from her flatmates, Marta wandered away from the crazy dancing tent towards a corner they hadn't yet explored. She wasn't worried about losing the others; she'd find them later. Holly's blue dress would be easy to spot.

A room had been constructed by partitioning off a stone corridor with swathes of fabric. Inside was a full gambling set-up: everything you'd expect to see in a real casino, only perhaps more colourful. Marta weaved between the roulette wheel and the poker table, watching the jovial carelessness with which chips were thrown away. It was just a game; the chips were worth nothing.

Marta was considering the possibility of trying her hand at Black Jack when she saw something that made her stop dead. There, standing only a couple of metres away, her blonde hair hanging in soft curls down her back, was Tash. She was standing side-on, clasping the arm of a suave young man who was placing a bet. He looked just like Jack, thought Marta, turning quickly and leaving the room before she was spotted. Trust Tash to get a Jack look-alike the minute he left her.

She was still shaking as she walked up the white steps that linked the courtyards. It shouldn't have come as a surprise. Of course Tash was here. Of course she'd come back to her old college for the 'May ball'. But for some reason, Marta had neglected to predict this. She had blocked that part of her life from her mind.

A disco was blaring from one of the larger halls. Marta hovered in the doorway, perching on a bench at the back of the room. The balls of her feet hurt and one of the straps was rubbing on her little toe. *You're the one the I want, you are the one I want – ooh, ooh, ooh, honey!* Even Marta knew the words. She had watched Grease about six times in English. She sat, nursing her feet and watching the terrible dancers lurch around the floor.

It took a few minutes for Marta to notice the person sitting next to her at the back of the hall. The only reason she did notice, in fact, was because the bench started wobbling. It was rocking as though… as though the person was sobbing. Marta could hear the sniffing between sobs. She looked sideways.

The sight nearly caused her to shriek. "Holly?"

The girl turned, dropping her hands from her face. Holly's eyes were barely recognisable they were so red. The sobbing stopped, briefly.

"What's wrong?" Marta shifted sideways along the bench so she didn't have to compete with Chesney Hawkes' *I Am the One and Only*.

Holly shrugged, biting her lower lip to stop it shaking. "Oh, I dunno." Another tear rolled down her cheek. "I just saw an ex-boyfriend with another girl."

Marta laid an arm gently around her shoulders. "Oh, Holly. That is so horrible. You still like the guy?"

Holly shrugged again. "No, not really."

Marta frowned. "Oh. So what is problem?"

Holly shook her head as though she didn't know where to start. "It just made me realise… It made me think about my old life, and my new one, and… well, I used to love it. I used to have loads of friends, do sport, go out with guys, have a laugh… Now I hate every moment of it. Everything's awful." Holly leant forwards on her knees, wiping her bare arm across her face. Her makeup was ruined.

"Let me get you tissue," said Marta, remembering a sign she'd seen for the ladies' nearby.

Holly nodded gratefully. It was strange, seeing Holly like this. She had always seemed such a strong person, so resilient, but she no longer seemed to have the energy to bounce back. Marta wondered what to advise. Quitting Andertons would seem like the most sensible option, but was that defeatist? What would she do if she did leave?

This career thing was so difficult. Marta had always assumed that it would be easy after leaving university. A degree was a passport to better jobs, career options… anything, really. And it was, in Holly's case. Not in Marta's, of course; she had the wrong type of degree. But for Holly, she could do whatever she wanted. The problem was, what *did* she want? Nobody talked about the issue of having too many options. Marta wrapped her fist in a bundle of toilet roll and raced back to the disco.

Someone had taken her place on the bench. Marta hung back. She recognised the tall physique of the guy next to Holly. With one hand on her arm, gently rubbing it, Rich was saying something to her. Something amusing. She was laughing through the tears and nodding. Marta slipped into the shadows of the hallway.

It happened just like in the movies. Rich produced a handkerchief from his pocket (What foresight! Where on earth had he got one of them?) and dabbed at her face whilst making jokes. Holly was cheering up. Then they moved closer. Holly reached out and cupped the side of his face in her hand. She pulled him near, and finally, they kissed.

Marta slipped out of the doorway and headed back to the mad folk-dancing tent with a massive grin on her face.

44

MARTA FROWNED AT HER HANDSET. *Withheld number* flashed at her as it rang. Eventually, after Tina and Rich had both turned to glare at her, she picked up.

"Hey gorgeous, how's things?"

"Good!" whispered Marta, recognising the voice instantly and hurrying out of the lounge. Her heart was thumping. Secretly, she'd been hoping Jack would call.

"Why are you whispering?"

"I'm not!" she replied, softly. She wasn't actually sure why she was keeping her voice down – it wasn't as though the others could tell who was on the other end of the line.

"Yes you are. Where are you? Not still at work?"

"No – am home."

"OK then. So yell, HI JACK, HOW ARE YOU, HONEY?" he goaded.

"No."

"You haven't told them, have you?" he asked, with mirth in his voice.

"No." She perched on the stairs, wishing – not for the first time – that she had her own room. The living room had all the material things she could wish for in a bedroom – bed, wardrobe, chest, desk – but it lacked privacy.

"Don't blame you. I'm not exactly flavour of the month there, I know. Hey listen, I can't chat as I'm in the office, but–"

"Still?" Marta interjected. It was ten o'clock on a Monday.

Jack sighed. "Don't ask. You're gonna regret choosing to go out with a banker, believe me."

Marta smiled. *Choosing to go out with a banker.* So far, she hadn't regretted a moment of it.

"But it's about the banquet on Wednesday."

Marta forced herself not to react like an excitable teenager. Inside, she was babbling her head off. "What about it?"

"Well, I just wanted to warn you."

"Warn about what?"

Jack hesitated. "About my colleagues."

"Are they as bad as you?" asked Marta, pleased with herself for remaining so aloof.

Jack laughed. "Worse, I'm afraid."

"And you think I won't manage?" she asked, smiling. She wasn't quite sure what Jack was warning her of, exactly, but she felt confident she would cope fine. She had come across most types since moving to England.

"N-no," Jack replied, uncharacteristically hesitant. "No, I just mean... well, they're animals, to be frank. Predators."

"And you think I will be scared by that?" asked Marta, remembering back to her night out with Tina and the traders. Shocked, she may have been, but she certainly hadn't been scared.

"I just mean... well, you're an attractive girl, Marta—"

"Thank you," she interrupted, quite enjoying the conversation.

"And they'll try it on with you – even though they'll have another girl on their arm – so be prepared for some harassment, OK?"

"Sure," said Marta, wondering why Jack was feeling so protective, all of a sudden. It was nice to know he cared, of course, but really, she could fend for herself.

"And they'll say all sorts of crap about me," he added.

"What sort of crap?"

"Oh, they'll call me Jack the Stripper, and they'll probably make up loads of stories about me and other women."

A brief wave of anxiety flitted through Marta's mind. *Was* Jack a womaniser? He might be – she wouldn't know. "And why would they do that, Jack?"

"Oh, because it's funny. Because in banking it's supposed to be cool to have eight girls on the go at any one time, so that's what everyone pretends. I've somehow got myself a reputation as a bit of a player, and the boys don't let it lie."

"How?"

"Well..." Jack tutted. She could picture his muscular shoulders lifting as he shrugged. "By making stuff up, mainly."

Marta laughed. "Like in school!"

Jack laughed too. "Yeah, I guess. Goldmans is a bit like school."

"Well as long as I can make up some stuff too," said Marta, already starting to plot her introductory line. *Hi, I'm Jana Bogalov, daughter of Russian tsar...*

"Of course," said Jack, sounding reassured. "I just didn't want you to be shocked by all the bollocks they come up with."

Marta was grinning. "It is them who will be shocked."

"Oh really? I can't wait. Are you going to wear a transparent dress?"

Marta laughed. "Maybe."

"You could," he said, "as it's a masked banquet, so no one would recognise you."

"I said, maybe," Marta replied, with no intention of wearing a transparent dress. She already had her outfit – a perfectly opaque outfit – planned out.

"See you Wednesday, then. The Zetland Arms at six."

Marta was tempted to say something about how excited she was, but she restrained herself. "See you then," she said coolly.

"'Bye gorgeous."

45

"MARTA, THIS EES BRILLIANT. I really appreciate your help."
Carl finished skimming through the print-offs and smiled at her.

"At least someone does," she said, shrugging.

Carl frowned. "What do you mean?"

Marta shook her head and slipped down in her chair, letting the
monitor eclipse his view. She didn't want the whole office to know
the problem. "Doesn't matter."

Anka seemed to have disappeared. She'd been online all morning,
keeping Marta amused with silly stories of comings and goings in
Łomianki, but now she wasn't responding. She must've gone back to
the bakery. Jack wasn't around either; he was flying to Germany for
some hugely important business meeting. He had his Gooseberry but
it didn't feel right sending naughty messages when he was in the
middle of handling a major global transaction.

The problem was simple: She didn't have anything to do. Other
than the tit-bits Carl had passed on, on her request, she'd had no
assignments for a whole week now. Ever since the day after the
Unilight run-through, in fact. She was beginning to wonder whether
the two things were connected.

Her computer bleeped. She brought up her email, anticipating
Anka's reply.

> *From:*   *David Lyles, Director*
> *Subject:*   *Re: Marta's performance on Unilight*

> *Marta,*

Sorry not to do this in person but I am extremely busy at the moment and am out of the office until next week.

I am sorry to say that the purpose of this email is to give you an official warning about the quality of your work at Stratisvision. Whilst your deliverables in the trial two-week period were of sufficient quality to guarantee you further employment for the duration of June and July, it has been noted that your output since the extension of your contract has been of a considerably lower standard – with reference to the Unilight project. It has also been noted that your attitude has been nonchalant when probed on this matter.

Just so you know: under UK law, employers are obliged to give three official warnings before an employee is asked to leave.

Kind regards,

David

PS – A word of advice, Marta: please don't let me issue you with any more warnings. Your initial appraisal showed real promise, and I feel sure that with more consistent diligence on your part, you could go far at Stratisvision. (You are a Pole, after all!)

David Lyle, Director
Stratisvision. Helping companies stretch and grow through strategic marketing innovation.

Marta stared at the email. She re-read the main paragraph. For a moment, she wondered whether David was joking. He was a bit of a clown – he might think it was funny to send this to the new girl. But then she thought about the language. It was all formal, as though he'd copied it and pasted it from some official handbook. And the PS – there was nothing funny about that. He clearly wasn't fooling around.

Marta thought about forwarding it to Carl and asking his advice. But then, what could he say? Of everyone she knew, Carl was the one person who would almost certainly never have received anything like this in his life. She played with the scroll button on her mouse. Down, up. Down, up. How could they be warning her about the quality of her work? She wasn't perfect, sure. But she was good. Good enough. She felt certain about that.

As she scrolled, Marta noticed something. There was more text in the email, below David's signature. It looked like… It looked like correspondence between David and Dean. Marta leant forward.

> *From:*   *Dean Johnson, Associate Director*
> *To:*   *David Lyle, Director*
> *Subject:*   *Fw: here you go*
>
> *David,*
> *See below. I have mounting concerns over this assistant analyst. She had two weeks to complete the task, and output (attached) is brief & shoddy to say the least. Late, too. My impression is that Kat had to pull out all the stops to get it into shape on time.*
> *Spoke with the assistant analyst after the mtg – she was nonchalant, as though nothing amiss. Proud of her efforts(?).*
> *…Official warning?*
> *I'll leave it with you.*
>
> *Dean*
>
> *Dean Johnson*
> *Associate Director*
> *Stratisvision*

Marta stared, horrified. She felt certain that David hadn't meant to include this exchange in the email to her, but she was glad that he had. 'Mounting concerns?' 'Nonchalant as though nothing amiss'? But nothing *was* amiss! How could they judge her so harshly? Carl had checked her presentation and said it was 'just right'. He wouldn't have lied. And how could Dean give Kat so much credit, when she'd done almost nothing in the whole two weeks? She read on.

> *From:*   *Kat Sneider*
> *To:*   *Dean Johnson, Associate Director*
> *Subject:*   *Fw: here you go*

Hi Dean,

Meeting went well, didn't it? I think we impressed the Unilight team ☺
Sorry to do this, but I feel I ought to share something with you. As you know, the Polish intern has been helping me on the presentation. Below is the email she sent me this morning – a day late and frankly, inadequate. Luckily we pulled together a half-decent pres in the end, but no thanks to her.

Let me know next steps following mtg. Happy to make changes etc.
K

Kat Sneider
Marketing Analyst, Stratisvision

Marta was shaking now – through anger or fear, she didn't know. Kat was more of a bitch than she'd imagined. Why would anyone send an email like this? And how could she dare rate the presentation as 'inadequate' when Dean would have seen with his own eyes that it was perfectly good? Marta scrolled down to the bottom.

From:	*Marta Dabrowska*
To:	*Kat Sneider*
Subject:	*here you go*
Attachments:	*<Unilight_presentation_MD_v3>*

Hi Kat,

Here you go – am sorry it is late and I didn't finish it. I have problems to be quick enough, but here you go. Is OK but I still need doing lots of work on it.

Marta
Marta Dabrowska, Stratisvision

Marta nearly choked. She stared at the screen, hardly able to believe what she was reading. This wasn't the email she'd sent Kat. She never wrote 'I didn't finish it' or 'I have problems to be quick enough'. Kat must have edited Marta's email to make her look bad, then forwarded it to Dean. And the attachment… Marta looked at the file name and closed her eyes. Of course. Kat had sent over an early draft of the presentation. A very early draft. No wonder Dean was unimpressed.

For a moment, she just sat, staring, unseeing, thinking about what she'd just learnt. Thank God David Lyle was careless with his emails.

The rationale for Kat's elaborate, vindictive ploy was a mystery to Marta, and right now she didn't have time to think about it. She just needed to work out a way of proving to David and Dean that she was good enough after all. After a few minutes, inspiration struck. She delved into her Sent Items.

Had Marta not had such a resilient personality, she might have cried on discovering that the email was missing. Instead, she sighed shakily and buried her head in her hands, staring at the screen through splayed fingers. Kat had somehow deleted the message. There was no way of telling David or Dean what she'd sent Kat that morning. Robotically, Marta rose from her seat and headed for the exit. She needed a place to think, and the ladies' toilets seemed as good a place as any.

Annoyingly, both toilets were occupied. As she toyed between waiting like an English person and going off in search of another option, there was a flushing sound.

"Oh, hi Marta. Nice belt," sung Kat, emerging from the cubicle and strutting towards the sinks. "Designer, is it?"

Marta swallowed. "Emily Norman."

Kat reached for a paper towel. "Blimey. They *are* paying you too much. You seem to have Emily Norman's entire collection."

Marta ignored the comment. She had two options: confront Kat now, whilst she had her at arm's length on neutral ground, or wait for another opportunity that might never come up.

"Kat, I have question for you."

A look of guilt briefly flickered across Kat's immaculate face. "What?"

"Why did you send fake email to Dean so he thinks I am useless?"

Kat frowned – quite convincingly, in fact. Marta wasn't deterred. "What're you on about?"

"You know. I did all the work for the Unilight presentation and you did a fake email to Dean saying I couldn't do it."

Kat glanced over her shoulder as though checking that the cubicles were empty, then stepped closer, pressing Marta up against the wash basins. "Listen. As I said before, I'm the analyst, you're the assistant analyst. You assist me. If I want to take credit for the work, I will. OK?"

"But you lied to—"

"And how exactly is that different to what you did, taking credit for the Italian Stallion's work?" She raised an eyebrow.

Marta was lost for words. It was *completely* different. She had tried several times to explain to Charlotte that it was Carl's work she was using, whereas Kat had deliberately misled her boss – fabricating emails, for God's sake.

"Listen," said Kat, stepping back from the sinks and heading for the door. "I suggest you just keep quiet, and keep working hard," she said. "There's nothing they hate more than a cry-baby here." With a toss of her über-blonde hair, she flung open the door and waltzed out.

46

"FUCK, I THINK I'M ALREADY PISSED," slurred one of the bankers' girlfriends, tripping as she tottered out of the pub.

"It's the masks," said another, whose face was covered by an elaborate Red Indian feathered affair. "I can't see a bloody thing out of mine."

The girls turned to look at her and burst out laughing. It was impossible not to.

"Where did you *get* it, Suze? It looks like it's got fully integrated wig plaits and everything!"

There was a moment's silence, then Susie replied. "That's my hair."

"Oh, right. Sorry."

They followed the men up the steps and into the grand, stone building. Marta had never been to the Natural History Museum before. She had no idea what to expect. It seemed like a strange place to hold a company summer ball, but then Goldman Sachs was a strange company. Any firm that expected its employees to work through weekends and evenings was strange, in Marta's books.

"Shall we retrieve our partners?" suggested one of the gorgeous men in bow-ties. All of Jack's colleagues were gorgeous. They reminded her of Tina's work mates: young, suave, attractive – and very rude. They had already assigned her the name 'Jack's Polska' – apparently to distinguish her from 'the others'. Marta had retained her composure; Jack had warned her of what to expect.

Jack stepped sideways and held out his arm. Marta nearly melted with pride. He looked adorable. His mask, which was subtle like hers, covered only his eyes, and did nothing to disguise his good looks.

"Shall we?" he said, guiding Marta across the pillared atrium towards the red carpet.

Marta grinned. "I feel like a movie star," she said, taking care not to trip in her exceedingly high heels.

"You look like one," Jack replied, glancing down yet again at the shimmering silver dress that hugged her body. It was long, but had a slit that ran all the way up the right hand side, revealing most of her leg. "No – you look better than a movie star."

Marta smiled. It was so nice to be going out with Jack. He was so different to anybody she'd ever dated. Different in a good way. Even though he'd been brought up in another country – in another class, perhaps – and even though he hadn't grasped exactly what Marta had been through, moving to England… he made her feel good. He had introduced her to his world – his ridiculous, affluent, exciting world – and he was letting her in. She squeezed his arm as they entered the hall.

The banquet room was like nothing she could have imagined – namely because in the middle of it, casting an imposing shadow over the decorative, candlelit tables, was an enormous skeleton of a diplodocus.

"Fuck me!" yelled Suze from behind her Hiawatha mask, before tripping over the matting and finding herself hanging off her boyfriend's arm.

Jack moved closer to Marta, so that their masks were touching. "He probably will, later on. That's why JD comes to these events."

Marta frowned. "For sex?"

Jack nodded. "Brings a different girl every time. They get hideously drunk then end up shagging in the loos or outside."

Marta cringed. Surely that wasn't the point of an evening like this? She looked around, marvelling at the impressive surroundings. The hall was like a cathedral: large and ornate, with gold candlesticks on each of the twenty or so tables, the whole room bathed in a warm, red glow.

They moved towards the swarm of gorgeous people at one end of the hall, behind which, apparently, was the table plan. Jack dived through the masses and emerged looking somewhat unimpressed.

"Shit." Jack looked at his mate, JD.

"What?"

"Roy Butcher."

Marta and Suze, JD's girlfriend, exchanged a look through their masks. Who was Roy Butcher?

"Oh, bloody marvellous." JD rolled his eyes. "Who else?"

Jack waved a hand. "No one important. Amit and his girlfriend, Porker and his mate and that quiet girl in Research, Hay-Chi, with some girl called Amy."

JD pulled a face. "Fucking Butcher. Great."

Marta noticed Jack stamp on his foot – quite hard, in fact – just as a large man in his forties stepped towards them wearing a batman-like mask. Jack switched on a smile as the man passed. "That was him, dickhead!" he hissed. Marta was still at a loss.

The seating plan was even worse than they had imagined. Marta was next to the big man himself, who had come with his wife, an equally sizeable lady with an equally loud, American accent.

"So!" bellowed Roy Butcher as soon as the table was complete. "I'm sure you all know me, but I don't know all your names!"

"Try *any*," whispered JD, rather too loudly.

"Let's do some intros! As you know, I'm Roy Butcher, Head of EMEA Banking at Goldmans."

"What's Emea?" whispered Marta.

"Europe, Middle East and Africa," Jack replied quietly. "Don't ask questions like that out loud."

Marta nodded. Perhaps tonight wouldn't be as much fun as she'd hoped.

"Hay-Chi Lu," said the Chinese girl opposite, so quietly that Marta couldn't tell whether she was lip-reading or hearing. "Telecoms and IT research analyst."

"And about as interesting as this napkin," added JD, again, loud enough for everyone to hear. Marta noticed he'd already poured himself and Suzie a glass of red wine and was almost through his.

"Suzie Ripley," giggled Suze when it was her turn. "JD's girlfriend and... well, I'm between jobs."

Marta noticed a sharp intake of breath from the large man on her left.

"I'm JD, mergers and acquisitions analyst and all-round

Goldman slave-cum-goffer boy," he mumbled through his mask, which has slipped down over his face. Suze giggled stupidly and topped up his glass.

Jack, thankfully, raised the tone with a flawless introduction involving the phrase 'leveraged buyout credit analyst' – whatever that was.

"Marta Dabrowska," she announced. "Strategic marketing consultant."

There were a few nods of interest before Rod's wife Marianne leaned forward and asked, loudly: "Where are you from, Marta?" at which point, Marta was forced to engage in the usual discussion about how many Poles there were in London now, and how they were very hard-working but – if the reports were to be believed – taking all the English people's jobs, especially in plumbing and construction – although luckily not in finance! Ha!

The masks came off as the starters arrived – strange, crispy parcels that looked like dumplings gone wrong – and Marta was relieved to note that Marianne's attention had turned elsewhere. Jack was engrossed in a cryptic conversation with JD about 'principle debt', although it had to be said, JD didn't seem entirely absorbed. He was more interested in his wine and the pastry parcels, which he was convinced came from KFC. Roy Butcher was boring the Chinese girl opposite with a very loud banking-related story.

Marta tucked into her starter, feeling out of place. Everyone else seemed to know about finance – apart from Suzie, of course, but she was off her head – and they seemed quite intent on discussing it all through dinner. Marta had no one to talk to.

The plates were whisked away and replaced by larger ones, accompanied by huge spinning dishes around the floral display of Chinese noodles, roasted meat, Italian noodles and Japanese rice, all in separate silver bowls. There was no Eastern European option, she noted, unsurprised. Maybe one day, when there were enough Poles to be classed as 'Londoners', not just 'immigrants', then pierogi would be commonplace.

"Will you get us another spoon?" demanded Butcher of the waitress – a slender girl of about Marta's age. "I said, get us a spoon!" he repeated as the waitress stopped to take instructions on how to pour wine from Marianne. The girl jumped, then nodded politely and scampered off. Marta's dislike for the man was growing. Poor girl – she was only doing her job. Marta knew how that felt.

Roy Butcher monopolised Jack for most of the main course. It was fascinating to hear the men talk, but somewhat frustrating for Marta, not being able to join in. After Jack's warning earlier, she didn't dare speak out – not in front of the Head of Europe, Middle East *and* Africa.

"And emerging markets?"

"Well, of course there's the increased credit risk which is what keeps the market so volatile."

"Indeed, although there's nothing wrong with a bit of volatility, eh?"

Marta's head was flicking to and fro like a metronome. She was thinking of suggesting she swapped seats with Jack when suddenly she felt his hand on her knee under the table.

"Mmm, quite. But the European markets have been so quiet," he said, finding the slit in her dress and expertly feeling his way up her leg.

"Which is exactly why we need to shake 'em up a bit!" cried Roy, as Jack's hand slid all the way up the inside of her thigh. Marta started to feel quite hot.

"Easier said than done," Jack replied, making contact with Marta's knickers.

"Not when you're Goldman Sachs," said Roy, leaning closer to Jack and ignoring Marta. "You know, I've seen plenty in my twelve years here…" Marta could feel Jack's fingers touching her. She leant back in her chair, feeling weak. "And I've learned that Goldmans can move markets!" he said.

"Move markets," Jack repeated, eyebrows raised. "Is that so?"

"Yes indeed," finished Butcher, obviously feeling his point was well made. Marta was wishing she was somewhere else – with Jack.

Suddenly, Roy's wife started screeching. "Where is it? I had it just a moment ago – that little waitress must've stolen it!"

There were baffled looks all round the table, until Roy explained how much money Marianne's handbag had cost – fourteen hundred pounds – and people started diving under the table. Jack's hand retreated instantly.

After much frenzied searching, the bag was found – on the back of Marianne's chair. No apologies were made to the waitress of course, although Marta managed to slip her a sympathetic smile as she provided Roy with his extra spoon.

Marta drank her way through the speeches, as did JD and Suze, who insisted on braying like donkeys whenever the CEO made a comment that was supposed to be funny, evidently oblivious to the glares of Roy Butcher and Marianne. Jack had timed his trip to the gents impeccably, and clearly didn't intend to come back before the droning was over.

"The legislative hurdles have been overcome, the banking reform complete and the firm on track for a record fourth quarter, pleasing not only our shareholders but – more importantly – the people who matter most to us: our employees!"

A rapturous applause may have been anticipated by the speaker at this point. In fact, all he got was a vague muttering from around the room and JD asking loudly, "Is he still talking?" It was a relief for everyone when another man stepped onto the stage and thanked the CEO, advising the roomful of bankers to "please put your hands together for Mr John Norris".

Jack slipped back into his seat as the desserts arrived.

"The rest of the room's having fun," he muttered, motioning to the tables around them, which were filled with drunk, gorgeous people falling off chairs, singing, yelling and throwing mini trifles at one another.

"You missed some great speech," she said, eyes telling him otherwise.

Jack tutted. "I'm devastated. But you know, when a man's gotta pee…"

"Where are toilets?" she asked.

Jack smiled. "At the back. Is that an invitation?"

Marta frowned. Was he implying… "No."

"Come on, Marta – we'd only be missing a discussion about the differences between US and UK financial reporting standards–" He nodded towards Roy Butcher, who was bellowing at anyone who would listen.

Marta rose to her feet. She couldn't tell whether Jack was joking, but she hoped he was. She wouldn't be spoiling the night by letting him ravage her in the disabled toilet, like the cheap English girls. "I'll be back in a minute."

On her return, the area around the diplodocus had been transformed into some sort of dance floor. A band was playing a cheesy cover of Brown Eyed Girl, and some of the more inebriated guests were lurching around the stone floor, unabashed. A few were wearing masks of some description, possibly to hide their identity when it came to the incriminating photos on Monday morning.

Jack was waiting for her at the edge of the ring, his bowtie loose around his neck, a glass of wine in each hand. He looked divine. As she approached, he unexpectedly tipped back his head and downed his drink in one.

"Why did you do that?" asked Marta, feeling drunk enough already but taking a sip all the same.

"So we can dance," he replied, gently placing her glass on a table and slipping a hand round her waist.

It was during the first lap of the dance floor – and it did feel like a lap – that Marta realised why Jack had polished off his wine. He was not made for dancing. It was surprising, she thought, given how good he looked standing still, but there was no doubt about it: he didn't have a rhythmic bone in his body.

Marta tolerated five minutes of being towed around, feeling like a puppet with a deranged handler, after which she feigned tiredness.

"You look so sexy when you dance," he told her as they retired to the bar.

"*You don't,*" Marta wanted to say, but then looked at his face – his glowing, handsome face. "Thanks. You too."

They discovered some armchairs and sofas at the end of the room, away from the watchful eye of the diplodocus.

"You did well," Jack said, as they sunk into the soft, brown velvet.

"What do you mean?" Marta asked, hoping he wasn't still talking about the dancing. That would've been a bit much, really.

"Dealing with Roy Butcher and Marianne."

"No silly questions," she said proudly.

"Not one. And I'm sorry I left you for half of it. JD needed saving – from himself."

Marta smiled. "I do fine on my own, you leveraged credit finance expert."

"Leveraged buyout credit analyst," Jack corrected, leaning forward and kissing her.

Marta wrapped one leg over his, leaving her glass on the table as they embraced. It felt so good. Jack was hers. He was her very own gorgeous, leveraged buyout credit analyst. Who cared if he couldn't dance?

One o'clock came around too quickly, and soon they were being swept onto the streets of Kensington with the other hundred wobbly, semi-masked banquet-goers. Jack held out his hand for a cab, keeping the other around Marta's waist.

"Mine's just round the corner, so we could walk," he said, questioningly.

Marta hesitated. It wasn't that she couldn't decide whether her heels were up to the walk. It was that she wasn't sure whether she wanted to go back to Jack's. She'd had a wonderful night, and she could see why he assumed they would be going back together to have sex. But it seemed wrong, somehow, to end it like that. Tonight was their first real date – the daytime ones didn't count – and there would be plenty of other opportunities for sex. She'd ruined plenty of relationships by moving too quickly; she didn't want this to be the same.

"I think I will go home," she told him.

He looked utterly shocked. "Was it something I–"

"No! No. I just…" Marta turned and kissed Jack gently on the lips. "Want it to be special. Not too soon."

Jack nodded, kissing her back. "I understand."

They stepped onto the road as a taxi approached.

"Here," Jack said to the driver, handing two twenty-pound notes through the passenger window.

"Jack, no!" she objected from the back seat.

"No choice," he said, smiling as he pushed shut the door and banged on the roof.

Twisting round in the back of the cab, Marta watched the broad-shouldered silhouette turn and disappear, wondering whether she'd made a mistake tonight. Then she thought of the prospect of next Thursday's date, and the one after that, and the one after that. No, she had plenty to look forward to.

47

"I CAN'T BELIEVE I used to do ten miles without even thinking about it. I'm so unfit!"

"Don't stress yourself," advised Marta, wishing Holly would ease up a little. The pace was too quick, even by her standards. They were planning to run a seven mile route around Hyde Park and Green Park, but they'd be lucky to make it half way without passing out at this rate.

"But listen to me! I'm panting like a dog," she gasped.

"You pant like any person running so quickly," Marta commented, reducing her stride and falling behind. "We are practically splinting," she yelled at Holly's back.

"Sprinting," Holly said, finally letting up and dropping to Marta's pace. "Not splinting."

Marta grinned back at Holly. They ran in amicable silence for a while, listening to the sound of their pounding feet above the background hum of Hyde Park in summer. Marta had chucked the stupid music player that Dom had found for her in the bin, preferring to hear the sound of real life while she ran: children shrieking, parents scolding, picnics in full flow.

"It's so good to be out in the sun," said Holly as they overtook a group of young power-walkers in flannel tracksuits. "I feel like a battery hen, cooped up in that office."

"Battery?"

"Oh, it's a phrase. Means intensively reared."

Marta nodded. Intensively reared. That said it all for her flatmate. Marta wondered whether now was the time to burden Holly with her own office dilemmas or whether she had enough on her plate as it was. She was also dying to know what had happened between Holly and Rich since the ball last weekend, but she wasn't sure how to bring up the subject. Neither flatmate had mentioned anything about the kiss – they weren't even behaving differently around the flat together. They clearly weren't aware that Marta had seen them.

"I should run more often," declared Holly, upping the pace again. "Makes me feel free. I forget all about the shit in my life."

Marta smiled. The spark was back in Holly's voice. Marta decided that now was the time. "Can I ask question?"

"Sure."

"What does it mean when you get official warning from your company? Will they do a sacking?"

Holly glanced at her, suddenly serious again. "You've had an official warning from Stratisvision?"

Marta drew a deep breath, wondering whether her lungs could cope with the lengthy explanation whilst running at such a pace.

"Is complicated." They skirted around a flock of children spilling across the path by an ice cream van. Then Marta told her. She explained about the forged email, the reprimand from Dean, the stern message from David Lyle. "…But there is no proof that I did the work, Holly. The email is gone."

Holly wiped her palm across her sweaty forehead. Thankfully, her spurt of energy hadn't lasted long and they were back to a reasonable jog. "What a fucking nightmare," she concluded. "I knew a Kat once. At Cambridge. She was nasty too. Only ever hung out with the beautiful crew. They spent all day flicking their hair and talking about lip gloss."

"Perhaps is same girl?" joked Marta. "Or perhaps all girls called Kat are like bitches. Was she called Kat Sneider?"

Holly smiled. "Dunno, I'm afraid. She was at a different college. Kings. I only knew her through Tash." They were nearing the corner of the park and they needed to navigate across a rather complicated main road in order to get to the other park. "But I doubt this Kat would've ended up in consulting." Holly led the way towards what looked like an underpass. "Hold your breath – it stinks under here. No, Kat spent three years shagging rich knob-heads from Eton in the Pitt Club, from what I remember."

"Pitt Club?" echoed Marta. Holly was right – the tunnel smelt like a urinal. There was a telling trickle of yellow liquid running along the gutter beside them.

"Oh, it's a society thing for public school boys in Cambridge. Full of rich, pompous prats – like Jack Templeton-Cooper, in fact. Tash's ex. I think he was a member."

Marta flinched. She looked across at Holly's flushed face to check she hadn't noticed. Jack wasn't a rich, pompous prat. He was just... well, rich. And a little bit pompous. Maybe. Marta was wondering how to steer the conversation back to her problems at work when something occurred to her.

"Holly? This girl... did she have long, white hair and little nose turning up like this?" Marta pressed the end of hers so it vaguely resembled that of the office Barbie.

Holly took a deep breath as they emerged in the relatively fresh air. "She was blonde, yeah. Can't quite remember her face. She was pretty, I know that – she made sure *everyone* knew it."

Marta followed Holly through a gate into Green Park. Holly didn't seem to get it. "Is the same girl, I think!"

"Why, 'cause they've both got blonde hair?"

"She knows Jack from this Pitt Society!"

Holly frowned. "What's Jack got to do with anything?"

"Well... Maybe she is jealous of me, so this is why she being horrid!"

"Hold on – I'm confused." Holly guided them onto a tree-lined track that followed the perimeter of the park. "Jealous of you in what way? Where does Jack Templeton-Cooper fit into all this?"

"He–" Marta stopped herself. She couldn't bring herself to tell Holly the truth. "Maybe Kat is friend of Tash, and Tash think I am doing the business with Jack! So Kat hate me for that. She is jealous."

Holly clearly didn't think much of Marta's reasoning, but that didn't matter. Marta had worked it out. This explained everything. Kat knew Jack from this Cambridge society and now, somehow, she knew that Marta was seeing him. She was jealous. Or maybe Tash *was* involved, and she was the jealous one. Either way, it explained why Kat was determined to make Marta fail.

Something else occurred to her. "Kat knows I lived with Tash, I think."

"What makes you say that?"

"My friend, Carl – he heard them talking about me once. They said Kensington."

Holly shrugged, clearly still not convinced. Marta didn't care. She was confident now. Finally, there seemed to be a reason for her victimisation at work. To prove her theory, she just had to find out one thing: which college Kat Sneider had gone to.

"Whoever she is, you need to get her out of your life," remarked Holly. "And you need to expose her for the fraud that she is – somehow. That's five miles, by the way."

Marta instinctively picked up speed. Only two miles to go. "Do I tell someone about the email thing, with no proof?"

"Well, in my experience of conniving little bitches – of which there are many at Andertons – they're not as hardy as they like to think. She'll crack under pressure, I reckon, if you get her in front of this David what's-his-face. Be brave. Drop her in it."

Marta nodded. She knew it was good advice; it was just a question of putting it into practice – not easy now she had this black mark against her name. Who would David Lyle believe: the slick, blonde analyst whose aunt was Chief Executive or the Polish assistant who'd been at the firm for less than five weeks? Without any evidence, it was a risky strategy.

"Now I have a question for you," Holly said. They had finally settled into a rhythm, their long legs striding in time as they veered off the path, leaving the crowds behind them.

"You want to know when I move out of your living room?"

"No!" Holly looked really upset. "No – we all love you being there! You're the only one who cooks proper food." She grinned.

"Oh, good. But I will pay rent to–"

"Shuddup about the bloody rent! We all work in the City, for God's sake – well, apart from Rich. And he's – well, he's fine with it too."

Marta glanced sideways. It was hard to tell whether Holly was blushing because her face was already red, but there was definitely a hint of awkwardness at the sound of her flatmate's name. That was no bad thing, though. A bit of secret romance was a great way to start a relationship.

"No – I wanted to ask about Poles. Poles in London. In fact, Poles all over the UK. Where do you get Polish food from, if you want, say bread or cheese like the stuff that you're used to?"

Marta pulled a face at her friend. "Why do you want to know this?!"

Holly shrugged. "Just wondered."

"Well, you can get most things from the Polskie Delikatesy. Everywhere in London now has them, but lots in Acton, Hammersmith – places like this."

"And what are they like, these Pole Skidela... what are they called?"

Marta smiled. "Polskie, Del-i-ka-te-sy. Polish delicatessen. They just like normal shop in Poland, only very expensive, in comparison. Always the same, with sad, grumpy woman behind counter, shelves filled with tins and cakes like back home. But prices much higher."

"And is there... is there a cheaper alternative? A chain? Like, a Polish supermarket that's moved over here?"

Marta frowned. "I don't think so. Supermarkets not gonna come here as setting up business is too expensive – property, marketing, supplies... not worth it for a Polish chain."

"But you can get Polish food in Tesco now, can't you?"

"Holly, why you asking me this?" Marta scrutinised her friend's face, smiling. It was as though Holly were planning something. Something involving Polish food.

"It's for... a project. A project I'm doing. Do you buy Polish food in Tesco?"

Marta shrugged. "Sometimes, but it is horrible. All long-living stuff. Not fresh." She had a feeling this wasn't for a project of Holly's. Not a work project, anyway. She was showing too much interest for this to be an Andertons assignment.

"Long life," corrected Holly. "So there's no single place that everybody goes to. Are you in touch with any friends from Warsaw?"

Marta gave up trying to understand Holly's motives. "Łomianki, yes. Not so many in Warsaw. Only some university friends."

"Right," said Holly, trying to sound nonchalant. They were

nearing a gate that led directly to Green Park tube. "Well, here we are. Thanks, running buddy."

They slowed to a stop, stretching their burning muscles in the sunlight.

"Same next week?" asked Marta.

Holly started to grimace as though work would dictate the answer, then her expression brightened. "Yeah. For sure. If I'm working, I'll slip out for an hour. I'm not a battery hen, after all."

48

MARTA'S HEART STARTED HAMMERING against her ribcage. She had been summoned for another 'catch-up' with David Lyle. The outcome of the last one had been an extension of her contract and a small pay rise; she had a feeling that this one would not be so positive.

This was not a good way to start the day. Marta opened up the spreadsheet she was supposed to be working on and scrolled idly down one of the columns. She couldn't concentrate. What if David was calling her in for a second official warning? That meant she had only one chance left. One chance to redeem her career.

Instinctively, Marta looked up towards Carl's desk. He wasn't there. Of course he wasn't. Today Carl was locked away in a series of Project Compass meetings with, among others, the cause of all Marta's troubles: Kat Sneider. Marta had set him a challenge. He was to find out which college Kat had gone to at Cambridge – not that she needed confirmation. Almost certainly, this was the girl Holly had mentioned. The girl who knew Jack from this Pitt Society thing.

What would David say at nine forty-five? Gosh – that was only half an hour away. Marta breathed deeply, trying to prepare herself. What if he had some new evidence to show that she wasn't performing well enough? Perhaps Kat had played another trick without her even noticing. Would this be the time to try and defend herself? It would seem a bit pathetic, piping up with accusations only when confronted with a second warning. Maybe that wasn't the best option. But then... she had to state the truth at some point. The questions were popping up faster than she could answer them, and staring at the spreadsheet wasn't helping. Marta got up and headed for the kitchen.

Her secret stash of fruit tea bags behind the microwave was diminishing at a suspiciously high rate; clearly it wasn't as secret as she'd hoped. Marta flicked on the kettle and inspected the smeary mugs as she waited for it to boil. There was something calming about the sound of bubbling water sloshing around in the plastic vessel. Her thoughts became more rational as she wiped the inside of the chosen mug with a paper towel. David's catch-up would not be disastrous. If anything, it might bring about an opportunity to 'spill beans' as they said over here. She'd make sure he came out knowing what had been going on between Marta and Kat.

The boiling water quickly turned pink as the juices escaped from the teabag. Marta was considering adding half a teaspoon of sugar when suddenly her contemplation was shattered. The screech was like that of a cat in pain.

"Awww! Get the fuck away from me! Why does it matter what fucking college I went to? Don't you think I've got other things on my mind?!"

Marta turned just in time to see Kat's slender figure storm, full pelt, towards the kitchen. Marta leapt sideways and yanked open the fridge, pretending to peer inside it. It was a tall fridge, so the door almost shielded her from the rest of the office.

"I can't be-*lieve* they're doing this to me," hissed Kat, clearly addressing the person whose footsteps were struggling to keep up. The pair of them stopped at the edge of the kitchen, presumably unaware of the person inside the fridge.

"Isn't there anything Patr – your aunt can do?" asked the other girl, whose voice Marta recognised as Kim's. She was Kat's left-hand woman.

"Yeah – and she's already doing it! She's the reason I've only been made *redundant* and not outright sacked, isn't she?"

The girl mumbled something sympathetic. Marta stared at the out-of-date yoghurts and half-eaten sandwiches. It was all a blur. Kat was being made redundant. What did that mean? Was it like being made sacked, only more polite?

"They say *I've* been conniving and dishonest and that *I've* not been pulling my weight... well try opening your eyes, that's what I say. Take a look at that Polish bitch who spends all day asking Carl what to do... *Fuck*, what's daddy gonna say?"

There was no reply from Kim. For a moment, there was nothing from either girl. Marta froze. She felt sure they had noticed her feet, which were visible beneath the fridge door – or noticed that the fridge was making a whining noise as a result of being left open too long. Then, much to Marta's surprise, there was a sniffle – a muted sniffle, as though Kat were crying into Kim's shoulder.

'Polish bitch'? Did they really think that? And did she really spend all her time asking Carl what to do? Marta pondered this as she listened to the muffled sobs. No, it wasn't true. She didn't ask him much – only the basics to help her get going. And Carl didn't mind, anyway. He liked it. Kat was just making excuses.

Eventually, the sniffs and Kim's soothing murmur receded as, presumably, Kat was led away. Marta tentatively stepped out of the fridge in time to see Kat's high-heeled boot disappearing through the office doorway.

On autopilot, Marta squeezed the last drops of colour from the teabag and tossed it into the bin. She could hardly believe what she'd just witnessed. Kat had been made redundant from Stratisvision. Redundant. That meant 'no longer useful', didn't it? Presumably that meant that she wouldn't be coming back. If so, this was excellent news. But the question was *why?* She'd have to ask Carl.

There was no opportunity to ask Carl. The office was in turmoil. Groups of girls were hovering in corners, whispering, pointing; senior managers were rushing around pretending not to notice the change and David Lyle was shut in his office with a woman who apparently came from 'HR'. Carl was in a meeting room with a project team that no longer included Kat.

"Er, Marta? Shall we do our catch-up now?" asked David, leaning out of his office. He was wearing electric blue corduroy trousers that almost distracted Marta from the intensity of his expression. She followed him in.

"So…" he began, leaning back in his leather chair and motioning for Marta to sit down. The door had been very deliberately shut behind them. "The news is out now, so there seemed little point in delaying our chat."

Marta nodded, trying not to look at the trousers. David Lyle seemed tense, but at least he was smiling at her – if a little awkwardly.

"I assume you're aware, this morning we had to let go of one of our analysts," he said. "Kat Sneider."

Let go of. As though Kat were a bird wanting to be set free. Marta nodded again.

"There will be an official email going out in due course to confirm the news," he said. "But the reason I wanted to speak to you in particular was… well, two reasons really. Firstly, to apologise. I understand you've had a tough few weeks. I sent you an official warning about the quality of your work, and I now understand that that was unwarranted, so please ignore its content and consider it retracted. Again, I'll send an email to this effect."

Marta was jumping up and down inside; this was the best news she could have hoped for. She had no idea how David had found out about Kat's campaign, but clearly he had, and now she was off the hook.

"In case you're wondering," he said, "you were overheard in the Ladies' talking with Kat about the Unilight project. We pulled off the emails from the server. You worked hard on that presentation, didn't you?"

"Yes." Marta smiled. She just couldn't help it. Which female, she wondered, had overheard them?

"In future, Marta, I'd advise you not to keep these things to yourself. Now, the second reason I wanted to speak to you," he went on, "was to ask whether you'd be happy to take on Kat's role on Project Compass. You'd be working alongside Carl Rossi, under the guidance of Charlotte and Dean."

Marta's smile widened. To be chosen to work on Project Compass was an honour. And working with Carl… It would be a party compared to recent experiences. "I would be happy," she said.

"Good! Well, that's everything. And obviously it'd be appreciated if you could be a bit discreet about the details of Kat's dismissal…"

Marta nodded reassuringly. She'd be happy never to mention Kat's name again. The whole episode was over. Forgotten already.

"Oh, and Marta?" said David, as she reached the door. "Good girl. I mean, well done. I always knew you were a hard worker – not just because you're Polish, uhuh! I'm glad we've still got you on board." He winked.

Marta nodded uncertainly. She just couldn't work David Lyle out. One minute he was prancing around the office in safari shirts slapping hands with his colleagues, the next he was sending out emails in scary, serious language threatening to sack her and now he was patronisingly endorsing the virtues of having a Pole on the payroll.

It was too early for lunch, but Marta needed to get out of the office. Girls were loitering around her desk: the members of Kat's entourage who were finding themselves suddenly without direction, hoping to glean an inkling from Marta about the circumstances surrounding their ringleader's fall from grace. Much to their annoyance, Marta was ignoring them all.

"You getting a coffee?" "Want some company?" "Fancy a chat?"

"Am meeting a friend," Marta lied, swiping her card and heading out.

She found herself heading up High Holborn and cutting down a road that ran parallel to Red Lion Street. Annoyingly, the memory of lunch with Dom in that café full of builders and lawyers popped into her head. She tried to eliminate it, but the image was vivid: the embrace, the chatter, the adoring looks, their knees touching beneath the table… No. It wasn't worth thinking about. Dom's embrace hadn't been real, his chatter had been false and his looks had meant nothing. He'd probably been thinking about that blonde the whole time anyway. Marta turned right and headed towards Leather Lane market. She could do without random flashbacks like that.

"Excuse me," said a voice from inside a motorbike helmet. For a fleeting moment, Marta thought it might be Dom and was irritated to find her pulse quicken. As the helmet came off, though, it transpired that the rider was a woman.

"I'm doing a shoot for the Metro on high street fashion," she said, holding up a camera that looked like the sort paparazzi used. "Would you mind featuring? We're doing a piece called Londoners Looking Hot."

Marta glanced down at the pencil skirt and tight-fitting blouse that, like most of her clothes, came from Emily Norman. "Sure," she said, breaking into a smile.

She was still smiling when the woman kick-started her machine and motored off towards the main road, a dozen photos later. Marta may have got her hopes up too soon in the past, but now, finally, it seemed as though things were going her way. Her new life in England was beginning to resemble the life she'd spent so many years dreaming about in her cramped bedroom back home.

49

IT WAS A PLEASANT WALK from Holborn to Bank. The air was warm and the pubs along the way were teeming with young city workers guzzling beer in celebration of it being Thursday. Marta had left work at seven, slightly later than planned, but Jack had seemed fine with the half-hour delay – in fact, he'd seemed more than fine, yelling something about 'one more with the lads' above an incredible din. He was clearly already in a bar.

It was difficult to know whether to talk to Jack about the matter of Kat Sneider. Of course, it would be good to find out how well Jack had known her at Cambridge, whether she and Tash had been friends… maybe Jack could explain why Kat had been so determined to bring Marta down at work. And it would be nice to have someone else to talk to about the situation who wasn't her flatmate. Poor Holly had enough of her own office problems. But what if… what if she discovered things she didn't want to discover? What if she learned that Jack and Kat had had some sort of fling whilst at university? It was quite possible, given the way Kat behaved. How had Holly put it? 'Three years shagging rich knob-heads from Eton in the Pitt Club'. Marta shuddered at the thought. If that were the case, she'd rather not know.

Marta took a short-cut around St Paul's, marvelling at the size and beauty of the three hundred year-old cathedral. She'd read about it in one of mama's university books. Apparently the bell inside was even bigger than Big Ben. Emerging from the shadow of the building into the sunlight, Marta felt a rush of happiness. She loved London. She loved her routine. She loved the fact that she was living a life that most of her Polish friends could only dream of back in Łomianki.

She wouldn't ask Jack about Kat, she decided. It would spoil the night. Who cared what had happened two years ago in Cambridge? Jack was Marta's guy now. Her initial doubts about Jack Templeton-Cooper had been so misplaced it was almost funny, looking back. She'd assumed him to be an arrogant, insecure English player who couldn't keep his hands to himself, but she'd been wrong. Jack was different when you got him alone. He was kind and generous, and funny, too. His wit was sharp – a little cruel sometimes, but brilliant. It was nice to be on the right side of his jokes.

She didn't mind that Jack was a bit of a snob, either. It was a consequence of his upbringing. He was humble enough to hear her point of view – well, most of the time – and besides, he did have an annoying habit of being right about everything. He was never openly rude, only voicing his opinions in private. Jack was a gentleman. She smiled. Jack was Marta's gentleman.

All Bar One was surprisingly empty. A few after-work drinkers were hovering outside in twos and threes, but evidently the establishment was second choice to the more interesting looking one next door – a mock Gothic tavern called the London Stone, outside which swarmed maybe a hundred suits. Marta checked her watch. Twenty five past seven. Jack was nowhere to be seen.

She wandered to the far corner of the empty bar, listening to the hypnotic ring tone and waiting for Jack to pick up. She couldn't help wondering how much thought had gone into the choice of venue; there was as much atmosphere here than in a dentist's waiting room.

"Hello, Jack, this is Marta. I am in the bar you said and it is half to eight – no, half past seven. I wait outside, OK? See you soon."

Marta sighed, assuming her position beside the fake greenery that spilled from the window ledges. She felt slightly rejected.

It was nearly a quarter to eight when Marta heard the cry from across the road. It sounded a little bit like her name, but all blurry, with no consonants. She looked up.

Jack's shirt was hanging out. His tie dangled loosely around his neck and a couple of shirt buttons were undone, exposing his tanned chest. He looked… well, gorgeous, obviously. But something else, too. He looked drunk.

"I'msorry!" he slurred, lunging at her, arms open. Marta accepted the embrace, finding herself locked in a kiss that was somewhat more passionate than she'd expected. His mouth tasted of beer. When he finally pulled away, Marta noticed several people pointing and nudging one another outside the London Stone.

"God, you're beautiful," said Jack, still holding Marta at arm's length and trying to focus on her eyes.

"And you are drunk," added Marta. "Where were you?"

Jack shook his head and slipped an arm around her waist. He seemed fairly steady on his feet, Marta noticed. That was promising. "Out with the boys," he said. "Completed a deal today so the client took us drinking. At lunch." He hiccupped. "Not drunk though. Just tipsy."

Marta nodded, allowing Jack to guide her away from All Bar One. She didn't know what 'tipsy' meant, but she could only imagine it was several stages after 'drunk'. Perhaps this evening wasn't going to be the romantic one she'd envisaged.

"Shit hole, that place. Sorry for making you wait there. Couldn't think of the name of…" Jack squinted up at the name of the bar next door, hiccupping again.

"The London Stone?"

"Yeah – oh yeah. Much better bar. Much better." He nodded.

Jack took her hand and led the way through the crowded bar. He seemed confident, if not sober, she thought. "What're you drinking? Wine? Bacardi?"

Marta looked at him. "Beer."

"Oh yes, of course. Sorry – can't get used to that. Never been out with a bird who drinks pints." He winked.

Marta rolled her eyes and went off to find some seats. Even Jack seemed to have preconceptions, she thought. Couldn't anyone just take her at face value – not see her as 'a bird' or 'a Pole'?

"I have something for you," she said, once he'd navigated his way back from the bar and placed the drinks on the table.

"For me? Really? Does it involve you getting naked?" Jack grinned as he took a healthy sip of beer.

Marta placed the newspapers on the table between them. "No." She opened Jack's copy on page fourteen and waited for him to notice.

"Marta why are you showing me the fashion section of the Metro?" he asked.

"Look close."

Jack squinted at the page. "'High waists are out and the classic tom-boy look is making a come-back'," he read. "Well that's good news, isn't it? For tom-boys, I mean."

"Look at the pictures," urged Marta. "London Looking Hot—" She pointed.

Jack suddenly slammed his pint down. "Fuck – it's you!"

Marta smiled, glancing again at the page. She could hardly believe it was her, either. The image took up most of the right-hand page.

"What... how did that happen?"

Marta shrugged as though this sort of thing was an everyday event. "A woman just came and took a photo of me in the street. It's because of Emily Norman's clothes. Everybody comment on them. My friend, Anka – she knows everything about fashion and she is so jealous!" Marta felt a stab of guilt as she thought back to Anka's last email. She'd been wild with envy over Marta's latest acquisitions and Marta had vowed to send her something in the post. Shit. That had been a week ago and she still hadn't sent anything.

"Can I keep this? God, you're so fit, Marta. Look at that—" He nodded at the image before folding his copy away. "People wonder why I'm going out with a Polish girl, I know they do, but if they could see you..." He shook his head, smiling.

Marta stared at him. He *was* drunk. *People wonder why I'm going out with a Polish girl.* He would never have said that sober. Marta bit back her response. He wasn't just seeing her because of her looks, was he? Jack wasn't that shallow. Maybe when drunk, yes – but all men started thinking with their dicks after a few pints. Surely she meant more to him than that? Jack was still gazing at her, confirming her theory. He couldn't help it, she told herself; he'd been drinking since lunchtime.

"So, what was the deal you did?" asked Marta.

Jack frowned. "Deal?"

"The deal you finished today – at work."

"Oh yes. Newstran. Newstran got bought by News International. Big media company. We advised on the transaction."

"Oh." Marta wasn't sure what to ask. It sounded rather dull. "What do they do, Newstran?"

Jack frowned. "Media."

"But I mean, what sort? Do they write newspapers? Magazines? Websites?"

Jack shrugged. "Don't know. No idea. They just do media."

Marta nodded. She wanted to take more of an interest in what Jack did every day to earn his thousands of pounds, but somehow she couldn't muster the enthusiasm – and neither could he, it seemed. Surely it wasn't purely the salary that inspired him to work at Goldman Sachs?

The conversation continued in a similar vein. Marta's questions were abundant and Jack's responses vague and random, lacking their usual sharpness and wit. In fact, most of their discussions – if you could call them that – led back to one particular topic: sex. Every time Marta steered them away from it, Jack found a way to bring them back. He clearly had it on the brain.

"Most people in banking tend to give up sport when they join – there's no time for outside interests. Except drinking – and strip-clubs, of course. Have you ever… danced? You know…?"

Marta sighed. She was about to suggest another pint – of water, in Jack's case – when something caught her eye. Walking past them with a tray of drinks was a guy with a very large nose. "Hey, isn't that–"

Marta didn't get to finish her sentence. Jack's hand, which had been resting gently on top of hers, suddenly tightened. Marta winced as her fingers were crushed in his fist.

"Let's go," said Jack. "I've just remembered, we should be in another bar. Come on – let's go."

Marta frowned, trying to escape his grip and noting that Jeremy was heading for a large table full of Cambridge-like people. "Jack, why–"

"I'll explain in bit – let's go." Jack stood up, releasing her hand just for long enough for Marta to grab her bag, then whisked her out of the bar. Marta followed, bemused and slightly angry.

"Where we going? Why, Jack? Why?" demanded Marta as he led her round the corner from the pub and up the street towards Bank.

"I just realised we should be going to this other bar… in fact, no – even better. Let's go back to mine."

Marta wriggled free of Jack's grip and stopped dead on the pavement. She could only think of one plausible explanation for Jack's behaviour, and she didn't like it: Jack hadn't wanted to be seen with Marta in that bar.

"Tell me why you ran off like that? You didn't want Jeremy to see us? Yes?"

Jack looked utterly confused, and for a moment Marta felt guilty for making the accusation. "No… I just wanted… There's this other bar, and I thought… oh, never mind."

Marta waited, but nothing more seemed forthcoming. Jack was drunk. Maybe he had a reason for whisking them away like that and maybe he couldn't tell her now. Maybe his reason was quite innocent. Marta looked at his face. His eyes were darting all over the place and for a moment he seemed quite vulnerable – his shirt dishevelled, hair slightly tousled.

"Marta, come back to mine," he said. It was like a plea. Marta felt herself drawing closer, his arm in the small of her back. He was looking at her, blinking, as though he couldn't bear for her to object. Poor guy, it wasn't his fault they'd made him start drinking at lunchtime. He was trying to sober up, she could tell. His fingers were reaching under her shirt at the back, tickling her bare skin. She let him kiss her. It was so gentle – much gentler than before. Marta nodded.

In the cab, the desire for conversation seemed less; mere looks, kisses, comments were enough. Marta's imagination ran wild dreaming up visions of Jack Templeton-Cooper's house. Would there be pillars and flames outside, like in Egerton Square? Would he have long, winding staircases? Her questions were answered abruptly when the taxi lurched to a halt outside a row of tall townhouses, most of which had multiple doorbells. Marta hid her disappointment. Jack lived in a flat.

"Is this yours?" asked Marta, knowing the answer. All the rich people in London owned their own place. Jack nodded, leading her up the steps.

As soon as she stepped inside, Marta realised: Jack did not live in a flat. He owned the whole building. Marta gazed up at the high, ornate ceiling and peered through the half-open doors to the sides.

Jack walked backwards through the echoing hall across the floor that looked like an ice rink, grabbing Marta's waist and smothering her with kisses. His body smelt delicious – of aftershave or maybe his own scent, she didn't know. Backwards, he mastered the stairs – surprisingly well, noted Marta. The unpleasant thought that he might have done this before – with Tash, or some other girl – crossed her mind.

They entered what looked like a lounge – slowly, because it was difficult to walk whilst kissing and being caressed so intensely. Jack's grip on her was firm, but she didn't mind; she was his girlfriend, after all. They collapsed on a brown leather sofa, Jack on top of her. Marta tried to swing her legs round to the floor – it was too early to be doing that stuff – but Jack's knees were in the way.

"Going somewhere?" he asked, pressing himself down on her and kissing her more.

Marta wriggled and realised she was trapped; Jack was stronger than her. She tried once more, again with no luck. It didn't feel right. "Jack—"

"What?" he asked, looking down at her. His eyes were full of passion. Drunk passion.

"I want a drink," she lied. She just wanted some space; a break from the intensity.

"Good idea," he replied, sliding off her and reaching for a couple of shot glasses that were barely out of arm's reach. "Whisky? Brandy? Something else? I've got everything."

I'm sure you have, thought Marta. "Vodka?"

Jack poured two large splashes and looked at Marta. "What is it you say?"

"Na zdrowie," she said, reluctantly taking hers. More alcohol was the last thing Jack needed.

"Na zdrowie," he repeated, chinking her glass and downing his in one.

Marta obligingly did the same, and was surprised at the ease with which it slid down her throat. Expensive stuff, evidently.

Jack was on top of her again, stroking her hair and pawing gently at the buttons on her top. Marta could smell the vodka fumes on his breath. His eyes were wandering down her body and up again, clearly undressing her in his mind. He was hot and heavy on top of her, his weight suppressing her breathing, his mouth on hers, kissing her forcefully.

It was only later, when Marta surfaced for air, that she realised his left hand had been making progress on her shirt buttons. Jack's hand slid down to her breasts and opened the blouse to expose her bra – a flimsy, lacy affair. She hadn't worn it deliberately. She hadn't met up with Jack tonight with the intention of having sex with him; the thought hadn't crossed her mind. She wanted to do things in the right order with Jack – go steady, not mess it up too soon. She pressed on Jack's chest, hoping he'd ease up a bit. It had no effect. Her strength was negligible compared to his.

"Jack, please—"

Marta pushed on his shoulder, which yielded a little, lifting Jack's face from her body. "What?" He sounded aggressive now. The vodka had been a bad idea.

"Please, no," Marta begged, trying the other shoulder and hoping that Jack might roll off her altogether. She was sober and he was drunk – surely she had the advantage?

Her efforts were futile. Jack was firmly on top of her, and with one hand he was reaching round and unclasping her bra. Marta's shirt was keeping everything loosely in place, but Jack was finding his way underneath, reaching down and massaging her breasts. Marta tried again to twist free but Jack's weight was bearing down on her hips. Tears of frustration – maybe fear – started rolling down the sides of her cheeks. Jack didn't notice.

"Jack, please, no," she wept as he pushed her skirt up around her waist, keeping one hand on one of her breasts. Her legs were pinned to the sofa beneath his; he ignored her sobs as he pulled the fabric of her knickers aside with his other hand. In desperation, Marta screamed. The shrill noise pierced through the silence, shocking Jack for a moment and causing him to ease off a little. Marta seized the opportunity and twisted round, still screaming, so that Jack lost his grip.

To her horror, she felt Jack's hand on her mouth, clamping her head against his body. He was still on top of her, his other hand still in her pants.

"Shuddup!" he uttered, in between screams.

She did, but only to bite Jack's hand. He yelped like a boy and let go, but his weight was still pressing down on her. She was too weak to escape.

Then, miraculously, her phone rang. Jack heard it too, and for a moment seemed distracted. Using all her strength, Marta wrenched herself free of his clutches and dragged herself across the carpet to her bag. Perhaps it was Holly or Tina, she thought hopefully. Maybe they'd come and rescue her.

She only caught a glimpse of the number, but it wasn't one she recognised. "Hello?" she gasped. Jack was moving towards her, one hand on his trouser zip. She shuffled backwards towards the door.

"You little peasant bitch!" screamed a voice that Marta recognised instantly. It was her former housemate. Jack's ex-girlfriend. "First you try and steal my boyfriend from right under my nose, in *my own house,* then you go and monopolise my friends, and now you have another fucking go at my boyfriend! Have you *no* shame? You've got a *fucking nerve,* you have, Marta. Why don't you just take my advice and fuck off back to your Polish farmyard?"

Marta gasped. She tried to react, but it was too late. Tash had hung up. *Another go at my boyfriend?* Did she think she was still seeing Jack? Marta looked at Jack, who had frozen, mid-crawl, half-way between the sofa and her. The lust had gone from his eyes, and in its place was a mixture of fear, guilt and anger. Suddenly, Marta realised why Jack hadn't wanted Jeremy to see them together.

"You are still going out with Tash."

It was a statement, not a question. Marta understood now. She knew Jack's motives. She knew, finally, what type of guy he was: he was the sort who wanted it all – and thought he could get it.

"No – not exactly. It's just – No, don't go Marta. It's not like…"

Marta's expression killed off his sentence. She started doing up her buttons. Never in her life had she felt this angry, this hurt… this *stupid*. It hurt more than the sight of Dom with that blonde. God, what kind of idiot was she, falling for cheats like this?

She was downstairs with her hand on the front door when her phone rang again. She whipped it out, still glaring at Jack. This time, she was ready with an explanation for Tash. Her fear of Jack had turned to pure hatred.

312

"Hi Tash, I want you to know that—"

"Kto to jest? Marta?"

Marta pulled the handset from her ear and looked at the number. It was mama.

"Sorry mama. I thought—"

"Listen Marta, I'm sorry. Bad news." She sniffed. "It's tata. He's had a heart attack."

50

"BACK AGAIN?" Jack leered down at her from the top step. "Change your mind did you?"

Marta looked at him, horrified, through the tears. "Jack, my dad is in hospital. I need to fly home and my phone has no money. Please, I need yours." She stayed on the bottom step, sobbing, waiting for Jack to agree. She didn't care about what had just happened between them – she didn't care about Tash, or any of the other trivial things in her life. She just cared about getting to tata.

"It might cost you," said Jack, raising an eyebrow.

Marta yelped hysterically. Tata was in a critical state in Kosciusko hospital – maybe dead now, for all she knew – and Jack was still thinking with his dick. "My dad has had a heart... Heart attack." The sobs were choking her as she tried to explain. "Please Jack, I need telefon. Let me in."

"Oh. Shit." Jack's cocky grin vanished. "Well, fuck knows where I put it..." He opened the door.

Marta ran up the steps, pushing past him and storming up to the room with the sofa. All she could think about was tata. He had collapsed saying goodnight to her sister. Mama had been out at the shops. Ewa had called 999 and watched him being put in the ambulance, poor girl – she must have been petrified. Marta's tears started flowing more heavily, blurring her vision. Where was Jack's phone? And why hadn't she been there when tata had needed her?

Jack appeared in the doorway. "I'm not sure where I left it," he said, idly lifting a copy of FHM from the arm of the sofa as though expecting to find the phone underneath.

"Jack, help me. I need phone. Do you have house phone?"

Jack shook his head. "Only for internet – and that's down at the moment. Bloody Orange."

Marta finished scouring the lounge. "You had it in the bar with the friends… where did you put after that?"

"I really don't know," he replied, shrugging. "Can't you just top yours up?"

"Have to go to a shop for that. Is there shop near here?"

Jack scratched his head. Marta watched him, desperately wishing he'd sober up. He was no use at all.

"Can't think of one. Why d'you need a phone, anyway?"

Marta sighed, leaving Jack in the room and rushing back downstairs. "I need to buy flight to Poland!" she called back to him. She was beside herself now; she could hardly see through the tears.

"You're not gonna get a flight tonight, are you?" he cried, following her down and nearly tripping down the last few stairs. "It'll be midnight by the time you get to an airport. Just stay here. Leave early tomorrow."

Marta yanked open the front door, turning back briefly to glare at Jack, her eyes full of loathing.

"You think I want to spend any more time with you? Ever?" She shook her head, lost for words. "I go to Poland now. I hope I never see you again."

Marta slammed the door shut and ran down the street.

315

51

IT WAS GETTING DARK. Marta ran, eyes streaming, only able to see as far as the next pool of light on the road. Her high heels were slowing her down. Which way had the taxi come? Marta didn't know where she was heading; she was just trying to escape from this residential area. She needed a shop, a tube station, a bus stop… anything that got her closer to finding a flight to Warsaw.

She came to a junction and stopped to wipe her eyes. Up ahead there were lights – more than just street lamps. Headlights in traffic jams. She reached down and pulled off her shoes, setting off at a sprint and taking advantage of the momentary clear vision.

The tears didn't stop for long. As she ran, images kept flashing through her mind: Tata teaching her to drive in their rusty old Volkswagen, Tata singing tunelessly on car journeys to keep Tomek and Ewa amused, Tata getting everyone lost on his infamous walks in Kampinoski park. He *had* to be OK. He was too young to have a heart attack. It was impossible to imagine him lying in hospital, frail and helpless like an old man… Marta wiped a sleeve across her face. She was approaching the main road.

The bus stop was vacant. Marta could see the tail lights of a number 209 disappearing into the darkness. She checked the map. It was covered in graffiti but she could just about make out the details she needed. She was in Fulham, on Castelnau Road. All the buses went towards Hammersmith. How ironic, she thought. She'd always wanted to go to Hammersmith.

It was only as the bus pulled up that Marta remembered she had run out of money on her travel card. She swiped it on the little button, knowing that it would turn red and give a tell-tale double-bleep. The driver sighed and looked at her. He sighed, opened his mouth to ask for the one pound fifty, and then stopped and just waved her on. Marta mustered a grateful smile. He must have seen her red eyes. Maybe he was Polish, thought Marta, perching on the edge of a seat and watching the world flash past. A fresh wave of sobs engulfed her as she thought about tata's job; was he still working at Polkomtel? Would he still have a job when he got better? *If* he got better, she thought, collapsing against the bus window in anguish.

They were stuck in a traffic jam. Marta had been looking out for a shop or a cash point, but there was no sign of either. She was desperate to top up her phone. It was ten o'clock now; she'd never get a flight tonight unless she called easyJet now. Maybe Jack was right. Maybe it was too late already.

A man sat down next to her, filling his seat and a large part of hers with his ample backside. Marta wiped her eyes.

"Excuse me," she said. "Can I please use your mobile phone?"

The man looked at her face and then glanced down at the dirty shoes in her lap. "So sorry – don't have it on me," he said, shifting sideways on his seat as though Marta might be contagious.

Marta turned back to the window. She was too distraught to be ashamed. She didn't even care that he'd mistaken her for a Romanian tramp – she just cared about making the phone call. Marta bit her lip, trying to stop her mind wandering to visions of tata. Maybe she should get a taxi straight to Kilburn? She had no money on her, but maybe she'd find a cash point. Would there be cabs in this area? Where the hell was she, anyway?

Finally, the bus pulled up at a stop where lots of people wanted to get off. There were shops and bars on both sides of the road and the streets were heaving with drunk people. Marta joined the throng and pushed her way off the bus.

The queue for the cash point seemed to last forever. At one point Marta considered asking the guys in front of her to switch places – they were Polish and she felt sure they'd understand, if she explained – but as her hand rose up to the shoulder of the leather jacket, she lost her nerve. Nobody seemed to understand.

The newsagent was pulling blinds down over his magazines as

Marta approached. He shook his head at her. "Closed," he said, drawing a blank with his hands.

Marta yelped in protest. "Please! I only need phone top-up! I will pay double – here!" She waved a twenty-pound note at the man. "I need it so bad."

The man rolled his eyes and reached behind the counter.

"Thank you!" cried Marta, already starting to dial Holly's number as she left the shop.

Holly's phone was off. Either that or she was under ground. Most likely, she was at work and didn't want to be disturbed. Marta tried again, knowing it was futile. Infuriatingly, Holly was probably sitting in front of a computer right now, with access to the easyJet website and everything else. But her phone was off. Maybe Marta could find the switchboard number for Andertons. What was the directory number in this country? She didn't know, which meant... which meant that she couldn't call the easyJet booking line either.

Tina's phone, predictably, rang on and on – the ringtone no doubt drowned out by the sound of drunk traders in a city bar. Marta needed an internet café. Or maybe she just needed to go home and use Holly's computer. She had to go back for her passport anyway. A quick scan of the area revealed a couple of internet cafés, both of them closed.

Marta headed for the blue and red sign that looked like a metro symbol. She would go home. Her head was such a mess she could barely concentrate on the plan. The flashbacks kept reappearing: tata playing with Tomek behind the sofa, Tata making clever contraptions out of string when mama moaned about the lack of drying space in their flat... how was he? Marta couldn't bear not to know. She pulled out her phone again and dialled Ewa's number. Mama, despite their appeals, refused to carry a mobile phone. It didn't ring. Of course it didn't – they'd be in the hospital. Marta upped her pace and started running towards the station.

Her phone rang just as she was going underground. She scrambled back up the escalator and snatched it out of her pocket.

Dom-home, said the display, flashing at her as she stared at it. Marta hesitated. Dom was the last person she'd been expecting to hear from. So desperate was she for someone to talk to, someone to help, she nearly picked up. Then she stopped, remembering her last sighting of Dom. Then an image of tata with Ewa on his shoulders slipped into her mind and she pressed the green button.

"Słucham?"

Too late. The line was dead. Marta desperately scrolled down to Dom's number and called him back, but it was going straight through to voicemail. She'd lost her chance. The tears started again. She'd had one chance to speak to a person who might have been able to help get her out of this country, back to tata, and she'd blown it. She'd blown it because of her own selfish wrangling. What a fool.

Her phone bleeped as she lowered it from her ear. The bowtie symbol was flashing. She had a voicemail.

"Hi, Marta," said Dom's voice – quiet, gentle but strong. It brought back memories. "I haven't heard from you for a while, so I'm assuming you met someone else and you don't want to see me, but I just wanted to call and say goodbye. I'm sorry it didn't work out between us. I thought we were great together, and… well, I don't know what went wrong. Anyway, I'm going back to Poland tomorrow – for good, so I guess I won't see you again. Things didn't happen the way I wanted in England, as you know. That job I got… ugh. I won't go into details but basically they needed a scapegoat for a big fuck-up, and the company's gone bust now. My sister came over and I realised how much I miss home, so that's where I'm going. Well… 'bye Marta. Good luck with everything."

Marta's face was wet with tears. She could barely see the right button to press on the handset. *God* she missed Dom. His calm manliness, his cheeky grin, his voice, his hair… Why had he fucked everything up for them? And now he was going back to –

She froze. Of course. Dom was going to Poland tomorrow. She pressed redial and waited, every second seeming like minutes.

"Marta?"

"Dom! Sorry – I got your voicemail and I need to ask you something. A favour. Sorry, I'm desperate. I need to fly home as soon as I can. My dad's had a heart attack. He's in hospital. Please, Dom – are you near a computer? Can you check? I'm nowhere near home and there are no internet cafés."

"Calm down," he said. For some reason, his words brought fresh

319

tears to her eyes. "Yep, I'm at home. I'll check for you. I might be able to change my flight into your name, although we'd be pushing it as I think they need twenty-four hours' notice. I fly at seven-thirty. It's to Krakow, too, so you'd have to get the train to Warsaw."

"Is there anything before then?"

"Hold on… I'm not logged in yet. To be honest though, I doubt it. In fact, hmm, nine fifteen. No chance. How long will it take you to get home?"

Marta looked at the tube map behind her. She'd have to use two green lines then the brown line, which always stopped randomly between stations. "An hour?"

"Tomorrow it is then. I'll look into changing my flight, and failing that I'll book you another one. Get yourself home and call me from there."

Marta didn't know what to say. She wanted to fling her arms around him and not let go. "Thank you so much."

"No worries – but you will call me, won't you?"

"Of course." Marta suddenly realised what he meant. "Sorry for not calling." She wasn't sure whether to explain or not. Her brain was a mess. Part of her wanted him to know that she'd found out about the blonde, but then she didn't want to start an argument with him now. "The reason–"

Suddenly, something occurred to Marta.

"The reason what?" he asked.

"Um…" Marta was beginning to work it out. "Dom, what does your sister look like?"

"Random question. Er, she's blonde. Tall – about your height. Pretty, I guess. Wears too much makeup and thinks she's some kind of movie star…"

A wave of immense happiness washed over Marta, just briefly, before the image of tata in hospital reappeared.

"Why d'you ask?"

Marta sighed, shakily. She felt so guilty. "Um… long story. I'll call you when I get home."

"Make sure you do."

52

"HAVE SOME MORE TEA," mama urged, reaching down for the pot.

"No – I won't sleep." Marta shook her head.

"You won't sleep anyway," said mama.

Marta smiled wryly, passing her cup over. "You're right."

They were sitting beside the fire on the tatty armchairs that had been there for as long as Marta could remember. The television was on, but neither was watching it. Tata was in a stable condition in hospital but the doctors didn't know whether he'd make a full recovery. It was too late for visitors – even despite Marta's pleading with the nurses.

"You looked tired, kochana."

Marta nodded. She was exhausted. The flight to Krakow – Dom's flight – had been delayed by four hours. She had missed her connection at Krakow and used up nearly all her energy fretting about the state of tata and the possible implications of the delay, then the rude men in the station had told her that express trains weren't running to Warsaw so she'd got on some sort of pre-war minibus that had rattled and shaken its way round most of the villages in eastern Poland until it finally arrived in Łomianki. Without her sister's hourly text message updates, she might have worried herself to death.

"You do too," Marta replied. "Did you sleep at all last night?"

Mama shook her head. "I put the children to bed then came down here. I couldn't sleep so I tried to read. Then I tried watching television – I even tried to do housework but I couldn't concentrate on anything. In the end, Ewa came down and kept me company. We watched the sun come up over the hills."

Marta nodded again. "Is she OK?"

Mama smiled a little. "She's a brave girl. It was a horrible thing for her to see, but she's doing alright." Tears were welling up in her eyes as she spoke. "You know she wants to be a doctor when she grows up?"

Marta shook her head. She wasn't surprised. Ewa had always wanted to help people. She helped mama all the time without even knowing it. She was tough, too. If anyone could get over seeing her father collapse on her bed, it was Ewa.

"She'd make a good doctor. And Tomek?"

Mama nodded. "He hasn't said much, but I think he's OK."

"He's a teenager. They never say much. He'll be fine, as long as tata's fine." ·

Mama nodded tightly, as though she didn't dare speak for fear of bursting into tears. Marta looked away and tried to think of something else to talk about.

"I thought I said to clear out all my old stuff?" She tugged at the fabric of her old towelling dressing gown. It was actually rather nice to be wearing it again – comforting, as though nothing had changed since she'd left.

"You know me," replied mama. "Can't throw anything away. Anyway, you need it in this place."

It was true. The flat, although cosy and warm in spirit, was always cold. Even now, on this balmy July evening, the fire was on.

"Tell me about England, kochana," said mama, clearly determined to occupy her mind with something other than tata.

"Well…" Marta didn't know what to say. There were things about England she didn't want to say – things that mama wouldn't understand, or that Marta was ashamed to tell. "My job is good! I think they like me, and they'll ask me to stay after my contract is up."

"Of course they will," mama smiled.

"Well… I can't assume that, mama. It's not that easy to get good jobs in England."

"Yes, for most people, I'm sure. But you came top of your year at SGH, didn't you? That sets you apart."

Marta nodded. Tonight was not the time to try and explain (again) the truth about working in England. This was not the time to make her point with tales of doctors packing boxes in warehouses and airline pilots picking strawberries, or the ignorance of English employers when it came to foreign qualifications. She would not talk about the latest Government report on how the UK didn't need Eastern Europeans. Tonight, she'd tell mama what she wanted to hear. "Yes, I think I am doing well."

"And are there nice men in your office?"

Marta rolled her eyes. It was a question mama asked every time they spoke. "I told you – only Carl, and he's nice but a little bit odd."

"Oh. But what about the young man who gave you his flight?"

"Dom." Marta felt a rush of guilt, just saying his name. How could she have been so cruel? "He's Polish."

"Oh! Oh right." Mama sounded disappointed. She had clearly been hoping for her daughter to meet a nice English man – like most other mothers in Łomianki. Marta wouldn't be telling her about Jack. "But he works with you too?"

"Um, no. Well, he works somewhere else. Sort of."

"Oh, right."

Mama clearly wasn't herself, thought Marta. In other circumstances there would have been a formal inquisition following Marta's vague response, but not today.

"Anyway, I don't think I'll be seeing him again. He's moving back to Poland."

"Oh?" There was a brief flicker of interest.

"Well, things didn't really work out for him over there, and… he missed his family and stuff. And I don't think I helped much."

"What d'you mean?"

"Oh, nothing. I was just…" Marta was torn. Maybe she should tell mama about Dominik – an abridged version, obviously.

"Just what?"

Marta sighed. "Horrible. I was horrible to him."

"Why?"

"Oh, well… I didn't mean to be horrible. I thought… well, we were going out for a bit. It was great. I really thought he was – you know, the type of guy who…" Marta was struggling to explain. She didn't usually confide in her mum about this sort of thing. For that, there had always been Anka.

"You liked him," mama concluded.

Marta nodded. "Yes. But then after a few weeks I went round to this place he goes to on Sundays – a Polish café – and he was there…" She cringed, thinking about it. "With a girl. She was gorgeous, and they were all over each other, and I assumed, well… I assumed that he was cheating on me."

Mama pulled a face, pouring more tea. "Don't tell me, you went off and sulked instead of confronting him, and it turned out to be a big misunderstanding?"

Marta stared at her. "How did you know that?"

She half-smiled. "I didn't know that, but I know you, kochana. I know your sulks. I know how you go off all defiant and proud – too proud to open up to the problem."

Marta leaned forwards and pressed her fingers into the corners of her eyes.

"So, who was the girl?" asked mama.

"His sister."

Mama tutted. "Oh, kochana."

There was a moment of silence. Marta cursed herself for being so pig-headed – something she'd inherited from her mother.

"But you're friends again now?"

Marta shrugged, leaning back in the chair. "For what it's worth, with him going back to Krakow."

"And you've talked about the misunderstanding?"

"Um," Marta hesitated. She hadn't been in any state to discuss relationships with Dom last night; she'd barely managed to take in the flight details.

Mama groaned quietly. "Marta, when will you learn?"

"What? Learn what?"

"To share your worries! To talk things through! You don't have to take all the world's issues onto your shoulders! If you'd confronted this boy then he would have explained, and you wouldn't have gone through – what, weeks? Months? – of torture!"

Marta looked at her. "What about you? Did *you* share your worries about tata, when you knew he was getting chest pains?"

Mama's face fell. Marta instantly regretted saying it. "I'm sorry, mama. I didn't mean that."

"No, it's OK. It's true." Tears were welling up in mama's eyes. "I did worry, you're right. And I didn't share it – not even with tata." The tears started flowing. "I should have talked to him. If I'd said something, maybe he would've seen the doctor and not–" She choked on her own tears.

Marta felt awful. She crept out of her chair and moved over to her mother's. "No, I didn't mean that, mama. You couldn't have prevented–"

"Maybe I could," muttered mama into the fabric of her daughter's dressing gown.

Marta hugged her more tightly. "Shh, shh. You couldn't have done anything. He'll be fine, anyway."

In that moment, as Marta crouched beside the old armchair, stroking her mother's hair and squeezing her heaving body against her own, she realised something: Since moving to England, she had changed. She had lost track of the bigger picture – no, worse than that: she had become totally self-obsessed. She no longer thought about anyone but herself.

Stroking her mother's back, Marta tormented herself with flashbacks from the past six months. She had hurt Dom so badly that he was fleeing the country. She had forgotten her best friend's birthday. She had failed to notice how unhappy Holly had become – Holly, who listened to all her trivial dilemmas and solved them whenever she could. She had used Carl to advance her career without giving anything back – not even friendship. And worst of all, she had gone out with Jack – against everyone's will – just so she could live a life of country clubs and expensive wine bars… Why? Why did it matter whether her clothes were from Emily Norman or a market stall? Why had she opted for fancy restaurants when she could have gone to the polskie delikatesy with Dom? Marta felt awful.

Eventually, mama pulled away. Marta stayed by her side, holding her hand.

"Promise me something," said mama.

"What?"

"First thing tomorrow, you'll do something for me."

"Go to the hospital?"

Mama shook her head. "As well as that. Promise me you'll call this boy and explain everything."

Marta nodded.

"And apologise."

She nodded again. Mama always knew what was the best thing to do. "I will," she said. "First thing."

53

"ANYWAY, SO I CALLED HIM THIS MORNING – mama told me I should. Poor guy – he must think I'm a lunatic now. I mean, he'd made up his mind to leave England, forget about everything and move on, and now I pop back into his life after ignoring him for nearly two months. I'm an idiot, aren't I?"

Tata didn't respond. Of course he didn't. He had an oxygen mask covering his mouth and plastic tubes coming out of his nose. His eyes were shut. Marta looked down, unable to watch his face any longer. There were needles coming out of his hands with more tubes attached, and the bedding had been pulled down over his chest to expose a blood-stained, flimsy cotton gown.

"Anyway, he's moving back to Poland so that's that. I've got to move on – like him. Luckily, I've got these amazing flatmates – oh, tata I'm so lucky to have found them – I don't know what I would've done if I hadn't met Holly…"

Marta prattled on. She preferred to talk than stay silent. It helped take her mind off her father's wheezing and the state of his face: grey and papery, as though the blood had been drained away.

Walking in this morning had been such a shock. Mama had warned her, but Marta hadn't listened – or at least, she hadn't prepared herself. The nurse had updated them on tata's condition, which hadn't changed since yesterday, and run them through the procedure for emergencies. If tata stirred, or if any of the machines started making a different noise, they were to pull the red cord by the side of his bed. Then the nurse had whipped back the curtain. Marta hadn't managed to suppress her gasp.

They'd arrived at seven – mama, Marta, Ewa and Tomek – before mama had taken the children to Saturday school. Poor things – they hadn't wanted to go, but mama had insisted. She was adamant their education wouldn't suffer. Marta wasn't convinced – she doubted that Ewa could focus on long multiplication or Tomek on German grammar when they'd started the day in here – but she'd said nothing. Mama was usually right.

It had been interesting watching Ewa this morning. She'd listened intently to the nurse's update and then picked up the clipboard at the foot of tata's bed and pored over his medical notes. When Marta had expressed concern about the number of wires sticking out of his chest, Ewa had silenced her with a sharp look and an explanation. Of course, she was anxious, too – Marta had noticed her little body shaking as she'd leant forward to kiss him goodbye – but there was a matter-of-factness about her manner that defied her years. She was going to make a great doctor. When she left, telling tata he would make a full recovery today, somehow, Marta believed it.

"...But Holly and Rich are just *made* for each other. That's the thing. Rich has known it for ages, but Holly hasn't realised. She's too preoccupied with work. In fact, everyone in London is preoccupied with work – that's the way they are over there. Everyone with *proper* jobs..."

Marta brought her hand up to tata's side and softly stroked his palm – avoiding the needle and clamp-thing on the end of one finger. His skin was cold and dry, like an old person's. It was impossible to believe that this was the hand that only months ago had been pressing bank notes into her hand so authoritatively. This was the hand that grasped Ewa round the waist and flung her in the air, the hand that built clever contraptions for mama around the house and lobbed that old, deflated football across the park.

"Tata, you have to help me. You have to explain to mama about my job. She thinks it's easy to get work in England – easy for me, because I came top of my year. But it's not, tata. My background is irrelevant. No one over there has heard of SGH. They can't even pronounce the name. I'm just a Polish girl to them – a girl who's come over to be an au pair or clean toilets. That's all they think we can do."

Marta paused. She wasn't sure, but she thought she heard a slight change in the rhythm of tata's wheezing. She listened, watching his chest and its dressing move up and down. Yes – another interruption. It was like a short, dry cough from inside the oxygen mask. Marta leaned forward to within reach of the red emergency cord.

"Tata? Are you OK? Can you hear me?"

The wheezing returned to normal. Maybe it was nothing. "I hope you can. Sorry I'm talking so much – I just had a lot to get off my chest. Oh God – no, sorry, that wasn't a joke. Tata, I'm sorry. Oh…" Marta found herself thinking too much about the words and felt warm tears start to roll down her cheeks.

"Tata, are you OK? Was that a cough?" Marta was sobbing. "Just… wake up, will you? Open your sodding eyes and look at me! I need you! We all need you!" Marta let out a shaky sigh and wiped her cheeks with a sleeve.

It was through watery eyes that Marta saw the movement – so watery that she didn't quite trust what she'd seen.

"Tata?" She stared at his eyes, where the movement had been. Tata remained still. "Can you hear me?"

Still nothing.

"Well, if you're not gonna wake up now then you'll have to listen to more of my twittering," she warned, still looking at tata's pale face and trying to steady her voice. "Yeah, so I'm relying on you to explain to mama how hard it is over there. She just doesn't get it."

Marta pulled her chair right up to the bed and leaned towards tata's head. "Listen. Mama needs you. She's a wreck right now. We all are – well, except Ewa who's the only one managing to hold herself together. You have to get better, and stop worrying about work. Mama told me about Polkomtel – I know about the redundancies. But really, tata, I've been thinking about this. I know it means lots to you, but it's only a job. I know you think it'd be the end of the world if you lost it, but it wouldn't – it really wouldn't. The end of the world would only come if you lost… if you – anyway, don't let me get all upset, tata." She sniffed away a fresh batch of tears. "Just get yourself better, OK?"

This time, Marta knew she wasn't mistaken. There was a movement. A flutter. His right eyelid moved slightly, then the other one. Then they both closed again.

"Tata?"

Marta reached out for the red cord, her hand hovering next to it.

There was a short groan from inside the mask. Marta pulled the cord. A low-pitched wailing noise filled the room.

"Can you hear me?" asked Marta, frantic with worry but at the same time hoping this might be a positive sign.

There was another groan that sounded like "'Course I can," but could have been a grunt of pain. At the same time, tata's eyes flickered open and blinked. Slowly, his drowsy gaze turned to Marta.

"He's awake!" cried Marta as two nurses hurried in.

For a moment there was mayhem. Marta stepped back as they moved around quickly on either side of the bed, pressing buttons, checking figures and peering into tata's eyes. One of them lifted the gown from his chest, revealing another tangle of tubes and needles, some of them stained with dry blood. Marta looked away.

"Is he OK?" she asked, when their activity died down.

"Ask him yourself," replied the nurse who had greeted them this morning. She seemed pleased about something.

Marta could feel her bottom lip wobble as her vision went blurry again. "Tata?" she asked, rushing forward and looking down at him.

"Stop crying," he replied, the mask dislodging itself as tata's face broke into a smile. "You're dripping tears on my lovely new outfit!"

54

THE QUEUE WEAVED ITS WAY OUT OF THE SHOP and into the market square, where it curled to avoid the main dog-walking route. Marta assumed her place and waited, inhaling a whiff of freshly baked bread.

The town was quieter than she remembered it. The square had always been bustling on a Sunday – full of children playing chowanego and young parents running after them. That's how Marta remembered it. Now the scene was more static: old folk hobbling about, poking at the crumbling pavement with their sticks and looking up only to moan at one another. Mama was right; it was different without the young people.

Nobody seemed to be in a hurry for their bread. The old women chatted and grumbled about the heat, the couples argued over how much they'd spent and the loners just stood, staring out through their thick-lensed glasses. Marta found herself getting agitated at the lack of progress – and then cross with herself for feeling that way. She never used to be so impatient. Maybe that was another thing London had done to her. Everything happened so quickly over there. If you wanted a loaf of bread in London you would go to the nearest Tesco and use an 'Express Checkout', which took less than a couple of minutes. What would Holly say if she could see Marta now, standing in line all morning with these old people?

Maybe she was just impatient to see her friend, Marta reasoned, straining to see how many people were ahead of her inside. She hadn't seen Anka in over six months, and she had so much to tell – most importantly, the news about tata. Perhaps that was why she felt agitated.

Finally, Marta arrived at the counter. She could barely suppress her excitement as the porcelain doll's face, hidden beneath a shapeless blue hair net, looked up to greet her.

"Hi, could I get—"

"Marta!" screamed Anka — much to the disdain of the clientele. "You're here! Oh my God — I tried to call you before but... oh, hang on. Paulina, could you cover for me? Thanks so much. Marta, come through here." She lifted a portion of the counter up for Marta to crawl through.

"Yeah, sorry I missed your call," said Marta as they settled on the steps at the back of the bakery — just like old times. "I was in the hospital."

"How is he?" asked Anka, anxiously.

Marta tipped her head to one side then the other. "Actually, I think he's gonna be OK."

"Oh, thank God!"

"Well, when I left him today he was conscious — speaking a little — and the doctor said he might make a full recovery if he's careful."

Anka was smiling. "I knew it!" she cried. "I prayed for him last night but even as I said the words, I thought, 'why am I doing this? He'll be fine.' And he is! You Dabrowskas are tough as leather, you are. Nothing gets in your way."

Marta leaned over and hugged her friend. "I think the heart attack had a pretty good go."

Anka squeezed her. "I'm so pleased he'll be OK. I worried all night for you — and you didn't call me!"

Marta pulled away gently. "God, I've been all over the place these last few days. I'm so sorry, Anka. I didn't even know you knew."

Anka smiled. "Nothing stays secret in this town for long. Mama found out from some woman at church whose son is in Tomek's class."

Marta nodded. She should have called Anka. Why hadn't she? Perhaps she'd been too busy worrying. It was as though, in her mind, by talking about tata before she'd seen him, she'd somehow alter his prognosis.

Anka was looking at her. "You OK?"

Marta nodded vaguely. She wasn't actually sure. They'd said that tata *might* make a full recovery, but what did that mean? Would he have another attack? Would he get made redundant from Polkomtel? "I think so."

"How's your mama?"

Marta shrugged. "Not great. She seems…" Marta couldn't think of the word. "Old. They both seem old."

Anka nodded. "That's the thing about parents. They get old."

Marta could feel her eyes filling with tears. What was wrong with her? Why did she keep crying? Everything was supposed to be alright. Well, for now. Tata was fine *for now*. That was the thing. Nothing was guaranteed any more. When she was younger, it was simple: whatever Marta did, mama and tata were there, like rocks, if she needed them. In fact, that had been the case until the end of last week. But it wouldn't be the case forever, and Marta was only just beginning to realise that.

"Come here." Anka moved closer and hugged her again. The tears spilt onto her cheeks and sunk into Anka's apron.

Marta tried to explain. "I thought I was being so grown-up, going to England and starting my own life. My own career. So independent…"

"You were. You are." Anka looked at her. "You're one of the bravest people I know."

Marta shook her head. "No I'm not. I'm not brave. Look at me. I do all these things that make me *look* brave but inside I know I'm not doing it alone – I've got mama and tata. And now… I've just realised that I can't have them forever. I'm not independent after all."

"Sorry to disagree with you, Marta, but that's bullshit. Everyone's allowed to get upset if something happens to a person they care about. You'd have to be made of… of metal to cope with what happened and not show any emotion. You're perfectly independent – you're just a kind person, too."

Marta shook her head. "But I'm not kind. I'm horrible. I've turned horrible," she protested. "Ever since I started to settle in England I got more and more self-centred. I never think about anyone else now – only my job and my new life!"

Anka looked puzzled. "Jesus, Marta. You've got to stop beating yourself up or you'll have a breakdown. Listen, you've had a lot on your plate since you moved, so it's hardly surprising you don't have much time to think about anyone else. For God's sake… that's what you're like. Ambitious. Successful. That's why you go off and do exciting things while I'm left stuffing dumplings!"

Marta started to smile. Anka was exaggerating, as always, but maybe there was some truth in her words. Maybe Marta just had a lot on her plate. That was why she'd forgotten – "Oh my God! I nearly forgot again!"

"What?"

"Your birthday present!"

"Yes, you sent me–"

"No – no, that was just a little something," said Marta, remembering guiltily that she'd never actually paid Tina anything for what she sent over. "This is your proper gift." She reached into her bag.

"But I don't want–"

"Open it," instructed Marta. "It's not much, but…"

Anka squealed. "Oh my God!" She extracted the beads from the Emily Norman clothes. "Loads of stuff! Gorgeous stuff!" She trailed the necklace over her skin and tried on the belt. "I love it! Thank you!"

Marta smiled, rising to her feet and admiring yet again her friend's effortless style. "It's not Gucci, I'm afraid, but it should last longer than the stuff you get here."

Anka shook her head, beaming. "I don't want Gucci, silly. I just want my friend back! My ambitious, successful friend."

55

MARTA WAS TOO TIRED TO DO ANYTHING about the broken wheels on her suitcase, or the fact that her left shoe was rubbing the top layer of skin off her ankle. She was too tired to reply to Holly's text message asking when she'd be back and she couldn't even muster the energy to stop off at the corner shop and buy some soup for supper. All she could think about was her makeshift bed.

It wasn't as though she'd done anything particularly energetic these last five days. She'd barely moved except to make the journey between the flat and the hospital by bus. No, this wasn't a physical exhaustion. It was an exhaustion caused by a sickening rollercoaster of emotions – oppressive lows, dizzying highs, small ups and downs when the doctors broke this news and that, the feeling of being plunged into darkness, not knowing what direction the future would take, and the complete lack of control. Marta had never understood the phrase 'sick with worry', but now she did.

He was going to be fine. That's what they'd told her as she'd left the hospital eight hours earlier. She believed them – at least, she wanted to believe them. She had to, to keep herself sane, but at the same time there was this looming black cloud hanging over everything: the possibility that he might have another attack. Marta plodded on, her stubborn suitcase making a grinding noise on the flagstones. Everything would seem fine in the morning. She was just tired. Problems always seemed worse late at night.

Marta stopped a few doors down from her flat and listened. She hesitated, looking up at the window next to the door – the lounge window. Yes, as she suspected, there were silhouettes of bodies moving around behind the curtains, moving around in time with the beat that was pounding out onto the road. Marta breathed deeply and continued towards number nine. They were having a party.

Before she had even located her keys, the door was flung open and someone from inside yelled, "Marta's back!" There was a chorus of screaming and whooping, and even as Marta stooped to retrieve her suitcase, she found herself being tugged down the hallway towards a kitchen that was brimming with laughter and alcohol. Who were all these people?

"My bag—"

"I've got it!"

"Who is—"

"It's a homecoming party for you!" replied Holly, who looked... well, radiant. She never usually wore slinky dresses or makeup.

"Why…"

"That's not strictly true," Tina interjected. She, as ever, was wearing small slivers of fabric strategically placed around her body. "It's a general all-round celebration. Holly, have you told Marta your news?"

Marta waited for Holly's response, accepting the drink that was thrust into her hand.

Holly looked at Marta as though she couldn't hold it in any longer. "I've quit my job!"

Marta rushed forward to hug her friend. The relief washed over her as they squeezed one another, Marta possibly even happier about the news than Holly herself.

"Finally!" she said as they drew apart.

"Yeah, well, it's been a year. I think I've done my time. Come on – let's go through."

They migrated into the lounge, where yet more faces that Marta didn't recognise turned to greet them.

"That lot are traders, in case you didn't guess," Holly explained, pointing to the group of well-groomed young men setting light to a line of shots on the coffee table. Tina was just settling down to join them. "And these are uni mates…" She moved towards a less organised bunch – more of a rabble, in fact – who seemed to be trying out break-dancing moves in front of the speaker.

Marta nodded politely at those who caught her eye and laughed as a guy collapsed on his head at her feet. It was only as they moved away that she noticed the girl in the corner, standing slightly to one side in a chic fitted dress and clearly in no mood for getting down with MC Hammer. Staring expressionlessly at Marta was Tash.

Marta stared back for a second, then felt Holly's hand on her elbow, guiding her away. She followed, not sure what else to do. Why was she here? Surely Holly hadn't invited her? Marta wanted to ask, but Holly was already busy with the next set of introductions.

"This is Tim, this is Sara, and – oh, I'm sorry. I don't know…"

Marta smiled at Tim and Sara and turned to the two strangers who were leaning awkwardly against the dining room table. She nearly gasped.

"Carl!" she cried, trying not to stare too blatantly at the fact that his arm was around the waist of the other young man. "Hi!"

Holly looked at her, eyebrows raised.

"Oh, sorry," said Marta, still in shock. "This is Carl, from work. And…"

"Davey," said the other guy, offering his hand and a beautiful smile. He was gorgeous: dark-skinned, like Carl, but perfectly proportioned with a carved jaw line. Marta accepted his handshake – more of a gentle brush of fingers – and winked at Carl. He was beaming. A huge weight lifted from her mind.

"These are Rich's mates – I'm sure you've seen them around the house in various states of consciousness and undress," said Holly, turning to the next bunch of lads and smiling. "Ben, Doug, Chris, Mark and Damo… Where is Rich, anyway?"

The lads looked at one another and one of them – Chris or Mark – muttered something under his breath.

"No," replied Holly, rolling her eyes. "He's not in my pants. God, your wit knows no bounds… Come on Marta. Let's sort out the sausages." She turned on her heel and whisked Marta into the kitchen.

"Where's Rich? She's after some sausage!" yelled one of the guys, triggering dirty laughs from the others and a one-fingered salute from Holly.

Marta wished, in a way, they hadn't gone to the trouble of

337

throwing a party. It was a nice gesture, and of course she'd sacrifice her much-needed sleep for the occasion, but actually she would rather have sat down with Holly and Tina over a cup of hot chocolate and talked. There was so much she wanted to ask – about Rich and Holly, about what Holly was going to do now she'd quit, about whether they'd found out about Jack – but now didn't seem like the time.

"Holly?" she asked as they ripped the mini sausages from their packaging. "Why is Tash here?"

Holly opened her mouth to respond, then seemed unnerved by something behind Marta.

Marta turned. Tash didn't say anything; she just stood there and motioned for Marta to follow her into the hallway. They sat on the stairs, away from the din and the glare of the party.

"Marta, I'm sorry."

They sat there, looking at one another. Marta wasn't going to say anything until Tash had explained. Right now, she wasn't sure what Tash was apologising for.

"Look… I think it's been pretty tough for you, these last few months, and I don't think I helped by making you homeless and blaming you for something I now realise wasn't your fault."

Marta studied Tash's expression. It was fairly blank, but that was probably because Tash never moved many muscles in her face when she talked – it dislodged her makeup.

"God, I'm hopeless at this. Help me out, will you? Say something?"

Marta frowned. Tash was so complicated. So English. "What do you want me to say?"

Tash frowned. "I don't know – tell me you're fine and you forgive me and we can be friends again! Or something."

"Why are you suddenly coming and saying sorry for things that happen months ago? I don't understand."

"Because I only just realised!" yelped Tash, showing her first sign of genuine emotion. "I only just found out about Jack! I thought it was *you* tricking him – not the other way round. But then I found out about Plum… and Kat… and probably hundreds of others–"

"What? Plum and Kat?" Marta wasn't sure what she meant.

"Yes! For months, apparently. God knows how many others there were… I hope they all get Syphilis," she spat.

"So… he was doing… doing the business with all the girls, at the same time?" asked Marta.

"Yes!" hissed Tash hatefully. "Stupid bastard. He just couldn't help himself, could he?"

Marta let out a deep breath, thinking about the implications of what Tash had just said. All the time Marta had been 'with' Jack, he'd been equally 'with' Tash, *and* Kat, *and* Plum too. She thought back to the time at Hurlingham when Charles had accidentally called her Kat. Jack must have been talking about his girlfriends – his *harem* of girlfriends – quite openly behind their backs.

Then another flashback appeared: the image of Tash with her Jack look-alike in the casino at the Cambridge ball. She couldn't believe she hadn't registered then. In fact, more incredible was the fact that Jack had managed to deceive all four girls – or, at least two of them – into thinking that they were his real girlfriend. How long did he think he could keep this thing going?

"Did they know about you?" asked Marta.

Tash rolled her eyes. "Well, Plum did, obviously. Fucking bitch. Took him from right under my nose. And to think that she'd had the nerve to tell me about *you*. I guess Kat would've known, too. Not that it would've bothered her. You didn't know, did you?"

Marta shook her head. "First I knew was when you called me, eating my head off."

Tash's anger seemed to ebb for a moment. "Biting, not eating," she said, smiling slightly. "Yeah, I'm sorry about that."

Marta watched Tash as she continued to gnaw at her finger nail. Her eyes looked sunken and red beneath the makeup. Marta moved closer and gave her a sympathetic nudge. She herself had got over Jack pretty quickly. She had realised, despite having convinced herself that they were a great couple and that Jack was her man, that they had almost nothing in common and Jack had some serious character flaws that she'd overlooked. She felt nothing either way for Jack – except perhaps for a small amount of wonder at his audacity. He was a blip in her past, a learning, a silly mistake. For Tash, though, he was more than that. He had been her boyfriend for years – or so she'd thought.

She'd assumed, quite reasonably, that they'd be together for ever, and now this had hit her like a pan in the face: the realisation that he was sleeping with at least three other girls. Ouch.

For some reason, and it wasn't something Marta had been expecting to do today – or ever, in fact – she leant over and hugged Tash. Perhaps it was the effect of an emotional week. She pulled her tight, rubbing her back and messing up her immaculate blonde locks.

"How did you find out?" asked Marta as she pulled away.

Tash sighed. She looked sad now, not angry. "Holly, actually. She told me about what had happened to you with Jack and that stuff going on with Kat in your office and I pieced it together. He broke down as soon as I confronted him – that's when I found out about Plum. Stupid fool let it slip."

Marta sat there, shaking her head and marvelling at Jack's nerve – and his thoughtlessness, too. Poor Tash. She was not a strong person. Surely Jack knew of her insecurities? Of all the girls he could have chosen to be the 'real' girlfriend, why had he picked Tash? Well, of course, it was obvious why: it was because Tash would always come back to him. She needed him more than he needed her. Like a yoyo, she'd come back to Jack no matter what he put her through. Except this time, thought Marta. This time he'd gone way too far.

Thank God for Holly, thought Marta. If she hadn't stepped in, the rift between Marta and Tash would have grown and Tash might never have realised who she was going out with. It was nice of her, too, not to make a big deal of the Jack thing. Marta could imagine her reaction when she'd found out who the 'mystery man' really was.

"He's going out with Kat now, apparently," said Tash, smiling a little in her up-tights way. "They're well-suited, I'd say."

Marta smiled and rose to her feet. "Come on – let's get a drink."

Tash had just filled their glasses when she suddenly gasped. "Oh God – I nearly forgot! Here–" She handed over Marta's drink – something posh, like what they used to drink in Egerton Square – then bounded off down the hallway.

She reappeared, brandishing a bulging plastic bag, taped up at the top. "I had to take it into work before I came here – they nearly sacked me for the fashion offence." She smiled.

Marta knew what it was even before she'd ripped open the plastic.

"Oh, thank you!" she cried, as soon she glimpsed the turquoise fabric. Her beautiful Malina Q jacket fell into her hands. "I thought you burned it or something!"

"I should've," replied Tash, looking disdainfully at the garment as Marta rubbed it fondly against her cheek.

"Ooh! Ah!" cried Rich, practically throwing a tray of hot sausages onto the kitchen surface and nursing his hot fingers.

"Don't be such a girl," said Holly, turning to him and slipping a hand around his waist. It was such uncharacteristic behaviour that Marta couldn't help staring. She exchanged a sideways glance with Tash. Her most burning question had been answered: Holly and Rich were official.

Marta grinned as the pair of them moved towards the sink and Holly gently numbed his burn under the tap. Part of her wanted to slip back into the lounge and leave the pair of them alone, but she had one more unanswered question.

"Holly, what will you do now you left Andertons?"

Holly turned, smiling. "Well… I've got some ideas," she replied. "Some ideas I need to run past you."

Marta frowned.

"Don't worry," said Holly, "you won't be left in the dark on this – quite the opposite."

Marta's bewilderment grew, but she wasn't given any more clues.

"I'll explain when we're sober. Oh yeah–"Holly leapt across the kitchen. "These came for you–" She lifted the huge bouquet of flowers that was leaning against the window, their stems wedged in a shampoo container. "Yeah – sorry about the vase."

"Who is it from?" asked Marta, reaching for the envelope.

"I dunno. Open it and find out," replied Holly, shovelling the sausages onto a plate.

Marta tore at the paper and pulled out the card – a typically English affair with a tasteless watercolour dog on the front.

Dear Marta,

We were so sorry to hear about your father; you are in our thoughts every day. Everyone at Stratisvision sends their fondest regards, and we look forward to seeing you when you are back.

Let us know when you think you'll be ready to return to work. I'd like to discuss the possibility of taking you on as a full-time employee.

Best,
Patricia and the team x

"Is from the CEO!" cried Marta. "They want me to work for them!"

"'Course they do. Why wouldn't they?" Holly rolled her eyes.

Marta stared at the card, letting all the images of the last few months crash through her mind: the countless job interviews, the patronising comments, the blank looks at the name of her university, the knock-backs, the gentle suggestions that she find other work... Finally, here was a decent company in her chosen field who valued her. The management of Stratisvision – the CEO, no less – could see her potential. Finally, she was building up a career.

The words on the card started to blur, and she realised she was crying.

"What's up?" asked Rich.

Marta laughed through the tears. "I don't know! I am happy, but crying!"

"Here," Tash handed her a tissue. "I think you're tired."

Marta nodded. "Maybe I go and lie down on your bed, Holly?"

Holly looked at her watch. "Um, yeah. Sure."

The response was strangely lukewarm, but Marta didn't have the energy to find out why. She stumbled out of the kitchen, looking for her broken suitcase and thinking about the crazy events of the last twenty-four hours.

As Marta deliberated between opening the case in the hallway or lugging it up the stairs first, the doorbell rang. "I'll get it," she cried, peering through the frosted door panel and hoping it wasn't a neighbour coming to complain.

At a point when Marta thought she'd reached her emotional limit for the day, here, on the doorstep, was the one person who had the potential to tip her over.

"Dom!"

He stood there, grinning. "Well? Can I come in?"

Marta opened the door, like a zombie. She hadn't even realised Dom was still in the country. After their brief, awkward phone call the other morning, she'd assumed he would catch the next available flight and never be seen again. "You're still here," she said, stupidly.

"Well, you took my ticket home, didn't you?" He pretended to look cross.

"But…" Marta lingered in the hallway, not keen on re-entering the noisy lounge.

"You look knackered," he said.

She nodded. "Was just about to go and lie down. But…" She couldn't quite ask Dom the question: was he still here because of her?

"Your bed's taken, I see—" He nodded through the wall to where the break-dancing competition was taking place. "I've got one you can use."

Marta smiled. It was so tempting.

"Just for sleeping, I mean," he added. His hair was a mess, just as she remembered it. His brown eyes grinned back at her, innocently, invitingly.

"I'll get my jacket."

56

MARTA TURNED HER HEAD on the pillow and smiled. Dom was beside her, his naked torso propped up on an elbow. He was watching her.

"Morning," she stammered, trying to remember the details of the night before. Her memory was hazy through tiredness. Had they…?

"Just about," he said, glancing up at the clock in the tiny room. Sunlight was pouring through the flimsy curtains.

Marta squinted and realised, with horror, that it was nearly midday. "Południum?! Shit!"

Dom shifted closer and gently touched her bare arm. "So? Doesn't matter. It's the weekend. You needed sleep."

"Tata! I need to find out how he is!" gasped Marta, feeling around under the bedclothes to discover that she was wearing her underwear. To the side of the bed was a crumpled pile of clothes and beside it, her wallet and phone. Yes, now she remembered: Dom had been a gentleman last night. He'd helped her undress, kissed her goodnight and then left her to sleep. No sex – just a bit of a cuddle. It was almost disappointing, she thought, reaching out for her phone. But then, she'd been too tired for anything last night. There were two new text messages – one from last night and one from this morning.

From: Tina
Thought you were
supposed to be tired,
you dirty tart!
Have fun xxx

From: Ewa
Tata much better today –
laughing & joking &
annoying the nurses.
They're moving him
to another ward!
Miss you. Ex

"Is he OK?"

Marta moved back into bed. "He's fine. Pissing everyone off with his bad jokes I think."

Dom smiled, his eyes wandering between her face and her breasts, which she'd accidentally left exposed. She pulled the duvet up over them. Dom pushed it back down again. She pulled it up. He suddenly disappeared under the covers and popped up right next to her, his face just above her chest. Marta couldn't help smiling. She felt so happy, all of a sudden. Dom, the cutest, most lovable guy she'd ever met, was lying on top of her, his erection digging into her leg. Tata was going to be fine. She had a good job. Holly and Rich were going out. Tash and she had made up, and Jack was finally out of her life for good. Everything, finally, was working out.

"Why did you decide to stay?" she asked, feeling brave enough now to ask the question. Last night, she hadn't been sure. Now, she thought she knew the answer – she just wanted to hear it from him.

Dom's body tensed up. "Let's not talk about that now." He pulled away at the fabric of her bra to expose her nipple and tickled it gently.

Marta could feel herself numbing, relenting to his physical presence, his touch – but the rational part of her wanted to know *why*. Why wouldn't he talk about this?

"Tell me, Dom."

His tongue made contact with her nipple, which went hard instantly. "Not now," he uttered, "it can wait."

Something was niggling Marta as Dom's head slipped beneath the duvet and her body became all but powerless. *Maybe Dom wasn't planning to stay after all.* That was the only explanation she could think of. Why else wouldn't he answer her question? All he needed to say was, 'I'm staying because of you', so why wouldn't he?

All rational thoughts flew from her mind as her body was stripped – of clothes and of control. She lost the power of reasoning as he entered her, her body arching and shuddering, her brain numbed with pleasure.

They were lying beside one another, hot, panting, exhausted, ten minutes later when Marta's thoughts came together again.

"Dom?"

He rolled towards her again.

"You're not going back to Krakow, are you?"

Dom exhaled, slowly. The hesitation answered her question.

"You are!" cried Marta, unable to control her voice. He couldn't go back to Poland – not now! Not after... after *that!*

Dom shook his head and wiped the beads of sweat from Marta's cheeks, one by one. "I don't want to. Especially not now. But I made up my mind."

"But that was–" *before I came back,* Marta wanted to say. Perhaps that wasn't reason enough. Perhaps it was arrogant to assume it was.

"I know. That was when you were off shagging your rich Englishman and I didn't have anything to live for here."

"I wasn't–"

Dom smiled. "I know. But you're right. That was before, when I had no job and nobody I cared about over here." He brushed a strand of hair off her face. Marta felt like crying. Surely he couldn't walk away, when things were this good?

"It's different now, isn't it?"

Dom hesitated. "Of course it is. But the thing is... I find it hard over here. It's not how I imagined it. I know I laugh and joke about Barry's place, but really... it was getting me down. That was the best I could do – handing out sodding flyers in the street!"

"But you got a proper job–"

"Yeah, for about four weeks. I told you they went into liquidation, didn't I?"

Marta nodded. "There'll be other firms," she said tentatively.

"Other firms looking for a cheap scapegoat to blame for a management fuck-up? Yeah, sure. Plenty."

Marta closed her eyes for a second. The outlook couldn't be this bleak. "Don't you think... I mean, we've had our fair share of shit work here, but don't you think we might have a chance? I feel as though we're finally starting to make it over here – to fit in, to–"

"No," Dom cut in. He was shaking his head. "No, *you're* starting to make it over here. You're fitting in. *I'm* not."

Marta couldn't think of a come-back.

"It wasn't an easy decision to make," he said softly. "At least, it wasn't easy once you reappeared." He smiled wryly. "But I made it. It's the right thing for me to do. I've got to go back."

Marta stayed silent for a while. She was cooling down. The passion of the last ten minutes seemed like an age away, and now, with the realisation that Dom was going back to Poland, it felt almost worthless.

"I thought you were ambitious," she challenged quietly. It was a new tactic – a last-ditch approach.

"I am. At least, I was. But I'm not Michael Marks. I'm an ordinary Pole, just like the other million. Nothing special. Nobody wants me here."

"I do," whispered Marta, so quietly she wondered whether she'd spoken it or just thought it.

"I know."

The news was sinking in. Marta stopped arguing. She reached out and touched his bicep, wrapping one leg over his. He was leaving. These would be her last moments with him. She'd have to get on with her life in England without Dom.

It was possible. She could do it. She was an independent-minded young woman. She had a bunch of friends over here, a place to live and a good job where she was beginning to earn some respect. People liked her here. She fitted in. Holly had hinted yesterday that she might even need to involve her in whatever it was she planned to do after leaving Andertons. She had plenty to live for in England.

"You'll be fine here," said Dom, reaffirming her thoughts. "You'll do well."

Marta nodded.

"And Krakow's not far away, is it?"

Marta shrugged. "Not with easyJet, I guess."

Dom rolled on top of her again and kissed her on the lips. "You will visit, won't you?"

Marta ran her hand through his messy hair and smiled. "I'll think about it."

57

"REMEMBER, I don't pay you to be enterprising!" growled Holly, as Marta came back to replenish her supply of leaflets. "In fact," she went on, maintaining her angry look, "I don't pay you at all!"

They both burst out laughing. Marta picked up a batch from the corner of the office – a cramped, box-like room not dissimilar to Barry Roffey's hovel, but neater – and passed behind Holly's chair.

"What d'you think?" asked Holly, tilting the computer screen upwards.

The website looked great. Simple, easy to use yet professional, and in perfect Polish as well as English. Marta rested her leaflets on the desk and crouched down to try out a few things.

"What shall I buy? Mmm, some chleb, I think, and ziemniaki… and kapusta. Does the check-out work? Can I order these now?"

"Of course," replied Holly. "If you log in as you, it'll remember what you last ordered. What's kapusta?"

"Cabbage, of course."

"Of course. Yeah, it all works – the only bit that doesn't is the one-hour delivery slots. We can only get it down to two hours at the moment because of the firm we're using. That'll improve though, as we get more users."

Marta played around on the site, filling her basket with all sorts of goodies she missed from back home: ciasto, ciastko, barszcz czerwony… gosh, it was easier than shopping back in Łomianki! Everything was here, on one website – no need to queue at the bakery for bułka.

"I better go," said Marta. "Will give these out and then back to work." She grabbed the flyers and headed out.

"Hey, Marta," said Holly, as she opened the door.

"What?"

"I've been thinking."

"I know. You always think, Holly. Think, think, think! Never stop thinking – even when you asleep!"

Holly smiled. "Yeah, I know. But I've had a particular thought that affects you."

"Oh, right."

"Well, I realised that you've done so much for me on polskisklep, and I owe you big time."

Marta screwed up her nose. "I owe you bigger time, for giving me a place to stay and an agency that give me a job!"

"No – that was nothing. Really. I mean, you're here in your lunch hour, giving out leaflets... I want to repay the favour. I want you to have my bedroom in the flat."

Marta stared, taking in the meaning of Holly's words. "You moving out of the flat?"

Holly smiled, shaking her head. "No, I'm not moving out."

"Then..."

Holly looked a little sheepish. Suddenly, Marta understood.

"You moving in to Richard's bedroom?!"

Holly nodded. "But you wouldn't need to pay any more rent than–"

"Ah ha!" Marta grinned wildly. So *this* was what it was about. Holly and Rich were a real couple! "That is so good news, Holly. Am so excited!"

"Yeah I thought you would be. The furniture can stay, and if you need more hanging space–"

"Not about that!" cried Marta. "Am not excited about that – well, I am, is very exciting to finally have my own room – but am excited for *you*!"

Holly was blushing. "Well, yeah. Anyway. So... thanks again. I'll see you later."

"See you later!" Marta yelled as she leapt, two by two, down the rotten staircase. She was still grinning when she reached street level and started to hand out her last wad of leaflets.

It was amazing how quickly the website had come together.

Three weeks. Three weeks of hard work and long hours on Holly's part – but she was used to that. She had continued to lead an Andertons lifestyle since leaving the firm – barely sleeping, working weekends and eating her lunch one-handed at her desk – but it was no longer a bad thing. She was no longer working for the good of some huge, hierarchical American machine; she was working for herself.

polskisklep.com had been Holly's secret brainchild for months, it turned out. She'd been working on an e-commerce project at work when it had occurred to her that all over London, Polish delicatessens and supermarkets were making good money from the thousands of immigrants like Marta who wanted familiar food from back home. But nobody was doing it online.

Somehow – and Marta still hadn't worked out how – Holly had built a prototype website whilst she was still at Andertons, and tested the concept with random Poles outside Hammersmith Broadway before revealing her plans to the flatmates.

With Marta's help, she had teamed up with some Polish suppliers who sent over weekly shipments – small at the moment, but enough to pack the refrigerated warehouse in Acton and keep the local delivery firm busy. It was a modest operation, but it would grow as more people discovered the website – which was why Marta was spending her lunch hours pounding the streets with flyers.

Holly hadn't done it all by herself, of course. Ironically enough, after a week of scouring CVs for a potential business partner and finding no one who fitted the bill in both commercial awareness and technical know-how, Holly had found the solution in her own flat – holding hands with Marta.

That solution, a qualified accountant and native Pole with a love of computers, was leaping around outside the Hammersmith Primark as Marta slammed the door shut behind her.

"Cześć," she said, laughing as Dom instinctively offered her a leaflet.

"Oh, it's you." He retracted the leaflet and drew her closer.

"How's it going?" she asked, pulling away from an over-zealous kiss. "No straying out of your zone?"

"Oh no."

"No dumping?"

He grinned. "No."

"No funny business?"

"Not yet. Maybe later."